TOO FAR GONE
A GREY JUSTICE NOVEL

BY
CHRISTY REECE

Too Far Gone

 A Grey Justice Novel

Published by Christy Reece

Cover Art by Patricia Schmitt/Pickyme

Copyright 2017 by Christy Reece

ISBN: 978-0-9967666-5-4

To obtain permission to excerpt portions of the text, please contact the author at Christy@christyreece.com.

PROLOGUE

Valencia, Venezuela
Twenty-one years ago

The man tiptoed down the hallway. Holding his daughter tightly with one arm, he used his other arm to keep his wife by his side. At three in the morning, the only sound in the monstrous old house was the tick-tock of the giant clock in the formal parlor. The old children's rhyme, *Nothing was stirring, not even a mouse*, came to him. But this was no children's story. If anyone put a name to it, horror would be the most appropriate genre. Because if he failed, there was no doubt what would happen to him and his family.

How he had allowed things to advance this far was something he would regret until the end of time. He had promised to protect his loved ones. Instead, he had been on the verge of following in his father's footsteps and in the process had almost lost his wife and daughter. To his everlasting shame, he had already lost his son to that soulless monster. He refused to lose any more. If it was the last thing he did, his wife and little girl would be safe. This he swore.

"Papa?"

The childish whisper, barely a sound, tickled at his ear. He squeezed her tighter and spoke softly against her ear, "Shh, baby girl. You have to be quiet till we get to the car."

Held in her father's arms, the child felt safe and snug. Even though it was the middle of the night when everyone else was asleep, she was wide awake, excited for the adventure to come. They were going on a magical, secret trip. Just she, Mama, and Papa. Her brother wasn't going. She knew Mama was sad about that, because when she had asked if he was going, her mama had started crying.

She should probably feel guilty that they were going on a trip without her big brother, but she couldn't help but be glad he wasn't coming along. He'd been mean to her lately. Just a few days ago, he'd taken one of her favorite dolls and torn it apart, right in front of her. Then he'd laughed and called her a bad-word crybaby. She knew it was a bad word, because he'd said it in front of Mama one time, and she had smacked his bottom and made him go to his room.

Maybe when they returned from their trip, he would be nicer to her. For now, she couldn't wait until they started on their new, big adventure.

"Someone's coming," Mama whispered.

"Come on." Papa took her mama's hand, and they ran into the library.

"Going somewhere?" The familiar voice behind them had both her parents whirling around with a gasp.

Papa's arms tightened around her. Though recognizing the owner of that voice, she twisted in her father's arms so she could see him. He wasn't big like Papa, but when he smiled, like he was now, he was as scary as any giant closet monster she'd ever imagined. He was her grandpapa…her papa's papa. And he wasn't a very nice man.

"Get out of our way, old man. We're leaving."

"Is that right? And where will you go?"

"That's not your problem. We're taking nothing with us that belongs to you."

"Oh, but you are."

Grandpapa looked right at her when he said that. Shivers started at her toes and raced up her body. Why was he looking at her like that?

"You've already taken one of my children," Papa said. "You cannot have the other one."

Grandpapa smiled, one of his scarier ones. "I blame your mother for your melodrama. She coddled you too much."

"My mother would have been disgusted by what you've done."

"Your mother understood more than you think. Besides, what is there to worry about? Your son will be my heir. He'll inherit an empire. Want for nothing."

"Yes," Mama hissed. "And you'll turn him into a heartless fiend, just like you. You cannot have my daughter, too."

"*Your daughter* is my granddaughter," Grandpapa snapped. "She will lack for nothing. Will have the best of everything. If you take her away, she'll be penniless. A nobody like yourself."

"She'll have love."

Tears streamed down her mama's face. She hated it when her mama cried.

"Leave her alone, Grandpapa."

Grandpapa's eyes zeroed in on her, and the shivering she'd felt before grew stronger. She'd heard her mama say once that Grandpapa had the eyes of the devil, black and lifeless. She thought maybe that was true, because right now they gleamed like one of the monsters in her fairy-tale books.

"I'm pleased you have spirit, little one. It will see you through much." Without moving his eyes from her, he said, "Take her back to her room, Stephan."

Her entire body stiffened with fear as she looked over her papa's shoulders at the man who had just entered. If there was anyone who scared her more than Grandpapa, it was Stephan.

"No!" Papa shouted. "We are leaving!"

She clung to her papa's neck, but Stephan's big hands pulled her away. Mama was hanging on to her, too, pleading with Grandpapa to leave them alone.

Kicking and screaming, she scratched and bit, trying to get away from Stephan. With one arm holding her legs and his other securing her arms, Stephan carried her out of the room like she was a sack of laundry.

She squirmed and screamed. Just before he got to the stairway, she managed to free one leg and kicked as hard as she could. Stephan grunted, and his arms went limp as he dropped to his knees. The instant he set her free, she ran back to the library. She pushed open the door and then froze.

Papa stood in front of her mama, tears rolling down his face. She heard a little pop, and then Papa fell on the floor.

"Papa!" she screamed.

Her mama cried out, "Don't look, Gabby!"

Another small popping noise sounded, and then Mama fell on top of Papa.

The shrill, anguished sound of a little girl screaming echoed through the house.

CHAPTER ONE

Present Day
Dallas, Texas

The elevator glided noiselessly up to the penthouse. Jonah Slater stared straight ahead, leashed violence evident in the rigid set to his shoulders. He told himself he was ready, more than ready, to find out the truth. The news would lead him down a path he never thought he would take. At one time, the thought of destroying another life would have been an abomination to him. But for justice, for honor…for Teri, he would carry out his promise.

With only a slight jolt, the elevator reached the top, and the doors slid open. The man he had come to see—more friend than employer—stood before him. The solemnity of his expression was normal. Grey Justice wasn't known for his easygoing personality.

Dark blue eyes swept over him in an all-encompassing sweep. "I'm glad to see you're in one piece, even if you do look like you tangled with a pack of rabid coyotes."

Unable to hold back, Jonah asked, "You have something?"

"Come in and let's talk."

Knowing he would get nothing until Justice was ready to speak, Jonah wasted no time on protests. Having been in the man's home many times, he knew his way around. He made his way into the living room, cursing the pain in his left thigh. The last op had been a hairy one, and he'd come out of it better than he deserved. Mostly bruises, really, but his body was telling him to take it easy for a while. His mind and heart said no way in hell. Not until he had what he needed.

He stopped in the middle of the room. "What do you have?"

"You want coffee or something stronger?" His eyes zeroed in on an ugly bruise on Jonah's jaw. "Or maybe some aspirin?"

The instant the offer was made, Jonah knew he wasn't going to hear what he wanted...what he needed.

"You don't have his name, do you?"

"Yes and no."

"What does that mean?"

"I have a first name, I have a general location."

First name? Hell, what good was a first name? He asked anyway, "What is it?"

"Peter." Justice held up his hand. "I told you going in it would be a slow process. This group is well organized and good at hiding in plain sight."

"What's the location? I'll go there and find someone who knows something."

"Up north."

"The US?"

"Yes."

"Could you be more specific?"

"No. Unfortunately not."

Wrenching disappointment slashed at his heart. When he'd gotten the call to come for a private meeting at Justice's penthouse, his gut had told him something monumental was imminent. The knowledge that, once again, Teri was being denied justice was infuriating.

"Then why'd you call me here?"

Justice cocked his head and raised a questioning brow. Jonah blew out a soft curse. "The Starling incident."

"Incident is an interesting word for it. You almost got yourself killed."

"It worked out fine."

"Someday it won't."

"That's my problem, not yours."

"For everyone who cares about you, yes, it is a problem. Eli deserves better."

Guilt slammed into him, and Jonah looked away from his boss's piercing stare. The man was right. Eli, Jonah's older brother, and the only brother he would claim, did deserve better.

"I'll go see him."

"And what? Explain why you don't care if you die or not?"

Justice was wrong about that. He didn't want to die...at least not until he'd found Teri's killer. After that? Hell, he didn't know.

"The situation was resolved. Other than a few bumps and bruises, no one got hurt."

"This time."

"Look, Justice, I know you're pissed. I—"

"I don't get pissed, Jonah."

That was true. Justice rarely lost his cool. His control was legendary. Jonah reached for his own control. Yeah, he knew he'd almost screwed up last week, but in the end the job got done.

"If you think I'm upset about how the op went down," Justice continued, "you're wrong. You made the decision based upon the information you had. No one, especially me, will fault you for that."

"Then what's the problem?"

Justice's voice went to a steely growl. "You went against protocol and ran into that building like some kind of Lone Ranger vigilante. You left your team behind. If they hadn't disobeyed orders and followed you, you'd be dead."

"I was leading the op. My choice, my decision."

"You were leading a team. I don't think you understand the concept of teamwork. You're not one lone man trying to save the world. You're no longer one lone man trying to bring down your father's corrupt empire. You have people depending on you, just like you depend on them. One day it's not going to work out. You're either going to burn yourself out or get yourself killed."

No, not yet. And other than a few nicks and the occasional near miss, he had encountered no real problems. Staying busy kept him sane. And looking for Teri's killer kept him alive.

"It worked out fine."

"You got lucky this time."

Luck? He didn't believe in it. Especially not good luck.

"So, if you have no real info for me, why am I here?"

"I have a job for you."

"You're not firing me?"

"No. Despite your rashness, you're damn good at what you do. Besides, this is more than a job. It's also a favor. And it'll give you some thinking time."

Hell, all he had was thinking time. Staying busy, on the edge of danger, was the only time the demons of regret didn't eat at him.

"What kind of favor?"

"Bodyguard. Interrogator. Watcher. Keeper." Justice shrugged. "However you want to term it."

"Sounds like some kind of made-up bullshit to keep me out of trouble."

"It's neither made up nor bullshit. It's a legitimate and important job. If you don't do it, I'll have a difficult time finding anyone else."

Jonah cast a narrow-eyed doubtful look. "You're telling me that out of all your thousands of erstwhile employees, you can't find someone more suitable than me?"

"Yes. Out of my thousands of employees, you are at the top of my list for this particular job. And before you claim that it's not legitimate, let me remind you that I don't have time for bullshit."

Couldn't argue with the man there. If there was anyone who didn't have time or the inclination for BS, it was Grey Justice. Jonah had met Justice a few years ago. After discovering that his father, Mathias, along with his oldest brother, Adam, were up to their eyeteeth in a multitude of illegal activities, he'd gone to Justice for some advice.

At that time, Jonah had believed that discovering the vileness behind much of his family's wealth would be the darkest moments of his life. Little had he known that uncovering those misdeeds would lead him to an even greater darkness. That had been just the beginning, a starting point. He came to realize that there was darkness and then there was the total absence of light. Nothingness. All hope gone. That was where he'd ended up. Since that day, he had yet to see even a glimmer of light.

Grey Justice, with his obsession for righting wrongs, had helped him immeasurably. Without him, Jonah would be dead. That was fact. He owed the man a helluva lot. So, instead of turning him down outright, he asked, "What makes me so suitable for this job?"

Grey watched with interest as myriad emotions flickered across the hard planes of Jonah's battered face. For a man known for quick action, including making decisions, Grey had stalled considerably on this particular assignment. Going back and forth, he had weighed the consequences if this thing went south against the benefits if it worked the way he hoped. In the end, he trusted his gut. Jonah Slater might be a hothead, but he wasn't without compassion. Life, in the way of his father and brother, had screwed him royally. What better way for him to get past his own pain than to meet someone who had been dealt an even more rotten deal? Jonah had one focus—vengeance. What would happen if he could channel that need into something more worthwhile?

Having manipulated people and events to get the desired results for most of his adult life, Grey had no compunction in skirting the truth. "She's an asset in danger.

"What kind of asset and what kind of danger?"

"The details will be sent to you. Right now…" He glanced at his watch. "You've got a plane to catch."

"Babysitting is not exactly one of my strengths."

"I think Sophie and Violet would disagree."

At the mention of Jonah's two nieces, his stern face softened. "They are the exception. I doubt being an expert in hide-and-go-seek or sipping fake tea is what you have in mind."

"Acting as a bodyguard differs vastly from babysitting. She will be in extreme danger. I'm counting on you to keep her safe."

Grey locked gazes with the man in front of him. He knew full well that Jonah didn't need to work, for Grey or anyone else. Money had nothing to do with his employment with the Grey Justice Group and everything to do with his need to quiet the demons of guilt and grief inside him. Being no stranger to those types of monsters, Grey knew better than most that the only way to combat them was to meet them head on.

Jonah gave a grim nod. "Fine. I'll grab my gear and—"

"No need. Lily's on the roof, waiting. You'll find a go bag already on the chopper, along with the information you'll need."

"I'm impressed. You have your ace pilot waiting for me."

"She'll take you to the landing strip and fly you to your destination."

Jonah went to the elevator door and then turned back to give Grey an enigmatic look. "I've shelved the questions for now."

"You'll learn all you need to know soon. I'll be in touch."

The door closed on Jonah's frowning face. He knew the man hadn't missed the veiled nuances of Grey's promise. Jonah would learn all he needed to know. That didn't necessarily mean he would learn everything, though. At least not yet.

And when he did? Who knew what he would do?

CHAPTER TWO

London, England

Waiting to be kidnapped was a little like sitting on a keg of sizzling dynamite. She knew the where, she knew the when. That was all. Who and how it would go down were nerve-rattling mysteries.

In one way or another, Gabriella Mendoza had been working and planning for this event for most of her adult life. Dreaming and scheming, but without any clear idea of how she could accomplish her goal. By happenstance, design, or small miracle, she wasn't quite sure yet, she'd been given the opportunity to make her plans a reality.

For a girl who had been told what to do for most of her life, that had been a heady, mind-blowing experience. Directed where to go, what to say, what to think, smothered to the point of insanity. Her every action analyzed, judged, discussed, and corrected. She had always consoled herself that she had never given in, not really. But with each day that passed, she could feel herself disappearing more and more. One day she would no longer exist, and she would become a shell-like version of her original self.

Some would look at her life and laugh or sneer in disgust. What did she have to complain about? They would see the house she lived in, the clothes she wore, the food she ate, and see nothing more. She lived a life of wealth and privilege few people could fathom.

If one were willing to look closer, the evidence of a miserable, lifeless existence was apparent.

Raiza, her friend, mentor, and teacher, would be thrilled for her. With stalwart determination, Raiza Torres had combined methodical training and incredible wisdom to prepare her charge for this day. And though her friend was no longer with her, Gabriella could feel her spirit driving her, guiding her toward the freedom they had both wanted for her.

If this didn't work? No. She wouldn't even think that thought. There were no other options. She would never have another chance. It was either this, or accept the invisible chains she would never be able to shed. She would not, could not, fail.

Knowing worry would get her nowhere, she pushed it aside. Crossing the bedroom suite, she went to the window looking out at the vast estate. The winter had been a cold and bitter one, but like a little schoolgirl full of mischief, spring was teasing with tiny buds on the trees. From the ground, hardy crocus heads were popping up, and little blades of green were shooting out in the dead brown grass.

Spring was her favorite season. Rebirth and renewal…a farewell to the old and the cold. So much hope lived in the spring. It was where she lived. No one knew of her hopes, of her plans. They, like her thoughts, were carefully guarded secrets stored away in her head, held close in her heart. She might have no privacy, and her daily activities might be planned from dusk till dawn, but there was one thing no one could invade or take away from her. Her dreams. They were hers alone.

A guard, one of the many who patrolled the perimeter of the estate, clomped across the ground. Gabby winced as his heavy boots stomped the fragile new grass. She had felt that way more than once.

But that would soon change. Hiding her bubbling excitement behind a composed, placid veneer had been more difficult than she'd anticipated. She was so used to disguising her real thoughts, she had believed this would be no different. But this was completely different. The hope she'd held on to for so long now had a solid foundation. She was finally going to be free.

Last night, she had gone through her studio and said goodbye to her work. Her paintings had been her only outlet, the only freedom of expression she had been allowed. Her art held her spirit, her essence, her very being. And she knew to her soul that the paintings would be destroyed. Her grandfather would see to that. She felt as though she was turning her back on them, but she had no choice. If she were to survive, she had to leave everything behind, including the work that had sustained her.

She had woken this morning sad but resolved. She would look to the future, and to have a future, she had to leave everything behind.

"Are you ready?" a harsh voice barked.

Unstartled by the abrupt intrusion, Gabriella turned. Having someone burst into her room without knocking was normal. Prisoners didn't deserve privacy.

"Yes, I'm ready." Her calm statement gave no hint of just how ready she was. In her handbag were all the things she could not live without. How very odd that there was so little. A photo or two of her parents, a necklace that had once belonged to her mother, and her favorite drawing pen. If anyone looked inside, and it wouldn't surprise her if someone did, they would see nothing out of the ordinary. Treasures to her would mean nothing to these heartless men.

"Let's go. I have more important things to do than escort my little sister to a doctor's appointment."

She had learned the hard way that Mendoza women were to act in a certain way. At age fifteen, when most young girls were dreaming of their future and all the possibilities, she had learned of her grandfather's plan for her future. The reinforcement of that news had put her in the hospital for two weeks.

For years, she had followed the rules, biding her time. But soon, very soon, the bird would leave her gilded cage and fly away forever. The time for wishing was over. Now was the time for action.

"If you don't get moving, I'll be glad to give you some incentive."

Carlos's oily voice, with his evil reference, made no impact. She knew why he was here. Raiza was gone. Until a replacement companion could be found, she would be under heavier guard. Her brother had been charged with seeing to the reinforced security. Little did they know that this worked into her plans as if heaven sent. Giving Carlos the responsibility of her security was laughable. Not only was her brother an idiot, he was also lazy. Which made it that much easier for her plans to succeed.

Admittedly, having him here had been unpleasant. Carlos had made numerous threats, but hadn't, as yet, made good on any of them. Gabriella had already decided that if he tried, it would be the last thing he ever did. She might not survive whatever punishment her grandfather devised for such a sin, but it would be much better than having the monster who was her brother touch her in any way.

To know this man was her blood relative was a nauseating fact she had worked hard to forget. She had been successful for many years, mostly because Carlos was occupied with his own pleasurable pursuits. Little did he know that his life was about to take an abrupt plunge to the bottom.

"You know, if I wasn't quite sure you hate me almost as much as I despise you, I'd assume you were delaying so I could carry out my new duties."

Unwilling to deal with the confrontation and its aftermath on a day that would be challenging enough, Gabby allowed herself one lethal glare as she passed him to go out the door. His mocking laughter sent chills of revulsion up her spine, but she quieted them with the reminder that, very soon, his vileness would disappear from her life forever.

***

Sitting in an unobtrusive tan-colored panel truck he'd parked behind a large clump of trees, Wyatt Kingston held the high-powered binoculars to his eyes as he spoke into the radio mic. "They just left the estate."

The British-accented voice of his employer was crisp and clear. "How many following?"

"One SUV. Three guards inside."

"The brother is definitely with her?"

"Yes. They're in the back of the limo together."

"Your recommendation?"

"Looks good."

Silence followed the statement. Wyatt wouldn't act until the go-ahead was given. His team was doing the heavy lifting, but this was all Grey Justice's mission.

"Take them."

"Copy that."

Seated at his desk thousands of miles away, the Dallas skyline at his back, Grey listened as final preparations were made for the abductions of Gabriella and Carlos Mendoza.

If the op went down as planned, both would soon be living very different lives. If this thing went sideways, Carlos Mendoza would be out of their reach forever. As for Gabriella? He didn't kid himself. A failed mission might be the end for her as well.

CHAPTER THREE

London, England

The large waiting room was filled with people, both standing and sitting, but the instant Gabby appeared, a nurse rushed forward and ushered her into an exam room. Not having to wait was a perk she probably didn't fully appreciate. She supposed being related to the doctor was an advantage, but it was one Gabby would gladly do without. When they were small children, she and her cousin Antonia had been occasional playmates. But the adult Antonia, having had all her education paid for by their grandfather, followed his dictates. She did his bidding in all things. Gabby trusted her as much as she trusted anyone in her family, which meant not at all.

The reason for this appointment was a mystery. She had no health issues and had endured a physical exam only a few weeks ago.

Gabby had barely sat down when Antonia glided into the room. Her black Dior dress probably cost more than the monthly rent on the high-priced office space. Her face beautifully austere, she gave an impersonal smile. "And how are we today, Gabriella?"

She couldn't allow Antonia to know that this appointment, no matter the reason, had been a godsend. If she didn't put up at least a little resistance, there would be speculation. She could afford none.

"Why am I here, Antonia? I was here only a few weeks ago."

"Yes, and you were quite ill. I'm just following up to make sure you've recovered."

Gabriella rolled her eyes. "I had a little cold. It was nothing more than that."

"Your health, just like everyone's in our family, is of paramount importance."

"As you can see, I'm perfectly healthy. Feel free to take my temperature or whatever, and you'll see."

"Nonsense." Her gaze shifted to someone standing behind Gabby. "Martha, please help my cousin remove her clothes. I'll be back in a moment."

Gabby turned and faced the sternest, most dour-faced woman she'd ever seen. Gabby had been to her cousin's office many times and had never seen her before. "Are you new?"

The woman's expression never changed. "Please remove your clothes."

An inkling of concern rose inside her. This suddenly felt like more than a casual *let's see how you're doing* exam. Why would she need to take her clothes off for a simple recheck?

Not liking where this was leading, Gabby took a step toward the door. The nurse placed herself in front of Gabby, preventing her from leaving. With a *just try it* expression on her grim face, the woman was as intimidating as any of her grandfather's armed guards. Gabby knew she could fight her way out of here, but then what? All the plans she had made would be for nothing. There might never be another chance.

She drew in a breath. Very well. As frustrating as this might be, she would endure a pointless, useless exam, and then she would be on her way.

She nodded at the nurse in dismissal. "I don't need any help taking my clothes off."

Thankfully, the woman took her at her word and went to stand in front of the door. Leaning against it, the nurse crossed her arms and waited.

As her heart pounded with anxiety, Gabby tried to reassure herself. Antonia would never hurt her. There would be no reason.

She turned her back to the nurse and undressed, her shaking hands and trembling knees slowing her a bit. When she was nude, she felt a soft robe descend on her shoulders. Grateful for the warming comfort, Gabby wrapped the robe around her body, then sat on the edge of a chair, trying to prevent her teeth from chattering.

Seconds later, Antonia returned, holding a steaming cup. "Sorry for the chill. Here's your tea, prepared just the way you like it—one sugar, no cream."

Telling Antonia that the chill in the air had nothing to do with her shivering would do no good. Taking the cup, she breathed in the aromatic fragrance of spring flowers. At least this felt normal. Their love of tea was one of the few things she and her cousin had in common. Antonia always gave her a cup of tea during an office visit.

Sipping the brew, Gabby gave a grateful hum. "It's delicious."

Antonia smiled. "It's my new favorite. I'll have my office manager get you a tin of it to take home with you."

Gabby took another sip and sighed. With the warmth of the soft robe and the delicious tea, she was feeling much more relaxed. There was no reason for her to worry. Antonia would give her a quick exam, note that she was indeed perfectly healthy, and that would be that. She would leave here and begin a brand-new life.

The feeling of happy anticipation was the last thing she remembered.

***

Gabby walked out of the doctor's office under her own steam, but it took every ounce of determination to do so. Her body ached, but for some odd reason, she couldn't determine the location or the reason. Her mind was a blur of vague images and soft words, but she couldn't piece together who had said them or what had happened.

Though all she wanted to do was lie down and take a long nap, she struggled to comprehend what had occurred. She remembered sipping tea, feeling warm and cozy, and then nothing. When she woke, Antonia had been standing over her, and Gabby was once again fully clothed.

When Gabby had asked if she'd been drugged, Antonia had given her a slightly guilty look and admitted slipping a light sedative into the tea. She claimed that because Gabby had seemed so anxious, she had drugged her to make her feel better, nothing more.

A harsh curse came from Carlos, who was standing at the door of the elevator, glaring at her. "Would you come on already? I have important people waiting on me."

One guard followed behind her, and two guards flanked her, but unless she tripped no one would touch her. The rule of the house—no men outside the family could touch a Mendoza female.

She made it to the elevator just as the doors opened. Carlos stepped on and then watched with a smirk as she followed, stumbling. The instant she entered, Gabby grabbed the bar to steady herself. Their faces as expressionless as robots, the guards stepped inside, and one pushed the button for the ground floor. The car moved, and a wave of nausea rolled through her. With every bit of determination she could muster, she fought the sickness. Admittedly, while throwing up all over Carlos and her guards would give her a sense of satisfaction, the temptation was one she dared not indulge. The guards would take the insult like any loyal soldier, but humiliating a Mendoza in public would not be tolerated. Swallowing back the nausea, Gabby gripped the bar tighter.

She arrived at the first floor without humiliating herself and breathed a prayer of thankfulness. Carlos was the first one out of the elevator. Two of her bodyguards went ahead of her. Gabby stepped out, followed by another guard. Too sick to notice the stares and whispers from a lobby filled with strangers, Gabby kept her eyes focused on the prize. The limo waited on the street, the back door already open. She walked through the revolving door and onto the sidewalk. Just a few more steps, and she could collapse into her seat and take a nap. That was all she needed, just a short nap, and she would be fine.

Three feet from the car, she heard a slight whisper of sound and turned.

Chaos erupted.

The targets exited the building and headed to the limo. Taking them on the street in front of dozens of witnesses held risks, but an open-road abduction held more danger. The chances of a target being injured were greater. The mission was abduction without harm. This scenario was the only way Wyatt could ensure their safety.

His men waited for the signal, and Wyatt spoke quietly, "Go."

The van jerked to a stop beside the limo, obstructing its exit from the front. An SUV stopped a few feet behind the van. The limo was blocked front and back. The only exit was the sidewalk, but a parking meter and concrete post prevented escape that way.

Wyatt's men jumped from their vehicles and surrounded the small group. Three men went for the bodyguards. Wyatt went for Gabriella. Another man reached for her brother Carlos.

A second from securing his target, Wyatt jerked to a stop when Carlos grabbed hold of his sister. Showing just what a sleazeball he was, he jerked Gabriella in front of him and yelled, "Take her. She'll bring you more ransom money than I would."

Wyatt wrapped his hand around Gabriella's arm and snatched her away from her brother. Holding her with one arm, he used his other arm to shove the asshole toward one of his men. A yelp of pain erupted from Carlos, and Wyatt smiled. The tranquilizer needle jabbed into the idiot's neck had apparently hurt. *Good.*

Gabriella began to struggle in his arms. Whether she did it to make the guards believe she had no part in the abduction, or she really was afraid, he didn't know. Easily holding her, Wyatt pushed a pressure syringe filled with a sleeping agent against her neck. She slumped like a wilted flower in his arms. Surprised at the quick reaction—the drug wasn't nearly as potent as the one her brother had received—Wyatt made a quick check to make sure she wasn't faking. Sure enough, she was out like a light. Deciding she must be a total lightweight, Wyatt covered her face with a hood, lifted her into his arms, and carried her to the SUV. He placed her in the back of the vehicle and quickly tied her hands and feet together.

Another man carried Carlos to the van. The three bodyguards, all in various stages of consciousness, would be transported to a densely wooded area miles away. After a few hours, they would be set free.

Gabriella should stay unconscious until he was out of the city, but if she didn't, she was restrained and shouldn't cause any problems. Since he didn't want her to be able to identify him if things went south, she would remain blindfolded and tied up until the transfer. Then she would become another man's problem.

Heaven help her.

CHAPTER FOUR

She woke to darkness, head pounding, stomach roiling, arms and legs bound. A cloth covered her entire head. Her mind felt fractured, her thoughts so chaotic that for a moment she feared she had amnesia. Did she know her name? Yes, yes. She was Gabriella Mendoza. Her parents, beloved and long dead, had been Javier and Meredith. The evil and powerful Luis Mendoza was her grandfather. Carlos, her brother, was rapidly following in their grandfather's wicked footsteps.

So she didn't have amnesia. Where was she? What had happened? Her memory was still blurred. Men had attacked them. The bodyguards had been knocked out. She and Carlos had been abducted. Was her brother here with her, too?

She struggled against her bonds. Even as her mind told her to stay quiet until she figured things out, she couldn't stop the whimpers of distress.

"Relax," a gruff male voice said. "You're safe."

Two observations hit her at once. She was in a vehicle—she could feel the vibration of movement beneath her back. She was lying on a cushioned seat, likely the backseat of the car. And she didn't know the voice of the man. He'd spoken Spanish, but his accent held a slight oddity to it. He was an American. Why would—

If her hands had been free, she would have slapped her forehead for her stupidity. The truth of what was going on finally penetrated her fogged brain. She hadn't been kidnapped for nefarious reasons. This was her rescue. The deal she'd made months ago. The abduction she had arranged and anticipated had finally taken place.

She moved her shoulders to ease the tension and then stiffened again. Her purse. When she'd walked out of the building, her purse had been draped over her right shoulder. Where was it now? With her hands bound and her eyes covered she had no way of searching.

"Do you know what happened to my purse?"

"It dropped on the ground when we grabbed you. Did you have medication inside it? Something you have to have?"

"No...no. Nothing like that." Behind the hood, Gabby squeezed her eyes tight but tears seeped out anyway. The photos of her parents, her mother's necklace. Getting them back would be impossible. It had been all she'd had left of them.

She drew in a breath, then another one. Crying over what could not be changed was pointless. Her parents were in her heart. The memory of their love would remain within her forever.

She had to look to the future. Everything would be all right. No, she didn't know the name of the man who'd spoken. No, she didn't know where she was going. And no, she had no clue what her future held. But one thing she did know was that she now actually had a future. One that didn't involve her grandfather's autocratic rule or his cruel schemes.

She was free from the Mendoza curse. At last.

Even though she was lying in the backseat and he couldn't even see her, Wyatt sensed the tension leave Gabriella's body. They'd had to make the abduction as realistic as possible. When witnesses were questioned and the guards found, all would report that masked men with powerful-looking guns had abducted Gabriella and Carlos Mendoza. No one would suspect that Gabriella had been the one to instigate the event. Carlos was headed back to the United States, where he would finally face justice. And Gabriella? He didn't have a clue, but if he knew Grey Justice, the man had an agenda for her, too.

"Could I know your name?" she asked in perfect English, with only a trace of a British accent.

"No."

She drew in a sharp breath and didn't breathe for several seconds. His answer had startled her, but having her fearful was all right for now. She needed to be alert and on guard. Just because they had come this far didn't mean they were out of danger. She needed to be wary—even of him. He was not her savior.

"Could I at least remove the hood?"

"It's best for both of us that you can't see. Be assured you're all right."

"I'm having difficulty breathing."

"No, you're not."

"Shouldn't I be the judge of whether I'm breathing fine or not?"

He grinned, pleased. She didn't sound scared anymore. She sounded decidedly aggravated.

"We'll be at our destination soon. You can take it off then."

"Where are we going? How do I know you are who you say you are?"

"I didn't say who I am."

She went silent, and he knew he had made her afraid again. Strange, but he felt bad about that. Couldn't be helped, though. He was doing the job he'd been paid to do. Mollycoddling his captive wasn't part of the op. When he heard a slight noise that sounded like a soft whimper, he relented. "You're going to be fine. No one will hurt you."

"Thank you."

Wyatt wasn't known for his kindness, but he was human enough to want to reassure her. Besides, the last thing he needed was for her to panic and try to escape.

This time of night, with the exception of the occasional trucker, the two-lane highway was empty. He was making good time and should be at their destination ahead of schedule.

What lay ahead for his passenger once they reached the drop-off place wasn't something he would speculate about. She would be out of his hands and someone else's responsibility. The fact that Justice had advised him to take extra care with her was an indicator that she was under the man's protection. Despite the need to distance himself from any kind of softness, Wyatt was glad she would be safe. The instant before he'd covered her head with the black hood, he'd glimpsed a surprising vulnerability in her dark brown eyes. Surprising, since her family was some of the worst scumbags in this world. Had Gabriella Mendoza managed to escape from that evil? Or was that, like everything else in this world, just a lie?

Headlights in his rearview mirror barely gave him a warning. A loud speaker blared the dire words, "Pull over or die." A blast of piercing light exploded, almost blinding him.

Wyatt slammed his foot to the accelerator and growled, "Stay down."

He kept one eye on the road, another on the rearview mirror as he pressed a button on his steering wheel. The moment the call was answered, he said, "I've got trouble."

"Where are you?"

"Route 23. About ten minutes away from the drop-off."

"I'll head your way."

The call ended. Wyatt knew not to go to the original destination. Best he could do was outrun them until backup arrived.

"Are you going to pull over?"

The soft, quivering voice coming from the backseat barely penetrated Wyatt's consciousness. His concentration lay on staying alive and on the road.

"No. Just stay down and keep quiet. You'll be fine."

"That voice belongs to a man named Horatio Powers. He's in charge of my security. He won't give up."

"Yeah...well, I'm not big on giving up either."

Wyatt adjusted the rearview mirrors to block out as much of the piercing light as possible. If he could elude them, he would. He had his doubts that would be possible, but he'd do his dead-level best.

Luis Mendoza would not want his granddaughter injured, of this he was sure. They wouldn't shoot at them while the Jeep was moving, and since he wasn't about to pull over, he figured they'd just follow him until he had to stop. The man coming would take Gabriella to the safe house, and Wyatt could leave her in the capable hands of her protector.

The SUV behind him lightly bumped the Jeep. Wyatt cursed. They might not be willing to kill Gabriella, but that didn't mean they wouldn't try to run him off the road. If that happened, he was a dead man. No way would they allow him to live.

"Do you have a gun?"

The question startled him. "Yes, but shooting while driving on an icy unfamiliar road isn't—"

"I can shoot."

"You?"

"You needn't sound so surprised. I am proficient in many things."

"Okay, sit up and lean forward so I can uncover your head."

She popped up, and Wyatt reached back and jerked the hood from her head. He didn't have to look at her to see the relief she must feel.

"Turn around so I can untie you."

It was a little tricky with one hand, but he had her hands loose in a matter of seconds. Pulling his secondary weapon from his ankle holster, he handed it to her. "This is a SIG Sauer with a—"

"No need for instruction. I know its capabilities."

Impressed at her calmness, he put both hands back on the steering wheel and glanced in the rearview mirror. "Hopefully, you won't have to use it."

"I don't care what they try. I am not going back. I'll take death over returning."

Gabby took a brief second to look around and get her bearings. They were on a two-lane, winding road. It was midnight dark, but the spotlight from the truck behind them cast a brilliant glow. Her vision wavered. She squinted at the vehicle, cursing the drugs she'd been given. She had bragged about her proficiency with a gun, and while her claim was true, she wasn't sure she could hit the broad side of a slow-moving train in her condition.

The interior of their vehicle was so bright that she knew if anyone had been trying to kill them, they'd be easy targets.

Fortunately, her grandfather's men wouldn't shoot for fear of her getting hurt by a stray bullet or a car wreck.

"How much farther to our destination?"

"Doesn't matter. I can't lead them to where we're going. We'll keep going until we—"

As abrupt as a light switch, bright lights exploded from the opposite direction. A cellphone buzzed. The man behind the wheel pressed a button. A voice that was gravelly low and hard as steel said, "In three seconds, switch to the other lane. Three. Two. One. Now!"

Before Gabby could ask what was going on, the man behind the wheel had switched lanes and the oncoming car was now heading straight toward the SUV carrying her grandfather's men.

Kneeling on the seat, she looked out the back window, watching in horror. "What is he doing?"

"Playing chicken."

"He's going to get himself killed."

His eyes on the rearview mirror, he growled a low curse. "Probably someday."

The two vehicles came closer and closer to each other. Seconds from crashing head on, the SUV swerved off the road and disappeared down a steep embankment. The car with the daredevil driver jerked to a stop and made a U-turn in the middle of the road.

The voice spoke again. "Let's go ahead and make the exchange up ahead." This time, he sounded bored, maybe a little annoyed. She was supposed to get in the car with *him*? This man who'd had the nerve to play chicken with her grandfather's men?

They traveled a few more yards and then pulled into a clearing on the side of the road. The other man pulled in behind them.

The adrenaline rush now draining from her body, Gabby felt the world whirling around her. Drugs, along with fear and exhaustion, were rapidly taking their toll. She told herself she couldn't let go. She didn't know these people. Just because they had helped her escape didn't mean they didn't have their own agenda. She needed to stay alert and wary.

The door beside her opened, and she looked up into eyes the color of dark green moss. A memory hovered, just out of reach. Her blurred brain reached frantically for it, as if letting her know this was important information.

Without a word, the green-eyed man extended a hand. Gabby took it, vaguely noting how warm, large, and rough it seemed as she was pulled from the backseat.

Her feet touched the ground, and despite her self-lecture about staying awake and aware, she collapsed into the man's arms. She was conscious only long enough to hear the man say, his gruff voice sounding slightly amused, "Hello, princess."

CHAPTER FIVE

Colorado Mountains

Jonah stuck his head inside the bedroom. This wasn't normal. She was still out. When she collapsed in his arms, he had assumed she'd fainted and would wake soon. During a ten-hour flight, plus an hour of traveling to get to the safe house, she hadn't made one single indication of consciousness. Something wasn't right.

Closing the door, he punched speed-dial on his phone. The instant it was answered, he said, "What the hell did Kingston give her?"

"A mild knockout drug. Nothing dangerous. Why?"

"She's still out of it."

"Kingston said she looked a little glassy-eyed when she came out of the building. If she had something already in her system, that might account for it."

"She have a drug problem?"

"My intel says no. Maybe whatever she had done at the doctor's office required a sedative."

"Could be. Her breathing's okay, as is her pulse."

"A double dose of sedative, plus the anxiety of the abduction, might've put her system in a tailspin."

"Yeah." He glanced at the closed door. He hoped that's all it was. Babysitting the granddaughter of a notorious crime boss was bad enough. Having her die in his charge would be a damn sight worse.

"You haven't seen anyone suspicious?"

Striding to one of the small windows on the second floor, Jonah looked out at the stark-white landscape.

"No. We got handed a full-on blizzard a little after midnight. Even if they knew where she's stashed, anyone looking for her would have a helluva time getting here."

"Yeah. I heard the area was hit hard. It'll be a few days before I can pay her a visit."

There were worse things than staying holed up in a luxury mansion in the middle of a large forest while winter raged around them, but Jonah felt the restrictions like a tight chain around his neck. The noise he made was meant to sound like a nonverbal affirmation. It came out more like the growl of a rabid wolf.

As if he hadn't heard the frustration in Jonah's response, Justice went on. "That'll give you time to ease into the questions. If she knows something about her grandfather's activities, it's best we find out before the feds find her."

The minute Jonah had boarded Justice's private jet, he'd been handed a thick file filled with facts, suppositions, and suspicions of what the Mendoza family had been involved with over the last thirty or so years. Murder, drug trafficking, and arms dealing were just a few of the suspected activities.

Having had a father and brother mired in a multitude of illegal and sickening crimes, Jonah was way past being shocked by another man's evil ambition. He was, however, more intrigued than he'd planned to be.

Unable to stop himself, he went back to the bedroom and opened the door. Even though he'd gotten only a brief glimpse of her before she'd lost consciousness, her eyes had gleamed with both determination and vulnerability.

She was beautiful, too. The file had been filled with multiple photographs taken over the years at the events the woman had attended. She reminded him of a young Catherine Zeta-Jones. It was her eyes that struck him the most. Even when she was at her most glamorous and smiling, the sadness in them told a different story.

If he was going to do the job he'd been tasked to do, he was going to have to ignore that vulnerability. When word spread that the granddaughter of the notorious Luis Mendoza had been taken, every alphabet law enforcement agency in the US, along with agencies from numerous other countries, would be working to find her. They'd want to know what she knew. Jonah intended to find out first.

"How long do we have before the feds come calling?"

"Luis Mendoza will try to keep the abduction a secret as long as possible while he searches for her. Unfortunately, the event was somewhat public, so it won't be a secret for long. Good thing is, only three people know your location. You should be safe, but best not to take anything for granted."

Jonah grunted again. He'd learned the hard way to never take anything for granted. If shit was going to find you, it'd seep into any crack or cranny it could find.

With the promise to notify Justice when he learned anything of value, Jonah ended the call. He turned away from the sleeping beauty on the bed and went to the window facing the back of the house. The pristine purity of the snow was in direct contrast to the darkness of his thoughts. While he was locked up in this wood and rock mansion, watching over a crime princess, Teri's killer roamed free. The bastard was out there somewhere, breathing, eating, and sleeping. Every day he was allowed to draw breath was a day he never should have had.

Her killer hadn't known her. Teri had been nothing more than a job to him, a contract to fulfill. To Jonah, she'd been everything good and fine. If not for her, he would have been alone, looking for a way to bring his father and Adam, his oldest brother, to justice. In the end, their plan had destroyed them both. Jonah had been framed and imprisoned. Teri had been murdered. A hit, ordered by his own father, Mathias Slater.

The instant he was released from prison, Jonah had been on a quest to bring her killer to justice. So far, all he had were odd, vague leads that had led him nowhere. A man named Peter who resided up north was not much to go on. And if not for Grey Justice, he might not even have had that. He had known going in that getting justice for Teri would be slow going. While he waited for a lead to pan out, he worked his ass off conducting various missions for the Grey Justice Group. But in the downtime, when all he had were his thoughts and his demons, guilt sliced through him like a fiery knife. Teri had died because of him.

So yes, there were worse things than being holed up in a fortress protecting a beautiful woman.

The sooner he got the info they needed and Gabriella Mendoza went on to start her new life, the sooner he could get back to gaining justice for Teri.

***

Gabby frowned at the unpleasant sensation. She'd been existing in soft, dark oblivion, surrounded by brilliant emerald stars. But now an irritant, like a buzzing gnat, threatened her peace. She batted her hand to shoo the thing away and made contact with something much bigger than a gnat. Something that growled a curse.

Her eyes, still heavy, blinked and tried to open. When that proved too much trouble, she stopped trying and searched for beautiful oblivion once more.

"Oh no you don't. You've been out of it way too long. Wake up, princess. It's time to face reality."

Gabby frowned at the brusque voice. She didn't recognize it, but she had a vague recollection of someone calling her princess. Squinting, she peeked through her lashes and caught her breath on a gasp. The man's eyes were the same color as the stars in her dreams. Only they didn't look nearly as friendly as her stars.

"Who are you?"

"Your babysitter for the foreseeable future. Think you can sit up?"

Confused, she glanced around the room. She was in a large, lovely bedroom with walls the color of a peaceful ocean. It wasn't her bedroom. Gabby scrambled to remember what happened.

"Whatever the hell drugs you were on did a number on you, didn't they?"

Insulted, she snapped, "I do not take drugs."

Though he didn't smile, something gleamed in his brilliant eyes, making her think she had amused him. "Then why don't you remember what happened?"

"How do you know I don't remember?"

"Because you look confused."

Refusing to stay in a supine position in the presence of the unfriendly stranger, Gabby moved to sit up. Thinking the man would back away, she sat up quickly, and her head connected with his chin.

"Dammit. First a slug and now a head-butt. No one told me you were so violent."

"I'm not violent. You just happened to be in the way. Now who are you and where am I?"

"You're in the US. Colorado, to be exact. I believe you requested this, shall we say abduction, in exchange for your brother. Do you remember that?"

Breath gushed from Gabby as memories returned in a flood of images. Masked men. Guns. A car chase. And then this man had been there. She could piece together most of it, but there was one thing she didn't know.

"My brother...Carlos. Where is he?"

"Your concern would be touching if not for the fact that you set him up. Having second thoughts?"

She didn't bother to explain to this unfriendly stranger that concern for her brother's welfare was not the reason for her question. If Carlos were anywhere nearby, he would do his best to take her back to her grandfather. She had to know so she could be prepared.

She asked again, "Where is he?"

"He's in police custody in Dallas, Texas."

Massive relief rushed through her. At last Carlos would receive the punishment he deserved. He was far away and locked up. He would never hurt any innocent woman again. And she had escaped her grandfather. Her plan had actually worked!

"Are you going to pass out again? If so, warn me so I can get out of your way."

"Are you an ass by nature, or is this special treatment just for me?"

His stern mouth twitched this time, giving her the idea he had almost smiled. He didn't look like the type who smiled much. That was fine with her. Having been surrounded by smiling people most of her life, she knew a fake smile could hide a multitude of sins. This man's surly attitude was actually quite refreshing.

"You've been out a long time. Over twelve hours. I would imagine you're hungry."

The grogginess was rapidly wearing off, telling her she was both hungry and in desperate need of the bathroom.

As if reading her thoughts, he stepped away from the bed. "The bathroom's through that door over there. You should have everything you need. If you don't find it, let me know. I'll go round us up some grub, then we can talk."

She swung her feet to the floor and stood up slowly. Thankful the room was no longer swirling around her, she went toward the door he'd indicated. The man stayed close for a few seconds, and though he wasn't within touching range, she got the impression that if she stumbled, he could grab her in a second. She wasn't sure why that image both terrified and excited her.

Apparently satisfied she wasn't going to pass out again, the man headed out of the bedroom.

She stopped at the bathroom door. "Wait. You haven't told me your name."

"The name's Slater. Jonah Slater."

He threw the answer over his shoulder, so he didn't see the shock or hear her small gasp. Jonah Slater? Really? After all these years? How had she not recognized him?

Had she escaped her grandfather only to end up in the hands of a man who had every reason to hate her?

CHAPTER SIX

Valencia, Venezuela
Mendoza Estate

If he didn't let loose the fury boiling inside him, Luis Mendoza knew that any moment now he would have a stroke. His grandchildren had been taken from him. And what had his people told him? Nothing so far. The only answer he'd received from even his most trusted advisers was, "We have no idea who took them or why."

"This is intolerable. I will not stand for it."

Striding to the phone at his desk, he pressed a series of numbers. The instant the call was answered, Luis released a battalion of verbal threats that might be laughable if they hadn't been all true. He would have every damn one of them carried out if his grandchildren were not returned. Secondly, and just as important, he wanted to know who was responsible. When he found them, he would unleash a hell unseen in modern times.

"I'll do my best, Señor Mendoza. But my sources say that the cameras malfunctioned all over the city that day. The eyewitnesses said the men spoke fluent Spanish, and all wore ski masks to hide their faces. They had no other information to share. With so little to go on, finding the culprits will—"

"I don't want excuses, I want results. If you can't give me what I need, I'll make sure that young trophy wife you're so proud of doesn't get the chance to get any older."

"Señor Mendoza, you are threatening a government official. Surely you realize that—"

"Don't you dare act as if you have clean hands. You have taken more bribes than I can count. Get me the name of the person responsible and you stay alive. Get it within the next forty-eight hours and your wife can live, too."

Luis slammed the phone into its receiver. He had several cellphones, but when it came to certain calls, he trusted only an old-fashioned landline. Plus, there was something so very satisfying about slamming a phone down. Couldn't do that to a damn cellphone without breaking it. He had broken more than his share.

His fury still at the boiling point, Luis bellowed, "Stephan!"

As silent as a lizard, his friend and right-hand man slid into the room. With a face on the wrong side of ugly and a body a championship wrestler would envy, Stephan Conti was the one person in the world whom Luis trusted completely. They had grown up together. Had attended the same schools and knew each other better than their spouses could ever imagine. They'd shared secrets, women, and when they were younger, they'd killed together. These days, neither of them had the energy to do much more than share memories of the grand old days. But just because they were old didn't mean Luis was any less powerful or Stephan any less deadly.

"What am I to do?"

No one, not even his dear wife, Flora, had ever been privy to seeing Luis in a vulnerable position. Only Stephan had been allowed that privilege.

His ugly face wrinkled with fury, Stephan commiserated the only way he could. "We will find your grandchildren. Then we will hunt down the bastards who did this and disembowel them in front of their entire families."

A rattling rush of air expelled from Luis's lungs. No one could ease his worry or bolster his confidence like Stephan.

"Thank you, my friend. You always put things in the proper perspective."

With renewed energy, he ambled to the bar across the room and poured two fingers of scotch for each of them. Offering a glass to Stephan, he took his drink and settled on a leather sofa. He took a sip of the smoky liquid, swished it around his tongue, and swallowed. He could feel his muscles relaxing at last. It would all work out. He'd worked too hard, waited too long, to fail now.

He allowed himself a moment of silent peace, then said, "All right. Tell me everything."

"They were taken in front of Antonia's building. Gabriella had just undergone her procedure."

Stephan paused long enough to give Luis a disapproving glare. In all the years they'd been friends, Luis's decisions regarding Gabriella had invoked the most disagreement. Stephan had vehemently opposed Luis's most recent choice for her life.

Luis really didn't see what the problem was. It wasn't as if he was planning on killing the girl. He had provided Gabriella with the best of everything. She owed him this one small favor. And as her grandfather and leader of the Mendoza family, it was his right.

Ignoring the barely veiled censure, Luis made a sweeping hand motion, urging Stephan to continue.

"According to the witnesses we've talked to, Carlos and Gabriella, along with three guards, walked out of the medical building. The instant they stepped onto the sidewalk, they were surrounded by seven masked men. Vehicles blocked the limo. One man took Carlos, another took Gabriella. The other men took the guards. They all left in separate vehicles."

"And no one could give any descriptions?"

"No. Again, they all wore ski masks. In less than a minute, they were gone. This was a well-planned and expertly executed abduction. They were obviously professionals."

"What about license plates, identifying marks on the vehicles?"

"None were reported."

"I was told that cameras all over the city malfunctioned."

"This is true and cannot be a coincidence. This was a strategic strike against you. The men were heavily armed and disabled our guards without one shot being fired."

"All the guards have been found?"

"Yes. They were released about a hundred miles outside London in a remote area. Unharmed."

For now, Luis thought. He needn't state the obvious. The men would be reprimanded, and their families would be threatened. If they didn't find his grandchildren, they would lose their lives, and if he felt like it, he'd have their families killed, too. It was as simple as that. They had failed in their jobs. If they didn't rectify the situation, punishment would be swift and brutal.

"What are the guards saying? Have they nothing useful to share?"

"Nothing more than what the witnesses have already told us. They claim no words were exchanged while they were being transported to their drop-off point."

"Is this Bianchi's doing?" The question had gnawed at him ever since he'd learned of the abductions. Would Rudolph be so bold, so daring? It was something he had feared for so long. If Bianchi gained Gabriella, where did that leave him and their agreement? He couldn't even bring himself to contemplate the answer. But if this were Bianchi's doing, why take Carlos, too? That didn't make any sense.

Darkness flickered in Stephan's eyes. "Based on what I just learned, I don't think it's Bianchi."

"You have news?" Luis snarled. "Tell me. Now!"

"Carlos is in the custody of the Dallas Police Department in Texas. He was found, bound and gagged, inside a police car with a note attached to his shirt."

Seething, Luis asked through clenched teeth, "And what did this note say?"

Stephan glanced down at his phone and read the message. *My name is Carlos Luis Mendoza. I am a rapist and a scumbag. I escaped justice once before. If you allow me to escape again, you won't ever find me. Don't let me out this time.*

"Dammit, I was afraid this would happen. I told him he needed to take extra care."

"Perhaps sending him to London was not the best idea."

"Gabriella needed extra eyes until I could find her another companion. Besides, he was getting bored and restless here. It was only a matter of time before the boy got into trouble again. I had no choice."

Stephan nodded. "You're right, of course."

He and Stephan had discussed Carlos many times. They had argued over what to do about the young man and his predilection for getting into trouble. Luis had no issues with his grandson having a bit of fun, but his stupidity in not hiding his less-savory misdeeds had caused a world of problems for the family. The last time he was in the States, the imbecile had actually had the audacity to return the girl to her home after keeping her for a few days.

Carlos had taken no precautions. The girl had known his name and how to find him. Within hours, Carlos had been arrested and charged with a multitude of offenses. If not for Luis's contacts and connections, the boy would have surely faced years of prison time. Luis had arranged bail for him and had spirited him back to his home country.

Luis's sources had reported that the girl, Stephanie something or other, had taken her life after Carlos's escape. While he could comprehend the girl's family wanting vengeance, he couldn't allow his grandson to be imprisoned. Besides, the girl had obviously had too much freedom, or she never would have been with Carlos.

"I don't think there's anything we can do to save him now."

Stephan's words made the scotch Luis had consumed turn sour in his stomach. No, he wouldn't give up on his grandson. He would do all he could for Carlos, but it would take time. He would let the boy stew in a jail cell for a few months. Maybe it would do him some good, teach him some humility. His main concern now was getting Gabriella back home. She was his only priority.

"Gabriella is the one we need to concentrate on."

"Of course."

The way Stephan responded made Luis's heart leap with optimism. "You have good news. You found her?"

"Not yet, but we're working on it."

"Working on it how? What do you have?"

A slow smile spread across Stephan's face. "Did you forget the other procedure Gabriella went through several years ago?"

How could he have forgotten? This was actually something both he and Stephan had agreed upon. In fact, it had been Stephan's idea.

"So we know how to find her?"

"Yes. Worry not, my friend. We will be bringing your granddaughter home soon."

CHAPTER SEVEN

Colorado Mountains

Shoving two frozen dinners into the microwave, Jonah set the timer and waited. The pantry and freezer were well stocked, which was a good thing since he couldn't cook worth a damn. They had plenty of frozen meals and canned foods to last them through the summer if need be. Not that he planned to be here that long. Once he got the information he needed, he'd be out of here, and Gabriella Mendoza would be on her way to a new life.

He had to admit she had surprised him. Most people would be at least a little apprehensive to wake up to find a complete stranger standing over them. Instead, once she'd regained her composure, she had acted as if nothing unusual had happened. Hell, with her family, maybe things like that happened all the time.

He'd read her file and had been prepared to dislike every person who shared the Mendoza name. Even though the crimes were somewhat different, there were too many similarities to his own screwed-up family to have any kind of good feeling about meeting Gabriella, much less being her caretaker.

He still didn't plan on liking her, but at least she wasn't completely disagreeable.

Hearing a noise behind him, he twisted around. Three years of prison meant no one got the drop on him. So how did this woman suddenly appear without him knowing? He told himself that lack of sleep blurred his concentration and that the noise from the microwave had obscured her sounds. His lack of wariness had nothing to do with the beautiful, doe-eyed creature who looked far too innocent for her own good. She had been exposed to a cesspool of human vermin her entire life. No way had she escaped without some kind of corruption. Just because she wanted to get away from her family didn't mean she didn't carry that evil inside her. Wasn't he a prime example?

"So what now?"

He couldn't fathom why, but she was looking much more cautious than she had before. He switched his expression to neutral. He was here to gain her trust and learn what secrets she might harbor. Glaring at her like she was his enemy wouldn't exactly inspire trust.

"We eat."

"Thank you. I'm starving." And with that, she sat down at the table, folded her hands in front of her, and looked up at him expectantly.

Jonah raised a brow at the obvious sign that she was waiting to be served. "You'll find the plates in the cabinet behind you and the silverware in the drawer to the left."

Confusion flickered in her eyes, and then she caught his meaning. Flushing a lovely shade of pink, she jumped to her feet and went to the cabinet for the plates.

He held back a sarcastic remark. Wasn't her fault that she'd been pampered and waited upon her entire life. Going from a privileged background to fending for herself was going to take some adjustment.

After the plates and silverware were placed on the table, Jonah pulled their meals from the microwave. Placing a tray of food in front of her, he took his own tray and transferred his food to the plate.

Out of the corner of his eye, he watched as she copied him. Something odd clinched his heart at her obvious attempt to do exactly what he was doing. He knew how it felt to be a fish out of water. He'd been a privileged young man thrown into a prison filled with the most-hardened criminals. It had been sink or swim for him. And if he'd thought about it too hard, he knew he'd have never fully emerged.

They ate in silence. She had a healthy appetite, greedily scraping up the last bites of the plate of salmon, wild rice, and broccoli until there was nothing left.

"Want anything else?"

"No. Thank you. It was delicious."

"Let's get this cleaned up." He took his plate, silverware, and glass to the sink. Rinsed them and then placed them in the dishwasher. He walked across the room to look out the window and figured she would copy him in that, too. He listened as she took care of her dishes and wasn't surprised to have her come stand beside him.

"You said we're in Colorado. What city?"

"A few miles outside Grand Junction."

"I've never seen snow like this."

"Supposed to be like this for at least a couple more days."

"It feels so isolated."

He glanced at her, wondering if she was nervous about being alone with a stranger. He didn't see fear in her eyes, but there was definite guardedness in her manner.

"Is there any way my grandfather's men can find me?"

"We're thousands of miles away. No one followed us. We're isolated, with plenty of safeguards. If anyone does venture here, friend or foe, I'd know about it in advance."

She nodded her head in agreement, but her body language said something else. She was still uncertain about things. Maybe this would help. "Follow me."

In silence, Gabby followed Jonah Slater from the kitchen into a small, efficient-looking office. He had been coolly polite. She was thankful he hadn't laughed at her when she had sat down at the table. Setting a table for a meal was something completely out of her realm of experience. Other than dressing herself and taking care of her personal hygiene, she wasn't allowed to do much of anything else. Some people might think that was a blessing, but she'd always seen it as a curse. Helplessness was abhorrent to her. It was a feeling she'd had most of her life and the one thing she was determined never to feel again.

She stood in the doorway while Jonah clicked a laptop keyboard on the desk. She didn't trust him...not completely. She knew too much about him and his family to feel remotely comfortable with him. He hadn't given any indication that he remembered her. No, he wasn't overly friendly, but he didn't seem to hate her. If he had remembered, she was certain there would have been animosity.

"There's someone that wants to talk to you."

A spurt of panic burst through her. She had been betrayed. He was going to contact her grandfather. Gabby backed away one step, on the verge of running for the door. She'd rather take her chances in a blizzard than be returned to hell.

"Gabriella?" A female voice called her name.

She'd heard that voice only a couple of times, but she recognized it immediately. She rushed to the desk where the laptop screen revealed the one person she did trust—the woman who had arranged her abduction—Kathleen Callahan.

The relief made her practically gush her words. "Kathleen, it's so good to see you."

"It's good to see you, too. How are you? Is Jonah taking good care of you?"

"Yes, of course. I—" She threw a glance toward Jonah, uncomfortable talking in front of him.

Giving her a slight nod, telling her he knew exactly what she was thinking, he backed out of the room. "I'll give you two some privacy." Surprising her even more, he closed the door.

Feeling as though the air had been sucked out of the room, Gabby felt her legs give out, and she dropped into a chair.

"Are you okay?"

"No, but I will be."

Kathleen's face scrunched up into a frown. "I had hoped to be there to greet you, but I'm a little indisposed."

"What's wrong?"

"Nothing other than I'm pregnant and can't fly."

"Oh! Congratulations."

"Thank you. It's been a while since we talked. I'm sorry it took so long to get you."

A few months more of waiting had been hard, but that was behind her now. "My brother...what's happened to him?"

"He's in jail in Dallas. For now, he's been charged with the rape and kidnapping of Stephanie Pierce, but there are three other women who have come forward with the same allegations."

Even though she was still exhausted and more than a little emotionally overwhelmed, she recognized the significance of the timing. Kathleen and whoever she was working with had been prepared for this.

"I don't think you'll ever have to worry about him again."

The compassion in Kathleen's voice brought tears to Gabby's eyes. At least one evil was locked up where he could no longer hurt the innocent.

Gabby had feared Carlos would never be punished for his crimes, but during her visit to Dallas to attend the McGruder Art Show, she had been approached by a beautiful red-haired woman named Kathleen Callahan, and a liaison had been born. It had taken almost a year, but Gabby had never given up hope. Mostly because hope was all she'd had left.

"Thank you, Kathleen. I'm glad things worked out the way we wanted."

"Without your help, we never would have been able to get justice for these women."

It was obvious Kathleen had some strong backing and influence, but she still couldn't help but worry. "My grandfather—"

"Your grandfather will not have the chance to intervene."

She said the words with such conviction, Gabby believed her. Carlos really would never get a chance to hurt another woman again.

"Now," Kathleen continued, "let's talk about you."

"What about me?"

"What are your plans?"

Plans? She chewed on her bottom lip as her gaze skittered away from the screen. She had no plans, not really. Only dreams.

For years, getting away from her grandfather had seemed like such a nebulous idea she had never really believed it could happen. Yes, she had planned and dreamed, but deep down inside, she hadn't believed it could ever be a reality. Then, when she'd realized escape was possible, she'd had no resources. Her clothes and food, her every necessity, had been provided by her grandfather. She had no money and nothing of value. Even the clothes she was wearing now were not her own.

Gabby took a breath and straightened her spine. Kathleen had kept her end of the bargain and owed her nothing. The next step was hers alone. The time had come to stand on her own. "I don't have any concrete plans, but not to worry. I'm resourceful. I'm sure I'll be fine."

"I'm sure you will be, too, but we'd like to help you get settled into a new life."

"We who?"

"Let's just say you have a wealthy benefactor."

She had known Kathleen had influential and possibly wealthy contacts. Arranging for the successful abduction of two people couldn't have been an inexpensive endeavor. The men who'd carried out the event had been professionals. That kind of expertise didn't come cheap.

"Can I know his or her name?"

"It's best for both of you if you don't. At least not yet."

Unable to help herself, Gabby looked over her shoulder at the closed door. Was it Jonah Slater? His family was almost as wealthy as her grandfather. If so, why? Did he have a vested interest in sending Carlos to jail? Had her brother hurt someone in the Slater family?

Correctly interpreting her thoughts, Kathleen said, "It's not Jonah."

"Why is he here? How does he fit into this?"

"He works for the same organization that I do. He's there to watch out for you until you get relocated."

She could accept that, but she sensed there was more.

"What else?"

For the first time, Kathleen looked slightly uncomfortable. Before she could answer, Jonah spoke from the open doorway. "I'm here to find out what you know."

She hadn't even heard him open the door. And it was obvious that he'd been listening in the entire time. Whirling around, she stared at him. "Know about what?"

"Your grandfather's activities."

Gabby didn't know why this news surprised her. Of course they would want to use her. Didn't everyone?

"Don't look like that, Gabriella. This is for your own protection as much as anything," Kathleen said.

"How so?"

"There are government agencies, including several in the US, that know about your disappearance. They're looking for you."

"But why?"

"Your grandfather is a dangerous man. Many countries would like information on him to bring him to justice. Some think you know things. Others likely want to use you as leverage or to ransom. Finding out what you know can help ensure your safety."

Exhaustion dropped on her like a silent bomb. She had wanted to disappear, have a normal life. She should have known that wasn't a possibility. People like her didn't get to be normal.

"Jonah will lead you through a series of questions. He'll—"

"Begin tomorrow," Jonah finished.

"But we need—" Kathleen said.

"It can wait until tomorrow, when everyone is fresh."

Too tired to comprehend all the nuances of the conversation, Gabby sat in silence. Her mind was a kaleidoscope of thoughts and worries. What would they want to know? What should she tell them? What if they decided to return her after she told them what she knew? What if this had been their plan all along? A trap to get to Luis Mendoza. Kathleen was the only person she'd dealt with, and just how much did she know about her? Almost nothing.

A hand settled on her shoulder, grounding her back in reality. Jonah stood at her side. Though his face showed little emotion, she saw something in those remarkable eyes that told her he understood what she was feeling.

"Why don't you go back to your room and lie down?"

Though a part of her wanted to run out the door and into the night, disappearing forever, she knew that was a ridiculous notion. No money, no transportation. Plus, there was a blizzard roaring. She wouldn't get twenty feet before she was completely lost. Escape had been her goal, dying was not.

Even though her legs felt like they were made from gelatin, Gabby walked out of the office with her head held high. She knew Jonah watched her from the doorway. She might be weak as water, but she was bound and determined to not need his help. She'd been dependent on people her entire life. Getting away from her grandfather was supposed to be about gaining her independence. She didn't care what others had planned for her. She had finally escaped. There was no way she would ever return. One way or the other, she would survive.

Jonah waited until Gabriella disappeared up the stairs before turning back to Kathleen. He had come to this job with the intention of getting it done and leaving. That was still his intent. However, after spending only a few moments with Gabriella, he was planning to adjust his timeline. Not only was she physically exhausted, she was much more vulnerable than he had anticipated.

"We need to give her a few days, Kathleen."

"We may not have that much time."

"How so?"

"The news of the abduction broke a couple of hours ago. Since then there have been more than a dozen law enforcement agencies scrambling for information. Between the FBI and Interpol, plus numerous other foreign government agencies, the frenzy is just beginning. Everyone is accusing one another of being responsible. And everyone wants to get hold of Gabriella Mendoza."

"I would've thought Carlos's abduction would cause the biggest uproar."

"That's what we thought, too. And that might have been the case if it wasn't for a tiny bit of information that Gabriella forgot to mention."

"What's that?"

"She's engaged to Rudolph Bianchi."

Jonah snorted his disbelief. "The man's eighty if he's a day."

"Ninety, to be exact. It's his grandson she's engaged to. Goes by Rudy."

His stomach revolted at the thought of Gabriella within a thousand miles of Rudy Bianchi. "Isn't he in prison for murdering a half-dozen young girls?"

"Yes. After tons of legal wrangling and years of delay, they finally got a conviction. Life sentence, no parole. There were reports that the engagement was called off after that, but there are some who think the thing's still on. Apparently, the arrangement was made years ago."

No wonder Gabriella had wanted to escape. Jonah had done extensive research on the Mafia and crime families throughout the world. His father and brother had had ties with several. The Bianchi family of Rome, Italy, was one of the more mysterious and frightening ones he'd delved into.

"And she didn't say anything to you when you collaborated on her abduction?"

"No, but to be fair, we've only exchanged a handful of words. We wanted Carlos…however we could get him. Gabriella was the one who created the opportunity."

This put a whole new spin on the questions Jonah needed to ask. What did Gabriella know about Bianchi? Could she provide information to bring down a Mafia family as well as a crime boss?

"I'll get started in the morning. She's not going to be able to give me anything tonight. She needs to rest."

"She did look a little shell-shocked. What do you think of her so far?"

What did he think of her? How was he to answer that? She was a job, nothing more.

"Jonah?"

"What the hell should I be thinking?"

"Okay."

Though her expression remained serene, the way Kathleen answered told Jonah he'd overreacted. Hell, that was nothing new. But treating Kathleen unkindly was uncalled for. Not only was she just doing her job, she was his sister-in-law.

"Sorry, guess I'm tired, too." Forcing a pleasant demeanor, he gave her his assessment of his charge. "She's scared and uncertain. Entrusting your life to strangers can't be easy, especially for someone who's had it easy for so long."

"You think she's had it easy?"

The file he'd read had given him only the barest facts on Gabriella and almost nothing on her personal life.

He shrugged. "Doesn't really matter what I think about her personally. I'll get the information you and Justice want, and then she's all yours."

"I wish I could be there. But—"

Another face appeared on the screen beside Kathleen's. "But her husband and her doctor want her to stay healthy."

As usual, Eli, Jonah's older brother, brought a calming influence. When they were kids, Eli was the one who stood up for him against his old man. Mathias Slater had been a mean old buzzard, and for whatever reason, his youngest son had often been his favorite target. Eli had saved Jonah from multiple beatings. Neither of them had known that Mathias's cruelty to his children was just a precursor to what he'd do to them when they were adults.

Eli had endured hell because of their father. Since Kathleen had come into his life, a remarkable transformation had taken place. Jonah admired his sister-in-law for her kindness, quick wit, and intelligence, but he loved her for the happiness she'd brought his brother and his nieces. Violet and Sophia adored their new mother.

"Hello, big brother. How are things there?"

"Good. I spoke with Mom last night. She's coming home soon so she can be here when the baby arrives. She's ready to sell the house in Dallas. Wants to get a place close to us."

Jonah nodded, a momentary lump in his throat preventing speech. Their mother had suffered much over the years, but the last year had been the worst. A dead husband, an incarcerated son, and a tragic secret that could never know the light of day.

"That's good to hear. She's been hidden away long enough. It's time for her to come back home and get on with her life."

They both knew a normal life for their mother was probably not in the cards. The past would always lie heavily on her, shrouding her happiness, but she deserved to have as much of a good life as she could.

"Lacey has decided to stay in Europe a little while longer."

Their baby sister was like a beautiful hummingbird, flitting through life without any clear direction. Even as much as he believed that each person had to make their own way in their own timeframe, he hoped to hell that Lacey found her way soon. Who she was and what she stood for was a mystery that even Lacey herself didn't seem to know.

"Maybe that's for the best. She's been on the front lines, taking care of Mom. Spreading her independent wings might be good for her."

"I agree."

"But you have someone watching over her. Right?"

Eli raised a brow. "Of course."

Jonah huffed out a laugh. They both knew that if Eli hadn't taken care of it, he would have.

Returning to the business at hand, he said, "I'll call you tomorrow, Kathleen, after the first interview. Once we get what we need, what's the next step for her?"

"Depending on what she wants to do, Grey will make arrangements for her."

That was good. Justice would see that she was safe, far away from her grandfather's evil reach. She would be fine.

Saying goodbye, Jonah clicked off the call and sat back in his chair. He would do the job...get the information he'd been tasked to get, and then he was out of here. He ignored the odd, ominous feeling that told him it wasn't going to be that easy.

CHAPTER EIGHT

Valencia, Venezuela
Mendoza Estate

"Are the news reports true?"

Luis rubbed the aching tension in his neck. He had barely slept last night, knowing this call was coming. Although he now doubted that Bianchi was behind this thing, Luis felt the need to question him all the same. How easy it would be for Bianchi to take what he wanted and leave Luis out altogether. That wasn't going to happen...not while he still had breath.

Problem was, how to ask without offense? Insulting the man could be disastrous. "Yes. It is true. My grandchildren were abducted."

"Why wasn't I informed? Why did I have to learn about this from media outlets?"

"I had hoped to have her back before you found out. Your health—"

"You dare, Luis?"

He was glad that the man on the other end of the line couldn't see his expression. The fear was something he'd enjoy, but it was the bitter hatred that would probably get Luis killed.

"I meant nothing other than I had hoped to get the matter resolved without alarming anyone."

"And is it resolved?"

Of course it wasn't. More than twenty-four hours had passed, and he still didn't know the identities of Gabriella's abductors or their intent. If not for the fact that Carlos was in jail in Dallas, he might have thought the kidnapping was for ransom. That was something he understood and could handle. But this? He felt helpless, and the feeling didn't set well on his broad shoulders. Things like this didn't happen to him…he made things like this happen to other people.

"We have several leads."

"Don't patronize me, old friend. It cheapens our friendship."

Luis held back a sarcastic reply. Friendship had never existed between them. Not only were they too much alike, but their rivalry had lived for decades, the hatred growing only stronger. Whoever had said, *Keep your friends close but your enemies closer*, had known exactly what they were talking about. Their fake friendship was based upon mutual distrust.

However, they both shared one specific goal. And Gabriella was the key.

"We will find her and soon."

"I will send men to help."

"No need. Too many will get in the way. She's my grand-daughter, not yours. I'll find her and bring her home."

"I don't have to tell you what's riding on you finding her, do I?"

"No reminder is necessary. I know what is at risk."

"And you know the consequences of failure."

If it had been possible to reach through his phone and grab hold of the decrepit bastard's neck, Luis would have done so at that moment. How dare he be lectured like a youngster?

Luis held his temper, saying evenly, "I will keep my end of the bargain, as I promised."

"I understand the arrangements for transfer were made. Was the transaction completed?"

Inappropriate laughter threatened to erupt inside Luis. *Transfer? Transaction?* Rudolph did have a way with words.

"Yes. Which makes our urgency even greater."

"I agree. You're sure you don't need help? My men are fully capable of hunting down anyone."

"Again...there's no need. I have things well under control." Unable to continue the pretense, Luis said, "As soon as I have news, I'll contact you."

Ending the call gave him no pleasure. With a roar of fury, he hurled the offensive cellphone across the room. The sound of glass breaking and a cracking case gave him a small amount of ease. But not enough. Not nearly enough.

How was it that he had been successful in every aspect of his life except the one that mattered most? He had wanted a large family, as had his dear Flora. After miscarriage after miscarriage, she had finally carried a baby to term—a beautiful boy. Flora had been happy, and Luis, at last, could have what he truly wanted.

Although he had been a stern disciplinarian, there had been no real need. The boy had been affable and agreeable. Luis had not seen any worries in achieving his ultimate goal. But then, what had happened? The obedient boy had grown into a rebellious man. From an early age, Javier had known his destiny. Instead of fulfilling his purpose, he had rebelled in the worst way possible.

Falling in love with an American nobody had been bad enough, but he had married the girl, destroying Luis's carefully laid plans.

Once again, his goal had been denied.

The only good thing his useless daughter-in-law had managed was to bear two children. He might have lost his son, but Luis had consoled himself that he had two more chances. Of course, one of them hadn't turned out the way he had intended.

Carlos, his only grandson, was weak. An idiotic young man who had allowed his baser desires to control his life. Luis had plenty of people to run his businesses and see to his legacy. Maybe a short incarceration would make a small amount of difference in Carlos's personality. However, the boy would never have the self-discipline to assume any kind of leadership position. He didn't matter.

Gabriella was the key. She was what he needed. His final hope. His last-ditch effort to achieve his dream. Luis refused to accept defeat. He would find his granddaughter, and she would fulfill the destiny he intended. The one her father had failed at so miserably.

Those who tried to prevent it from happening would pay.

CHAPTER NINE

Colorado Mountains

Gabby started her day with a curious mixture of both elation and dread. She hadn't expected to sleep. Fortunately, exhaustion had gotten the best of her. Even though her sleep had been restless, she felt better this morning and ready to deal with what came next.

Silly not to expect there would be questions. After all, no one except those closest to her grandfather knew the kind of relationship she had with him. Most probably thought there was affection between them or, at the very least, some sort of closeness. Nothing could be further from the truth.

The knowledge that her grandfather no longer controlled her life was an intoxicating feeling. Part of her wanted to fly, she felt so free. Another part, the cautious, trust-no-one side of her, knew it wasn't going to be that easy. Jonah and those he worked with wanted to know what she knew. And she had to decide what she was going to do about that. If she told them everything, what would happen?

Just because she had been "rescued" didn't mean she could give her blind faith to these people. What if this was all a setup? What if her grandfather had suspected what she'd been planning, was aware of what she had been doing, and had created this elaborate scenario to trap her? To find out everything she knew?

And she knew a lot.

When she'd been given her first computer a few years back, it had been to take her online college courses. In a little over four years, she had earned a bachelor's of fine arts and a master's in art history. Each year that she was pursuing those degrees, she had been presented with a new laptop.

Having online access had opened up a world of possibilities. Everything she knew about research was self-taught. Her grandfather was savvy enough to know that knowledge was power. Gabby knowing too much could be detrimental, so he made sure that her Internet usage was carefully monitored. But she had learned how to circumvent his control. Gabby knew more than he could ever have believed possible. More than anyone could have believed possible.

She had decided she would be philosophical about the whole thing. Jonah would ask questions, and she would answer what she felt she could until she had more information.

That her inquisitor was Jonah Slater, from the wealthy and powerful Slater family, was worrisome. Not only was the family known to have been involved in illegal activities, she knew that on one occasion at least, her family and his had socialized. How far did their association go? The Slater patriarch was dead, and one of the brothers was in prison, but what about the other Slaters? Were they associated with her grandfather? Were they in business together or perhaps rivals?

In her research, she didn't remember seeing them linked, as friend or foe. That didn't necessarily exonerate them, but it did give more credence that Jonah was actually on the right side of things.

She had a few questions of her own to ask. How he answered and what she learned would determine how she would respond.

"Good morning," a male voice, morning rough, grumbled out. "Did you sleep well?"

Gabby stood at the kitchen door and worked to compose herself. She had come downstairs with what she considered her bland expression, but the moment she spotted Jonah standing in the kitchen, she could literally feel her face change. She was sure her mouth was open and could only hope there was no drool.

He had been working out, that much was obvious. He stood in the middle of the room and gulped down water while sweat rolled down his naked and very excellent chest. He was lean and muscular with some of the most impressive abs she'd ever seen. Wearing only a pair of faded blue sweats that hovered just below his belly button, Jonah Slater was a work of art. As an artist, she told herself it was only natural to appreciate such a superb specimen of the human form. Her pounding heart and flushed skin were harder to explain away, so she ignored them.

Deluding herself had never been her thing, but in this she had no choice. No way could she allow herself to become attracted or infatuated with Jonah Slater. That would be a disaster.

"Gabriella? Everything okay?"

Hoping to explain away the moment of weakness, she shrugged. "Guess I'm still a little groggy from yesterday. But I do feel better."

Giving her a look that said he didn't quite buy her story, he nevertheless let it go. "Maybe breakfast would help. Cheese omelet and toast sound okay to you?"

"Sounds perfect."

Determined to not feel like the idiot she had last night, she went to the cabinets to pull down plates for their meal, then withdrew cutlery from the drawer. Jonah said nothing about her initiative, as if he hadn't expected anything different. She appreciated that. Being normal, acting like an average, ordinary person, was going to take some time. This was a good start.

She was grateful he pulled on a T-shirt before he started cooking. Her concentration needed to be keen and watching a shirtless, still glistening Jonah Slater prepare breakfast was a distraction she didn't need.

The meal took him all of five minutes to prepare. He performed the task with such ease, she knew he had done it many times.

She wanted to do that. To feel comfortable in the kitchen. To feel comfortable with herself in the kitchen. That was just one of her many goals. She had so much catching up to do.

They sat in silence and devoured the meal. Jonah didn't seem to be a morning person, which was fine with her. She had way too much on her mind to try to come up with idle chitchat.

After breakfast, they did another cleanup like they'd done last night. Knowing what to do and where things went made things easier this time. She liked that the procedure now felt like a routine.

With a restful night's sleep behind her and a full belly, she was prepared to face whatever he threw at her. The table clear of breakfast things, she sat across from him and watched as he set up for the interview. Spending most of her life alone had given her exceptional observation skills. She couldn't read minds, but she was good at reading people and determining whether they were telling the truth. So far, she hadn't been given any indication that he wasn't being honest. Wouldn't he try to be more agreeable and likable if he was trying to gain her trust? He definitely hadn't put much effort into that. Grunts and one-word answers seemed to be the norm for him.

That didn't mean she couldn't be pleasant herself, though. Maybe she could disarm him with charm.

"Before we get started, I wanted to thank you for your involvement in this."

He looked up quickly, apparently startled by her words. Remarkable eyes shimmered with confusion. "My involvement in what?"

"In helping me escape."

An emotion flickered on his face that told her he wasn't comfortable with gratitude. He acknowledged her answer with a customary grunt, then said, "You ready to start?"

Quickly recognizing that charm wasn't going to get the job done, she went for broke. "Could I ask you a question first?"

"Sure. I guess."

"How do I know I can trust you?"

Cynicism curled his lip as his eyes darkened to a hunter green. "Are you asking because of my family or because I'm an ex-con?"

"But you were innocent."

"How do you know that?"

"I read articles." She wouldn't tell him she had followed his case daily. Nor would she tell him she had cried when she'd learned he had been exonerated. There were certain things he didn't need to know.

"Then you know I was framed."

"By your brother Adam. Yes?"

"No. By my father."

She straightened her shoulders. Now that was something she hadn't known. "Your father? But why would your father do something like that?"

"Why would a corrupt man do anything? It was to his advantage. He learned I was delving into his illegal activities, and that was his way of not only stopping me, but also punishing me."

"What were you going to do with the information you uncovered?"

"Destroy him."

The words were stark, said without an ounce of emotion. She saw the steely determination behind the handsome face. This was a man who had been resolved to bring down a powerful empire, no matter what. And it had cost him. She could definitely respect a man like that. Maybe she and Jonah Slater had more in common than she'd first thought.

"Your father...he never faced punishment?"

"Not publicly, no. But he received his punishment all the same."

She remembered the story. Every news outlet had carried it for days. Mathias Slater had been killed by an employee, but there had been nothing in the news about his own illegal activities. The fact that Jonah was telling her something that wasn't public knowledge went a long way in helping her trust him.

"Your family has had many tragedies. I'm very sorry."

Surprise and something like warmth flared in his eyes. For a brief moment, she saw behind the implacable façade to the humanity he worked so hard to cover. It was gone in seconds, and the veneer was once more in place.

"You ready to talk?"

He had answered only a few questions. If she was going to share what she knew, he was going to have to do better than that.

"Why are you involved in this?"

"You mean your rescue?"

Gabby had been manipulated with words too many times not to recognize the ploy. His use of the word *rescue* had been deliberate, meant to remind her that while she had instigated this event, she owed gratitude to the ones who'd brought it to fruition.

Playing along, she said, "Yes."

"I work for the man who arranged it."

"My so-called benefactor?"

"You doubt that he is? After what he arranged for you?"

"If he is indeed on my side, why can't I know his name?"

"You will, in time."

She didn't like the mystery, but did she have any other choice? She couldn't leave here—a blizzard raged outside. She had no money, no way out.

As if he knew exactly what she was thinking, Jonah said, "Look, Gabriella, you can look at this as your prison or your temporary safe house until we can get you where you want to go. That's up to you."

"Gabby."

"What?"

"The people I trust call me Gabby. I need to be able to trust you, so therefore, please call me Gabby."

If he was surprised at her words, he didn't show it, just gave her one of those infuriating grunts again and said, "You ready?"

Holding back a frustrated breath, Gabby nodded. "Very well. What is it you want to know?"

Placing a small recorder between them, he stated the date and time, and then, "This is Jonah Slater interviewing Gabriella Mendoza regarding the activities of her grandfather, Luis Mendoza."

His green eyes piercing with intent, he said, "Gabriella, are you answering these questions of your own free will?"

She told herself that his not using her nickname meant nothing. Compared to what she had experienced in her life, one little slight made no difference.

And even though she didn't feel she had any choice in the matter, she answered, "Yes, I am."

"Are you aware that your grandfather is considered one of the most notorious crime bosses of this century?"

Gabby had no feelings of loyalty, admiration, or the remotest affection for anyone in her family, most especially her grandfather. Still, her strong sense of self-preservation made her cautious. Trusting too soon could lead to her doom.

"I see my grandfather only a few times a year. He shares nothing about the family business with me."

"So is that a yes or a no?"

She refused to be bullied. "It is my answer."

He gave a little nod of concession and said, "When you see him, what do you talk about?"

"At the end of each year, he invites me to his home and gives me his list of expectations for the next year."

"What sort of expectations?"

"He has a list of approved social activities for me to review. I look them over. If I have questions, I ask. If not, I leave."

"And that's it?"

"When I return from my trips, I go to his home and give him a report of where I went, what I did, and what I learned."

"That's all?"

He didn't believe her. On an odd level, it bothered her that he thought she was lying. She wasn't lying...she just wasn't telling everything. Not until she was sure.

"So you're telling me you never attended family gatherings? Christmas? Easter? No holiday or birthday parties?"

"I stopped having birthday parties after my parents were killed." The correct word was murdered. She didn't trust Jonah enough to tell him this truth.

"And there were no other get-togethers? Holiday parties or social events you attended?"

Even now, years later, the memory of that first social event had the power to cause a minor panic attack. Hearing the increase of her heartbeat, knowing dizziness and nausea weren't far behind, Gabby took controlled, measured breaths. This was not a good time to reveal her weaknesses.

"Gabriella, do you need to stop? Take a break?"

The sound of Jonah's deep voice, the concern in it, had an amazing calming effect. She took in another controlled breath and shook her head. "No. I'm fine. What was your question again?"

His eyes narrowing slightly, he watched her in silence for several more seconds. Then, apparently satisfied she wasn't going to keel over, he said again, "Holidays? Birthdays? Family gatherings?"

That again? "We're not exactly a close-knit family."

"You're telling me that after your sixth birthday, you spent all the rest of your birthdays and holidays completely alone?"

"With the exception of paid companions and my guards... yes, I spent them alone."

"I find that hard to believe."

"That's because you're looking at the people I'm related to as a real family. We are not. My grandfather, brother, and various aunts, uncles, and cousins are related to me by blood. Nothing more. I have no relationship with any of them."

"So you've been like a princess in a castle, held prisoner until the prince comes to rescue you?"

If not for the mocking amusement glittering in his eyes, the blatant sarcasm would have been much more palatable. His doubt was understandable. Who would believe that in these modern times she had been held a prisoner? His amusement hurt. Her life was no joking matter.

As she did with every other unpleasant ordeal in her life, she dealt with it by pretending it didn't matter. Her voice was cool and emotionless. "Believe what you like. You will anyway."

Jonah cursed himself silently. He had hurt her feelings. She had been willing, if not eager, to answer his questions. But now her face was as remote as a mountaintop, her lively eyes now blank.

"I'm sorry, Gabriella."

In the few hours he'd known her, he knew that Gabriella Mendoza liked to maintain a calm façade. He was quickly learning something else. Beneath that feigned serenity was a mass of emotions.

"Why are you sorry?"

"Because my comment obviously hurt you. That was not my intent."

"You have a job to do. You have nothing to apologize for."

Jonah realized he was going about this the wrong way. He had been approaching this as if she had lived a normal life. Even with the bare facts in her file, he had known her life wasn't typical.

"Let me ask you a few more questions, and then we'll take a short break."

"All right."

"Who would you say is your grandfather's closest adviser? And before you say you don't know, who is he with when you see him?"

"Stephan Conti. They've been friends for years."

"Anyone else?"

"He has numerous acquaintances but no true friends. He does have a handful of bodyguards, but they change frequently. As far as I know, Stephan has been the only constant."

"And when you see your grandfather, what does he talk about?"

"As I said, he gives me my agenda for the year."

"Your agenda?"

"Yes. He reviews my events for the upcoming year. He hands me a calendar and allows me to look at it. As I do, he asks questions about my year before. When we're finished, if I have questions, I'm allowed to ask. If I don't, I leave."

"And that's it?"

"On rare occasions, he'll send word via one of my guards."

"And what would a word from him be like? What's the last message he sent you?"

She frowned as she replied, "That I had a doctor's appointment with my cousin, Antonia Rojas."

"That was an unplanned appointment?"

"Yes. I have a physical every year, but that was months away. A few weeks ago, I had a slight cold, and she insisted I come in, which I did. I recovered quickly. This new visit was unexpected." She shook her head. "I didn't question it too thoroughly since it was so fortuitous. I knew my brother would be accompanying me, which gave your people the chance to make the abductions."

"Do you have health problems?"

"No. I'm very healthy."

Despite the fact that he was asking questions to learn more about her grandfather, the oddity of this gave him pause. Why would a seemingly healthy woman need to see a doctor unexpectedly and at her grandfather's instigation?

"What did the examination entail?"

"I don't know."

"What do you mean, you don't know?"

"Antonia gave me tea with a sedative. I slept through the exam. When I woke, I was dressed and ready to go."

"Why would she drug you?"

"She said I was acting nervous and she thought the sedative would calm me." She lifted her shoulders, shrugging. "I probably was acting nervous. I knew what was going to happen once I left the doctor's office."

"Did you ask anyone what the exam entailed?"

"No. I was so out of it, I had no real thoughts other than going home and taking a nap. I had even forgotten about the abduction."

Why the hell had she been drugged?

He could tell she was uncomfortable with this line of questioning. Even though he wanted to know more, he wouldn't pursue it. He might be offended on her behalf, but her doctor visits would not provide any information about her grandfather's business dealings.

"Is your brother involved with your grandfather's activities?"

"I don't believe so, but can't say for sure. I try to stay as far away from Carlos as possible."

Jonah could certainly understand why. Had the bastard ever physically hurt his sister? Even though it was none of his business and not relevant to what he needed to learn from her, he had to ask, "Has your brother ever harmed you?"

Her mouth tightened, and even before she spoke, he knew she was not going to tell him the truth. "No. My brother stays away from me and I from him."

"He was with you at your home. Had been there for several weeks. Why?"

"He claimed that he had been charged to oversee my security for a while. It might have been as punishment. I don't know."

So she assumed she was her brother's punishment for his misdeeds? Hell, no wonder she had no affection for her family.

"Did he indicate what he had done?"

"No. As I said, I stayed as far away from him as possible."

"You didn't have meals with him?"

"No."

"Very well. Did he bring anyone with him?"

"If you mean like a friend, then no. Carlos has no friends. That's one of the few things we have in common."

The statement was matter of fact, with no evidence of self-pity. Jonah had no idea why that bothered him. Hell, other than his brother and Justice, he had no real friends either.

"What do you do on a daily basis?"

He told himself the question was pertinent. She could reveal something inadvertently that would be relevant.

If she thought the question was off base, she didn't let on. "If I'm not traveling, I have a routine. Exercise, breakfast, painting, lunch, reading, gardening, dinner, Internet browsing, television, and then sleep."

"As restrictive as your grandfather is, I'm surprised he allows you to travel."

"It surprised me at first, too. He claimed he wanted to enhance my knowledge of other cultures and have a chance to practice my language skills."

"And you're allowed online access?"

"My browsing history is monitored daily."

Her full lips lifted, and he was momentarily distracted. Forcing his eyes away, he pushed himself to get back on track. "So you don't have friends, not even boyfriends? Now or in the past?"

The laugh she gave was incongruent with the beauty of her face. The sound was both ugly and mocking. "Boyfriend? Mr. Slater, please ask a serious question."

Anger surged through him. He didn't know whether it was the way she tried to put distance between them by coolly referring to him as Mr. Slater, or the fact that based on Kathleen's intel, her words were a lie. She'd once had a fiancé. Possibly still had one.

He practically barked his next question. "Not even Rudy Bianchi?"

Surprise and then anger flared in her eyes. "That's a vile, wretched thing to ask."

"Why?"

"Because Rudy Bianchi is a murderer. A madman. A psychopath. A...a...disgusting piece of human filth. He's in prison for the rest of his life. I haven't seen him since...I haven't seen him in years."

"Then you want to tell me how it is that you were once engaged to him?"

The chair made a screeching noise as she sprang up. Her face was almost as white as the snow outside. "How dare you say something so revolting? I have never been engaged to Rudy Bianchi."

Jonah forced himself to stay seated. Her reaction was extreme, her voice shaking with insult. Either she was the best liar he'd ever come across, or Kathleen's intel was wrong.

"I have it on good authority that you were once engaged to marry Rudy Bianchi. Your engagement ended when he went to prison. Some think it's still on."

"You have been misinformed." Her voice was less forceful, more uncertain than before.

"Is it possible that your grandfather arranged the engagement without telling you?"

Gabby put her hands behind her and gripped them together, her fingernails digging into her skin. Of course that was possible. For more than half her life, the man had dictated every second of her waking moments. He would have had no hesitation to arrange a marriage for her, even to a murderer.

What would have happened if Rudy had never been convicted? Would she have been forced to marry the monster?

The very thought of what might have happened had the breakfast she'd consumed churn in her stomach.

"Gabby, look at me."

Whether it was because he called her by her preferred name or because of his steady, deep voice, she didn't know, but something calmed her down enough to look at him.

"Just because he arranged it means nothing. It's over. You've escaped. You're going to start a new life. He can't make you do anything ever again."

She nodded. Jonah was right. It didn't matter what her grandfather wanted. She had escaped. He would have no control over her life ever again.

"Thank you. You're right. I was panicking over nothing."

"Why don't we take that break now?" He glanced out at the falling snow. "It's snowing too heavily to go out, but there's a gym downstairs and an indoor pool. Some physical activity might make you feel better."

Yes. She needed to move, to work out all these emotions bubbling inside her.

"There should be something in your room to wear."

"Thank you."

She was grateful he didn't follow. That he didn't want to show her how to get to the gym. She needed to be alone. Needed to absorb what she'd learned and come to terms with the fact that she'd had even less control of her life than she'd thought.

Even though she was far away from him now, the knowledge of what her grandfather had planned was impossible to accept. Had he actually intended for her to marry Rudy Bianchi? The monster who had almost killed her?

Chapter Ten

Dallas, Texas

"I don't think we're going to get any useful intel from her until she knows she's safe."

"Do you think she knows anything?"

"Hard to say. She's good at answering questions without revealing a damn thing."

Kathleen studied her brother-in-law's face. Jonah was only slightly easier to read than their enigmatic employer, Grey Justice, which meant close to impossible. Darkness sat heavily on Jonah's shoulders. Today, however, something else seemed to enshroud him.

"How can we make her feel safer?"

"I'm going to talk with her about what she wants once she leaves here. Where she'd liked to go once this is behind her."

"Justice has people who do that. He was planning to schedule a session as soon as the snow lets up."

"She needs to know that she has choices."

"You think that's all she needs?"

"Hell, I don't know. Her file gave no real indication of the life she's been living. She's been held like a prisoner. No holidays or social occasions with family or friends. Other than the traveling she does, she's alone or surrounded by her grandfather's hired goons. Everywhere she goes, everything she does, is monitored."

"You asked her about Bianchi?"

"Yes. She seemed more shocked than we were."

"How is that possible?"

Kathleen had met Gabriella Mendoza only one time, and that was more than a year ago. The young woman had been attending the McGruder Art Show in Dallas, one of the few events she was known to participate in every year. Justice had deemed it their only chance to get close to the reclusive young woman who just happened to be the sister of Carlos Mendoza. The serial rapist had been out on bail for the rape and kidnapping of Stephanie Pierce. Instead of allowing Carlos to face the consequences of his actions, Luis Mendoza had spirited him back to Venezuela. Extradition, especially tricky when dealing with a country run by an unpredictable dictator, hadn't been an option. Making contact with Gabriella and pleading their case had been their only hope to bring Carlos to justice.

Gabriella had been sitting alone at a table but her bodyguards had been hovering close-by. Kathleen had sat down with her, pretending she didn't know who the young woman was. Gabriella would have nothing of it. The wisdom in her eyes went eons beyond her age. They hadn't talked long, as one of the guards had come along and insisted it was time for Gabriella to leave. But they'd talked enough for Kathleen to encourage Gabriella to help bring her brother to justice.

Since then they had communicated three times, once via an abbreviated phone conversation in which Gabriella had asked to be abducted along with her brother. The other two times were through encrypted text messages. It had taken days for them to decode the text.

"Where's Gabriella now?"

"In the gym working out. I thought it might help her deal. I'll give her some time and some space."

"But you don't think you'll get anything."

"Not until she knows we're not going to double-cross her."

"I'll talk with Grey."

She was about to click off when Jonah said, "Something else. Can you dig into her medical records?"

"Possibly. It'll take some time, though. Why?"

"She mentioned that her grandfather was the one who arranged for her visit to the doctor. It was an unscheduled visit. She said she'd had a checkup only a few weeks before."

"What was the appointment for? What did the doctor do?"

A blaze of fury ignited in his eyes, and Kathleen thought it might have been the first time she'd seen him so incensed. She was used to the dark and brooding Jonah.

"She doesn't know. She was sedated."

Outrage swept through her. "She doesn't know what was done to her?"

"No. The doctor dosed her tea. When Gabby woke, the exam was over."

Kathleen had known that Gabriella was dealing with a lot, but she was beginning to see there was so much more that the young woman had endured.

"What's the doctor's name?"

"Antonia Rojas. She's Gabriella's cousin."

"As antiquated as Luis Mendoza is, I'm surprised a female family member would be allowed to have a medical degree."

"I'm sure it's more of a convenience for him. Having your own doctor in the family to do your will would be helpful."

"I'll see what I can find out. I'll be back with you soon."

Clicking off the call, she turned and watched her stepdaughters, Violet and Sophia, run around their playroom, giggling with carefree abandon. This was what a childhood should be like for every single child. Safe, happy, and loved beyond measure.

Her own childhood might have been unconventional, but at least she had known she was loved. How had Gabriella survived? And just what the hell did Luis Mendoza plan for his granddaughter? Whatever it was, it would be to his advantage and not Gabriella's.

A tiny fist punched, and she touched her swollen belly, savoring the unique feeling of having a little human being inside her. It was hard to determine who was the most excited to meet the newest family member. His upcoming arrival was all Violet and Sophia could talk about, and Eli practically beamed with excitement and pride every time she entered a room. And Kathleen was overjoyed that she would soon be giving birth to a beautiful baby boy. Nothing was more precious than an innocent child.

At that thought, she glanced back at the screen where she'd been talking to Jonah. Was that the reason there had once been a match planned between a Mendoza and a Bianchi? To create a child with both of the families' blood running through him or her? Were Mendoza and Bianchi that cold and heartless?

She already knew the answer to that question.

CHAPTER ELEVEN

Colorado Mountains

Rudy Bianchi. Her heart pounded with every step she took on the treadmill. She hadn't uttered his name aloud in over twelve years. Even having that name in her mind caused bile to surge into her throat.

The very idea that her grandfather had apparently been set to marry her off to the fiend shouldn't have been a surprise. But it was. Thankfully, the monster was in prison with no hope of parole. Even if he hadn't been, she would never have gone through with a marriage. She would have killed the bastard herself before she'd allowed that to happen.

"Feeling better?"

Lost in horrific memories, Gabby shrieked as she whirled around, almost falling from the treadmill.

"Whoa." Jonah reached out for her and then, as if realizing she wouldn't want to be touched, held his hands still as if to catch her if she fell. "Sorry. I didn't mean to startle you."

"That's okay." She grimaced a smile. "Just have a lot on my mind."

His eyes flickered over her and then swiftly moved away, but not before she saw the heat in them. He was attracted to her. She didn't know what surprised her the most—that he found her attractive, or that she'd felt a wave of heat herself. After one brief, disastrous fling with the son of one of her bodyguards, she had learned to shut down those kinds of feelings. But now that she was free to have them, wasn't it just her luck to be attracted to a man who had every cause to dislike her?

"Did the exercise help?"

No, not really. Overcoming the knowledge that her grandfather had planned to marry her off to a sadistic murderer was going to take more than a three-mile treadmill run.

She gave her best fake smile. "Full speed ahead."

She could tell he didn't believe her cheery attitude. It hadn't been her best lie, but she was thankful he didn't give her false platitudes. That her grandfather's treachery included giving her to a serial killer couldn't be sugarcoated.

"For someone who's lived in London for most of your life, you have a very American way of speaking."

"I watch a lot of American television and movies. Also, my mother was from the US."

"Maryland. Right?"

"How did you—" She shook her head. "Silly question. Of course you know everything about me."

"Not everything. In fact, other than the most basic information, you're a mystery."

"My grandfather's doing. Besides, there isn't anything interesting about my life."

"Why do you say that?"

"I don't really do anything."

"Events don't make a person interesting. It's who they are and what's inside them that makes them interesting."

His words surprised her. Jonah Slater seemed so tough and hard, but his answer had been insightful and sensitive.

She didn't want to like this man. Their acquaintance would be temporary. Once the snowstorm passed, she would start a whole new life, far away. Yet she found herself being drawn to him. He really was quite handsome with his green eyes, dark, slightly unkempt hair, and unsmiling, sensual mouth. A few inches over six feet, broad-shouldered and hard-bodied, but not overly muscular. The image of his half-nude sweating body wasn't one she'd be able to get out of her mind for a long while. Not that she wanted to.

If she were a normal girl with a normal life, she'd definitely be interested in knowing more about him.

She took a breath. She might not trust him enough to tell him what she knew about her grandfather, but she needed to tell him this. He deserved to know. "I have a confession."

His eyes went sharp. "What kind of confession?"

"We've met before."

"Now that's something I think I'd remember."

She had never considered herself particularly brave. Arranging her abduction and Carlos's arrest had been the first true act of grit she'd shown since she was fifteen years old.

She swallowed a nervous lump. "It was years ago, at your home. A birthday party for your oldest brother."

Something grim tightened his face, and Gabby swallowed harder. His memory of that day was probably horrific. And she was responsible for it.

"It was my fault."

Confusion replaced the grimness. "What was your fault?"

"That you were caught. That you and your brother were... disciplined."

"I still don't—" Comprehension finally hit and was quickly followed by a surprising amusement. "So that's how the old man found out Eli and I had gotten into the liquor cabinet. You ratted us out."

"I'm so sorry. My brother had pushed me down and told me to go away. I was mad at him and wanted to get him in trouble. But that's no excuse for what I did."

"Carlos was there, too?"

"You don't remember?"

"I had a belly full of alcohol and got my ass beat. Things like who was around to witness my humiliation got put on the back burner."

"I never would have told on you if I'd had any idea what your father would do."

"How did you even know about what Mathias did?"

"I was looking in the window."

"Sorry you had to see that, but getting my ass beat by Mathias was almost a daily thing that year. If you hadn't ratted us out, he would've found some other reason."

"Why?"

"Because my old man was a sadistic bastard who thrived on being a bully."

"But why?"

"Haven't you figured that out by now? People like Mathias and your grandfather don't need a reason to do what they want. They live by their own perverted rules. People are pawns to use or victims to destroy."

"Were you ever close to your father?"

"No." He glanced around the gym. "Are you through down here?"

"Yes."

"Come eat. I put together some soup and sandwiches."

"You don't have to fix my food. I can do it."

"Good. You can do dinner."

The panic must've shown in her eyes, because he said, "Don't worry. All you have to do is throw it into the microwave."

"Learning to cook is on my list, but I'd hate to use you as a test subject."

"You have a list?"

"Absolutely." She grimaced and added, "Actually, it's a mental list. I never wrote things down since I knew it could be confiscated at any time."

"What would have happened if your grandfather had discovered your plan to escape?"

She shivered at the thought. "The small amount of freedom I had would have become nonexistent. And I'm sure he would have brought in more men to guard me."

"Was he physically abusive?"

Jonah waited for her to call him out on the inappropriate question. He couldn't say why he asked. It sure as hell was none of his business, but for whatever reason, he needed to know.

"No, he wasn't. Not really."

"What does that mean?"

"When I was younger, I had what he called a 'wild spirit.' On occasion, he would shake me until my teeth rattled. Other than that, he never touched me."

He was glad to hear she hadn't suffered physical abuse, but there was something she wasn't telling him. The tension around her mouth hadn't been there until he'd asked the question. He wanted to delve further, but once again was reminded that it was none of his damn business.

"Come eat lunch."

"Okay if I shower first?"

"No problem. Twenty minutes enough time?"

"Yes. But you can go ahead. I'm used to eating by myself."

"No problem. I'll wait for you."

Another tightening around her mouth told him she didn't like his answer. Tough shit. They still had things to discuss.

She walked from the room with effortless elegance. The little he had read in her files included the training she'd received from some of the world's most-famous tutors. Had that training included how to conduct herself in any situation? Perhaps even to lie?

Still, wouldn't she be more willing to talk about herself to one of the people who'd helped her escape? The things she'd shared were flimsy and uninformative. She had to know more. It was Jonah's responsibility to get that information from her before she began her new life.

He'd been gentle with her, allowing her to set the pace. After lunch, that would have to change.

***

Refreshed after an abbreviated shower, Gabby dressed in a long-sleeved white V-neck pullover and black jeans. She was amazed at the amount of clothing in her closet. Most was casual, but there were sweaters, shirts, and blouses, along with slacks and jeans. Several pairs of shoes lined the bottom of the closet. The dresser drawers held lingerie, nightgowns, bathing suits, and workout wear. The bathroom was equally well equipped. Whoever had supplied these things for her had gone to a lot of trouble and expense.

She entered the kitchen and found that Jonah had managed to surprise her once again. Sitting beside a bowl of steaming vegetable soup and a thick ham sandwich were a notebook and pen.

"What's this?"

He turned from looking out the window and gave her his usual solemn look. "You said you never wrote your wish list down in case it was found. Thought you might want to start. You've got a lot of catching up to do."

A lump formed in her throat. Ridiculous that a spiral-bound notebook and a cheap pen could cause such an emotional reaction. But it did. For the first time in years, someone had given her a gift out of thoughtfulness and nothing more.

"Thank you."

As if he realized she was feeling overwhelmed, he sat across from her and dug into his lunch. Gabby did the same, keeping her eyes on her meal, but every so often, her gaze would veer to the notebook, and she would imagine how she would fill the pages. She couldn't wait to get started.

Chapter Twelve

Rome, Italy
Bianchi Compound

Rudolph Bianchi half shuffled, half hobbled to the brown leather recliner, his favorite chair in his den. He eased into it, letting out a loud groan once he landed. He was alone, so there was no need to hide the pain his aching joints were causing him. If he had been in public, he would have put on a healthier façade. There was enough speculation that he was in poor health. There was no need to add fuel to the fire. Filthy buzzards would love to go ahead and bury him so they could take over his empire. As long as he had breath in his body, no one was touching what was his.

With shaking hands, he lifted the cellphone and pressed a speed-dial key to call his oldest enemy. He hated Luis Mendoza with an all-consuming passion. The man had stolen what was rightfully Rudolph's. Forgiveness was a foreign concept to a Bianchi, but that didn't mean he wouldn't barter, trade, or cheat to get what he wanted. He and Mendoza each had something the other one wanted. It had taken years, but they had finally been on the way to achieving their respective goals. And now, he didn't know anything. Being in the dark did not sit well with him.

The instant the phone was answered, Rudolph demanded, "Well, what have you learned?"

"Hola, Rudolph. How are you?"

"Don't play games with me, Luis. Where's your granddaughter?"

"I don't know."

"And why not? I was under the assumption that she would be easy to find. It's been two days since she was taken and you still know nothing? I'm sending men to help you look."

"No!" Luis said sharply. "Too many men will attract unwanted attention. We've narrowed down the location. There are obstacles impeding our reaching her. It's only a matter of time before we have her."

"What kind of obstacles?"

"Nothing to be concerned with. It's just a slight delay. My people have assured me we will have her soon."

"Very well. But you will bring her here when you find her. She needs to be close-by anyway, in case complications arise. I will ensure this never happens again."

"She's my granddaughter, Rudolph. I say where she goes."

"And I have a vested interest in her welfare."

"I'll keep you updated. The instant she's been secured, I'll notify you."

"I'll give you another week. If she's not found, I'm taking over."

The silence on the other end of the call was telling. Rudolph knew Luis was barely holding on to his infamous temper. All of this would have been amusing if it hadn't been so infuriating. The girl had to be found!

"I'll call you soon."

Rudolph opened his mouth to offer more advice but snapped it shut when the line went dead. Insufferable bastard!

If the girl wasn't found soon, he would take the matter into his own hands. Agreement be damned. He should have taken over long ago instead of allowing Luis to have a say in the matter. Gabriella might well be the man's granddaughter, but she was much more to Rudolph. Once she paid her grandfather's debt, Luis could do with her what he wanted. What happened to her afterward was of no interest to him. If anything, her death would make things easier all around.

But first... He nodded unconsciously. Yes, first she would make right what her grandfather had stolen from him decades ago.

***

Valencia, Venezuela
Mendoza Estate

Luis unlocked the door and entered his private sanctum. After speaking with that lout Bianchi, he needed the jagged edges of his temper soothed. Nothing could do that like a walk through his glorious treasures.

He used to allow others to come in and take in the beauty. Flora had often enjoyed their private time together here. On occasion, Stephan had dined with him here, too. He had once invited Carlos, but the young idiot hadn't appreciated the beauty. He had wanted to know the value of each piece. Greedy, ungrateful young whelp! Luis had demanded he leave and had never invited him to return.

If there was a family member who might appreciate the beauty, it would be Gabriella. He had thought once to invite her inside, just so she would understand, perhaps be less resistant when the time came. He had changed his mind. Her understanding wasn't a necessary thing. Besides, he would ensure her cooperation quite easily without making any kind of concession. The girl was like clay, malleable and easily manipulated.

Many people knew of his collection. His home was filled with fine art and priceless artifacts from all around the world. Often, when he held his famous parties, his guests were given a tour of his home. Showing off his riches was one of his few vanities.

Few, however, knew of his secret obsession. The ones who did—private collectors like him—understood his need to hide and protect what he valued most. Appreciating the incredible beauty of each piece, as well as the intense desire to own more.

The walk through the softly lighted hallway and into the main room took longer than it used to take. Luis couldn't decide if that was because he was older or because he stopped more frequently to admire one piece or another. He did know that the older he became, the more he enjoyed being here among his treasures. The quiet solitude soothed him like nothing else could. There was history, romance, and wealth in each piece. He had carefully chosen each item for his private collection. He knew each one's history, where it had come from, who it had once belonged to, and in some instances, who had touched it. Each item had been chosen for its beauty, simplicity, or elaborateness, as well as its significance in the world. Collectors all over the world would kill to have his treasures.

He loved each item as if the seed from his loins had created each of them. They were his one and only love, his one true passion.

At last, he reached the center of the room. The soft glow of the spotlight shone down on the silken pillow. The emptiness mocked him, called him a failure. He refused to rise to the bait. The self-censure would do no good. Yes, he had made mistakes, but he had done everything he could to rectify them. The emptiness was a reflection of other's failures, not his own. Had his son lived up to his promise and obeyed his father, this pillow would possess what it had been meant for. Instead, selfishness had cost Javier his life, and Luis had lost what he wanted above all things.

Gabriella was the key to his goal. She alone could achieve his dream. Her disappearance put a hitch in his plans, but he had overcome many obstacles already. This was just one more that he would triumph over. Great achievements were never reached without suffering and trials. He wouldn't fail this time. He had waited too long, endured too much.

The most maddening part about not having this particular treasure wasn't that it was taking so long to acquire. It was that the piece really belonged to him, not Bianchi. Luis had earned it. The lack made him feel common. Like any other collector who sought to obtain an item and lost out to another bidder. He wasn't like any other collector. What was contained within these walls was his, only and always his. That was why this elusive item was so infuriating. He coveted what already belonged to him, yet was possessed by someone else. Rudolph Bianchi, with his wrinkled ugly hands, got to touch what should have been his. That wasn't right.

Sighing with longing, he reached out and touched the empty space. Coldness penetrated his fingers, and rage exploded within him. It wasn't right or fair. The indignity was unbearable. He had to have what belonged to him!

The fury fueling him, he marched back through the room with the energy of a much younger man. He would find Gabriella, and she would fulfill her destiny. Whoever got in his way would die.

***

Colorado Mountains

Chewing her lip in concentration, Gabby scribbled in her notebook. For the past few hours, she had been immersed in the delightful pastime of not only dreaming of the future but also being able to write it down. There was something so satisfying about putting her thoughts and desires into words.

For so long, she had carefully guarded all her thoughts, hopes, and dreams, knowing if they were discovered, she would be guarded even more carefully. Even Raiza hadn't known about all of them, though that was more for her protection than Gabby's lack of trust. If it was discovered that Raiza had not only encouraged Gabby to dream about her future, but had worked hard to prepare her for that eventuality, she would have been dismissed, or worse.

She missed her friend more than she could say. For almost twelve years, Raiza had been her mentor, teacher, and only confidant. With her unique blend of compassion and no-nonsense realism, she had prepared Gabby in the only way she knew how. With a military and secret-police background, Raiza had trained her protégé to be ready for any eventuality. Unbeknownst to her grandfather, Gabby had learned what she needed to know to survive. Thankfully, her friend had also taught her patience, claiming that waiting for the right time to strike was just as important as knowing what to do when that moment came.

But last year, not long after Gabby had returned from her trip to the United States, where she'd met Kathleen, her dear friend had suffered a fatal heart attack. The shock and grief had been overwhelming, but the event also had given her the impetus to finally make her escape. She'd had no one left.

"Feel like talking?"

Jonah stood in the doorway. He had been surprisingly sensitive, seeming to understand her need to be alone with her thoughts.

She tried to see the young boy in him—the one she had met years ago. Other than his eyes, an unusual shade of deep green, she saw no similarities. A decade and a half had passed, so maybe that was the reason. She got the feeling it was more to do with Jonah's life experiences than anything else. He looked tough and uncompromising without a hint of innocence or softness.

"How long were you in prison?"

If the question surprised him, he didn't let on. "Almost three years."

"Was it difficult?"

"Some days more than others."

"I don't remember the details about what happened. I just remember seeing the news that you'd been convicted. Can you tell me about it?"

For several long seconds he didn't answer. She figured when he did speak, he would tell her to mind her own business. Instead, he said, "If I tell you, will you answer some questions, too?"

That seemed only fair. "Yes."

As he eased into a chair across from her, his gaze shifted and became unfocused, as if he was watching the past unfold. "My brother's executive assistant, Teri Burke, contacted me. We had met a couple of times, but had done nothing more than flirt a little. One day, she called and asked me out. I met her at a restaurant a few miles outside Dallas."

A small, wistful smile played around his mouth. "I had my mind on romance, but that wasn't the real reason she'd contacted me. She had worked for my brother for a little over a year and had discovered some disturbing things. She thought I should know."

"How did she know she could trust you?"

"Adam and I had no use for each other. We rarely saw each other, but when we did, neither of us hid our disgust. The only time we tried to get along was when our mother was present. Teri was around the family enough to know who she could trust."

"What did you do then?"

"I was already doing my own investigating. I had been working for my father and had seen some things that didn't seem right. Her suspicions ramped up my own. I went to a man I knew I could trust. Turns out, he'd been working his own angle against my father. Then I brought my brother Eli on board.

"We thought we had been so discreet…that we would never get caught."

"But you did?" Gabby said.

"I was overseeing a shipment of goods for my father. It was completely legal, but the feds showed up and uncovered a boatload of heroin and cocaine. I got busted. Didn't matter how innocent I was. My father was determined to teach me a lesson. My trial barely lasted a week. After my conviction, Teri disappeared. Almost two years passed before her body was discovered."

"You loved her."

"Yes."

"I'm sorry. Do you know what happened?"

"Only that my father ordered the hit. I'm still looking for the man who killed her."

"What will happen when you find him?"

"I'll kill him."

He made the statement without a hint of hesitation, not bothering to hide his intentions. The idea of taking another person's life was disturbing to her, but she appreciated Jonah's honesty. He could have lied and told her he'd make sure the killer was arrested and convicted. He chose to tell her the truth. Oddly enough, that made her feel better about him. If he could tell her this...trust her with this, could she trust him, too?

"I guess all families have a few bad apples, don't they?"

"Yeah, but I doubt there are too many families who make it a point of killing the people they don't like, including their own relatives."

"Your family had some of their relatives killed?"

"Teri was my fiancée. Also, my father had arranged for me to be killed in prison. Fortunately, the plan went awry."

"I'm sorry about your fiancée. I hope you find the man responsible."

"The man responsible is burning in hell. The man who carried it out will join him soon."

He said it with such surety and clarity, she believed him.

Apparently deciding he had shared enough and it was now her turn, he gave a little go-ahead nod. "Now you."

In between writing down her goals for the future, Gabby had given this a lot of thought. She had decided that she would either trust that the information she gave Jonah would be used to destroy her grandfather or it wouldn't. They could take her back or kill her whether she gave them information or not. At least this way, there was the chance that one day Luis Mendoza would pay for all that he had done.

And telling him the truth seemed only fair. He had given her ample time to settle in and feel more comfortable with him and the situation. He had truthfully answered what she had asked of him. It was now her turn.

She took a breath and a leap of faith. "My grandfather has quarterly dinners with many of his associates. I arrange those events and act as hostess."

"So you know who he does business with?"

"Yes. But I know more. Remember I told you that I do a lot of Internet surfing?" She waited for his nod before continuing. "I learned how to hack into not only his accounts but the accounts of his associates. I can give you names. Events. Shell corporations. Dates. Partnerships."

To say her revelation surprised him would be an understatement. Jonah didn't know if he should hug her for her ingenuity or shout at her for putting herself at risk.

"Why would you do this? What if you'd gotten caught?"

"The risk was worth it. Besides, what would my grandfather have done if he'd caught me? Nothing more than take away my computer."

He wasn't so sure about that, but there was no point in chastising her for something she'd managed to get away with.

"How can you remember so much?"

"I have a good memory. And for the last year, since I knew I would finally be able to escape, I've concentrated on memorizing as much as I could."

The treasure trove of information inside her head could be of infinite value, but it could also put her in much more danger than any of them had ever imagined. Not even Justice could have anticipated what Gabby might know.

"Did you plan on getting even with your grandfather someday?"

"Perhaps. The first time I snooped, it was more of a game. Just to see if I could actually get away with it. When I realized I could…that no one would ever suspect that meek, malleable Gabriella was intelligent or gutsy enough to do such a thing, I decided to learn everything I could. Knowledge is power."

For someone who had felt the powerlessness of having no control over his life, Jonah could certainly identify with her need for knowledge.

He stood and headed toward the door.

"Where are you going?"

He glanced over his shoulder as he walked out of the room. "To get you another notebook."

Her brilliant smile slammed into him with the force of a speeding train. Jonah felt the effects all the way to his feet. His heart pounded, and an uncomfortable and unfamiliar emotion swept through him. Oh hell no.

If a mere smile could do this to him, then he was getting in too deep with her. Other than a few members of his family, he hadn't cared about anyone in years. His only focus was to find Teri's killer. Damned if that was going to change.

He didn't care how beautiful, intelligent, or sweet she was. Gabriella Mendoza was a job to him and not one damn thing more.

CHAPTER THIRTEEN

"Out of all the men who came to my grandfather's last gathering, Donald Benson is probably the scariest."

Jonah glanced down at his notes. "Businessman out of Chicago?"

"Yes. I hacked into one of his bank accounts." She shrugged. "It's not under his name but his stepdaughter's. Anyway, a couple of years ago, he sent twelve payments over a three month period, all under ten thousand dollars, to a bogus company in the Caymans. I think he had someone killed."

Depositing a hundred thousand or so dollars to a secret account in the Caymans could mean just about anything, including payment for a hit, but Jonah was learning that Gabby had excellent instincts about her grandfather's business associates.

"Why do you think he had someone murdered?"

"His first ex-wife died in a boating accident that same year. The boat exploded. The authorities blamed faulty wiring."

Jonah jotted another note beside Benson's name. Even though he was recording the conversation and Gabby had already written some of this stuff down herself, he was making his own notes, too. With all the info she had provided over the last couple of days, Justice was going to have a field day.

They were sitting in the first floor den. Gabby was curled up in a chair, sipping a cup of cocoa, gazing into the fire. After that first, uninformative interview, Jonah had moved their location to a more relaxed setting. And those types of interviews were over. They'd progressed from his blunt questions and her vague answers to real conversations.

He had made a mistake, treating her as if she were in some way responsible for her family's antics. Gabby had no involvement in their illegal activities and without a doubt the things she was sharing would go a long way toward ending them.

"Oh, and there's Marcel Dubois. He hasn't been to a gathering in a couple of years. I'm not sure if he and my grandfather had a falling out or what happened, but about three years ago, the two had a secret meeting in Paris. About two weeks after that, my grandfather made a sizeable investment to Marcel's corporation. About a year after that, my grandfather received a payment that was more than double his investment."

"And you know this, how?"

"My grandfather uses an accounting firm in Caracas to handle many of his international transactions. I hacked into their system and accessed his accounts."

She said the words casually but he saw the gleam in her eyes. She knew the information she was providing would cause an uproar. As much as he was glad to get the information, he wasn't nearly as happy with the danger that would follow Gabby, not only from her grandfather, but other, possibly even more dangerous men.

"Did it ever occur to you what you might be opening up by digging into these men? The danger you'd be placing yourself in?"

"Yes and no." Her eyes took on a distant look as she continued slowly, "At first it was like solving a puzzle. Seeing all the different pieces and figuring out how they fit together. The more I uncovered, the more outraged I became. Then it became a quest."

She refocused on Jonah and gave him a solemn look. "It just wasn't right."

And that was the Gabby he was coming to know. She had a distinctly high moral code. It was little wonder she had been so isolated from her family. They were opposites in every way.

She set her empty mug on the table beside her and then shifted in her chair, reminding him that they'd been sitting for several hours. A break was definitely called for.

"Why don't we take a breather until this afternoon?"

She sent him a grateful look. "Thank you. Talking about these people always makes me tense and out of sorts."

"There's a hot tub and sauna in the gym. That might help."

"Sounds perfect." She lifted her slender arms above her head and stretched in an effortless, graceful movement. The white turtleneck sweater she wore tightened against her chest, outlining her full breasts.

And just like that, Jonah was no longer thinking of criminals and the shitty things they did. Instead, his mind veered to the image of a beautiful woman with long, black hair, golden creamy skin, and luscious breasts. She was sitting in a steamy hot tub, her eyes were closed and a sensuous, dreamy smile was curving her lovely lips.

He surged from his chair like a rocket. "I need to do some things. I'll see you later."

"Wait."

He'd already been striding toward the door but her words stopped him. "What's wrong?"

"Nothing. I was just wondering if there are any books or magazines here that I could read?"

Jonah cursed his lack of foresight. He'd been so focused on getting what he needed, he hadn't given much thought to the restlessness Gabby must feel. She had asked for nothing since she'd been here. When he'd given her a spiral bound notepad and a writing pen, she'd acted as if he'd given her keys to a castle.

Glad to be able to give her something else, he said, "Follow me."

Without hesitation, Gabby followed. Each day she knew this man, the more she liked him. She couldn't say he was easy to get to know. He didn't use pretty words or fake emotions. There was no double meaning to his statements. In fact, on more than one occasion, he had been painfully blunt. His lack of artifice was both refreshing and exhilarating.

They walked across the large foyer and headed up the stairway. "I can't believe I still haven't explored this house."

"Go anywhere you like. The third floor's got some good views of the mountain range. Kind of hard to see with the snow we've been having."

It had been snowing for days. Even for a person who spent the majority of her time in seclusion, Gabby was feeling closed in. She had walked out onto the balcony of her bedroom a couple of times but had only been able to stay for a few minutes. The icy wind had almost taken her breath.

"It's a beautiful house. Does it belong to the organization you work for?"

"Actually, no. This one belongs to the man himself."

"And I still can't know his name?"

"I think he wants to introduce himself. As soon as the weather calms down, he'll come meet you."

Before she could ask more questions, Jonah opened a large door on the second floor. Speechless, Gabby walked into one of the loveliest libraries she'd ever seen. The room was huge and circular in design. As she made a slow 360 degree turn, she gazed up in wonder at the tall wooden shelves stacked with more books than a person could read in several lifetimes.

On one side of the room, a beautiful spiral staircase led to a second level. On the other side were a massive stone fireplace, a large leather chair, and a giant sofa. From the gleaming cherry-wood shelves to the thick Persian rugs on the dark, hardwood floors, the library screamed elegance, grace, and comfort. Whoever had designed this library had the soul of a dreamer.

"I can't imagine owning all of these books." She returned her gaze to the silent man who still stood at the door. "Do you like to read?"

"Used to. Hated it when I was a kid but it grew on me when I got into college. Haven't had time for it lately."

"What did you study in college?"

"Business."

"Did you go to a large school?"

"Yes. University of Texas."

"Longhorns. Right?"

"How did you know?"

"Just a bit of useless trivia I picked up."

His mouth tilted in an almost smile. "Hey, there's nothing useless about the Longhorns."

A shiver of excitement zipped up her spine. If just a half smile had that kind of impact on her, she could only imagine what a full smile from Jonah would do to her.

"So you think you can find something to read?"

She laughed, gazing up at the treasure trove. "I'm sure I can find one or two I haven't read."

She looked at Jonah again and almost stumbled. Any trace of amusement had disappeared from his face. She had no idea what he was thinking but his granite hard expression told her something was bothering him.

"Jonah? Are you okay? Is something wrong?"

He stood silently for several more seconds, his eyes almost burning into hers. Then he abruptly shook his head and backed away. "Nothing's wrong. I'll see you later."

"Thank you, Jonah. For this."

Shrugging, he said, "Sure," then disappeared out the door, closing it behind him.

Gabby stared at the closed door. She had never felt like this before. She was breathless and lightheaded but also felt amazingly, wonderfully alive. Exhilarated. All because of one intense look from Jonah Slater. If the man ever really did turn on the charm, she wasn't sure she would survive. She was, however, quite sure she would enjoy every single moment.

Turning away from that sizzling thought, Gabby took in her surroundings again. She took in a deep breath, inhaling the wonderful fragrance of books, and smiled.

Chapter Fourteen

The snow continued to fall. Gabby had never seen anything like it. A part of her wanted to go out and play in the icy wonderland. Another part wanted to stay inside, snug and safe, and just enjoy the pristine, otherworldly beauty. Jonah had promised that once the heavy snow ended, she could go out, build snowmen, have snowball fights, and play to her heart's content. She opted for staying inside and waiting. She was learning that Jonah Slater was a man of his word. He could be trusted.

The oddity of trusting anyone, especially a man, was both scary and liberating. For so long, she had lived in an isolated world of distrust and skepticism. What she had seen and experienced had molded her into a person she didn't particularly like. She didn't want to be distrustful and suspicious. She wanted to be free of all those doubts. She would soon start a new life—she wanted a new attitude, too.

The cautious, inhibited Gabby told her to be careful. Reminded her of all the betrayals of the past. Getting her hopes up only to have them destroyed had happened too many times to have high expectations. She told herself to set her sights on what was achievable and acceptable. Anything higher was just going to disappoint. That included Jonah Slater.

But her heart, which, much to her dismay, seemed to be calling the shots lately, told her to stop with the caution and distrust. There were men worthy of her trust. Honorable men with courage and integrity. Just because they weren't in her own family didn't mean they didn't exist. Her heart told her that Jonah was one of those men.

Hard to believe she had known him for only twelve days. Even as taciturn as he was, he'd shared things with her she suspected he hadn't told anyone else. Horrible things that had happened in prison. The absolute emptiness he'd experienced each morning that he woke was something she could definitely identify with. Lack of hope was soul destroying.

She ached for him when he described how he had learned of his fiancée's disappearance, the helplessness he'd felt. In turn, she had shared with him her own hurts and fears. The heartache of losing her friend and mentor, Raiza. The ache of loneliness had been almost unbearable.

Still, there were things she hadn't told him. Some of the more painful experiences were just too hard to verbalize. She would tell him someday, she knew. Perhaps talking about them would help her heal. So yes, she would tell him. Just not yet.

"What would you say to a snowball fight?"

Turning away from the window she'd been gazing out of, she practically shouted, "Really? Seriously? We can go out?"

"Forecast says blue skies and sun. No more snow, at least for the foreseeable future. Temps are in the thirties, so you'll need to bundle up."

With her mind on the new adventure ahead, all caution scattered like ashes in the wind. She had never played in the snow, never once had a snowball fight. This was one of the items on her list.

"I'll be back in a flash."

"No hurry. I don't think the snow will melt anytime soon."

The instant she disappeared from the room, any amusement vanished with it. Jonah swore softly. He had to get out of here, away from her, as soon as possible. After twelve days of doing nothing but talking with her, learning about her, he had a boatload of information and knew one immutable fact—he was more attracted to her than he'd been to any woman, ever. That knowledge, more than anything, made him want to howl with fury. Teri's killer was still out there breathing. Instead of finding him and meting out justice, Jonah was isolated with a beautiful temptress whom he couldn't stop thinking about.

He was not only attracted to her, he was starting to like her. She was different from any woman he'd ever met. Her interests were eclectic, her enthusiasm for the ordinary was contagious. How long had it been since he'd sat down, read and enjoyed an entire book? Since he had shown her the library, he had rediscovered the simple pleasure of getting lost in a good book.

Very few things interested him anymore whereas Gabby was interested in everything. Each day was a new adventure for her, something exciting to be enjoyed and shared. What he looked at as mundane and boring, she viewed as delightful and different.

In the last few years, Jonah's view of the world had taken a sour turn. He knew this. Even without his family telling him, he recognized the signs. But Gabby, with her amazing attitude, was making him see things with a different perspective. Her sheer joy of living made him realize how empty his life had become.

Despite his need to get away from her, he was actually glad he'd been given the opportunity to help her. People like Gabby were a rarity, and she deserved to have a chance at happiness. And if he ever got the chance to meet Luis Mendoza, he'd make sure the bastard paid for what he'd put his granddaughter through.

"I'm ready."

She wore gloves, boots, and a thick coat with a hood that obscured all but her bright smile. Anyone else would have looked ridiculous. Gabby, with her contagious excitement, was the exception.

The next few hours belonged to Gabby, and he wanted her to have the perfect day. Determined that her first experience of playing in the snow would be one she'd remember forever, Jonah put his dark thoughts aside. There would be plenty of time for those later.

The beauty stole her breath. Everywhere the eye could see was a brilliant, blinding white. The only color was the darkness of the giant trees, and many of them were almost bowed over, laden with inches of snow. A winter wonderland lay before her, and she was right in its midst.

Jonah had apparently done some major shoveling before he'd offered her the chance to go outside. The sidewalk was clear and had been salted. He'd even cleared a path around the grounds so they could walk some distance without getting bogged down.

"Wow, now I know where you go when you disappear for hours."

Wearing a dark blue coat and gloves, Jonah wasn't nearly as bundled up as she was, and oh heavens, he was attractive. Those mesmerizing eyes that seemed to pierce through to her soul were gleaming with a light she hadn't seen in them before. He actually looked as though he was enjoying himself. There was darkness in Jonah, but for today at least, he seemed to have put his worries aside.

"Keeps me busy."

"You're probably bored here."

An almost infinitesimal smile twitched at his mouth. "You're the least-boring person I know."

"Wow, a compliment from Jonah Slater?"

"Don't let it go to your head."

She wouldn't, but she would hold it close to her heart.

They reached the end of the short trail and stopped. Gabby whirled slowly. The cold, crisp air almost burned her lungs but also made her feel gloriously alive. Distant mountains surrounded them, their peaks seeming to reach past heaven. Their sheer beauty and magnificence left her breathless.

"I've never seen anything more breathtakingly stunning."

"You've been to some of the most beautiful places in the world."

"Not really. I've been to countries that had some of the most beautiful places in the world. I rarely got to visit them. If my grandfather didn't think they would benefit him in some way, I didn't go."

"I noticed you go to a lot of museums and art shows."

"Yes. Those are the things that interest him. And even though the locations are chosen for me, I know I'm lucky to have the opportunity to see them. I've seen some of the most priceless and beautiful art in the world."

"But nothing like this?"

"No," she agreed. "Nothing like this."

"You have seen snow before. Right?"

"Of course. I just never have had the chance to play in it."

A hawk squealed overhead, and she lifted her eyes to watch it glide. She was so enthralled at the sight, she didn't notice that

Jonah had left her side until something hard and cold hit her in the back.

At first, she was startled, and then when she realized what had hit her, she stooped and created her own snowball. Carefully packing it into a perfectly round weapon, she stood and was immediately bombarded. Snowball after snowball came at her like missiles.

Dodging and weaving, she could barely escape them, much less throw her own. "Hey!" she protested. "Not fair."

His grin unrepentant, he hurled another one. "All's fair in love and snowball fights."

Recognizing that she'd soon be buried if she didn't get into the spirit of things, Gabby grabbed another handful of snow. In between recovering from the ones she couldn't evade, she created her own arsenal.

"Are you just going to stockpile yours?"

He barely got the words out before she began her assault. Flinging the balls of snow like a major leaguer, she pummeled her opponent.

A deep roar of laughter erupted from Jonah, and instead of continuing to throw snowballs, he concentrated on avoiding her attack.

"You've been holding out on me," he yelled between dodges. "You're a pro."

She stopped to give him her best proud grin. "I hit what I aim for."

Deliriously happy, she picked up the last snowball. Determined to make it count, she targeted his chest. It landed with a hard splat and exploded outward.

Apparently caught off guard by the force of her throw, Jonah lost his footing and fell backward, landing with a resounding thud on the packed snow.

"Jonah? Are you okay?"

When he didn't move or make a sound, Gabby's heart went into her throat. Running forward, she cursed her precision. Raiza had taught her to hit what she aimed for, but the lesson had been for guns and knives, not snowballs. Had she hurt him?

She skidded to a stop beside him and went to her knees. His eyes were closed, and he looked almost peaceful. How on earth had she knocked him out?

Leaning forward, she cupped her hands over his face and tapped lightly. "Jonah? Are you okay?"

Quick as a flash, he grabbed her forearms and twisted her around until she was lying flat on her back. Looking up at his grinning, arrogant face, she burst into uncontrollable giggles.

"What's so funny?"

"My snowball must have been awfully powerful to bring down something so big."

"You do pack a wallop, especially for an inexperienced snowball thrower."

She gave him a cheeky grin. "I never said I hadn't thrown other things before. I've just never thrown a snowball."

"Then let me tell you, you could be a champion thrower of snowballs."

"Thank you, Jonah."

"For what?"

"For this. I have so many wishes and dreams, and you just made one come true."

The smile dropped from his face, and his gaze focused on her mouth. Suddenly nervous, Gabby licked her lips.

Jonah leaned closer, his breath warming her cold cheeks. "You're an amazing person, Gabriella Mendoza."

"Jonah?" she whispered.

"Yes?"

"Kiss me."

It was a plea, a command, a hope and a dream. And with a groan that sounded both tortured and angry, Jonah complied. His mouth touched hers gently, and then when she opened her lips, he took hers boldly, expertly. His tongue swept deep into her mouth, tangling and dueling with her own.

Gabby grabbed his shoulders and held on tight, reveling in his taste and the extraordinary experience of being in this man's arms. Never had anything felt so right...so perfect.

The kiss ended much too soon. He raised his head, and she saw the regret immediately. It was in his eyes, in the grim set to his mouth. He shot to his feet and held out his hand, his expression once more cool and impersonal.

Gabby refused to feel the same. It didn't matter that he wished he hadn't kissed her. It had been a perfect ending to a perfect moment in time. She'd had much too few of them to have an ounce of regret.

"Thank you for a wonderful day, Jonah."

He gave a curt nod, acknowledging her gratitude.

They trudged back to the house in silence, Jonah with his regret and Gabby with her delight in the experience. No one could take her happiness away, not even the man who so obviously wished he was anywhere but here.

Chapter Fifteen

Gut-twisting outrage tore through him. Jonah could only stare at his sister-in-law as the horror of what she just told him penetrated his brain. How the hell could something like this happen?

He'd been headed up to bed, practically patting himself on the back for another successful day of gathering intel and pushing aside any kind of tender feelings he had for his charge. Yesterday's kiss had never been mentioned and wouldn't. It had been an anomaly and one he was determined not to repeat. Gabriella, no matter how charming and beautiful, was his charge, his job, and nothing more.

And now this call had come through destroying all of his carefully built defenses.

He and Kathleen had gotten into the habit of talking with each other every morning before Gabby came down for breakfast. Usually, it was to review what he'd learned the day before.

In less than two weeks, Gabriella had given them information that would have taken years to gather on their own. Once this information came to light, a massive shitstorm was going to come down on dozens of scumbags.

But Kathleen had news now...news that couldn't wait for their morning call.

On a scale from one to ten, with ten being the very worst news possible, this came in at a stone-solid eleven.

Jonah said again, "You're sure?"

Tears glittered in Kathleen's compassionate eyes. "Yes, we're sure."

"There's no way that this could just be speculative...something that they might do in the future? Could the notes have been misconstrued, read the wrong way?"

"I read them myself, Jonah. There's no other way to interpret the information."

Jonah rubbed the sudden dull throb at his temple. When he'd asked Kathleen to have someone hack into Antonia Rojas's patient files to find out why Gabby had been drugged at her doctor's appointment, he hadn't had a clue what the reason might be. But this... Holy shit, who the hell would've even considered this?

"But who...what...why?"

"I think we can both speculate with some degree of accuracy on the answers to all those questions."

"The last time we talked, you said that Rojas's firewall seemed impenetrable. That her computer security was extremely sophisticated. That it could take weeks for Charlie to be able to hack into the records."

"Another strange thing. And in a way, it makes me believe this even more. Charlie's been working day and night trying to break in, and then just a few hours ago, there it was. Clear as day. Almost as if the information was put there deliberately. She said it looked as though the entry had been made today."

"Could this be a trick, a trap of some sort? Could Mendoza have set this up so he could follow a trail that might lead to the person who took his granddaughter?"

"I asked Charlie the same thing. She said she didn't think so. And even if it were a trap, there's no way anyone could trace her. Charlie's the best there is...I believe her."

As one of Grey Justice's top investigators and cyberexperts, Jonah had seen the expertise of Charlotte Nolan, aka Charlie, firsthand. She *was* the best.

"I agree, she is. So the question is, do we believe what she uncovered?"

"I don't think we have a choice but to assume it's credible. At the very least, whether it's true or not, this is something Gabby needs to know, Jonah. ASAP."

She was right about that. This information couldn't be ignored or swept under a rug. But holy, holy hell. This was going to devastate Gabby.

"I'm wondering if her cousin did this for her as a favor."

He gaped at his sister-in-law. "A favor?"

Kathleen gave a rapid shake of her head. "Not the procedure, of course. But revealing the information might be Antonia's way of helping Gabby the only way she knows how."

Jonah had a lot of thoughts about Antonia Rojas. None of them good. "If the woman actually did this to Gabby, she deserves to be behind bars."

"What Antonia did was wrong and horrendous, but from what we know about Mendoza, the man may not have given her a choice. He is beyond ruthless."

How messed up was it that the more he learned about the Mendozas, the better his own screwed-up family looked?

Jonah didn't question whether Luis Mendoza could actually be so cruel or selfish. Having seen this type of narcissism and lack of morality in his own father, nothing surprised him. To achieve a goal he was pursuing, Mathias Slater would've done the very same thing without the slightest twinge of conscience.

But what was Mendoza's reasoning? What could be so important that he would do something of this magnitude? What could be so imperative that he had approved something so vile and wrong, so damn invasive, for his own granddaughter?

"Do you want me to tell her?" Kathleen asked.

That would be the easy way out. Let Kathleen deal with the heart-wrenching news of this monumental betrayal. He told himself it would be better coming from a woman, especially one Gabby knew and trusted. But how the hell could he even assign the word *better* to this? There was no easy way to tell her. Nothing, no matter who told her, could make this better.

"I'll tell her. She'll want facts."

"I'll send you her cousin's notes." Her expression one of sympathy, she asked, "Will you tell her tonight?"

He thought about how happy she'd looked a couple of hours ago, right before she'd gone up to bed for the night. Being able to write down her hopes and dreams instead of holding them in her head had given her a serenity and optimism that showed clearly in her face. She had almost filled up one notebook. He'd found two others for her to use. Soon, she'd have a library filled with everything she wanted to do in her life. And dammit, he wanted her to be able to live out every one of her dreams. But this... Shit, shit, shit. This news would destroy all of that peace. All of her hopefulness would disintegrate.

As much as he hated to deliver the killing blow, he refused to wait. Putting off telling her would be wrong and self-serving. Even waiting until tomorrow morning wouldn't be right.

"Yeah. I'll tell her tonight."

CHAPTER SIXTEEN

Jonah stood beside Gabby's bed. He had knocked and when she hadn't answered, he'd eased the door open. Finding her asleep wasn't unexpected. She'd played in the snow for hours. After yesterday's debacle, he hadn't dared joined her. Thankfully, that hadn't seemed to mar her enjoyment. She had built her own snowwoman and had even created several smaller figures she'd described as snow pets. He had watched her from the window, mesmerized by the almost childlike pleasure she took in something so simple.

After dinner, she'd said she was going to her room to write in her notebook. Apparently, she had settled in to write after slipping into light blue flannel pajamas and fallen asleep in the process. The notebook lay by her side.

He re-evaluated his earlier decision. To wake her would be criminal. He would destroy what might possibly be her last peaceful sleep to relay information that would demolish that peace. Tomorrow would be soon enough to break her heart.

He bent down, intending to put the notebook on the night-stand so she wouldn't inadvertently knock it onto the floor. Moonlight reflected into the room, revealing the words she'd written. Without the least amount of guilt, Jonah glanced over her notes. And as he read, the hard shell around his heart cracked even further.

It was a bucket list of sorts, but unlike any he'd ever seen. These were things most people did on a daily basis, many of them mundane. To Gabby, who'd rarely gotten the chance to do anything for herself or by herself, they were goals to achieve, new joys to experience.

He smiled at the first item on the list. She wanted a puppy. Why would Luis Mendoza not allow his granddaughter to have something that to him should be small and insignificant but to a young girl could mean the world? Was he that heartless?

Stupid question. After what Jonah had learned tonight, that went without saying. The man was a monster.

Continuing down her list, Jonah noted she'd listed things from the silly to the downright dangerous. Spitting off the top of the Empire State Building was right under climbing Mount Everest. Number twelve on her list was something he would make sure she got to do right away.

He placed the notebook on the nightstand, took one last look at the peacefully sleeping Gabby, and turned to leave.

The sound of an alarm from his phone halted his steps and his breath. They had visitors. The question of how they'd been found would have to be answered later. For right now, they needed to move.

Jonah shook Gabby's shoulder hard. They had little time to waste. "Wake up."

She blinked up at him. "What's wrong?"

"Someone's here. We've got to leave."

Whether it was the fear that she kept inside her that never went away or the urgency of his voice, he didn't know. Whatever it was, she didn't waste time on questions. She jumped out of bed.

"Don't turn on any lights. The moonlight should be bright enough for you to see. Dress in layers. Wear two pairs of socks. Meet me in the hallway in two minutes."

He didn't wait to see if she was surprised by the lack of time. They needed to get the hell out of here. The alarm that had gone off was three miles away. If the intruders were walking, it would take more time, but if they had snowmobiles or a truck with a snowplow attachment, then his and Gabby's time to escape would be considerably less.

Jonah went to his room and dressed with quick efficiency. Prison life had been hell but had taught him some important lessons and skills. Getting dressed fast was one of them. It had taken only one beating from a sadistic guard to learn that lesson.

He unlocked the weapons closet and withdrew a couple more guns. He was already armed, but according to Kingston, Gabby had said she was an excellent shot. He hoped to hell that was true. She needed to be able to defend herself if something happened to him.

He pulled out a go bag from the closet. It was a little heavier than normal since he'd added a few additional items Gabby might need. If they got stranded, the contents should last them at least until they were able to arrange for pickup.

Hyperaware of time tick-ticking away, Jonah took the extra seconds to text Justice a brief message. His employer would begin the preparations. Just because they'd believed they couldn't be found didn't mean they didn't have a contingency plan.

He strode out of the room and was relieved to see Gabby waiting for him in the hallway.

He handed her a pair of sturdy snow boots. "Put these on."

She took the boots and quickly slid off the boots she'd worn earlier. Her face was as white as the snow outside, and her dark eyes were filled with worry. She was, however, calm. Almost too much so. Had she been anticipating this, too? Damned if he would let her down. She had gotten away. No way in hell was he letting her go back.

"You have your notebooks?"

"Yes. Beneath my sweater."

"Good. Let's go."

"What about a coat?"

"I have a snowsuit for you in the garage."

She followed him down the stairs and stood at the door of the office while he collected the laptop. He wouldn't leave anything incriminating behind.

Turning back, he gave her a nod, and they headed to the basement. Parked beside the black SUV was a white, top-of-the-line snowmobile. While he'd prefer the SUV for warmth and safety, they wouldn't get a hundred yards from the house. This vehicle could drive through snow better than anything he'd ever driven.

He handed Gabby a white snowsuit. While she slid into it, he pulled on a larger one. As soon as they were zipped up, he gave her a white ski mask. "This will protect your face. Keep your hood on and your head down as much as possible."

He pulled on his own mask and then jumped on the leather seat.

"Ready?"

"Yes."

"Get behind me and hold on tight."

Gabby climbed on behind Jonah and wrapped her arms around his waist. The engine roared to life just as the garage door slid open. She was surprised to see a narrow path enclosed within two solid white walls. He had obviously been preparing in case they were found. Gabby took comfort in that. Just because her grandfather's men had found her didn't mean this was the end of the line.

"Hold on!" Jonah shouted. And they were off.

Her heart pounding in a frenzy, Gabby tightened her hold around Jonah's waist and prayed.

Jonah had sworn that no one knew about their location. Was there a leak in the organization Jonah and Kathleen worked for? What would happen if they were caught? She wouldn't be hurt. She knew the only reason they'd come was to take her back, but they wouldn't hesitate to hurt Jonah. They would either kill him outright or take him to her grandfather. She couldn't let either of those things happen. Her grandfather would take pleasure in questioning Jonah and making him suffer.

"Hang on. We're going over!"

She had barely registered Jonah's words before they were airborne, soaring over a giant snowbank. Suspended in midair, Gabby lost all breath. Seconds later, they landed with a jolt, and she took in a breath of icy air. In another time, another situation, she would have been yelling and whooping with happiness, delirious at the exhilarating and exciting experience. The dark cloud of what would happen if they were caught squashed any enjoyment in the moment.

She glanced over her shoulder. It was still dark, but the full moon against the brightness of the snow made it look like it was almost daylight. She saw nothing but a stark-white landscape of gently rolling hills and trees.

"I don't see anyone," she shouted into his ear. "Are you sure—"

"Keep your head down."

The terse warning was barely out of his mouth when the thump-thump of rotary blades roared overhead. Light exploded around them. The helicopter's searchlight seemed brighter than the sun. There was no way to escape.

Gabby's frantic mind began to create stories about how she'd come to be with Jonah. She had escaped her kidnappers and had been injured. Jonah had come along and found her. Maybe she had been knocked unconscious and suffered temporary amnesia. That's why she hadn't called her grandfather. She would make Jonah out to be her savior. She would still have to return, but at least Jonah would be safe.

"Okay. Hop off."

Three things registered at once. They had moved into a thick grouping of giant evergreens. The snowmobile had stopped. And though the helicopter could still be heard above them, the light from the searchlight barely penetrated the dense coverage from the trees.

"What now?"

"We walk from here. It's only about half a mile."

"What's only about half a mile?"

"Our ride."

Stunned, Gabby watched Jonah grab the bag he'd stored beneath the seat. The instant he held out his hand to her, she took it and followed him deeper into the woods.

"You already had this planned out, didn't you?"

"Contingency plans save asses."

"I'm going to embroider that on a pillow for you." When he didn't smile or even acknowledge her joke, she knew they still weren't out of danger. She shivered, more from nerves than cold. "How do you think they found us?"

"That's something I don't know, but I'm sure as hell going to find out."

***

Valencia, Venezuela
Mendoza Estate

"We lost them."

Despite his age, Luis jumped up from his chair. Gripping the phone in his hand with all his might, he ground out the words, "How is that possible?"

"They went into the forest for cover. Don't worry. We've got the place surrounded. The minute they emerge, we'll grab them."

He released an easy breath. Once this was over, he'd talk with his head of security about his dramatic turn of phrase. His words *we lost them* had carved at least a year off Luis's life.

"How many are there?"

"Just one man and the girl."

Just one man? Either this was a small operation, or they hadn't anticipated being found. One man to guard her? Yes, they should have no trouble getting to her. He could feel the tension in his body melting away. Gabriella's recovery was only a matter of time now.

"Good. The priority is Gabriella. Her captor is secondary. Take him alive or dead. If he gets away, we'll find him later."

"Yes, sir. I'll contact you as soon as we have her."

The line went dead but rang again immediately. Luis answered, "What do you have?"

"The house is registered to the government of Mantoballah."

"I've never heard of it."

"There's good reason for that. It doesn't exist."

He shook his head. This was getting more and more strange. First, Gabriella was taken, but no ransom was demanded. And now she was found in a mansion in the United States in the middle of the Colorado mountains.

"What about fingerprints?"

"We're getting them analyzed. It may take some time, and if the man has no record, we may not be able to identify him."

That was unacceptable. "A ten-thousand-dollar bonus will go to the first man who identifies the monster who has my granddaughter."

"Yes, sir."

Luis heard the surprise in the man's voice. Mendozas weren't known for their generosity. And though it galled to have made the concession, finding Gabriella and bringing her home would be more than worth the extra outlay of money.

"Call me when you have something."

Luis ended the call and resumed pacing. It was only a matter of time until Gabriella would be returned. When she was back home safely, he would ensure this never happened again. He would have her brought to his home, where she would stay under lock and key until she had fulfilled her purpose. He had been careless with her care. Had allowed her the freedom of not only living on her own but also traveling around the world. Yes, he had made sure she had armed guards at all times, but what good had they been? She had been taken right under their noses.

His office door opened, and Luis stopped pacing. Already knowing the answer but asking anyway, he said, "Anything?"

His face barely flushed from his morning activities, Stephan shook his head. "Nothing, as we predicted. They'd already given all that they knew. There was no point in prolonging the inevitable."

That was what he had figured, but he had needed to make sure. Traitors surrounded the most powerful. He had learned that lesson early in life and would never forget it. One of Gabriella's guards could have been in cahoots with her captors. Now that they knew none of them were, the guards had been duly chastised.

"Everything is complete?"

"Yes. Their bodies are being disposed of as we speak."

"And their families?"

Stephan's face scrunched up into what looked like a grimace but was actually a smile of triumph. Luis had seen that smile many times over the years. "Properly compensated and warned."

Luis whirled away and resumed pacing. At least that had been done to his specifications. But nothing was solved. Nothing would be right until Gabriella was found and brought back to where she would stay securely behind locked doors.

"I have other news."

Luis stumbled to a stop. "What?"

"Rudolph Bianchi has left his estate."

Bianchi was a recluse and had not left his home in years. If the old bastard was on the move, that could mean only one thing.

"Have the guest suite prepared."

"You don't seem surprised."

"I'm not. Rudolph has always been a single-minded individual. This is the only thing he has to live for. He's determined to see it through. As am I."

Luis rubbed in chin reflectively. If he played this right… "Perhaps this is for the best."

"How so?"

"He needs to see we're in control of the situation. Besides, having him here in my home puts him in my territory. He believes he's been calling the shots all these years. It's time for Bianchi to see who is really in charge."

CHAPTER SEVENTEEN

Colorado Mountains

He glanced over at Gabby, who sat huddled in the passenger seat. "Have you thawed out yet?"

After a half-mile trek in sometimes waist-deep snow, they had both been slightly frosty when they arrived at the old shed where he'd stored their next ride.

"I'm getting there." She shook her head. "I can't believe you had this planned."

Justice had given him only eleven days to set everything up, so the ramshackle shed had been a risk. One he'd had no choice but to take. The nearest storage rental facility was a twenty-mile hike. No way in hell would they have made it. He'd taken the chance that no one would discover this hiding place. The weather had helped in that regard. Not too many people out and about to notice a beat-up old shed sporting a brand-new lock on its decrepit door and an old but in excellent condition Range Rover hidden inside.

"Preparation eliminates disaster."

She frowned. "Who said that?"

"Me. Just now." He sent her a mock look of concern. "Uh oh. Did you hit your head on a tree branch?"

The emotions flitting across her face were both amusing and poignant. Her first expression was one of high insult, and then as she realized he was teasing, her dark eyes glinted with laughter. He was also pleased to see light pink color bloom in her pale cheeks. A definite improvement.

Had anyone ever gently teased her? She had been alone and isolated for so long, he doubted that she had experienced anything so normal.

"Where do we go from here?"

To blend in with the rest of the vehicles and hide in plain sight, they'd gotten on the highway as soon as possible. Problem was, it was still a few hours till dawn. They'd passed only a couple of cars, but since no one should suspect that they were now driving a completely different vehicle, they should be fine. They had a five-hour trip ahead of them, but if the weather held up, it should be an easy, scenic drive to his place in Utah.

"I have a cabin in—" He grabbed the vibrating phone from his coat pocket and glanced at the screen. *Kingston*.

"Hey, we're just—"

"You've got a problem, buddy."

"What?"

"You've got a GPS signal coming from inside your vehicle."

"That's not possible." His mind scrambled for a reason. The Range Rover had been locked up for over three weeks. Alarms would have been set off if the hiding place had been compromised. No one, other than himself, had access to it.

"I don't—" He glanced over at Gabriella, a dark foreboding in his gut. "Can you scramble it?"

"Doing my best. But you need to find and destroy the device ASAP."

Jonah slid the phone into his pocket and blew out a breath. They had only a few minutes, if that, to find the tracker. There was no easy way to do this.

"Gabby, are you wearing any jewelry?" He could see she wasn't wearing a watch, ring, or a necklace, but there were other places jewelry could go.

"No. Why?"

"No belly button ring, toe ring? Piercings of any kind?"

She was smart enough not to need an explanation for such a personal question. "I don't have anything like that. What's wrong?"

"We're transmitting a GPS signal. I'm one hundred percent certain that the Range Rover is clean. As am I. That only leaves you."

"You think there's a tracker on me somewhere?"

"Or inside you."

He had never seen anyone go so pale so fast. The absolute horror on her face told him she fully comprehended what he meant.

Her emotions would have to be dealt with later. For right now, they needed to locate the tracker and figure out how to disable it.

"Do you have any idea where it could be?"

Trying to get a grasp on this bizarre development, Gabby shook her head slowly. "How would I even know something like that, Jonah? I don't know what one would look like. Are they large...or..."

"Do you have any soreness anywhere on your body? Anyplace that looks like a small incision could have been made?"

"No. Nothing like that. I—"

"What?"

Instead of answering, her hands went to the waistband of her pants. "A few years ago, I had my appendix removed. When I woke, my doctor told me that in the process of examining me, they found a benign cyst on my right hip and removed it. I had never noticed anything there, but I believed him."

She swallowed thickly. How could she have been so stupid and naïve?

The SUV swerved to the right as Jonah pulled off the highway. The vehicle jerked to a stop, and Jonah switched on the overhead light. "Let me see."

Embarrassment might come later but couldn't be worried about now. Gabby unzipped her pants and pulled them, along with her panties, down enough to show him the small scar on her right hip. She swallowed a soft gasp when Jonah ran a long, callused finger gently across the scar.

"Could that be it?"

"Yeah." He glanced around as if searching for something.

"What are you doing?"

"We need to get this thing out of you. If I can find a doctor's office or hospital, they can—"

"We don't have time for that. They'll find us. You've got to get it out now."

For the first time, she saw a hint of alarm in his eyes. Jonah had been so calm and resolute in their escape, but now he looked almost as panicked as she felt. Silly, but his obvious fear of causing her pain made her feel less panicked.

"Either you do it, or I'll take care of it myself. Either way, that thing is coming out of me. Now."

"Hold on." He pulled back onto the road and zoomed down the highway.

"Where are we going?"

"We need to find a hospital." He gave her another grim look. "And fast."

They were in a remote area. Finding civilization, much less a hospital, was going to be hard. Finding one before her grandfather's men found them would be next to impossible.

Resolute, Gabby opened the compartment in front of her. There had to be something…

"What are you looking for?"

"A knife, if you have one."

"Hell, Gabby. You can't—"

He broke off as a familiarly ominous noise sounded above them. The *whomp-whomp* of a helicopter. Her grandfather's men had found them again.

"Hold on."

Gabby did as she was told but continued to look for something…anything that would get the tracker out of her body. And while the biggest reason to get the thing removed was whirring above them, likely shadowing their every move, it wasn't the only one. Something even more desperate was pulling at her. Something had been put inside her body without her consent. Didn't matter that it was an inanimate object. The object did not belong there, and she wanted it out. Now.

"Get down in the floorboard."

"They won't shoot me."

"No, but they might shoot at me. I don't want you getting hit."

Though she didn't for a moment believe the men would endanger her by shooting, Gabby didn't argue. She unbuckled her seat belt and slid into the spacious floorboard. She could feel the vehicle shift gears as Jonah sped up. They had to be going well over a hundred, but that wouldn't matter.

"You can't outrun a helicopter."

"Maybe not, but I'm sure as hell going to try."

She felt helpless to do anything. She had promised herself that if she was ever able to escape, she would never feel this way again. Dammit, she had to do something!

A black duffle bag in the backseat caught her eye. Jonah was the resourceful sort. Would he have what she was looking for?

Keeping her head low, she slithered over the console and into the backseat.

"Where are you going?"

"Don't worry about me. Just drive."

The whirring of the helicopter grew louder, telling her it was getting closer. Jonah cursed, and she noted absently that his language was both inventive and colorful. She was oddly thankful his attention was diverted, because she was quite sure he wouldn't allow her to do what she planned to do.

Unzipping the bag, she almost shouted with joy when the first thing she spotted was a lethal-looking stiletto knife. Refusing to give herself time to think about it and panic, Gabby slid her pants down over her right hip again and glided the knife across the scar. She told herself it was good that the blade was so sharp, because a dull knife would have hurt much worse.

Her fingers started searching. She drew in a silent breath. *Oh damn, damn, damn...*

The Range Rover roared down the highway, hugging the curves of the winding two-lane highway. Jonah was going as fast as he dared on the icy, treacherous road. He was now thankful for the lack of traffic since he would've had to do some major maneuvering. Still, as good as this vehicle was and as empty as the highway was, there was no way in hell he was going to outrun the helicopter. Wyatt Kingston was damn good at his job, but there was only so much he could do to scramble the tracker. And even then, unless the chopper lost track of them, they were toast. Jonah had to find cover and fast.

The silence in the backseat suddenly caught his attention. "Are you okay back there?"

"Yes."

The tension in her voice was understandable, but still he detected something else. "What are you doing?"

"Nothing for you to be concerned with. Just keep driving."

Now even more concerned, Jonah took his eyes off the road long enough to glance over his shoulder. The scene wasn't quite as gory as a horror movie but close enough.

"What the hell did you do?"

"I have to get this thing out of me. There's no other way."

"There sure as hell is. That knife wasn't even clean. Dammit, Gabby."

"I can get a tetanus shot later. The bleeding isn't that bad." She held up a tiny, bloodied fragment of metal. "Look what I found."

She had done it. Had actually dug the thing out of her body.

Jonah hit the power button for the backseat window "Throw it out."

He watched as her bloody hand snapped the small device in half and threw the offensive object out the window.

His foot slammed the gas pedal. Gabby had done her part, now he needed to do his. They had to lose the helicopter. Then, he had to find her some help.

"I'll be fine, Jonah. It doesn't hurt all that much now."

"Yes. After you get stitches and a tetanus shot, you'll be just fucking fine. Till then, put a bandage on it."

He knew he was being gruff with her, but dammit, she'd done something he hadn't expected. She wasn't the pampered princess he had assumed before he met her. Nor was she the vulnerable victim he'd thought she was after hearing how she'd been treated by her family. She was so much more than what he'd counted on when he agreed to do this job. And dammit, he didn't like it. This was not what he'd signed on for.

His grim mood lifted when he spotted the exit up ahead. He turned off the headlights, lifted his foot from the gas pedal, and took the exit. He was still going too fast, but he had no choice. Until he could find cover, speed was his only defense.

Turning onto the main road, Jonah blended in with the early morning traffic. It helped that it was a weekday. Work traffic, even in a small city, could get congested at times. They had lucked up and found one of those times.

He looked up, noting that the helicopter was already backing off. No way in hell would Mendoza's men risk getting caught by trying anything out in the open.

Jonah raced down the highway, the sound of the helicopter already fading. One crisis averted. Now on to another one. Finding a doctor before Gabby bled out.

CHAPTER EIGHTEEN

Gabby lay on her left side in the backseat of the Range Rover. Pretending she wasn't in pain was useless, but she kept her mind occupied. Dealing with what her grandfather had done to her would come later, when she was stronger. For now, she allowed herself to drift to the dreams she had buried for years. Things she'd always wanted to do, things she had never imagined she'd have the opportunity to try. She had filled two notebooks with them, and she still had so many more.

Every now and then, the sounds of an angry voice would penetrate her consciousness. In a way, that was a comfort. At least Jonah cared enough to be angry on her behalf—even though she knew some of that anger was at her.

"Hey! Gabby! Stay awake. You hear me?"

Her eyes blinked open. She hadn't been sleeping, only dreaming. "Have we lost them?"

"Yes."

The tenseness in his voice told her they weren't out of the woods yet.

"What's wrong?"

"We need to find another ride. The helicopter backed off, and they can't track us anymore, but they'll have everybody and their brother on the lookout for a white Range Rover."

She sat up and looked around. The sun was higher in the sky, but it was still early morning. She was surprised to see they'd entered a city. They were on a busy four-lane road. Vehicles swooped up and down the highway. After being in seclusion for so long, she noticed the activity seemed almost manic.

"Are you going to steal a car?"

A dry cracked laugh was his answer, and for a moment, she found herself longing to hear a real laugh from him again. He had laughed during their snow battle. The sound had been deep, slightly husky, and beautiful. Just in the short while she'd known him, she already knew nothing much amused him.

The Range Rover made an abrupt turn into a parking garage. After going up a couple of levels, Jonah pulled into an empty space between a sports car and a tan SUV.

"Are you going to steal the SUV? It doesn't look very reliable."

He barked out another laugh, this one sounding a little less rusty. "What is it with you wanting to steal a car?"

"I thought you said we needed another vehicle."

"We do. It'll be here in about half an hour." Surprising her, he opened his door, stepped out, and then opened the back door. "Move over."

She slid across the seat, doing her best to hide the wince of pain. The opening on her hip had stopped bleeding but still throbbed.

"Let's see what you've done to yourself."

His voice had turned low and gravelly, like the purr of an expensive automobile. Awareness flooded through her. She had been alone with this man for days, had even kissed him until she was breathless, but for some reason, this felt more heated and intimate than the kiss they'd shared. Then, they'd been outside in the cold, crisp air. But this enclosed space, along with that intense look in his eyes, made her aware of him on another level.

Jonah Slater was intimidatingly large, surly, and on occasion quite rude, and she found him both fascinating and enormously attractive.

He lifted her hand away from her hip and removed the cloth she'd been holding on the cut to staunch the bleeding. He hissed and then swore again. "You're going to need several stitches."

"At least it stopped bleeding."

He shook his head, and just when she thought he was going to give her another reprimand or at the very least a lecture, he instead smiled. In that moment, despite the pain in her side, the knowledge that she was being hunted like a wild animal, and the uncertainty of her future, a swell of happiness blossomed inside her. Without a doubt, Jonah Slater had a breathtaking smile.

"One thing you might want to mark off your list of possible professions is surgeon."

"Darn. That was number three on my list."

Their eyes met, and the awareness from before bloomed brighter. Emerald eyes darkened to jade as Jonah lowered his head. Her heart pounding, Gabby parted her lips. She knew his taste, knew the softness of his lips. Knew how it felt to have his mouth on hers. She wanted that again. Only longer, deeper, more intense. She wanted more.

His breath warmed her face as he moved closer. Every muscle tensed in anticipation, Gabby held her breath as she waited for his mouth to touch hers.

The obnoxious blare of a car horn several yards away destroyed the moment. Jonah cursed softly and backed away. Just what the hell had he been about to do? Had he been about to kiss her again? Hadn't he given himself a blistering lecture about this very thing not forty-eight hours ago? And he'd been about to do the same damn thing again? Where the hell had his mind been? He didn't bother to try to answer that question. He knew exactly where it'd been. *Damn idiot!*

"Let's get you patched up before our ride gets here."

He tried for an even tone, but his voice sounded as gruff as a hungry grizzly. Gabriella wasn't buying it either. The solemn, almost hurt look she gave him made him feel all the more shitty.

Figuring his best bet was to do the job at hand and ignore the rest, Jonah opened the first-aid kit and proceeded to clean the open wound. He forced himself to ignore her hiss of pain. His mind still reeled from what she had done to herself. How much courage did it take to slice deep into your skin and pluck something out of it? A helluva lot, in his estimation.

He pressed a fresh bandage onto the wound and gently slid her pants back up her hip. Ignoring the silkiness of her creamy skin was made easier by his stern reminder that he could not touch her. He was her protector, not her seducer.

"It doesn't really hurt."

Startled, he raised his eyes to hers. "What?"

"You look so grim. I just wanted to assure you that it looks worse than it is."

The fact that she was trying to reassure him didn't surprise him. In the short time he'd known her, he'd learned she had a deep compassion for other people's feelings. How the hell that was possible after what she'd been through was a mystery. Were some people born with those kinds of emotions as opposed to learning them from others? He mentally shook his head. This wasn't the time to have an internal discussion about nature versus nurture.

"Feel like sitting up?"

"Yes. Thanks."

Watching her face carefully, he pulled gently until she was sitting. The blood she'd lost hadn't been a great amount, but it was probably enough to make her lightheaded.

"Okay?"

"Yes." She blew out a breath and looked around. "Where are we?"

"Grand Junction."

"Where do we go from here?"

"Once we have our new ride, we'll find a doctor to stitch you up, then head out to another safe house."

"You knew this could happen. That we might be found."

"Always best to be prepared for the worst."

"I guess no one could have expected how they'd find us."

The devastation in her eyes told him she was still dealing with what her grandfather had done. And she still didn't know what else he had done. Something so much worse and so vile he could barely comprehend it himself. He had planned to tell her this morning, but now he would wait again. No way in hell was she ready to learn just how far her grandfather had gone.

"The good thing is, we escaped. And you removed their ability to track us."

"Do you think there could be another one inside me?"

"Doubtful. There aren't any other signals coming from the vehicle. You don't have any other scars?"

"No. That's the only one."

"Just in case, I've got a scanner coming with our new transportation. It'll just take a few seconds to make sure that was the only one."

"You must think I'm pretty stupid for not having known I had that inside me."

"No. I don't think you're stupid. I think your grandfather is an evil son of a bitch who will do whatever the hell he wants, no matter who it hurts."

"It sickens me to know his blood is inside me." She threw him a wry look. "Too bad there's no such thing as a blood transfusion for that kind of thing."

He knew exactly how that felt. Having Mathias Slater's blood inside him would haunt him for the rest of his life. Before he could commiserate and tell her he could identify with her thinking, his cellphone pinged once. Kingston had arrived.

"Our ride's here. Get on the floorboard again. I'll let you know when it's safe to come out."

She slid back down onto the floorboard and gave him a thumbs-up and a smile.

He gave her a nod and stepped out of the vehicle. He trusted this man as much as he trusted any man outside of his brother and Justice, but he was taking no chances. Mendoza had proved that he would do whatever it took to get his granddaughter back. Now that he knew a little more about why, it made Jonah even more paranoid. No way in hell was this the last they'd hear of Luis Mendoza. No way in hell was the bastard going to give up until he found his granddaughter and got what he wanted from her.

And no way in hell was Jonah going to let that happen.

Gabby crouched on the floorboard and listened as Jonah met the person who was bringing them a new vehicle. How Jonah had their escape so well planned still astonished her. How naïve she'd been to assume that once she was out of her grandfather's clutches, she would be safe from him. Now that the immediate danger had passed, the knowledge of what he had done to her was setting in. He'd had her tagged like an animal. She had known for years that he had no affection for her. Claiming concern for her safety had been his initial ruse for having her watched and guarded so carefully. When she had rebelled, the pretense had ended. He had made it clear that, as the head of the family, his word was law.

Was this her life from now on? Hiding, afraid that one of her grandfather's goons would appear out of nowhere and whisk her back to captivity? She had to figure out a way she could be safe without giving up the independence she so desired.

"Okay, Gabby. You can come out now."

She sat up gingerly. The cut on her hip was beginning to throb even more. The man standing beside Jonah looked slightly familiar. She frowned, trying to remember where she'd seen him before. Then it hit her. Though she'd gotten only glimpses of him, she recognized the man who'd abducted her. Odd, but she felt torn about how to act with him. How did one behave toward an abductor/rescuer?

Apparently, her ability to hide her thoughts had taken a hit over the last few days. He gave a reassuring smile, saying, "Relax, Ms. Mendoza. I'm just here to deliver a car. Nothing more."

"Okay. Let's get this done." Jonah held out his hand to her. "Step out of the car, and let's make sure there are no more trackers."

He held a metal-looking wand in his hand. "If there is one, this thing will beep."

She told herself she shouldn't be embarrassed. It wasn't as if she'd done anything wrong. But still she could feel herself blushing to the roots of her hair as Jonah took the small wand and, starting with her head, slowly moved the detector down her body.

Gabriella held her breath. She didn't know what she would do if the thing indicated she had another device inside her. She ground her teeth and waited to hear the terrible sound of a beep. Instead, there was blessed silence.

"Okay. Looks like we're clear." Jonah held out his hand to the other man and did one of those odd handshakes that men did. She had never understood them.

The other man gave her a solemn nod and said, "Ma'am," in that slow drawl she remembered. Seconds later, he jumped into the Range Rover and drove away.

She looked at Jonah. "What now?"

"Now we take care of you."

Chapter Nineteen

Valencia, Venezuela
Mendoza Estate

"We lost them again. They entered a populated area and we had to back off. We lost visual."

"But you're still tracking her, right? You'll be able to pick up—"

"No. The GPS tracker stopped working."

Luis hit the speaker button on the cellphone and laid it on the desk in front of him. If he didn't, he knew without a doubt he'd be throwing the damned thing across the room again. How could one small woman cause such aggravation? She was just a girl, and not a very bright one at that.

"How is that possible? The tracking device inside her is of the highest technology. The best money could buy."

"Unless it's damaged."

"You think something happened to Gabriella?" His mouth went dry with fear. Nothing could happen to his granddaughter. Not until he got what he needed.

"No. I think the person who took her discovered the tracker, removed and destroyed it."

Insult replaced the fear. "Someone dared touch her? Dared to cut Gabriella open?"

The fact that he had approved several invasive procedures himself was of no matter. Gabriella was his granddaughter—a Mendoza. She was his to do with as he pleased. Anyone else who had the audacity to touch her without his permission would deal with his wrath.

"That is our assumption, yes."

"So you've lost them completely?"

"We know the general area and the description of the vehicle. It'll take more time, but we will find them."

"Keep me updated on any new developments."

"Of course, sir."

Luis took deep breaths. Getting more upset would get him nowhere. Gabriella had been gone two weeks, and as much as it pained him that she had not been recovered yet, at least they had more information than before. Setbacks were bound to happen. They knew her location. She couldn't go far before his people spotted her again.

Luis eyed the man sitting on the sofa so quietly. Stephan was such a hulk that even in silence he made his presence known. His expression was both contemplative and sad.

"What is it?"

"The men said that Gabriella ran alongside her captor. She didn't resist?"

"No, but that's no surprise. Gabriella hasn't an ounce of gumption or guile. She hasn't had any since she was fifteen. I'm sure the man holding her has completely intimidated her. She's living in terror, waiting for rescue. She wouldn't know how to fight."

The lack of response from Stephan was irritating.

"You don't agree?"

"What if Gabriella instigated this entire event to escape?"

"Don't be ridiculous. The girl is a simpleton."

"I know you like to think of her that way, Luis, but you're wrong. Gabriella has a master's degree in art history. She speaks four languages fluently and is a gifted artist. She's much more intelligent than you've ever given her credit for."

"All right, perhaps she's not simpleminded, but even if she's not, how could she instigate such a thing? She had no contacts with the outside world. Even when she travels, she's watched twenty-four/seven. Besides, why would she want to escape? She lives in a mansion. Has the best of everything."

"And her life is organized and controlled by you."

"And your point is what? That she's unhappy? Her happiness is not a concern. She is a Mendoza. I make the choices that are best for her."

"What if she wants to make her own choices?"

"That's not for her to say." Luis surged to his feet. This kind of nonsense would get them nowhere. "She was taken against her will, and she's waiting for her grandpapa to save her. That's the end of this discussion."

Stephan saw no reason to continue an argument that he wouldn't win. When it came to his family, Luis was blinded by his pride and his own opinion of how things should be. He had lost his son because he refused to see the truth. His grandson had chosen a different path, but still just as destructive. And then there was Gabriella. Luis had smothered the girl, kept her under his rule and control since she was a child.

No, Gabriella wasn't known for her rebellion, but she had a brain, and Stephan assumed she had hopes and desires of her own. Luis had never taken the time to find out what those were. Nor did he believe that she should have them. If they didn't mesh with his plans for her, they weren't pertinent.

With no ransom demand and none of their enemies taking credit for the deed, Gabriella's disappearance was worrisome. Why would anyone take her without the possibility for either financial gain or leverage for power?

Luis Mendoza was brilliant in many ways, but in the way of his family, he was as clueless as a baby duck. There was more to this situation than met the eye, and it was Stephan's job to uncover the truth.

He had watched over the Mendozas from an early age. He didn't always agree with his friend, but Luis was the head of the family, and his decisions were final. But just because he felt that way didn't mean others did. And that included Gabriella.

As Luis continued on, talking about business as well as the upcoming visit from the man they both despised, Stephan made plans of his own. He had protected the Mendozas from every threat that had come their way. He would do so again. If Gabriella had anything to do with her disappearance, she would be returned home and duly punished. Luis could be quite creative in disciplining his family members. They almost never misbehaved again.

At fifteen, Gabriella had survived a punishment so severe she had almost died. Since then, she had caused almost no worries, which was the exact reason Luis discounted Gabriella's involvement in her own disappearance. But had that changed? Had Gabriella developed some backbone? Or had it never disappeared and perhaps had been lying dormant, waiting for the right time to exert itself again?

***

Colorado

Eight stitches. She had needed eight stitches. Even hours later, Jonah had a hard time wrapping his mind around that. In prison, he'd dealt with some of the toughest and meanest bastards imaginable, and he doubted even one of them would have been able to cut into their own flesh as she had. Not only that, she had done it with no fuss, no complaint. Hell, he hadn't even been aware of what she had done until it was over. Gabriella Mendoza had courage and then some.

The little out-of-the-way clinic had been expecting them. The influence of the Grey Justice Group reached far and wide, even into the remotest areas, such as Curtis, Colorado, population 292. He and Gabriella had walked into the tiny clinic and were immediately taken back to an exam room. Within ten minutes of arrival, a grizzled-faced but efficient doctor had sewed Gabby's wound and administered a tetanus shot. A pain shot had been offered, but Gabby had declined, saying the numbing salve the doctor applied would be enough.

Jonah hadn't been surprised at the refusal. Not only was she strong, she wanted to be fully aware of her surroundings and circumstances.

"How much farther?"

"Couple of hours."

He glanced over at his passenger and hid a smile. The expression on her face reminded him of his nieces, Sophia and Violet, when they were exhausted. She looked both grumpy and adorable. The remnants of the milk shake she'd consumed with her burger and fries had left the shadow of chocolate at the corners of her mouth

Number seventeen on the list he'd read last night had been eating a cheeseburger, fries, and a large chocolate milk shake. Not the healthiest meal in the world, but he imagined her strict lifestyle hadn't included anything remotely close to junk food.

When he'd driven up to the fast-food drive-through window, he'd placed the order and waited, anticipating her excitement. She hadn't disappointed. The instant he'd ordered, she'd laughed softly and said, "Something else I can check off my list."

She'd eaten only half her burger and fries but had lingered over her milk shake, drawing noisily on the straw until the cup was completely empty. He hadn't needed to ask if she had enjoyed it.

"Why don't you get some shut-eye?"

"I'm okay." The words had barely left her mouth when he saw her burrow deeper into her seat and she was gone. Just like his nieces when they dropped off to sleep. Only, she wasn't a child. She was a beautiful, vulnerable young woman. And he had no right to have the thoughts he'd been having about her. She was his to protect. Nothing more.

Teri's face appeared in his mind. She was his purpose. She had been his life and had died because of him. How damn selfish was he to forget that for even one moment?

Gabriella Mendoza was a job. Just like many others he'd had. Once this job was done, he'd go on to another one.

He glanced over at her again. She'd had a rough day. He wished he could say her bad days were over. She had more to come, possibly the most difficult she'd ever faced. He had seen her courage firsthand. She was going to need every bit of it to deal with what came next.

CHAPTER TWENTY

Utah

Gabby opened her eyes to darkness. They were still driving, but she must have slept for several hours. It had been sunny when she'd closed her eyes.

She moved her gaze to the man beside her. The dashboard lights gave off just enough brightness for her to see that his mouth was set in a thin, grim line and his jaw was clenched in tension.

Her heart going into overdrive, she sat up and looked around. "What's wrong? Are we being followed?"

"No. We're clear. We should be arriving at the safe house within ten minutes."

Asking why he looked so grim would do no good. She'd learned that Jonah shared only what he wanted to tell her. "Where are we?"

"Utah."

"What happens once we get to the house?"

"We lay low. Let the dust settle."

"And then?"

"Then I go on to another job, and you become someone else's problem."

The words made a direct hit. Before she could respond, he cursed softly. "I'm sorry, Gabby. I didn't mean that."

She wasn't so sure about that. Either way, it was a good reminder. Jonah Slater wasn't her friend. He was being paid to watch out for her and get information on her grandfather. For her to expect something more was both fruitless and naïve. She was through with naïveté.

"No worries. I'm sure you have somewhere else you need to be instead of babysitting me."

"I just meant—"

"I know exactly what you meant, Jonah. Further explanation isn't necessary."

She kept her eyes focused straight ahead. With the night so dark, he likely couldn't see the hurt on her face, but she would take no chances. The longer she was with Jonah, the more she let her guard down and the easier it was for him to hurt her. Perhaps all of this was for the best.

The man beside her expelled a lengthy sigh. "The thing is, Gabby, I—" Another sigh, this one held more than a hint of disgust. "Look. I'm attracted to you. Okay? More than I have been to anyone since Teri. And I know you're attracted to me, too. But there's no point in pursuing something that can't last. You've got a new life ahead of you, one that can't include me."

"Because, with my new identity, I can't have anything remotely associated with my past?"

"Yes."

"That's not the only reason, though, is it? You're still searching for Teri's killer. You won't stop until you find him and make him pay. Correct?"

"No, I won't stop."

"And what happens if he stops you instead?"

"I'll just make damn sure he goes with me."

"Do you even care if you live?"

The silence that followed was painful, awkward, and telling. He really didn't care if he lived once his fiancée's killer was dead.

She had no idea what to say. She wasn't going to change his mind about pursuing the killer. She actually admired him for his courage. She couldn't even lecture him on the sanctity of living the life he had been given. She had been living in limbo for more than half her life, waiting to live. Who was she to lecture?

Nor would she tell him that the thought of something happening to him was so abhorrent that it literally made her sick. He definitely wouldn't want to know that.

The quiet was uncomfortable. Ordinarily, Gabby would rush to fill the silence with something witty or amusing. She had honed her social skills while playing hostess for her grandfather's parties. Charming a room full of people, half of whom dealt with their rivals by killing them, took a special kind of expertise. She could easily say something that would ease the tension. She wouldn't. The painful silence would just have to stand.

"We're here."

The night was pitch dark, but lights blazed throughout the small structure, giving off a welcoming glow. The cabin was about a fifth of the size of the house they'd fled in Colorado. Gabby immediately fell in love. The other place had been a mansion, majestic with every amenity imaginable. This place, with its wide front porch, wooden rocking chairs, and tin roof, looked like a home. A place you could pull off your shoes and warm your toes by the fire.

"It's lovely. Is this someone's home?"

"Sort of. I bought it last year. Stayed in it a couple of times."

That the house belonged to him wasn't a surprise. Jonah Slater might be a wealthy man, but he had a down-to-earth quality that would look right at home in a small cabin in the woods.

The front door of the cabin opened, and Gabby lost her breath. "Who's here?"

"The man who arranged your rescue."

So she was finally going to know her benefactor. She felt both apprehensive and excited. She also felt messy and wished she could freshen up a bit before meeting the man who had been generous enough to change her life.

She had nothing, not even a comb. She resisted the temptation to look in the mirror on the sun visor. Since she could do nothing about her appearance, what was the point of knowing just how disheveled she looked?

Straightening her shoulders, Gabby reached for the door handle.

Jonah touched her arm. "Hold on a minute."

Surprising her once more, he reached into the console and handed her a small cloth bag. She unzipped it to find moist towelettes, a comb, breath freshener, and, of all things, lip gloss.

"Where did this come from?"

"My go bag. I once asked my sister what were the things she always had in her purse that she never traveled without. I thought they might come in handy."

A lump formed in her throat, and Gabby swallowed, wanting to tell him what his thoughtfulness meant to her. When she realized the lump wouldn't budge, Gabby settled for a quick smile and nodded her thanks. She made quick work of the contents of the pouch and felt a million times better.

Jonah, who had been staring straight ahead, giving her some semblance of privacy, said, "Ready?"

"Yes."

"Let's go."

He reached for the door handle, and this time, it was Gabby who grabbed his arm. "Wait. I might not get the chance to say it again. I just want to thank you for all you've done for me. You protected me when it would have been much easier and safer for you to leave and let my grandfather's men capture me. That was very courageous."

He looked at her for a long moment, and she got the impression he was fighting an inner battle. Finally, he lifted a shoulder in a careless shrug. "I'm no hero, honey. Let's go meet the man who really saved you."

Letting her hand on his arm drop away, Gabby opened her car door. Once again, she had been reminded that she was a job to Jonah, nothing more. This time, she swore the lesson would stick.

CHAPTER
TWENTY-ONE

Grey stood in the doorway and watched the exhausted couple trudge toward the cabin. Although he had met Gabriella a few times at various events, he wasn't sure she would remember him. If he had known what she had been enduring for most of her life, he would have done something for her sooner.

The instant he saw their expressions, he knew something had happened between them. There was both an awareness and a wariness of each other. Gabriella wore a proud and defiant expression. It was Jonah's face that Grey focused on the most. Despite his obvious exhaustion, this was the most alive Grey had seen the man in years. No, he didn't look happy or even particularly angry. Grey scrambled for a description and decided *engaged* was the right word. Jonah had been in shutdown mode for so long, but now he looked like he actually gave a damn.

Stepping out onto the porch, Grey sent Gabriella a reassuring smile. "Hello, Gabriella. I'm glad you're safe."

"Grey?" She threw a disbelieving glance at Jonah and then returned her amazed gaze to him. "You arranged all this? But why?"

"Come in. We'll talk once you get settled."

She stepped inside warily, as if expecting her grandfather or one of his goons to jump out and grab her. He couldn't blame her for that. Gabriella had learned distrust of powerful people at an early age. Though he and Luis Mendoza had nothing in common businesswise, they both wielded a huge amount of influence in their particular worlds.

Once inside, she went to stand beside Jonah, and Grey was pleased to see that his first impression was correct. She trusted Jonah as her protector, but he got the feeling it was more than that. There was a connection there. It wasn't what he'd expected. Nevertheless, he was glad to see it. Considering what they were each facing, that connection might be the only thing to save them both.

"Gabby," Jonah said, "why don't you go and freshen up? Your room is up the stairs, second door. You should have whatever you need. If not, let me know."

Throwing Jonah a grateful smile, she nodded at Grey and then sped up the stairway.

The instant the door closed, Grey said, "What happened?"

Jonah threw the duffel bag in his hand down and dropped onto the sofa. "She had a tracker inside her. I should've scanned her at the beginning, but it never occurred to me her grandfather would be that bloodless."

"Don't beat yourself up. It didn't occur to either Kingston or myself."

"What happened after we escaped the mansion?"

"Place was ransacked. Mendoza's men practically turned the damn thing on its side trying to find evidence."

"And you're sure they won't find my fingerprints on file?"

"I'm certain of it. Once you were exonerated, we made sure your fingerprints and all DNA evidence were erased from the system.

Jonah breathed out a relieved sigh. Among the many perks of having a friend like Justice were the connections he had and the influence he possessed. Even though Jonah had been innocent of his crimes, he would always have a prison record. Grey had seen to it that much of that record no longer existed.

"How did you get rid of the tracker?"

"I didn't. She did it herself."

As Jonah explained the details, he could see that Justice didn't look all that surprised, and he realized something. "You know more about her than you told me."

"I've learned more in the last few days. After we hacked into the medical records at her doctor's office, I feel I have a working knowledge of what she's been going through for most of her life."

"Care to share?"

Jonah told himself it wasn't an invasion of her privacy. He was protecting her. Finding out about her any way he could was justified.

"I don't—"

The sound of a door opening stopped their discussion. Whether Justice would have revealed what he knew was anyone's guess, but either way, Jonah intended to learn more.

He noted that her footsteps were lighter as she came down the stairs. Apparently, she'd taken a quick shower, because her hair was slightly damp. Her color was still a little off, but she looked a lot better than she had. A few moments of solitude, away from his grumpy-assed self, had likely been a welcome reprieve.

Justice had brought some clothes for her. The jeans were a good fit, molding her perfect ass and hugging her long, slender legs. The fawn-colored cashmere sweater brought out the golden tone of her skin and made her dark brown eyes seem deeper and even softer. Gabby was a beautiful woman and in no way looked like she'd just been through a traumatic experience. He only wished—

Jonah jerked himself out of those thoughts. He'd once again been going down a road he dared not travel. What the hell was wrong with him?

Gabby settled onto the sofa beside Jonah. There were other chairs in the room, but she had chosen to sit beside him. He told himself that was no big deal.

She gave Justice one of her bright smiles. "I still can't believe it was you all along, Grey. How is it that you know Kathleen?"

"She's my employee," Grey said.

"But at the art show in Dallas, you acted as if you barely knew her."

"A ruse so she could get close to you."

Her smile disappeared. "Because of Carlos. He is definitely in jail?"

"Yes. And will be for a very long time. No worries there."

"I'm sure I only know a portion of what he's done, and it's horrific."

"He's nothing for you to worry about anymore. That part of your life is over."

"So what now?"

"Jonah was just telling me how you dug the location device out by yourself. That took a lot of courage."

A light flush of color tinted her cheeks. Something else Jonah was learning. Praise embarrassed her. Considering her family, she probably hadn't heard much of it.

"I did it out of desperation. I couldn't let them catch us."

"Courage is sometimes the by-product of desperation but does nothing to lessen the significance of the act. You've shown your strength in many ways. Are you in pain?"

"Not really. The doctor told me to replace the bandage daily. The stitches will dissolve on their own." She shook her head. "I still can't believe I had that thing in me and never knew it. My appendectomy was five years ago."

"Your grandfather was determined to never lose control of you."

"Luis Mendoza is an evil fiend."

"Yes, he is. I'm sorry you had to live under his rule for so long."

"I'm here now. That's all that counts. And I thank you for that. Are you here to discuss what I told Jonah?"

"Not really. Unless you have more to share. The information you gave will bring irreparable damage to your grandfather and many of his associates. You've done more than your share of good work."

"I'm glad."

"I'm here, actually, to talk about you. About your future. Where you want to live. What you want to do in your new life." His gaze shifted to the coffee table, where several folders lay. "I brought questionnaires for you to complete. It'll give my people a chance to help you create the life you want."

Jonah frowned as he followed Gabby's gaze to the folders. There were several of them. He had a sick feeling that at least one held information that could demolish every good feeling Gabby had about starting her new life. She wasn't ready to have that discussion now. Not after the day she'd had.

"How about we have dinner?" Jonah said.

"Excellent idea." Justice's gaze shifted toward the kitchen. "I picked up some food from the diner in town."

"I'll see to the meal." Before he walked away, he gave Justice a hard, telling look. No way in hell did he want him to bring up the doctor's appointment and what they'd discovered. He'd let her get a good night's sleep and tell her tomorrow. Waiting one more day wouldn't make a difference.

Without Jonah's presence, Gabby felt somewhat self-conscious. She remembered describing Grey to Kathleen as Mr. Tall, Dark, and Dreamy. With coal-black hair, intense blue eyes, and a commanding presence, he was quite handsome. Still, there was something about him that frightened her. While she was quite sure he wasn't of her grandfather's ilk, she had the feeling he could be terrifyingly ruthless in his pursuit of what he wanted. Having a man like him on her side was a good thing.

"Jonah's told you about the various governments who are looking for you, hoping to get what information they can?"

"Yes." She grimaced. "Being wanted by both good and bad people is a little uncomfortable."

"I'm sure it is. We'll make sure they can't find you."

She believed him. Grey was known for his philanthropy and his advocacy for gaining justice for those wronged. Maybe it was naïve of her—something she had sworn was in the past—but she trusted his word.

"Thank you, again." She nodded at the folders in front of her. "Should I go ahead and start on these?"

"Why don't we eat first?"

Jonah appeared at the doorway. The grim set to his mouth had gotten even more pronounced. Something was bothering him. His words earlier about her becoming someone else's problem had stung. Was that how he really saw her? A problem? He had admitted to being attracted to her. Was that the reason for his grimness?

"Gabriella, after you."

Startled, she looked up, realizing both men were focused on her. She went to her feet, following the delightful fragrance of something spicy.

They gathered at a small round table in the kitchen. Jonah had set the table and put the prepared food out. The cheeseburger and shake she'd consumed in the early afternoon were long gone. She was ravenous.

She was halfway through with her meal before she raised her head. Though slightly embarrassed to know she'd been eating like a starving animal, she was pleased that both men seemed to be of the same mind. Glad she didn't have to pretend with them, she concentrated on her plate. Spaghetti and meatballs was one of her favorite meals, but she was rarely allowed to indulge. It tasted like manna to her. Running for one's life apparently increased the appetite.

"Have you ever tried to escape your grandfather before this?" Grey asked.

The pasta turned tasteless in her mouth. How many times had she tried? She had stopped counting. Having no real plan and nowhere to run had thwarted every attempt. She had just wanted to be gone. Her grandfather's men had always brought her back.

Then came the day when she'd tried something different—the one thing she had believed would work. At last, there would be retribution for her grandfather and an escape for her. It had been a disaster. Her naïveté had caused a chain reaction of events that she would never be able to forget. And it had almost gotten her killed.

That had been the last time she'd tried. Until now.

Jonah watched the light in Gabby's eyes die, replacing the contentment that had been there before.

"I haven't tried since I was fifteen."

"Why did you stop at fifteen?" Justice asked.

Her eyes dropped to her plate. She didn't know it yet, but that move was one of her tells. Jonah knew her next words wouldn't be the complete truth.

"Raiza came to live with me. She was hired to be my bodyguard but became so much more."

"You trusted her," Justice said.

"The only person I've ever trusted until…" Her gaze went to Jonah, and then, blushing, she shifted her attention back to Justice as she continued. "Raiza became my mentor, my trainer, and my confidant."

"And she's the reason you never tried to escape again?"

"Her husband was killed when an enemy tried to assassinate my grandfather. Raiza was left to provide for the family. She had three daughters and a son. If I had escaped, she would have been punished, possibly killed. Her children might have been punished, too. I couldn't take the risk."

Jonah asked the obvious question, though he already knew the answer. "And then Raiza died?"

"Yes. Not long after I returned home from my trip to Dallas, where I met Kathleen. With her death, my grandfather could no longer hold her or her family's welfare over my head."

"She was like a mother to you," Jonah said. She'd had almost no one in her life to really care about her and had lost the one person who did.

"That and so much more. Raiza was a wonderful person, and I miss her greatly."

"I'm surprised your grandfather didn't have someone waiting in the wings to take her place," Justice said.

"I'm sure he would have, but her death was unexpected. He was likely looking, but other things were occupying him at that time, which is probably one of the reasons my brother came to stay with me. For a little extra intimidation. Not that his presence made any difference. I was circumspect in my behavior so no one would have an inkling of my plans."

"I'm sorry it took so long to carry out the abduction."

She shrugged as if it didn't matter, but Jonah knew the wait must have been excruciating knowing the possibility of escape was finally within reach but having no idea how or when it would take place.

"It wasn't your fault. Getting my brother and me together so we could be captured at the same time took longer than I anticipated. The doctor's appointment was our first outing together."

Wanting to make sure they didn't go into dangerous territory, Jonah said quickly, "What things were occupying your grandfather?"

"What?"

"You said your grandfather was occupied with other things, or he would have found you another companion immediately."

"I don't know exactly what they were. I just know he was distracted the few times we talked."

Did that distraction have anything to do with what had been done to Gabby? Even though he knew it would never be possible, Jonah wished with all his heart that he could spend just a few moments alone with Luis Mendoza. That's all the time he would need.

The rest of the meal passed quietly, each of them lost in thought. When Gabby finished, Jonah suggested she go on up for the night. The fact that she hadn't argued was telling. After the day she'd had, she had to be exhausted.

She said good night. The instant he heard her bedroom door close, he shifted his eyes to Justice.

"We need to talk."

CHAPTER
TWENTY-TWO

Grey sat in the near darkness, across from Jonah. Their only light was a lamp in the far corner and the dying fire. He had been relieved when Jonah suggested that they get started early in the morning instead of continuing tonight. Gabriella had some hard news to face very soon. She would need all the rest she could get.

Besides, he had a damn hard task ahead of him tonight. He'd put off the telling for as long as he dared. He glanced over at the man sitting so quietly in front of the fire. He was so deep in thought, he'd barely said a word since Gabriella had left them.

Wondering what was going on with the two of them, Grey said, "She's quite different than what I anticipated. There's a depth I didn't expect."

"You didn't tell me you'd met her."

"Just an introduction once, and I've seen her at various functions over the last few years. She attends the McGruder Art Show each year. The only event she attends in the US. I've spotted her a couple of times at charity auctions in France. Other than the goons surrounding her, she was always alone."

"She's strong. A helluva lot stronger than her grandfather could ever guess."

"She's going to need to be."

"You have more information?"

"Yes, but you said you wanted to talk with me about something?"

"We'll get to that in a minute. Show me what you have."

Grey stood and went to a desk in the corner. Removing two folders from the top drawer, he put one of the folders on the coffee table in front of Jonah, and sighed. "It's as bad as we thought."

In silence, Jonah reviewed the material. Grey knew the moment his eyes hit upon one of the most horrific pieces of information they'd uncovered.

"Son. Of. A. Bitch," he snarled.

"My words exactly," Grey said grimly. "Along with a few more."

"You're sure?"

"One hundred percent. Seems he's been bragging about it."

"This is going to destroy her."

Before Grey could agree or argue the point, Jonah shook his head, refuting his own statement. "No, it won't. She's too damn strong for that. She'll make it through, no matter what happens. She'll make it through."

"You know her better than I do. Should I stay around? Should we tell her together?"

"No. I'll do it."

"You'll let me know her decision?"

"Yes. It may take her a few days to come to terms with everything."

"Understood. She can take all the time she needs. Be sure to let her know she has our full support."

"I will."

"So you wanted to talk?" Grey prompted.

"You need to get someone else to stay with her. Maybe a woman this time. I know you have trained female operatives who—"

Grey raised his hand to stop him. "You've established a rapport. She's given you a boatload of information I'm not sure anyone else would have been able to obtain so soon. She trusts you."

"She does, but I'm concerned she's projecting something onto me I don't deserve."

Grey cocked his head, genuinely confused. "How's that?"

"I think she's got some kind of hero complex about me. Sees me as something I'm not. I just think it'd be easier if she's not attached to the person protecting her."

"Easier for her, or easier for you?"

"Both."

"Well, God knows we wouldn't want her to see you as a hero or anything."

Disgusted with the conversation for some reason, Jonah asked bluntly, "Can you do it or not, Justice?"

"I have numerous men and women who could do this job. I still think you're the best one for it, though."

Restless and frustrated, Jonah rose from his seat and paced around the room. He felt like shit for doing this. It was going to hurt Gabby, and she had been hurt enough, with more to come. But if he didn't get out of here?

He whirled around, blurted, "I should be out looking for Teri's killer. We're close enough that I can go to—"

Justice blew out a heavy sigh, nodded toward the sofa. "Sit down."

His eyes drilled into Justice's. "You have other news."

"You're not going to like it."

Jonah swallowed a bitter laugh. Since he hadn't liked any news in the last few years, that didn't surprise him.

Instead of answering right away, Justice dropped another folder on the table in front of him. This one was thinner. A thick, ominous feeling settled in his gut. His eyes never leaving the folder, Jonah ground out the words, "Spit it out."

"Peter Tinsley was the name of the hired killer who murdered Teri."

"Was?"

"He's dead."

"How?"

"Bullet to the head."

"Who did it?"

"I don't know."

"You have an idea."

"Yes."

"Irelyn?"

"Yes."

Irelyn Raine, Grey's former business partner, had disappeared almost two years ago, but somehow always seemed to be in the background, inserting herself when needed. This was one time she hadn't been needed. It had been his right and responsibility to take down Teri's killer. Irelyn had taken that away from him.

"Did she know the bastard?"

"Not to my knowledge."

"Then why?"

"I would imagine to keep you from having to do it yourself."

"Dammit, that wasn't her place." Jonah dropped onto the sofa and sent Justice a steely glare. "Did you tell her to do it?"

"No. I won't deny that I didn't want you to have to kill the man. Killing a man, even one this evil, takes a toll on a soul."

Jonah didn't bother to ask Justice how he knew this.

"If Irelyn had asked, I would have told her to leave it alone. I didn't want her involved. But, as you know, Irelyn goes her own way."

"It was the one thing I wanted. The only thing."

"Yes, I know."

Jonah stared down at the innocuous-looking folders lying on the table. Two of them held offensive information. One could destroy Gabby's future, and the other just destroyed the promise he had made to himself and to Teri. He had sworn he would take down the bastard himself.

He heard Justice get to his feet. "I understand this is difficult for you. Just remember, there's more to you than vengeance, Jonah."

When Jonah didn't answer, he heard the man walk away. "I'm staying at a hotel in town. I'll see you both tomorrow."

Rage and pain slammed into him. The only thing he'd been living for had been done for him. He would never get the satisfaction of seeing death come to the man's eyes...the evil bastard who'd ended Teri's life.

The door closed quietly behind Justice and Jonah was left alone with his demons.

Hours later, the fire had long gone out and only cold ashes remained. He'd thought about getting up and starting a new fire, but hell...he didn't care. He was frozen on the inside. A fire, no matter how hot, would never penetrate the solid block of ice he had become.

It was over, finished. His goal, his purpose, was no more.

Peter Tinsley. An ordinary enough sounding name for a not-so-ordinary scumbag. According to the single sheet of paper inside the folder, the man had been forty-eight years old and, for over half those years, had been an assassin. A monster who hired himself out to the highest bidder to end another person's life. How did a person get to that point? Money for murder? When did life become so worthless, so valueless, that taking the breath from someone's body was an acceptable thing to do? Did the act become commonplace, like swatting a fly?

He let his mind wander. Focusing on the abstract was much more pleasant than accepting the inevitable. Cold, hard hopelessness was zooming toward him, and he fought it the only way he knew how, with cold, hard facts.

According to Justice's findings, Mathias's henchman, Cyrus Denton, had hired Tinsley several times over the years to do away with people who got in Mathias's way. One of those people Tinsley had been tasked to kill was Teri.

Why the hell had he allowed himself to fall in love with her? The minute she'd approached him about what she had found at Adam's office, he should have told her to quit and walk away. Should've told her that he'd handle things on his own. If he had, she'd still be alive.

Back then, he'd been so stupid, barely knowing his head from his ass. He'd been working for the Slater Corporation and feeling as useful as a knife at a gunfight. He'd been on the verge of leaving the family business altogether when he'd stumbled on something hinky on one of the shipping reports. He'd started an investigation. The more he dug, the more suspicious he became.

In his gut, though, he had known that the biggest reason he was digging was just to get dirt on his old man because he'd hated him so much. What a clueless fool he'd been.

Teri had been funny and sweet, and despite working for the second-biggest asshole in Texas—Mathias being the biggest—she'd been the most upbeat person he'd ever known.

They'd kept their relationship a secret for a long time. Adam had a tendency to want what his brothers had, and the last thing either of them wanted was for him to get interested in Teri. If he'd detected any kind of relationship between Jonah and Teri, he would have gone after her full force. Wanting what he couldn't have or what someone else had was just Adam's way.

In the last few months before it'd all turned to shit, their romance became secondary to the investigation. Looking back on it now, he could see that. All he'd been able to see, to concentrate on, was the dirt Mathias and Adam were embroiled in. The focus had been on digging up enough evidence that would bring them both down.

Then, without even a hint of thunder, the shitstorm arrived in torrents. Jonah had been framed for smuggling drugs into the country. Arrested, convicted, and sentenced in an extraordinarily short period of time. Mathias, with his money and influence, had made sure it was an open-and-shut case.

And then Teri disappeared.

It twisted his insides to think about how naïve they'd been. Without an ounce of training between the two of them, they'd thought they could bring down an empire. Justice had warned them to take all precautions. By then it had been too late. Mathias had somehow discovered what they'd been doing. And just as he had so many times before, he'd taken care of the problem in the cruelest way possible.

The day Eli had arrived at the prison to deliver the news that Teri's body had been found would rank as the worst day of his life, bar none. In his heart, he had known she was dead. Still, there had been that small kernel of hope that he was wrong. Eli's words had erased all doubt. But the agony wasn't over. That was the day he'd learned that there was devastating news and then there was pure, unadulterated hell. Only half of her body had been found. The fucker had decapitated her.

With a low, anguished growl, Jonah covered his face with his hands. Darkness descended, and grief overwhelmed him.

"Jonah? Is everything okay?"

Aw, shit.

Wiping his face with the backs of his hands, he cleared his throat, then winced at the huskiness of his voice as he said, "Go back to bed, Gabby. Everything's fine."

"Everything's not fine. What's wrong?"

"Nothing. I—"

She came to stand before him. "Please, Jonah. Let me help."

"You'd better get back to bed before you freeze."

Instead of doing what he asked—hell, that was no surprise—she held out her hand. That was it. Such a simple gesture, but one filled with compassion.

She was dressed in a long white nightgown that should have made her look like either a child or a spinster in a Victorian novel. Unfortunately, it did neither. Gabriella Mendoza looked both intensely beautiful and heartbreakingly innocent.

When he didn't take the offer of her hand, she dropped onto the footstool in front of him and spoke in a soft voice, as if she were talking to an injured animal. "You can trust me, Jonah. We've been through a lot together over the last couple of weeks. I've told you things I've never told another soul. There's nothing you can't share with me."

"Got some shitty news from Justice."

"Is your family okay?"

That she didn't assume the bad news had anything to do with her was a testament to this woman's nature. Considering what she'd been through, it would've made sense. Although his tears were probably a dead giveaway.

"My family is fine. I just—" He could tell her so many things. That it was none of her business. That he would be out of her life in a few days and they didn't really need to know anything more about each other. Or he could lie, come up with something vague.

Instead of doing any of those, which probably would have been the smart thing, Jonah opened his mouth and spilled his guts.

As Gabby listened to Jonah's heartbreaking story, tears filled her eyes. She had known most of it. That he'd been in prison and finally exonerated. That his father was behind everything. She also already knew that his fiancée had been murdered. She hadn't known the details, though. Death was sad at any point; murder was hideous. But the way the young woman had been killed was horrific.

"You feel guilty," she said softly.

"Of course I feel guilty. I am guilty."

"How?"

She knew she was treading on thin ice with him. This was a man in agony, consumed by guilt. Challenging him might not be the smartest course to take, but she couldn't stand seeing his pain. If she could help, even in some small way, she had to try.

"How am I guilty?" His eyes still glittered with tears but there was fury there, too. "It was my father who had her killed. How the hell could I not feel responsible?"

"But it wasn't you. Do you think I'm responsible for every person my grandfather killed?"

"It's not the same thing."

"No, but—"

"But nothing, Gabby. If I hadn't gone after Mathias, none of this would have happened."

"Wasn't Teri investigating on her own?"

"I should've told her to back off. Should've pushed her away. Made her leave."

"Would she have obeyed if you had?"

His mouth twitched with an almost smile. "Of course not. She had a mind of her own." Any humor vanished when he added, "It doesn't matter. I should have found a way to stop him on my own."

She would let the matter drop for now but hopefully she had given him something to think about.

"The authorities could do nothing to help?"

The bitter twist of his mouth told her how he felt before he even said the words. "The same ones who tried and convicted me based on my father's planted evidence?"

"Isn't that more your father's fault than the authorities? All they had was the evidence they uncovered. How could they have suspected your own father would set you up like that?"

He shoved his fingers through his hair. She could feel his frustration and hoped he wouldn't shut her out. It felt good to be discussing his situation with him. He was treating her like her opinions mattered. She was so used to having men, especially the ones in her family, dismiss anything she said. Jonah might not like what she was saying, but at least he treated her as a thinking adult with a right to her own views.

"If I'd had the chance to kill Mathias, I would have and saved my family a lot of heartache."

"You would have killed your own father?"

"Without an ounce of remorse."

Her mind veered away from similar thoughts. Yes, she'd been abused, both physically and mentally. Locked away, treated like a prisoner. Everything she held dear had been taken from her. She hated her grandfather with every fiber of her being. Yet the very thought of ending someone's life, even his, was a distasteful thought. Becoming what she knew him to be would be the height of hypocrisy, wouldn't it? In every way possible, she had strived to be the very opposite of what her family stood for.

Did Jonah really have it in him? He was a hard man...that was evident. But talking about the deed and actually carrying it out were two different entities. How did one get to that point? When did talk become action? When did hatred become an all-consuming goal to destroy? Had she been headed in that direction without even knowing it?

"You're freezing."

She jerked as Jonah's voice brought her back to reality. He thought her shivering was from lack of warmth in the room, but she knew it was more than that.

"It is a little chilly. The fire has gone out."

He stood and pulled her up with him. "We both need to get some sleep."

In a move that seemed like the most natural thing in the world, she went into his arms, and they held each other. The embrace was one of comfort. One damaged soul giving ease to another. She couldn't remember the last time she'd felt so safe and secure, so in tune with another human being.

She leaned back in his arms to say those exact words and caught her breath. Jonah's eyes glittered with heat, his expression one of need and desire. The thought of denying him never entered her mind. She lifted her hand and gently touched his cheek.

Jonah took her mouth with his, devouring her lips and taking her breath. Had he ever tasted anything sweeter? He heard a whispered warning in his head, telling him he was about to make a monumental mistake. He ignored the warning and shut down everything but the wild, hot need rising within him.

Gabby wanted him, he could feel her passion, the heat blooming within her. She was soft and pliant, pressing into him as if she wanted to get as close as possible. His body hardened, throbbing with lust, as a blazing heat threatened to explode. He needed. He wanted. He had to have her.

Gripping the nightgown, he pulled it up and slid his hands beneath. The soft cotton of the gown was no match for the silkiness of her skin. She moaned beneath his lips, and the fire burning within him heated to an inferno. His hands roamed over soft hills and silken curves. Had he ever wanted anyone more than he wanted this woman?

Trailing his lips down her neck, he breathed in the soft, subtle scent of aroused woman. Gripping her tighter, his mouth latched on to a taut, firm breast, and he suckled deeply. Her little groans of pleasure ramping up his own need, the soft sounds urged him on, telling him to take, to devour.

His hand swept up her side, pulling the gown up with him. He wanted her naked, on the sofa, on the floor, wherever he could get her. He would take her, ease the ache in his body, the deeper ache in his heart. She wanted him…she wouldn't deny him.

His fingers stuttered as they encountered an anomaly in her soft skin. The bandage on her hip, where she had courageously cut out a tracker. A tracker put there by evil men. Men who had used her, abused her.

Holy hell, what was he doing?

Releasing her abruptly, he backed away. His breath rasped from his lungs, and his body burned with desire, but he found the strength to say, "Go to bed, Gabby. Now. Please."

"But, Jonah, I—"

"Now!" The word was a command, a bark. She didn't deserve the treatment, but she had to go before he did something they'd both wake up regretting. She deserved better.

The hurt on her face almost made him change his mind, but no way in hell was he about to use her. People had taken advantage of her all her life. Damned if he would be one of them.

"Please, Gabby. For me."

She nodded and practically ran from him. He watched until she was out of sight, and then he dropped back onto the couch. What the hell had he been about to do?

CHAPTER
TWENTY-THREE

Valencia, Venezuela
Mendoza Estate

Stephan stood beside the window and peered down into the courtyard. "He's just coming through the gates."

"And everything is ready?"

"Yes. He'll not want for anything."

"Excellent. I want him leaving believing that everything is under control. He needs to see my commitment to our agreement hasn't wavered. Our relationship has always been turbulent, but since Rudy's imprisonment, it's grown even worse. Our agreement was forged long ago, but I'll admit that I delayed somewhat. Having my granddaughter mated to a serial killer isn't exactly a grandfather's dream."

"What we dream and what is necessary are often in direct contrast. Your goal can't be achieved without living up to your promise."

Yes, he knew that better than anyone. No man dreamed of making the decisions he had made—many of them, he'd been forced to make. Maintaining a reputation, retaining power, growing and achieving one's goals took sacrifices. Some great, some small. If others suffered, that was the way of the world.

Some might see this particular arrangement as selfishness on his part. He didn't agree. Bianchi had what rightfully belonged to him. The bastard wouldn't give it up without compensation. It was as simple as that.

"I'll be in my quarters if you need me."

While regrettable, having Stephan present when Bianchi was here was not advisable. The bad blood between the two would never be resolved. Years ago, Stephan had taught Rudolph's grandson, Rudy, a much-deserved lesson in humility. The lesson was one that the young man would likely never forget. His grandfather certainly hadn't.

The lesson had been harsh but necessary. Rudy had been given instructions, and instead of following them, he had improvised. Luis couldn't say he hated what happened or the results. Two young people had learned valuable lessons. Gabriella had learned the consequences of defiance. Her rebellious streak had ended that day. And Rudy had discovered that not following orders was a punishable offense.

In truth, he thought the event had been his most successful method of child-rearing. Too bad he'd never had the chance to have a similar experience for Carlos. If he had, perhaps the young man might not have veered so far off course.

Shrugging away the regrets, Luis walked with Stephan down the hallway and into the large atrium of his home. Stephan gave a small salute and continued up the stairway to his quarters. He would stay there, unless Luis called for him, until Bianchi departed.

With a concession he made to few, Luis opened the front door and went down the steps to greet his old rival. The day would come when they were united by more than enmity. Again, not what any man would dream of, but as Stephan so eloquently put it, what a man dreamed and what was necessary were often completely different. They each had something the other wanted. Their bartering system might be a bit archaic, but—what was the saying?—needs must. He desperately needed something that Rudolph possessed. And once Gabriella was returned to him, he would ensure the bargain went through. If he could have had what he wanted without going through with his agreement, he would. Since that wasn't possible, he would live up to his end of the bargain.

His best false smile in place, Luis held out his arms in welcome to the man he despised more than anyone he had ever known.

***

Rudolph glided through the arched entryway of Luis Mendoza's private museum, the hum of his wheelchair the only sound in the tomb-like mausoleum. He'd been inside the secret rooms only a few times. Each time he came, he left both impressed and disgusted. How many people knew that beneath the mansion was a collection of treasures that would rival that of many of the world's most-famous museums?

As a man grounded in practicality and reason, he found the objects pointless and somewhat vulgar. He also decided that many of Luis's most priceless treasures were remarkably ugly. He gave a mental shrug. To each his own. Luis's obsession was Rudolph's good fortune. Without it, he would have no hope for what he wanted.

"I've added several new items since you were here last."

The energy and enthusiasm in Luis's voice made the man sound like a teenager showing off a new sports car. Vanity and pride were etched on his face, while his eyes gleamed with avarice. Luis showing off his treasures with a childlike glee was in its own way amusing. The man really had no idea how ridiculous he appeared.

"This is an Egyptian vase from the eighth century. It once belonged to the Emperor of Japan. I purchased it two years ago last March for 60.2 million American dollars. My appraisers have assured me it's worth almost twice that amount now."

Rudolph grunted his acknowledgment. He could appreciate a bargain as much as the next man. If someone was insane enough to spend that kind of money for an ugly vase with a crack in it, that was their problem.

"And over here…" Luis pointed to a lighted alcove where a large painting hung of an old sheep farmer and a couple of goat-like creatures on a hillside. "This is an original Steinhardt. He painted it right after his wife died, and many think that—"

"Enough, Luis." Rudolph's weak lungs no longer allowed him to shout, but he could still put enough emphasis in his voice to let others know of his displeasure.

"What's wrong?"

"I haven't the slightest amount of interest in your so-called treasures. So far, you have done nothing other than try to impress me with food too rich for my belly, wine too expensive for my taste, and a tour of your useless baubles. I came here for one reason only."

Offense stamped an ugly meanness on Luis's face. "You insult me with your words while you hold my treasure for ransom. How dare you?"

"I dare because I have what you want. If you would stop playing with your silly toys and find your granddaughter, we wouldn't be having this discussion. Now tell me what's going on. Are you close to finding the girl or not?"

The gleam didn't leave his eyes, but Luis answered with more civility than Rudolph had expected. "We have gotten close twice. Whoever has her knows what they're doing. However, it's only a matter of time before we find them. Next time, we won't lose them."

"I've told you before. You gave the girl too much freedom."

"Her travels were important. As hostess for my parties, she was required to talk about a variety of things. She needed to be able to converse intelligently."

"From the moment the girl was conceived, she only had one real purpose. You should've seen to that."

"She was at the doctor's office, getting the procedure, when she was taken. I fulfilled my part of the bargain."

"Not yet you haven't. The girl is still missing. You should've had her under lock and key until she did her duty."

"If your grandson had not committed his crimes, this would not have been necessary. It could have been done and over with."

"My grandson can't help the way he is. His doctors have told me he's a sick young man. None of this is his fault. Besides, if you really want to place blame, you should look in the mirror. You're the one who brought this on yourself. Not me."

"You old buzzard. You have what doesn't belong to you. It belongs to me."

"It was given to me in exchange for what you took from me. It's rightfully mine, and you know it."

Luis drew in a breath. They were bickering like two children fighting over a toy. If he didn't get himself under control, he would pick up one of his priceless treasures and slam it into Rudolph's head. One misery would cease, but the ache for what he wanted most would never end.

"This argument is getting us nowhere. We each have what the other wants. If we work together, we can still make an exchange."

"Fine. I'll concede that without your cooperation I can't have what I want, so I'll agree to work with you up to a point. However, when the girl is found, she will come live with me in Rome. No more traveling or social engagements until I have what I want from her.

"And before you tell me no, old friend, listen well. The reason the girl is gone is because she initiated the entire thing. Your grandson was taken in exchange for giving the girl her freedom. Mark my words, she is behind this all."

"Who told you that?"

"No one. If you would get your head out of your ass, or your mind off your silly artifacts, you would see that clearly. Somehow, somewhere, she was able to negotiate this entire event. Therefore, when she is found, she's mine until I get my payment. Is that understood?"

This wasn't the first time it had been mentioned to him that Gabriella had instigated her own abduction, along with Carlos's arrest. The idea was so far-fetched and unrealistic, Luis had always ignored that theory. Rudolph's words made him rethink his opinion. Was the girl bright enough to have done something like that behind his back? She had been watched like a hawk every moment of every day. Who did she know who would have helped her? She had no friends. With the exception of him and Rudolph, not one single person cared if she lived or died.

Luis shook off his disquiet. The idea was still ludicrous, but there was no point in arguing the point with Bianchi.

"Very well. Once she is found, she can stay with you until her promise is fulfilled. But once she's delivered to you, that means I receive immediate payment."

"Agreed."

Triumph sparkled in Rudolph's watery eyes, and Luis wondered if he hadn't been too easy in his agreement. What was the old crone up to now?

CHAPTER TWENTY-FOUR

Utah

Grey arrived the next morning with a box of pastries and an agenda of getting to know Gabriella better. He had some preliminary suggestions on her next move, but he hadn't made any definitive plans for her yet. Creating a new life for someone wasn't the hard part. He had the money and contacts, plus a whole slew of experts who could make it happen. What he did need to know was what kind of life she wanted.

Rarely did he get so deeply involved in a relocation. There were dozens of people in his employ who could have come here and interviewed Gabby. For a couple of reasons, he was taking a hands-on approach. For one, Gabriella Mendoza had done him a great favor. Not only had she provided the opportunity to bring Carlos to justice, she had provided incredible intel that would put a stop to some very bad people. It might not completely destroy Luis Mendoza…time would tell. However, the information would damn well put a crater-like hole in his illegal activities, along with those of several of Mendoza's associates. Gabby deserved preferential treatment.

Another reason was because of the man he'd assigned to protect her. Jonah had been on the edge for so long. Last night, Grey had given him news that might just tip him over that edge into an abyss from which he might never return.

Jonah had been living for vengeance. Now that the chance was gone, his world could go dark again. Grey didn't intend that to happen. Assigning him to a new, dangerous job would give him the adrenaline rush he craved. Grey knew better than anyone that being in the line of danger kept the demons at bay. It was also a way to get yourself dead. When you stopped caring about life, death was an attractive alternative.

Few people knew that he'd once been in the very same place as Jonah. Living only for vengeance was a cold, barren place to reside. It had taken years to overcome the need. In truth, there were still dregs that popped up occasionally and corrupted his thinking. This was something Irelyn knew far too well.

Grey took a swallow from his mug and eyed the couple through the steam of the coffee. "Did you both sleep well?"

"Yes, thank you," Gabriella said politely.

Jonah grunted a yes.

They were both lying. Gabriella looked more exhausted this morning than she had last night. The grim man sitting next to her looked as though he'd swallowed a tub of cement. His face was carved in granite.

Grey hadn't expected cheerfulness from either one of them, but their expressions told him something had happened after he'd left last night. They both looked miserable. And that made him want to smile.

"I thought, over breakfast, we'd talk about your future."

Gabby cut her eyes over to the too-silent man sitting beside her. Was he even remotely interested in her future? He had barely even glanced at her this morning. Was what happened last night so terrible? Admittedly, she wasn't well schooled on the rules of this type of thing, but had it been that wrong? A kiss between two hurting people, each giving comfort in their own way. Okay, yes… it got a little heated. Okay, a lot heated, but still, was it a crime?

He certainly hadn't complained while it was happening. In fact, he'd participated quite eagerly. Her hands hadn't been the ones to pull up her nightgown and roam all over her body. It hadn't been her mouth that had bruised her lips, licked her neck, or suckled her—

Blushing to the roots of her hair, she ripped her thoughts back to the present. Remembering what had happened while Grey Justice sat in front of her, his keen eyes assessing, was not the appropriate time or place.

"Jonah said you've been making a list?"

A list? Her brain scrambled to get back on point. They were talking about the future. Her future. *Get with it, Gabby!*

The chair beside her squealed as Jonah pushed it back and stood. "Since this doesn't concern me, I'll go chop some firewood."

Ignoring Gabby's hurt eyes and Justice's angry glare, Jonah headed toward the door. Grabbing the ax leaning against the wall, he walked out.

After last night, he needed to get the hell out of here as soon as possible. Once Justice and Gabby discussed her future, he would have his own discussion with the man. There had to be a job coming up where his skills could be put to use. He'd done the job here, and it was time to leave.

Gabby had barely looked at him this morning. Not that he could blame her. What he had done last night was unconscionable. She had been offering him a gesture of solace, of comfort, and he'd turned it into something else. Didn't matter that she'd responded. Didn't matter that after a second, she had seemed to want more. That she had wrapped her arms around him and practically melted into him. It'd been a stupid-assed thing to do. And it could not happen again.

No use trying to deny something else that was eating at him. Only an hour after learning that the man who murdered Teri was dead, he had been kissing another woman. Just what kind of low-class sleaze did that make him? He had sworn he'd bring her killer to justice. And what had he done? Nothing. Exactly nothing. The bastard had escaped Jonah's vengeance. Instead of mourning that outcome, he had kissed another woman.

Lifting a log from the stack, he placed it on the chopping block and swung. The slam made a satisfying noise, echoing through the small canyon. Grabbing another log, Jonah swung again. He repeated the motions over and over, working up a good, solid sweat but only slightly easing the ache in his chest.

An hour later, he had a stack of wood before him and a satisfying burn in his shoulders. Wiping the sweat from his brow with his forearm, Jonah turned to find a pissed-off man standing behind him. Only, Grey Justice didn't show his anger in a normal way. The man was too controlled for that. But the icy blue glare left no doubt to his real feelings.

Jonah turned back to his pile of wood. "You and Gabriella get things worked out?"

Justice's silence was as loud as another man's screaming rage. Yeah, he was pissed. Well, so the hell what?

Turning, he glared at his boss. "You got a problem?"

"No, you do."

Jonah wasn't even going to pretend he didn't know what the man meant. "What do you expect me to do? My part is over. She's ready to move on. I need to do the same."

"I do have a new job for you."

"Good. Where and when do I leave?"

"You don't have to leave. The job's here."

"What the hell are you talking about? This job is over. She—"

"Is still being hunted. And depending on the results of the test she's going to have to take, she may need even more protection."

Jonah whirled around and hurled the ax, getting no satisfaction when the blade landed in a fallen tree several feet away, deeply embedded. Turning back to face Justice, he said, "What aren't you telling me?"

"We got word that Bianchi showed up at Mendoza's estate yesterday."

"The man never leaves his home. Why the hell would he risk it?"

"Could be nothing more than two megalomaniacs having a friendly get-together. Based on what they planned for Gabby, I'd say the reasons for a meeting were quite clear."

"Yeah," Jonah said. "Nothing messed up about that at all."

The tension in Grey's muscles eased a little. Jonah might not be happy that his job here was being extended, but he saw the seriousness of the situation. Until they knew exactly what the two equally evil and powerful men were up to, Gabriella needed to stay hidden away. Jonah could protect her better than anyone right now. She trusted him, and considering what she had gone through, that was a miracle in itself.

"Okay, you're right. I need to stay here. Hell, we'll bake cookies and watch movies."

"Oh, I'm sure you both can find something more productive to keep you occupied."

Jonah's expression went darker. "But first I have to tell her."

"Yes." Grey sighed. There was no easy way to do that. "Do you want me to stay?"

"No. I figure once I tell her, she'll either rip my head off or burn the place down. Best if only one of us is around."

"Just make sure she understands she's got friends. People who are here for her. She's not alone in this."

"I will. So where are you off to now?"

"Morocco."

"What's in Morocco?"

"Not what. Who."

"Irelyn's in Morocco? What's she doing there?"

"Other than pretending that I don't exist or that she ever knew me?" Grey shrugged. "Who the hell knows? Irelyn Raine is an enigma even to herself."

"If you find her, tell her…"

Jonah didn't finish the sentence, and Grey was glad of it. Yes, he had a right to be furious, but having anyone hurl insults at Irelyn, no matter the reason, would never sit well with him. He ignored the little voice that reminded him of all the times he'd hurt her himself. Their story was a complicated one that few, if anyone, would understand. They'd hurt each other as badly as could be done, but they always found their way back to one another. Eventually. It'd just been too damn long this time.

"I'll give her your regards."

"Yeah, you do that."

"I'll talk to you soon." Grey turned away. Both he and Jonah had a hard task before them. Jonah's was going to possibly destroy a woman who'd done nothing to deserve the pain she had coming. And Grey's job? To find the one woman he couldn't let go of or forget. In his heart, he knew that if he didn't find her soon, it was going to be too late for both of them.

CHAPTER
TWENTY-FIVE

Gabby watched from the window as Jonah and Grey talked. She couldn't hear what was being said, but neither of them seemed pleased with the other. After Jonah had walked out, making it obvious that her future wasn't his concern, Grey had apologized for his rudeness. When she had explained that there was no need to apologize, that she knew why Jonah was so upset, she'd seen complete shock in his eyes.

"What do you know?"

"That Teri Burke was his fiancée, and Mathias Slater hired a hitman to kill her. And since his release from prison, Jonah's been hunting her assassin. I know that Peter Tinsley, the man who murdered Teri, is dead."

"Do you also know that Jonah hasn't shared that kind of information with anyone? Ever?"

"Maybe he needed to tell someone who's an outsider."

"Maybe." His gaze had darted toward the door Jonah had walked out of, and then a speculative look had come over his face.

They'd gone on to talk about her future and her interests, but she got the impression that ideas and thoughts were being developed outside their immediate conversation. She was quickly learning that Grey Justice was a man of many layers.

She watched as Grey and Jonah continued their conversation. She noted that Grey gave Jonah a hard look and nodded toward the cabin. After a couple more minutes, both men's shoulders relaxed, and then Grey got into his SUV and drove away. The fact that he was leaving to begin the arrangements of creating her new life should have caused some sort of angst or at least excitement. Instead, her mind was focused on the brooding man standing beside the large woodpile, looking so alone. She wanted to comfort him.

With an abrupt movement, he went to retrieve the ax embedded in a fallen tree and then headed back to the cabin. Gabby jumped away from the window and looked around for something to do. She raced to the kitchen and pulled open the refrigerator door.

"What are you looking for?"

Gabby whirled around and tried to act like she knew what she was doing. "I was just looking for something to prepare for lunch."

Surprised he didn't call her out on the obvious lie, since she knew less about cooking than a toddler, she added, "Um… Maybe a sandwich or something easy?"

"We'll worry about that in a little while. Right now, I need to talk with you."

She followed him into the living room. "What is it? Has something happened?"

"I need to go into town for a few things. I don't feel comfortable taking you with me. You should be safe here."

"I'm sure I'll be fine."

"You told Kingston you can handle a gun." He placed a Glock and a box of shells on the coffee table. "Show me."

"You want me to shoot you?"

A spark of humor hit his eyes. "That won't be necessary."

She picked up the weapon and, with the ease of someone who'd performed the task hundreds of times, released the magazine and then pulled the slide back to check the chamber. She loaded the magazine with fifteen rounds, inserted it into the slot, loaded the chamber with another round, and slid it closed. She placed the weapon back on the table.

"Where'd you learn how to do that?"

"Raiza."

"Someday you're going to have to tell me all the things Raiza taught you."

She hid a smile. Jonah would likely be both surprised and delighted to know all the things her friend had taught her.

"Ever shoot anyone?"

"Of course not. But we used to do target practice at least three times a week. I hit what I mean to hit."

"Shooting a person is a lot different than shooting a target."

"I agree. Unfortunately, we could never get volunteers to let me shoot them."

"This is serious, Gabby."

"I know it is, Jonah. But I promise I will not hesitate to shoot if I'm threatened."

With an abrupt nod, he stood. "Good enough. I've got several errands, so it'll be a few hours." He handed her a cellphone. "It's a burner. My number is already in it. You have any concerns, you call me. Understand?"

"I understand."

With one last solemn look, he walked out and closed the door behind him.

Long after Jonah left, Gabby sat and listened to the silence. It had occurred to her that this was the first time in her life she'd ever been truly alone. Even though she'd had no friends and, not since her parents, any real family, she had never been by herself. For as long as she could remember, servants or guards had been within calling distance. It was a unique and wondrous experience to know that there wasn't anyone around to hear her. If she wanted to go out onto the porch and shout or scream, the only ones to hear would be birds and creatures of the forest. How liberating.

Instead of doing that, she decided to explore her new, temporary home. The cabin wasn't overly large but was a comfortable size for a small family. Two bedrooms, two baths, a kitchen, and a living room. The third floor held a giant room with more than a dozen windows and would make a wonderful art studio. She knew Jonah probably hadn't considered such a thing when he'd purchased the house, but her artist's eye could already see the possibilities.

The décor throughout was both modern and traditional with painted walls, hardwood floors, and a large, modern kitchen.

A person could find solitude and peace inside the sturdy, comfortable home and outside with the small lake, distant mountains, and gigantic trees that shaded the area.

She walked out onto the porch and leaned against the post. Drawing in fresh, clean air, a pleasant memory, one of the few from her childhood, flashed through her mind. Her parents had taken her and her brother on a holiday. They'd stayed in a villa in Spain that overlooked the sea. She couldn't recall the exact location, but she remembered the things that mattered most. Her beautiful mother's smile, her father's strong arms and deep laughter. She even remembered Carlos teaching her how to ride a bicycle. She had loved him then. He'd been her big brother, and she'd looked up to him.

She'd been only about five or so, but those few precious days were etched in her mind forever. Maybe she remembered them so well because not long after that, life went horribly, terribly wrong.

What was left of her family was the stuff of nightmares. A grandfather who murdered, destroyed people's lives on a whim. A brother who raped and did other vile things she didn't want to imagine. Various aunts, uncles, and cousins who toed the family line and did what they were told, either because they were just as evil or they were too scared to rebel.

Like Antonia.

Her thoughts went to the day of her abduction. So many things had happened since then, she'd barely given any thought to the reason behind the physical exam at Antonia's office. Now that she wasn't consumed by fear and the need for survival, she remembered several concerning things she should have questioned more thoroughly. Why had she been examined? Was there something wrong with her that she hadn't been told?

Why had Antonia felt the need to drug her? Admittedly, she might have seemed more anxious than normal. After all, she had known that within minutes after her exam ended she would be on her way to a new life. But had her anxiousness been so apparent that Antonia had felt the need to sedate her?

Deep in thought, she turned to go back inside the cabin. The instant she opened the door, her eyes locked on Jonah's laptop lying on the coffee table. Why hadn't she thought to do this before? She could hack into almost anything without leaving evidence that she'd been there.

Determined to get to the truth, Gabby opened the laptop and set to work. In five minutes, she had bypassed the weak security firewall. She had given her cousin more credit than she deserved. A five-year-old could have hacked into her medical records.

She found her file a couple of minutes later. Oddly enough, it was in a separate file and not in with any other records. Her eyes scanned the information. The first page showed her vital statistics. Nothing remarkable there. She clicked the next page and noted she had been slightly anemic a couple years ago. Of course, she hadn't been told, but she did remember the cook had started serving more green, leafy vegetables.

She clicked to the next page, which included notes about past visits. Nothing remarkable there, either. From what she could tell, she was in excellent health.

Her eyes scrolled down to the last entry—the day she saw Antonia for the last time. Her cousin noted that she seemed a little more anxious than usual. Her vitals were good. Blood had been taken to check her iron level, which had improved. Nothing alarming or noteworthy.

She clicked to the next page, to Antonia's last notation. She read the words, read them again, and then again. Surely she was misinterpreting their meaning. She read them once more.

No. No. No.

Her body went numb. All feeling from her head to her toes ceased to exist. She sprang to her feet, not even hearing the chair as it tipped over, slamming against the hardwood floor.

This had to be a mistake. This couldn't be possible. They couldn't do this…they could not do this. But they had. God in heaven, they had!

She had to get out of here. She couldn't catch her breath. Air clawed at her lungs but wouldn't come out. She flew across the room and opened the door. She had to get out of here. She could not…simply could not…

Gabby took one step onto the porch and slammed into a hard wall of muscle and sinew. "Gabby? What's wrong?"

She shook her head. She couldn't form words or make even a sound.

"Breathe, baby. Breathe." His hands gripped her shoulder, and he shook her. "Breathe, dammit."

She heard an odd gurgling noise and knew the sound came from her. She drew in for another breath, found one, and felt it explode from her body with a sobbing sound of anguish. How could they?

What the hell was wrong with her? Jonah looked around for threats or danger but saw nothing. Something had scared or upset her. But what?

He pushed her away slightly to make sure she wasn't injured or bleeding. He saw nothing other than a pale, terrified woman gasping for breath.

"Tell me what's wrong," he demanded. "Tell me, sweetheart. What happened?"

She still didn't answer, and Jonah looked around again, this time for clues. His eyes skittered and then stopped. The laptop he'd left on the coffee table was gone. He closed his eyes. Holy hell, why hadn't he given that any thought? He had known she could hack into any kind of system. Without a doubt, she had hacked into her medical records. And she knew what her cousin—and her grandfather—had done to her.

"She...she... They...they..."

"I know, baby. I know." Not knowing what else to do, Jonah pulled her into his arms and held her. After all the speech preparation and encouraging words he'd practiced on the way back to the cabin, his mind was blank. He had no clue what to say or how to comfort her.

Her face was buried against his chest, and she was trembling, but at least she was breathing and seemed to be getting calmer. There was still more bad news to come, but he would wait.

Gabby breathed in and out as steadily as she could. No good ever came from hysteria. She was far from accepting the information she had read. There had to be a mistake. And Jonah—

She took a step away from him, and her foot hit something on the porch. Looking down, Gabby's eyes took in an odd assortment of items. Jonah must have dropped what he'd been carrying when she flew out of the cabin. Candy bars, DVDs, books, magazines, more notebooks. And in the middle of the innocuous items were several boxes. Something she'd never had cause to purchase or need before. The labels screamed out at her: Home Pregnancy Kit.

Realization dawned as his words finally clicked. *I know, baby. I know.*

Blood rushed from her head again, and she heard a hoarse, horrified whisper. "You knew?"

"Yes. I—"

As if scalded, she sprang away from him and ran back into the cabin. She stopped in the middle of the room and turned in a circle, looking for an escape. *Get out, get out, get out* was an echoing drumbeat in her head. The betrayal was worse than any she'd felt in years. She had trusted him!

"Gabby, stop. It's not what you think."

She whirled around and snarled, "Not what I think? You knew what was done and you didn't think to tell me? How could you?"

"I didn't know until yesterday…actually, the night before that. I was waiting for the right time to tell you."

"Right time? Right time to tell me this? There is no right time. How could you?"

"Dammit, Gabby. I—"

"Tell me now, Jonah. Say the words. Say them!"

"You were artificially inseminated."

She closed her eyes. The actual words sounded even worse than reading them. How dare they? How. Dare. They.

She opened her eyes again. Jonah's expression was one of deep regret, and yes, anger, too. Knowing that the anger was for her helped a little.

"How did you find out?"

"It bothered me…what you said about being drugged at your doctor's visit. I asked Kathleen to see if Justice's people could hack into Antonia's records. I found out right before your grandfather's men found us in Colorado."

"So a whole slew of people knew before I did. Kathleen, Grey, his hackers. All these people knew what was done to me."

"I'm sorry, Gabby. I just—"

"You should have told me, Jonah. The minute you found out, you should have told me."

"You're right. I should have."

All the strength went out of her legs. She sank to her knees and wrapped her arms around herself. Numbness faded, and a raging tide of agonizing pain washed over and through her. Sobs tore from her chest as the hideousness penetrated her horrified mind. What had they done?

Jonah was no stranger to helplessness. He'd felt it all too often himself not to recognize the agonizing pain. What had been done to Gabby was an awful and disgusting crime, and he couldn't do a damn thing to make it go away. No matter what happened, no matter how she dealt with it, this was something that couldn't be undone. Enduring and getting through to the other side was the only way to cope. He knew all about that, too.

What he wanted to do was go to Venezuela, find her freak of a grandfather, and end him. That might come later. For right now, Gabby needed him. So he did the only thing he knew to do. He went to his knees beside her, held her, and whispered meaningless platitudes.

Her voice was thick with tears. "I told myself that he could do nothing more to hurt me. That no matter what he did, he would never destroy me." She swallowed and then whispered, "I was wrong. He has…he has."

"He damn well has not." When she didn't respond, he pulled away slightly and grasping her shoulders, he shook her. "You are stronger than this, Gabby. You know you are. You've got more guts and stamina inside you than that bastard can fathom. You will not let him win."

A long shudder went through her, and then she wept softly, despairingly, against his shoulder.

Jonah continued to hold her and let her grieve as much as she needed. Gabby, being Gabby, didn't cry for long. Within a few minutes, the sobs turned to shudders. As if she was gathering strength, she went still in his arms. Then, with a long, shaky breath, she pulled away.

He hated to leave her, but he had left something in the SUV that couldn't wait any longer. Something that he hoped would help immensely. "Stay here. I'll be back in just a sec. Okay?"

"Yes…okay. I'm fine," she whispered.

No, she wasn't, but every single day he knew her, this woman impressed him more and more. She was so damn strong.

He went out the door and gathered the things he'd bought and brought them inside. It took three trips, but when everything was finally inside, he shut the front door and turned to face her.

She was still sitting on the floor, shoulders slumped, head bent in defeat. It was as if all the hope she'd carried within her had left her body.

Dammit, the bastards would pay for this.

He looked down at one of the gifts he'd bought for her. This might not be the right time for her to meet anyone new, but hell, it wouldn't be the first time his timing was off.

He bent down and unlocked the cage.

The first sign that someone other than Jonah was in the room was the cold nose she felt on her cheek. She raised her head and looked into the deepest, darkest, most soulful and kindest eyes she could imagine.

"Hello," she said softly. "And who are you?"

"He doesn't have a name yet. That's for you to decide. I picked him up at the shelter in town. He was found wandering the streets a few months back. The vet thinks he's a variety of breeds, but mostly black Labrador retriever. He's about six months old. He's had his shots, been neutered, too. He's just been waiting for someone to love him."

Her hand shook as she reached out and touched the pup's head. Tail wagging, a goofy, adoring expression on his face, the dog looked up at Gabby as if he knew and loved her already.

"Oh Jonah, he's beautiful. But why—"

"That was the first thing on your list."

Her face was still pale, but her eyes shone with a brightness that had nothing to do with tears. "Thank you. This is the sweetest thing anyone has ever done for me and the most precious gift I've ever had. I love him already."

"I'll put his water bowl and food out while you get to know him."

As she petted her new friend, accepted his kisses and hugged him in return, an odd kind of peace touched her. Nothing was resolved, and hard times were ahead, but with this lovely act of thoughtfulness, this hard but generous man had helped tremendously.

"Thank you, Jonah. I'm sorry I lost control."

"There's no need to apologize, Gabby. But we'll figure this out. Okay?"

"Okay." She drew in a breath and nuzzled her new friend. "Okay...yes, we will."

CHAPTER
TWENTY-SIX

Valencia, Venezuela
Mendoza Estate

Luis took a sip of his wine and eyed his lovely dinner companion. Though his libido had long since disappeared, he could still appreciate a beautiful woman. Especially one with her impressive résumé.

Two different associates had recommended the private investigator. He had put off calling a professional, believing his people would be able to find Gabriella on their own. After this last failed attempt, he'd had no choice but to call someone who specialized in finding missing people.

"You come highly recommended."

Her smile was both confident and charming. "I assure you my reputation is well deserved."

"How do you propose to find my granddaughter? Many of my employees have tried and not succeeded."

"I have contacts others may not have. And"—she smiled like a feline who'd just consumed a sizable mouse—"I have skills they don't possess."

"Yes, so I've heard."

He had interviewed a handful of investigators before settling on this one. There were many out there, but few who could lay claim to being both an investigator and an assassin. He had need of both.

"At this point, I'm only concerned with finding my granddaughter. I will, however, have need of your other service later on."

"Understood. My investigative skills have no equal. Finding your granddaughter will be my number-one priority. Once she is secure, I'll be anxious to entertain other areas where my expertise lies."

"Excellent. You were provided the basic details regarding my granddaughter and her disappearance. What else do you need? As you might have already surmised, Gabriella is my greatest treasure and I'll do whatever I have to do to have her returned home."

All business now, she leaned forward. "I need every detail you can give me about the girl. Her favorite foods, what music she listens to. Her favorite places to shop, to visit. Is she adventurous and bold or shy and timid?"

"Why do you need to know these things?"

"To create a profile. People can change many things about themselves, but there's always one or two habits or peccadilloes, if you will, that trip them up. Things they can't or won't give up. Sometimes they think they're so insignificant, no one will notice. But I notice."

"My granddaughter lives a quiet life. She has no friends and doesn't do much of anything other than paint in her studio and putter around in her little garden. She serves as hostess for my events. She does a bit of traveling each year."

"What are her favorite places to visit?"

Irritation hit him. Not only did he not know the answers, he found this all very trifling and silly. What grandparent knew such things of their grandchildren?

"She goes to the same places each year. The Louvre in Paris, the Prado in Spain, and the Uffizi Gallery in Florence."

"That's all?"

"Don't forget about the McGruder Art Show in Dallas," Stephan said.

"Dallas? As in Texas, in the US?"

"Yes, I'd forgotten about that one."

"Are you sure these are the only places she goes? Perhaps she snuck away from her guards and met someone."

"Not only is she guarded better than any member of a royal family, Gabriella is quite sedate. She doesn't have an ounce of rebellion in her body."

"She sounds boring. Why ever do you want her back?"

Since she was being blunt, he would follow her lead and do the same. He answered honestly, "Because she has something I want."

"And that is?"

"None of your business." He would go only so far in his trust of this woman. How did he know that if he told her the truth she wouldn't take offense? Some women, especially sophisticated women of the world like this one, had strange beliefs about a woman's role.

"I understand." Her smile was sympathetic. "If you'll just start talking about her, I'm sure I'll be able to create an adequate profile to get me started."

He tried to remember the last time he'd seen Gabriella. The autumn party, perhaps. Who knew? She'd just flitted around, doing her duties as hostess. Her smile had been gracious, her laughter pleasing. Her knowledge on a variety of topics enabled her to engage in interesting conversations with all his guests, no matter how varied and odd. She had done the job to his satisfaction. The next day she was gone. They'd rarely spoken during the party unless it was about one of the guests. What else was there to talk about?

"She's about five-eight, slender but not thin, is in excellent health, has dark hair, almost black. Dark brown eyes and creamy skin. She's an attractive young woman."

"Yes. I have her physical description as well as several photographs. But what about her personality? Any eccentricities?"

"As I mentioned earlier, she paints and putters in her garden. Other than that..." He shrugged. "Who knows what young people do?"

Though her expression didn't change from one of pleasant professionalism, Luis got the impression that she found his lack of knowledge of his granddaughter disappointing. Not that it mattered, but the minutia of Gabriella's life wasn't his responsibility. He fed and clothed her. He gave her everything she needed. That was more than enough.

"What about her friends? Perhaps I could talk with them."

"As I mentioned before, she's an introvert. Doesn't have friends."

"I see."

Luis forced himself not to squirm in his chair. The conversation was making him feel more and more uncomfortable. Lovely though this woman was, she had no right to judge how he ruled his family.

"Will that be all? I have important matters to attend to."

She nodded and stood. "This will be sufficient to get me started. If anything comes to mind that you think I should know, you have my number."

Fearing she might not understand the extreme urgency in retrieving Gabriella as soon as possible, he urged, "I'd appreciate it if you would make this your utmost priority. Gabriella doesn't do well on her own. She needs constant supervision."

"This case is my number-one priority. I'll do everything within my power to bring Gabriella home safely."

"Excellent."

"I'll contact you as soon as I have a lead."

"Yes, yes. That's fine. Just bring her home as soon as possible."

***

She waited until she was driving away before she released a tinkling laugh. Oh, the games silly men played. Did Luis Mendoza actually believe the words he'd spouted? She certainly didn't. But that was no matter. A job was a job. And this one happened to pay more than any she'd had before. There were layers that didn't usually exist, along with twists and delicious secret turns. Even if Mendoza hadn't been paying her, the entertainment value alone made it worth her while. How long had it been since she'd enjoyed anything?

A year ago, she had emerged from the sea, damaged but not broken. Days had passed before she could even lift her head. Weeks had gone by before she had accepted that she would live. Recovery had taken a long time, but it had also given her a chance to plan, to dream. Revenge and retribution were powerful motivators.

Those who had caused her pain would pay. That was a given. She had been left for dead. Like some sort of refuse...like garbage. Yes, those who had treated her as such would suffer.

She was back in the game now, but it wasn't like before. Would never be like it once was. And she had only one family to blame. The Slaters of Dallas, Texas, would be punished for what they'd done to her. She had been unsuccessful in her attempt to eliminate them, but this time she wouldn't fail. This time, it was personal. The Slaters would die cursing the day they'd ever crossed paths with Ivy Roane.

In the meantime, she needed to work. For money, yes. One could never have too much of that. But also for the distraction. Her plan for the Slaters would take time to coalesce. Until that day came, she would keep herself busy. Hunting down one wayward young woman wouldn't normally be that interesting, but the parties and intrigues involved were beyond fascinating.

Yes, she could have a bit of fun until her day of retribution came. Pitting evil men against one another was just the type of entertainment she needed.

CHAPTER
TWENTY-SEVEN

Utah

They were seated back in the living room. After feeding and taking care of her new friend, Gabby felt more centered. She couldn't say she was one hundred percent ready to face all that lay before her, but she was further along than she had been. Putting it off wasn't going to solve anything.

Jonah handed her a brown folder filled with a dozen or more pages. "Justice brought this with him yesterday."

Her hands shook as she took the folder. So innocuous looking...so boring. But the information in it contained life-changing news.

"Do you want me to tell you what's in it?"

"No..." She drew in a deep, bracing breath. "I need to do this myself."

"Most of the pages are Antonia's records. You've probably already read everything. The last page is information we got elsewhere."

She knew what that meant. Just the thought brought bile surging up her throat. Hiding from the truth would do no good.

She had to know everything. Even though she already knew, she had to be sure.

She opened the folder, quickly reviewed the notes she'd already read, and then flipped to the back page. She held her breath as she read the three sentences.

Two guards confirmed your suspicions. Several weeks ago, two of Luis Mendoza's men came to the prison and retrieved a package from Rudy Bianchi. Without a doubt, he is the sperm donor.

The blunt words stabbed into her with the precision of a steel pipe, causing massive damage. She surged to her feet and slammed the folder with the vulgar, offensive information onto the floor. She gazed around wildly, needing an escape. She had to get out of here. Had to go somewhere…anywhere but where this hideous, outrageously disgusting piece of information resided.

Hands gripped her shoulders and squeezed firmly. "It's going to be all right, Gabby. Do you hear me? No matter what happens, everything will be all right."

"I need some air."

"Of course." His hands gentle on her shoulders, he steered her toward the door and opened it. Walking out on the porch with her, he looked over his shoulder at the pup wagging his tail hopefully. "Do you want to take him with you?"

She glanced down at her new friend. He looked so trusting, so very sweet. If she took him, he would comfort her, but she knew without a doubt she would scare him. She anticipated some major screaming and crying. He didn't need to see that. She didn't want anyone to witness the meltdown that was coming.

"No. I need to be alone."

"I know you need solitude. But don't go too far."

She barely acknowledged his warning with a nod as she strode down the steps. The sky was slightly overcast, and a cool breeze blew in her face. She was dressed in jeans and a sweater, so she was fine for now. She might get cold later, but she couldn't stand the thought of going back inside for a coat. She had to get away now. She had to think. She needed to breathe.

She walked around the perimeter of the lake. It wasn't a large body of water but was pretty and peaceful. Her frozen mind didn't allow for coherent thought quite yet. The wind was blowing, and the tall trees swayed, rustling the leaves. Birds cawed and tweeted above her, while small woodland creatures foraged in the underbrush for food or shelter.

She absorbed the sounds of nature, of innocence. There were no worries, no concern or awareness of evil. Their goals were simplistic, survival in its purest form. But they were wary, too. Danger lurked, and while they focused on their main goals, they were aware of outside forces that could rob them of their lives.

And she, with supposedly higher intelligence, hadn't been aware enough to prevent the horrendous thing that had been done to her. How had she not seen this coming? Okay, maybe not the actual event—because, who in the world would even consider such a disgusting act? But she should have seen something coming. People, to her grandfather, were lesser beings created to serve him in some capacity.

How dare he? How dare anyone think they had a right to do this to someone? Her mind went to Antonia. They had never been close. Antonia was more than a decade older and had never been overly friendly with her. But she—

No! Gabriella whirled around, shoved her hands through her hair, and yanked hard. No. She would not blame Antonia. She wasn't the one at fault. Her cousin had been following the directives of an evil, sadistic monster.

If Antonia had not done as directed, she would have been punished, maybe even killed. Her family would likely have been threatened, too. Antonia had two young sons. Like any mother, she would have done anything to protect her children, even something as hideous as this.

Luis Mendoza was responsible for this repulsive act. And Rudolph Bianchi.

What had they hoped to accomplish? A child with both their bloodlines? For what purpose? What reason? She wasn't royalty. Had no bloodline that needed to be preserved. For what reason would they even want to share a great-grandchild? From what she could remember, they weren't even friends.

Her hand went to her stomach, and for the first time, she allowed herself to absorb the consequences of this vile act. She might be pregnant. With Rudy Bianchi's child. She had no knowledge of this kind of procedure, no idea of the success rate with just one treatment. Did it take more than one? She would do research, she would study. She would find out and she would—

A baby. It hit her then. An innocent child who had no control over who conceived it or how it came about might be inside of her, depending on her to keep it safe.

As her mind unfroze and her thoughts became more coherent, one alarming truth became apparent. They would never stop looking for her. If Luis and Rudolph had gone to these lengths, there was no way either of them would ever quit. She had believed, stupidly, that her grandfather would eventually stop looking. That at some point, he would accept that she could not be found and would give up. After all, it wasn't as if there had been any affection there. But that was before she knew he wanted to use her in this odd, sickening way.

She drew in a breath. All right. She now knew everything. What had been done…what they wanted from her. There was no going back. The real question was, what was she going to do about the future? They might have gotten away with doing this thing, but she'd be damned if they had any more control over her life or her actions.

She took in the beauty of nature, let the peace wash over her, and knew her answer. If she was pregnant, then so be it. She would love this child as her own. The sperm donor did not matter. And she swore, with all the strength within her, that no one on this earth, not Luis Mendoza, not Rudolph Bianchi, or his repulsive grandson Rudy, would ever dare touch her child. She'd kill them all before she let that happen.

His heart heavy, Jonah watched Gabby walk away from the cabin. Her face was like white marble. The only color had been her eyes, which held a deep, wrenching agony. She had been betrayed in the worst possible way by a man who should have protected her. And Jonah had no idea how to help her.

He'd had to let her go. She needed solitude—something he understood all too well. But her safety was still his number-one priority. And while he was confident that no one could trace them here, he would not be blasé.

He waited until he could no longer see her and then turned to the stairway, taking three at a time. The third floor was one of the biggest reasons he'd bought the cabin. One giant room with fourteen windows that gave a bird's-eye view of the entire area.

Other than a lone chair and a small table, the room wasn't furnished. After his release from prison, he'd bought this place and had spent hours on end in this room, looking out over the

area and coming to terms with everything that had happened...
and all that he had lost.

He lifted the high-powered binoculars he kept on the table
and spotted Gabby within seconds. Her arms were wrapped
around herself, her shoulders slumped, her head downcast.
Working through her grief would take time.

He tried to imagine how she might feel and knew there was
no way he could. This was too personal and intimate. In a sense,
she had been raped. The lack of violence didn't change that this
thing had been forced on her without her consent.

It was all so unbelievable...sterile and revolting at the same
time. As much as he had firsthand knowledge of what a wealthy,
power-hungry, narcissistic man would do to further his agenda,
his mind reeled at the enormity of this.

Just what had the bastards intended? And why? Why the
hell would a child be so important that Luis would approve this
screwed-up way to create one? Why would a grandchild with
Mendoza blood mean anything to Rudolph Bianchi? What were
they missing?

And if a child was conceived, what would Mendoza and
Bianchi do to get their hands on it?

CHAPTER TWENTY-EIGHT

Two hours later, Gabby returned to the cabin. Though she was still icicle pale, the cool, determined look in her eyes told Jonah she was ready to move forward. He knew that feeling all too well. When shit rained down on you, you had two choices—let it cover you completely, or grab a shovel and dig your way out.

She sat on the sofa, and without any prompting, her new friend, all forty-two pounds of him, jumped up beside her and put his head on her lap. She laughed softly, and a delightful color bloomed in her cheeks.

"Have you thought of a name yet?"

"Chamo."

"Venezuelan for friend. Right?"

"Yes." She stroked his head and smiled. "Friend."

"That's a good name."

Her posture straightened, and the look she sent him said she was ready for more. "All right. Tell me everything you know. Don't hold anything back. I need to know what I'm dealing with."

"We thought it was strange that you didn't know the reason you were seeing the doctor. And as you said, you were drugged on the pretense of needing your nerves calmed. Justice's IT people are the best in the business. Charlie, one of his best hackers, said that it was alarmingly easy for her to get into your medical records."

"She's right. It was incredibly simple. I thought perhaps Antonia's office staff was just careless, although they have never struck me as being anything less than professional."

"Charlie said that was the weird part. She couldn't access any other patient records that easily. She tried, just to see. Everyone else's record was secure, as were yours until a couple of days ago. From what she could tell, the records had been recently uploaded to that particular file."

"Do you think Antonia did that on purpose? Perhaps to draw me out and then trace my location?"

"Possibly. Or it could be that she knew at some point you might try to find out what was done to you and she wanted you to know. She may have been trying to help you out."

She closed her eyes for a moment. Jonah wasn't sure if it was because she was weary or was considering his words. When she opened them, he thought it had been a combination of both.

"You could be right. My grandfather…Luis…would have had to coerce her to do this."

He noticed her stumble over calling him her grandfather. It was something he could identify with. He had stopped referring to Mathias as his father years ago. The word should be said with affection, not disdain.

"You think Luis threatened her?"

"It is the norm for him. The way he gets things done. He likely threatened to harm her family." She took another breath. "What else?"

"The chances of pregnancy are low. It often takes several procedures before conception can take place."

She flinched, but he wasn't going to stop. She'd said she wanted to know everything. Besides, sugarcoating the situation wasn't possible. There was no way to make this look better.

"Where are the pregnancy kits?"

In awe of her bravery and self-control, Jonah was happy he could at least give her something she asked for. "I put them in your bathroom upstairs. It might not show yet. You—"

She held up her hand. "I understand. I'll do this every day until I'm sure."

Noting that her hand was shaking and she'd had as much of this discussion as she could handle, Jonah backed off. She'd held up a lot better than he'd ever imagined.

"So what now?"

"Since we don't know the results, we can't—"

She held up her hand again. He was pleased to see that it was slightly steadier than before. "Just to be clear, if I am pregnant, I'm keeping the baby."

"That's certainly your decision, but don't you want to think about—"

"There's nothing to think about. A child is innocent, no matter who his or her parents are."

"Then we'll need to make special arrangements if that happens."

She took another breath. Something she did right before she said something difficult. "You say the pregnancy kits are in the bathroom?"

"Yes."

She lifted Chamo's head from her lap and went to her feet. "While I'm doing this thing, I'd like for you to find out as much as you can about Luis and Rudolph Bianchi's relationship. I knew they wanted a match between Rudy and me, but that was years ago, before he went to prison. Nothing has been said to me since then." Her mouth twisted. "No surprise, but still there's got to be more to this. Something I've missed."

"I can do that."

Jonah watched her walk away. He could not begin to imagine what might be going through her mind. The chances of her being pregnant were low, but there was still the chance. And the chances of finding out this quickly—though it could take up to sixteen days after this type of fertilization—could still be done. Either way, she was walking toward what might be life-changing news with her head held high and her shoulders straight.

And she wanted to keep the baby. That might be the most unsurprising news of all. Gabby had been hurt and rejected so many times. Protecting and defending an innocent child, her child, just made sense.

He'd decided long ago he would never have children. He would leave that responsibility to Eli and Kathleen. They were great parents and better equipped than he could ever be.

He couldn't deny another reason for his decision. How did one prevent raising a child to be like his grandparent or his uncle? People could argue the nurture-versus-nature theory till the cows came home, but that didn't negate that evil still found a way to grow and develop. Every single evil person had started out an innocent child. He damn well didn't want to be responsible for bringing another one into the world.

***

The instant Gabby closed the bathroom door, she spotted the kits. They were hard to miss...nine of them lined up on the counter. Either Jonah had known she'd want to check multiple times, or there had been a sale. Imagining Jonah Slater walking through a pharmacy looking for a bargain buy on pregnancy kits brought a little lift to her heart.

She took a breath. Time to face reality. When she was younger, she had dreamed of one day falling in love and marrying a wonderful man like her father. They would have at the minimum four children. Sweet little babies she would raise to be strong, independent adults. That dream had gone into hibernation, along with all her other hopes and dreams. But when she'd started planning her escape, many of those dreams had returned, that one included. But not in her wildest dreams or nightmares had she ever envisioned taking a pregnancy test to discover if she was pregnant with a serial killer's baby. Or that her child might have been conceived in such a cold, heartless way.

A sob built up in her chest as tears filled her eyes. No, dammit, no. She would not cry about this again. This was not death...nor was it an end. Yes, it was vile and wrong on so many levels, but as with most things in life, she had a choice. She could either let them destroy her, or find a way to make it work. If she was pregnant, then she would do everything she could to ensure her baby's health and safety. If she wasn't, then she would move forward.

She picked up the closest kit and read the directions on the back. Her mind parked in neutral, she followed them to the letter and then sat down on the vanity bench and waited. She'd laid the indicator on the counter several feet from her. While she waited and stared, she gave herself a moment of meditative encouragement. She was strong and brave. She had already endured much. She could handle anything else that came her way. Luis Mendoza no longer controlled her life or her destiny. She was free.

Five minutes later, Gabby stood. She'd given the test ample time. Now it was time to find out the results. Barely breathing, she forced her shaky legs to cross the room. She closed her eyes, whispered a fervent prayer for courage, and then opened them.

Negative. She wasn't pregnant. At least not that the test could yet detect.

A whoosh of relieved air left her body. She would take another test tomorrow. Until then, she needed to learn everything she could about Luis and Rudolph Bianchi's relationship. Just what were they up to?

What could be so important that they would go to so much trouble? What was Rudolph Bianchi holding over Luis to get him to agree to something so bizarre?

She headed back downstairs and then stopped halfway and watched Jonah. He was reading something on his laptop, his forehead furrowed in concentration. Despite the fact that he'd kept the news from her longer than he should have, he had been incredibly supportive. She remembered that among the pregnancy tests that had fallen from the bags, there had been chocolates, movies, and books. And he'd given her a beautiful dog for a companion. He'd done all of that in hopes of easing her pain.

How odd that only a couple of weeks ago she had thought Jonah Slater was one of the coldest men she'd ever met. And now she thought he might be the kindest person she had ever known.

CHAPTER
TWENTY-NINE

When Gabby came back downstairs, Jonah was relieved to see she looked calmer and less terrified. Before he could ask, she said, "The test was negative."

Every muscle in his body loosened. It was about damn time they had some good news.

"I'll take another one tomorrow."

"If we run out, I can get more."

"Thank you."

"Justice brought a whole folder of information on the procedure, in case you want to read up on it."

"No, I don't. The basic facts are I was inseminated with Rudy Bianchi's sperm and I could be pregnant. Anything beyond that doesn't interest me."

"Very well, then, let's talk about the why of it. Why the hell would Luis and Rudolph Bianchi do something like this? What are they to each other?"

"Business associates. Occasional enemies. Mr. Bianchi used to attend my grandfather's events, but he stopped coming several years ago."

"Our research indicates he's a recluse."

"That's my understanding, too. Even when Rudy was on trial, his grandfather never attended."

"From what I can tell, he did everything possible to keep him out of prison. After his conviction, he appealed the verdict. Thankfully, it didn't work."

"I read an article that Rudolph had issued a statement. I don't remember what he said, though."

"Wasn't much. Just that he still believed in his grandson and that justice would one day be served."

Gabby snorted. "People like Bianchi and Luis have a perverted sense of justice. It serves only them."

"I agree. So why would they cook up this scheme? What's in it for them?"

"I have no idea."

"Justice told me that Rudolph showed up at Luis's home the other day."

"That's significant in itself. The man can't be bothered to attend his grandson's trial, but he goes to Luis's home?"

"Yeah. So what about Rudy?"

"What about him?"

"Not to be too indelicate, but the man shot off in a cup. He's in the know on this. You're the only one who was kept in the dark."

"The man is a disgusting piece of human waste."

The man was definitely slime, but the way she spoke about him sounded much more personal. Her voice held a vehemence that said theirs was more than a distant acquaintance.

"How well do you know him?"

He had no idea what she was thinking. Her face had been pale before, but now it seemed even more so. An ominous, sickening thought came to him. Hell, the man was a rapist and a killer. Any woman around him would be in danger.

"Did he hurt you?"

Instead of answering, she dropped down onto the sofa and patted her lap. Chamo had been sitting by the fireplace but jumped up on the sofa and dropped his head into her lap. She smoothed her hand over his coat for several long moments.

Jonah waited her out. He didn't get the impression that she was refusing to answer as much as she was trying to determine how to form the words.

"What do you know about my parents?"

The basic facts of the accident that had taken the lives of Meredith and Javier Mendoza were a matter of public record, but Jonah knew next to nothing about what kind of people or parents they had been.

"I know they were killed in Switzerland while they were on a skiing trip. They were headed to the airport, returning to Venezuela from a holiday. Your father was driving. He lost control of the car on the icy road, and it went off the road and exploded on impact, killing both your parents. You and your brother were staying with your grandfather at the time."

"No," she said quietly. "With the exception of the last part, that my brother and I were staying with my grandfather, it's a lie."

She closed her eyes briefly, and when she opened them, he was astonished that instead of the sadness he'd expected, a simmering fury burned. "Luis Mendoza killed my parents. He shot them in front of me."

His entire body jerked at the news. Of all the things he'd thought she might tell him, this was off-the-rails crazy. And Gabby had witnessed it all.

Not doubting her for a moment, he shook his head slowly. "There were no questions or mystery surrounding their deaths. I read a couple of old newspaper articles. Even reviewed a copy of the police report detailing the crash. The son of a bitch got away with murder."

"Of course he did. He is Luis Mendoza. His hand is in the pockets of the most-influential and powerful people in the world. Covering up murders would be child's play for him."

"Do you remember what happened?"

Gabby nodded. The scene had replayed in her head for years. Even now, if she closed her eyes, she could recall it in vivid detail. "We were leaving. It was the middle of the night. I thought we were going away on holiday. Not until years later did I realize what was actually happening. My father was taking my mother and me away. We were sneaking out of the house and my...Luis caught us. I remember my father saying, 'We're leaving, old man.'"

"What about your brother? He wasn't with you?"

"No. I remember my mother crying when I asked her why Carlos wasn't going with us. And I distinctly remember my papa telling Luis that he had already taken one child, but he couldn't have me, too."

"Did you ever tell anyone?"

She tried to smile, knew it was a pitiful attempt. "As many people as I could, but I was only six years old. Who listens to a six-year-old? Besides, the only people around were the ones already owned or indebted to Luis. By the time I was seven, he had all but imprisoned me, telling people I was too grief stricken to be around anyone.

"I had teachers and tutors who ignored my pleas. I ran away several times in hopes of finding someone who would listen. I was always found. I eventually stopped trying. Until..."

"Until what?"

"When I was fifteen, Luis told me he wanted me to start serving as hostess for his house parties. My aunt Evelyn, who previously hosted them, had died a couple of years before that, and since then, he'd had no one to act as hostess. He told me he was giving me this one last chance. That I could have more freedom if I behaved. I wasn't to speak of my parents or anything personal. I agreed."

The warm, comforting body of Chamo soothing her, she lost herself in memories for a while. She hadn't spoken about these events in so long. Telling them now was sure to bring back the nightmares she'd fought years to control. That couldn't be helped.

"Gabby?"

"Sorry, got lost there for a second. The day of the first party came. I really don't know if I would have abided by Luis's wishes. By that time, I had become the quiet and submissive grand-daughter he wanted. I hadn't been around anyone other than the servants in years, so I might have never said anything to anyone. However, I didn't anticipate seeing the chief of police at the party."

She grimaced at the sheer naïveté of her actions. "My thinking was so basic and simple. I knew nothing about the man himself. I only knew that he was an officer of the law. As such, he was honor-bound by his position to enforce that law. Luis had murdered my parents, and the man needed to know this so Luis could be brought to justice. So, being the naïve little idiot that I was, I pulled him aside and told him."

"And of course he had no honor."

"None whatsoever."

Dark memories threatened to overwhelm her. Talking about this after the day she'd had wasn't easy, but she needed to get it said and out there. Maybe it wasn't necessary for Jonah to know everything, but for the first time in years, she wanted to speak of that horrific day when everything changed.

"Both Rudolph and Rudy were at the party. Within five minutes of talking to the police chief, Stephan, Luis's right-hand man, had me cornered. He forced me up to my room and locked me inside. Half an hour later, Rudy Bianchi unlocked the door and walked into my room."

Jonah held his breath, his gut clenching with dread. Just what had the bastard done to her?

Her eyes distant, as if seeing the past unravel, she said softly, "He was twenty-seven years old. I met him for the first time at that party. He had tried to talk to me, but he was so much older, we had nothing in common. Plus, there was something odd about him...something that frightened me. As hostess, I couldn't be rude to a guest, but I did my best to stay away from him." She shook her head. "A lot of good that did."

"What happened?"

"When I asked him why he was in my room, he said that Luis had given him permission, as my future husband, to discipline me."

An ugly curse escaped Jonah's lips, but if she heard, she didn't let on.

"At first I laughed and told him to get out or Luis would kill him. I knew Luis didn't care about me, but he had never allowed a man outside the family to touch me. The bizarre claim that he was to be my future husband barely penetrated my frozen brain.

"When I realized he wasn't leaving...and he just stood there smirking, I ran to the door. He got there before me."

She went silent.

Jonah felt as awkward as a bulldozer in a French restaurant and had no words to help her through the retelling of what he figured had been a horrific event. But he had to offer her some kind of comfort. He crossed the room and sat beside her. He didn't touch her, but if she needed human contact, he was there for her.

"He didn't rape me." She sent him a frozen smile. "I learned later that that was the one thing he was told he couldn't do."

"Luis allowed this?"

"He didn't just allow it, he arranged it. Rudy told the truth about that. Apparently, it had been decided years before that Rudy and I were to be married. No one had told me simply because I didn't have a choice in the matter, so I didn't need to know.

"Luis claimed later that his sending Rudy to discipline me had been a test for both of us. One that neither of us passed."

Rage surged through Jonah, and it was all he could do not to release a battalion of curses. The very thought of any man, much less a child's grandfather, doing such a thing was beyond disgusting. Luis Mendoza had sent a twenty-seven-year-old man to discipline his fifteen-year-old granddaughter. A man she barely knew. A man who would one day become a serial killer of young girls.

Still barely comprehending how messed up all of this was, Jonah asked, "Did he…"

"He made a lot of threats…of how things would be once we married. What he would do to me…" She waved her hand. "I can't…

"Anyway, I knew nothing about defending myself. I cried and screamed. No one came. I finally got lucky, and one of my puny punches landed in the right place. I got away from him. The door was locked from the outside. The only exit was the balcony. I ran out to it, screamed again. No one came. So I went over."

"Shit! That's just…" He had no words.

"Unbelievable, I know. There are screwed-up families, and then there's mine."

And he'd thought he had the worst family in the world. Compared to the Mendozas, the Slaters looked like a 1950s sitcom.

"It's a wonder you weren't killed."

"I came close to dying. I had a skull fracture and multiple broken bones. Stayed in the hospital for almost two weeks. When I was released, I went to England, to live in one of Luis's houses. I assumed he didn't want to see me, and I certainly didn't want to see him."

Still shaken by what she'd revealed, Jonah asked, "After all you'd been through, I can't believe you weren't a basket case."

"I give credit to one person for my recovery."

"Who?"

"Raiza."

"I'm surprised, given his archaic views, he would trust a woman to watch over you."

"She could go places a man couldn't go, such as restrooms, dressing rooms. Luis wanted to make sure I was watched every waking moment. He just never anticipated what she would teach me."

"I know she taught you how to handle a gun. What else?"

"How to survive." She smiled as she continued. "She had children of her own, but she wasn't exactly what you would call the motherly type.

"She was the first woman I'd been around since my mother. I thought she would sympathize with me, make me feel better. You know…mother me. So I told her everything. It was like a faucet had been turned on. Everything that had happened to me since I was a little girl came pouring out of me. My parents' murders, being a virtual prisoner for so many years. I told her about Rudy and their plans for me.

"Instead of giving me the platitudes I expected or hugging me and telling me things would get better, she did the unexpected. Turned out, it was the one thing I most needed to hear."

"What?"

"She asked me what I was going to do about it. Cry and moan or find a way out? I told her I had no way out, and she stared at me with the hardest, most determined look in her eyes and said, 'So you're a coward. I have no time for cowards.'"

Jonah knew Raiza had likely saved Gabby's life, but he couldn't imagine saying that to a young girl who'd been so damaged and hurt. She would have been vulnerable and scared.

"What happened next?"

"She walked away from me, and I lost it." She grinned. "I had a broken leg and a broken arm, but that didn't stop me from throwing myself into a wheelchair and going after her. I screamed, yelled, and cursed like a demon."

"What did Raiza do?"

"She stood there and watched me. When I'd worn myself out, she nodded and said, 'Now we're getting somewhere.'

"She walked off then. A few minutes later, she came back with books and DVDs, but they weren't for entertainment. She told me to read the books, study the recordings, and after I healed, she would teach me. She kept that promise."

Her smile was soft and full of affection. "She gave me something no one ever had before. She gave me hope."

Jonah had seen his share of strong people before, but he wasn't sure he'd ever known anyone with more strength than this woman. What she had been through could have destroyed her. She might give credit to Raiza, but if she hadn't had the courage already within her, she wouldn't have become the woman she was. And she wouldn't be here now.

He didn't remember how or when, but at some point, he'd put his arms around her shoulders. Her head was on his chest. It seemed like the most natural thing in the world to pull her closer and press a kiss to the top of her silky head.

"I don't know if I've ever met anyone more courageous."

She huffed out a little laugh. "Courage had nothing to do with it. It was sheer necessity. It took longer than either of us thought it would to make it happen. Even though she encouraged me to leave, I couldn't. My grandfather would have punished Raiza for allowing me to escape. If she'd come with me, he would have hurt her children or grandchildren. So I waited and continued to train, knowing that one day I would be free."

"Sometimes having the patience to wait until the right moment is one of the bravest things a person can do."

When she didn't respond, he looked down at her. She had snuggled into his chest and was breathing the shallow breaths of a deep sleep.

The shock of yesterday, coupled with the hellacious news of what had been done to her, had taken its toll. After what she had been through during her life, trusting any man would be difficult for her. He felt both honored and humbled that she trusted him this much.

With Gabby's head on his chest and Chamo's head on her lap, Jonah gathered her closer and, oddly content, closed his eyes.

CHAPTER
THIRTY

Gray mist swirled around her as murky and wet tendrils, like tentacles, wrapped around her body, slipping, sliding over her skin. Claws scored her legs and arms, blood oozed from her wounds, ribbons of red seeped from her bones. Blood gushed, spewing everywhere.

The ground shook, the world tilted, and she was tumbling upside down while hands, evil hands with claws instead of fingers, grasped at her. She batted them away, crying, screaming for help she already knew wouldn't come.

She was on her feet, running, running. Breath wheezed from her overtaxed lungs and fought with the sobs that wouldn't quit, wouldn't quit. She had to get away. Anywhere would be better than here. No one would miss her. She was just a pawn. A prize to be won…an object to be used and then discarded like garbage.

Something swirled around her, and she looked down. Rags covered her body. The dress she'd once been so proud of hung haphazardly around her, torn to shreds. But she had escaped. No one could ever touch her again. She was free!

Noises surrounded her, angry shouts and vile threats. She turned slowly around. Scarlet eyes, red-hot with evil, pierced the darkness. He had found her! No, no, no! She wouldn't go back. She wouldn't!

Fiery agony seared through her. Blood poured down her misshapen, mangled legs. Dizziness swamped her, and she fell to her knees. Darkness washed over her. She opened her mouth, screamed for help, for mercy. Voices whispered, told her to shut up. Told her she had a destiny. She screamed at them, for help, for deliverance.

Wicked, high-pitched giggles rippled around her. He was coming…he was here! A cliff appeared before her. She looked over her shoulder. He was so close! Her arms formed into wings, and she knew she could fly. She turned and launched herself toward the sky. Her wings vanished, and she was falling, falling. The shrill giggles followed her down into a bottomless, black pit. Hands reached for her, clawed at her, teeth gnashed at her skin, her bones.

She screamed her agony.

"Gabby. Wake up. You're safe. You're safe. Shh. Shh. You're safe."

Jonah didn't know how long he'd been saying the words. She was lost in some kind of nightmare that wouldn't let her go. He'd been ripped from sleep by a heart-wrenching scream of pain and had been out of the bed in an instant. His first thought was she had been found and they were taking her away. Gun in hand, he'd barged into her room only to find her gripped in some kind of death struggle with an invisible monster.

He should have anticipated nightmares. After what she'd endured the last few days—hell, most of her life—not having nightmares would have been abnormal.

Jonah held her trembling body, continuing his litany of comforting words. She still wasn't awake. The cries had lessened to whimpers, but her body continued to jerk as if she were still being tortured.

"Baby...sweetheart. It's Jonah. You're here, safe with me. No one's ever going to hurt you again. I promise."

He knew the moment she was awake and aware. Her body went stiff. She inhaled and then held her breath.

"Gabby, did you hear me? It's Jonah. You're safe with me."

"Jonah?" she breathed.

He was about to loosen his arms to give her some room when she wrapped herself around him as if she'd never let him go.

"He found me...I don't know how, but he found me. He was going to hurt me again. Do what he did before, only worse. He was going to do to me what he did to those other girls.

"People were there, watching. My grandfather, Rudolph Bianchi, my brother. They all watched. Did nothing to stop it."

"It's over now. Those men can never hurt you again."

"Is it?" She moved away from him then, but only so she could see him. "They'll never stop looking for me. I had accepted that I would always be hunted. As long as Luis lives, so will his quest to find me. But now? With the possibility that I might be..." She shuddered and buried her face against his chest again. "If there's a child, we'll never be safe."

"Yes, you will, sweetheart. I promise you, whatever happens, if it's just you or you and a child, I'll make sure you're safe."

Gabby closed her eyes, absorbing as much warmth as she could from Jonah's hard body, then she pulled away. What had happened to her strength and willpower? When had she turned back into this weepy, needy little girl?

"I'll be fine, Jonah. Don't worry about me. The nightmare caught me off guard. I haven't had one in years."

"With everything that's happened, I'd be worried if you didn't have a few."

She smiled up at him. "Glad I could ease your worry, then."

The smile wasn't returned. Not that she should be surprised. Jonah's smiles were rare, but the expression on his face was both fierce and searching.

"What's wrong?"

"When I came in, you were screaming for him to get off of you. Was it Rudy?"

Her head dropped onto her pillow. She had stopped denying what had been done to her long ago, but she had never talked about it to anyone but Raiza. What she had told him before was just the tip of the iceberg.

"You don't have to tell me. I just—"

If anyone deserved the truth, it was this man who had risked so much for her.

"He sexually assaulted me, but not in the way you're thinking." She swallowed hard and continued, the images as vivid now as they were when they were happening.

"He tied me down on the bed, then ripped off my dress and underwear. He told me things he would do to me once we were married, but since he had promised not to take my virginity, he would give me a sample of what to expect. He went away for a minute. I lay there, screaming and crying. No one came.

"When he returned, he had things...objects that he used..." She could do this. "To penetrate me. A hairbrush. A curling iron. A bottle of shampoo. He tried them all. The shampoo bottle was too large. I...couldn't..."

Suddenly, she was back in Jonah's arms, crying against his chest again. The words continued to pour from her, but in his arms, it was somehow easier to say them.

"He bit me, punched and slapped me. Strangled me till I passed out. I don't know how long I was unconscious, but when I woke up, he had ejaculated all over me. I was bloody and hurting so bad, but I was still determined to get away from him. At some point while I was unconscious, he had untied me and rolled me over on my stomach. I'm not sure why.

"When I realized I was free, I knew I would only have one chance to escape. I remember him hovering over me. I can still feel his hot breath…it smelled like rotting meat.

"I rolled over onto my back. His pants were open, and he was holding himself. I didn't think about the consequences. I only knew I had to get away from him. If I had stayed, I'm almost certain he would have killed me. He was like a wild, rabid creature…had lost total control of his senses."

"What did you do?"

She noted that Jonah's voice was hoarse and sounded as if he was in pain. His compassion and obvious horror of what had happened enabled her to continue.

"I fisted my hands together, swung up, and hit him as hard as I could. Unfortunately, my aim was off, and I missed my target. I did manage to hit his stomach, though. It knocked the breath out of him, and he fell backward, off the bed.

"Even to this day, it still amazes me that I had the strength to get up and run. I think my brain was in panic mode and couldn't register pain. I knew going back to the door and pounding on it would do no good. No one was going to come and save me, so I ran to the balcony. I didn't give it another thought. I simply flew."

"What floor were you on?"

"The third."

"How the hell did you survive?"

"I hit one of the balconies below me. I broke my arm when I hit the railing, but that slowed my descent. Otherwise, I'm certain I wouldn't have survived the fall."

"Please tell me something happened to the bastard other than a stomach punch."

"I really don't know a lot. It wasn't like Luis was going to admit he made a mistake and assure me that Rudy got what was coming to him. My feelings weren't important. But Raiza told me that she'd heard he received the beating of his life from Stephan." She grimaced. "Considering what he did to other young girls later on, apparently the lesson wasn't sufficient."

"I wish I could get to him for you."

That didn't surprise her. Jonah would want to punish anyone who abused a child. Any normal person would want that to happen. Too bad she'd never had normal.

"He's locked up and being punished for what he did to those other girls. Now that I know what he was capable of, I guess I got off easy."

He pressed a kiss to her forehead. "Only a strong person would say something like that. I'm glad you're a survivor, Gabby."

They were quiet and still for the longest time. Jonah's heartbeat against her own was a beautiful moment, and one she had never experienced. When she was twenty, she'd had a very brief fling with a boy named Juan, the son of one of her guards. The relationship had been short-lived, barely two weeks, and had ended abruptly when she had overheard him bragging about their tryst to the cook's son. There had been no intimacy, no real feelings attached, so when it ended, she hadn't grieved or even been hurt. Oddly enough, she'd felt gratitude. She had feared that after her experience with Rudy, she wouldn't be able to let another man touch her ever again.

But being here with Jonah, both of them fully dressed, felt much more intimate than anything she'd ever shared with Juan.

"Asinine question, but did you ever receive any kind of help for what you went through?"

"If you mean therapy, no, there was nothing formal. It's certainly nothing Luis would have given thought to providing. But Raiza helped me through much of it. She had been through something similar when she was younger. She made me realize I had done nothing wrong. His filth could not really touch me."

He squeezed her gently. "I'm glad." He moved as if to get up. "Think you can go back to sleep?"

Everything within her wanted to ask him to stay with her. The very thought of closing her eyes and seeing those images again was almost more than she could fathom.

"Probably not. I think I'll read for a while."

"Would it help if I stayed?"

"You don't have to."

"What if I want to?"

"Then I would appreciate it. I hate to be weak, but—"

His fingers pressed against her mouth. "You are the least-weak person I've ever known."

"I don't feel very strong. I keep thinking of what's been done to me. What's inside of my body and might be happening."

"Don't think about it." He propped several pillows against the headboard and then gathered her close. "Just close your eyes and drift off to sleep knowing that no one will ever hurt you again. What's done is done, and we'll deal with whatever happens. But for now, shut those thoughts away and rest."

He held her for a while, and then when she started drifting off, she felt him shift and heard the light click off. She thought he might get up and leave then. Instead, he pressed a kiss against her forehead and held her all night long.

CHAPTER
THIRTY-ONE

Chewing her lip in concentration, Gabby reread the article she'd just found and then glanced down at her notes. Strange as this seemed, this could be it. Bizarre yes, but what about her family wasn't?

She looked up when Jonah opened the front door. "I think I may be on to something."

Jonah headed over to the table where Gabby was working. They'd gotten into a surprisingly domesticated routine over the last few days. He would cook breakfast, and she would clean up. He would work outside chopping wood or doing the odd yardwork, while she dug into more of the mysterious relationship between Luis and Rudolph Bianchi.

They would spend time together in the afternoon, either playing with Chamo or taking walks around the lake. She found herself telling Jonah more and more of her hopes and dreams. She still didn't know if her future included a baby. Each morning, she took a pregnancy test, and so far, all had been negative. She was hopeful they would remain that way.

Considering the reason she was here, from whom she was hiding, and the uncertainty of her future, it was an oddly peaceful time for her. She knew she was living in a bubble and that it could burst at any moment, but she was learning to enjoy each day she was given.

Standing beside her, Jonah peered down at the screen. "What'd you find?"

"Luis and Rudolph and their strange connection to one another."

"Connection?" He sat down beside her. "Like what?"

She gave him a little background information first. "When I first started hosting Luis's parties, Mr. Bianchi...Rudolph... would attend on occasion. Rudy was the only one who ever came with him. His daughter had died under mysterious circumstances years before. I think Rudy was ten at the time."

"Mysterious how?"

"The official death announcement said she fell down the stairs and broke her neck, but I remember on the rare times her name was mentioned, there was an uncomfortable silence. After what Rudy did to me, I suspected he had something to do with her death. Maybe pushed her down the stairs."

"Sounds plausible. His thirst to kill might've started at an early age."

She shivered at the thought. When she had been locked in her bedroom with him, she had thought him to be only a revolting creep. Years later, when she learned he was responsible for the rape and murder of six teenage girls, she realized how very fortunate she'd been. If she hadn't jumped off the balcony, would he have done the same to her?

"You okay?"

"Yes. Sorry. Just realizing how lucky I was to get away from the monster."

"Not too many people would see a skull fracture and multiple broken bones as lucky."

"Compared to being raped and murdered? I survived, and they didn't."

Even though she had been sexually assaulted, she still recognized it could have been so much worse.

"After Rudy went to prison, I stopped worrying about him. Didn't do any research on him or his grandfather. I thought that part of my past was behind me. Luis never mentioned him again." Her smile was bitter as she added, "Stupid me assumed any future association was out of the question."

His hand covered hers and squeezed gently. Jonah might not be one for flowery words, but his actions spoke volumes.

Sending him a grateful smile, she continued. "Anyway, I always detected a coldness between Luis and Mr. Bianchi but never knew why."

She nodded toward her notes. "I think I've figured it out. My grandmother, Flora Rossi, was Italian. I don't know very much about her. She died when I was just a child, and no one spoke of her. But it turns out, she was once engaged to Rudolph Bianchi."

"But she married your grandfather instead."

"Yes. Theirs was apparently a whirlwind romance. Within a couple weeks of meeting, Luis and Flora eloped. The Bianchi family was completely humiliated. Even her own family disowned her."

"I would've thought a scandal between prominent families like that would be public knowledge. How did you not know?"

"The things I know about my family are the things I uncovered for myself. I've only been told what Luis wanted me to know. Plus, it appears that both families tried to downplay the whole thing. I guess to lessen the embarrassment.

"Anyway, I found an article from a gossip column from years ago. The references are vague, but I'm familiar enough with the people involved to recognize who they're talking about. The wedding between Rudolph Bianchi and Flora Rossi was supposed to be the event of the season. It was to be held in Altura, the little corner of Italy where the Bianchis summered. The day before the wedding, Luis absconded with my grandmother."

"That would definitely cause harsh feelings."

"But then it gets even worse. My father was expected to marry Rudolph Bianchi's daughter. No formal announcement had been made, but the arrangement was apparently understood. I don't know how my father felt about that, but when he was in the United States on a business trip, he fell in love with my mother. Another whirlwind romance developed, followed by another elopement."

"So that was strike two for the Bianchis. The last hope for a union was for you and Rudy to marry."

"Yes. I don't know why they didn't try to force a marriage earlier, before Rudy went to prison. Whatever the reason, I'm grateful. And since Rudy was behind bars, they chose another route."

Nausea surged up her throat, but she fought it back. She woke each morning with the knowledge that this could be the day she found out she was pregnant. She was late with her monthly flow, but her menstrual period was never reliable. She had been late many times before. Considering the stress she was under, not being late would have been a miracle.

The hand on hers squeezed again. Jonah's strength and compassion were comforts she had come to rely on. She knew they couldn't last forever. But she was grateful for them right now. She wasn't sure she would have gotten through this without him.

"Okay. I get the connection, but why would it be so important for you to bear Bianchi's great-grandchild?"

"That's something I still don't know. Maybe it's just something Rudolph can hold over Luis. Prick at his pride. But my question is, what's in it for Luis? I know him well. He wouldn't have agreed to this unless it benefitted him in some way."

"I agree. There's got to be more." He nodded at the laptop. "Does knowing this much help at all?"

"The more I know, the better-equipped I am. It also helps me to appreciate my mother and father even more. They were trying to take me away from him, and that's why he killed them. Luis already had plans for me. So yes, knowing this does help. But does it help me understand Luis better? Absolutely not. There's no way I can understand his sick, twisted thinking.

"I am finding, though, that with each new thing I learn, my hatred grows. I didn't think I could despise him more than I already did. I was wrong."

He lifted his hand and trailed his fingers over her face in a soft caress. "You've escaped. That's what you need to focus on."

She leaned into his hand. For the past couple of days, they had gotten more comfortable touching, being close with each other. She'd had a few more nightmares, and Jonah somehow always knew that. She'd woken several times to find him holding her.

He hadn't kissed her again. She wanted him to. Wanted him to do more than that…and in a way, that was incredibly freeing, too. She trusted him more than any man she had ever known. Even as hard and physically strong as he was, she knew to her soul that he would never hurt her physically.

He pulled his hand away and stood. "It's getting late. I'd better get going."

The moment was lost. She knew exactly what he was going into town for. She had used her last pregnancy kit this morning. She watched as he grabbed his jacket from the peg beside the door.

"You need me to pick up anything else?"

Pretending things were normal was impossible. Acting as if she had nothing more on her mind than starting a new life could not happen yet. A tiny new life could be growing inside her. That she could be pregnant was scary enough. Starting a new life with a newborn was mind-blowingly terrifying. She barely knew how to take care of herself. How was she going to care for an infant, too? She didn't know the answer. But no matter what happened, she would protect her child.

Some might find her attitude beyond strange, even insane. Opinions of others were not her concern. She had to do what felt right to her. It had taken her years to be comfortable with herself. Her choices were her own. She would do what she had to do, no matter what.

The information she'd been given said it could take up to seventeen days after the procedure before a pregnancy might show. She was already on day twenty-four. Excessive maybe, but she had to be absolutely sure. She had decided she would take the test five more days before she was completely positive she was home free.

"Hey, you okay?"

The concern in his voice reminded her she'd just been staring at him. "I'm fine. And no, I can't think of anything else. The freezer and fridge are still full."

"What about more books, movies, puzzles? More chocolate?"

"Yes!"

He smiled at her enthusiasm. "Any special requests?"

"Surprise me."

"Will do." The lighthearted moment over, he gave her a hard look. "Don't go out while I'm gone. Lock the doors. Stay away from the windows. Chamo can sense if anyone's close by, but keep your gun with you at all times. Anyone, other than me, tries to come through that door, you know what to do."

"I'll be fine."

Apparently satisfied, he backed out the door. "I'll be back in an hour, maybe less."

"Drive safely."

He gave her one more look, and this time, it gave her shivers. There was attraction there, and heat. Before she could do anything more than just stare at him, he turned away. She finally allowed herself to breathe when she heard the door close.

How had Jonah become so important to her? It wasn't as if he tried to charm her. He was blunt, often to the point of rudeness. Rarely smiled. And if she didn't engage him in a conversation, she got the feeling he could go days without speaking a word.

But he had been incredibly supportive. Listening when she needed to talk and not giving any kind of opinion on what he thought she should do. Having been surrounded by men all her life who believed their word was law and only their opinions mattered, Jonah Slater was a refreshing change.

It was more than that, though. She knew without a doubt that he would fight to the death to protect her. Not because it was his job, but because Jonah Slater was a born protector.

The kiss they'd shared was still there...the heat still simmering, waiting to be rekindled. With each day, the temperature seemed to rise. Jonah hadn't made a move to do more. She knew he wanted her. The few times they'd been in bed together, while he was holding her, she had felt his response. The hardness wasn't something he could hide. He was physically attracted to her, desired her. But he had yet to do anything about that desire.

And she, sadly lacking in experience herself, feared they were at a stalemate. Two people who wanted each other, but until one of them made a move, nothing would happen.

There were a million and one reasons not to get involved with him. It couldn't last. She knew that. She would soon be gone, with a new name, a new life. One that he couldn't be part of.

She still didn't know where she would be living or what she would be doing once she left here. She and Grey had talked over the phone and online about her future. She had some definite ideas about what she wanted, several he had disagreed with, which, oddly enough, was another freeing experience. Being able to disagree with a man and not have it turn into a bitter argument or dire threats was a new and exciting thing to her. Both Grey and Jonah treated her as if they valued her input.

She returned to her favorite place in the house. A padded window box, complete with a fluffy pillow she could lean against and a view of a lovely little birdfeeder Jonah told her he'd built with his own hands. She had spent hours watching a variety of birds and the occasional squirrel enjoy the birdseed Jonah filled it with each day.

Chamo had become her constant companion. It was as if he sensed her uncertainty and wanted to make sure she knew he was there. For as long as she could remember, she had wanted a pet. She had never asked for one, though. Her grandfather and likely her brother, too, would have used it against her. Putting an innocent animal in that kind of position would have been unfair. But now she was free and on to a new life. Chamo was her first pet, but he wouldn't be her last. As soon as she was settled, she'd see about that.

She glanced down at the notebook in her hand. When she wasn't researching the Bianchis and Mendozas, drawing, or gazing out the window, daydreaming, she continued to write down plans for the future. And though those would definitely change if she was pregnant, she continued to fill the pages with wishes, dreams, and hopes.

No one could take those away from her. No one.

CHAPTER THITY-TWO

Valencia, Venezuela
Mendoza Estate

The first indication that anything was wrong came without warning. Luis and Stephan were finishing up their daily business brief. Still no word on Gabriella, but his investigator had assured him that she was close. Weeks had passed since there had been any sighting, but Luis refused to accept defeat. It was only a matter of time before things returned to normal and they could proceed as planned. He had worked too hard and too long on this to give up now.

Besides, Rudolph wanted this deal to work almost as badly as he did. Between the two of them, they would make this happen.

"I anticipate we'll be hearing from Bianchi again soon. The old goat checks in at least every other day. I wish I had something substantial to tell him. This waiting is beyond irritating. I've put him off each time, but I'm considering taking up his offer of assistance in the search for Gabriella."

Somewhat surprised that Stephan had no response to what Luis thought was a major concession to his enemy, he looked up from his calendar. Stephan sat across from him reading something on his iPhone. His friend's face was even more wrinkled and harsher than normal. "What's wrong?"

Without looking up, Stephan said, "Were you aware that Marcel Dubois had his assets frozen?"

"What do you mean? Where did you hear that?"

"The news just broke online. Apparently, the French government is investigating him. Several of his businesses have been temporarily closed until the matter is resolved."

"That's a surprise. Marcel used to be so careful." Luis shook his head, feeling somewhat smug. "That's what happens when you don't pay attention to detail. It's good we haven't had any dealings with him in the last couple of years."

Stephan's answer was a grunt of acknowledgment. His focus was still on the screen in front of him.

"Why do you look so concerned? It's not as if we have any—"

"Alastair Kaufmann."

"What about him?"

"His assets in England have been seized. I saw the news yesterday, but it didn't register as a problem to me."

"Why does it now?"

Instead of answering, Stephan clicked several keys and then read aloud, "Donald Benson in Chicago is under investigation for smuggling narcotics and jury tampering."

Luis's heart beat a little faster. "How is it that three men that we've done business with over the last five years are all under investigation at the same time? This makes no sense."

Without looking up, Stephan said, "Francois Balogh in France and Gunnar Reiner in Germany."

"What about them?"

"They're being investigated by their governments."

Luis gave a rapid shake of his head. "No. No. This has nothing to do with me. I'm sure that—"

"You had both these men at your last gathering. This cannot be a coincidence."

His mouth gone dry, Luis swallowed hard and asked, "But who would—"

"Gabriella," Stephan whispered.

"What?" Luis gave a shout of hearty laughter, grateful for the comic relief. "That's the most ridiculous thing you've ever said. How could she know anything of their business dealings?"

"She served as hostess at many of the dinner parties these men attended."

"So what? She talks flowers, music, art, and current events with them. She's never sat in on the meetings. We've never discussed business out in the open where she could hear anything incriminating. There's no possible way she would know anything about them."

"Perhaps. But we should be prepared, just in case."

"Prepared for what? She knows nothing." Luis nodded at the phone Stephan seemed glued to. "I admit all of these occurrences at the same time are quite unusual and even a little alarming, but coincidences happen all the time. All of these men play dangerous games with very dangerous people. This has nothing to do with us. Don't go getting paranoid in your old age."

Ignoring his protests, Stephan continued to read out name after name of present and past business associates who were being investigated by the authorities. Despite himself, a growing concern tingled up his spine.

The cellphone in front of him buzzed, and Luis grabbed it up, grateful for the distraction. The caller ID display ignited the concern into a blazing alarm.

"Señor Mendoza?"

"Si."

"I've just received word that a criminal investigation is being opened regarding the deaths of your son and daughter-in-law."

A hot flush of heat swept up Luis's body. Shock momentarily numbing his brain, he gripped the desk to help focus his thoughts. "For whatever reason?"

He asked the question, puzzlement in his voice. But he knew...he knew. Damn the little bitch. Damn her to hell.

"There are questions regarding how they died. The medical examiner is discussing the possibility of exhuming the bodies."

"Don't be ridiculous. The bodies were cremated. They can't be exhumed."

"According to the medical records, your information is not correct."

Could this be true? He had ordered the bodies cremated. The memorial service he'd held a few days after their deaths had featured two vases that contained their ashes. Most of the people involved in the cover-up were either retired or dead. Who would have had the audacity to not follow his dictates?

"This is the most ridiculous thing I've ever heard. I'll—"

"I just wanted to warn you, sir. As per our arrangement."

Luis didn't bother with thank-yous or any further questions. He ended the call and then looked at Stephan in bewildered fury. "You were right. Gabriella has betrayed us."

***

Three days later...
Mendoza Estate

"So you have some information? Leads?"

Ivy nodded, noting that the man behind the massive desk wasn't nearly as confident or arrogant as he had been when they first met. In fact, Luis Mendoza looked quite sickly. A person might assume that the stress of having his darling granddaughter still missing might have taken a toll on a grieving grandfather. But Ivy knew things...far more than anyone would have guessed. This was no worried grandpapa anxious to have his beautiful granddaughter back home because he loved her. There was evil, and then there was perverted evil. Without a doubt, Luis Mendoza belonged in the second category.

"That's true, Señor Mendoza. I do have a few leads, and I'll review those with you in a moment. However, you indicated you had something to show me."

Luis turned to his computer. "I do. It isn't much. The helicopter that was aiding in the chase of my granddaughter and her kidnapper picked up some images. I had them enhanced, but I still can't tell much about them. The images are too blurry. Both Gabriella and her abductor were wearing hoods and kept their faces down. Perhaps you'll see something that we didn't."

Ivy glanced over at the silent man sitting on the sofa. She knew his name was Stephan Conti and that he had been with the Mendozas for years. She knew he was loyal to the death to Luis, which made this part of her job that much easier.

"Whatever you have that might aid in me finding your granddaughter and her abductor would be most helpful. I'll combine them with what I have so far."

Luis turned the monitor around, and Ivy stared at chase photos, twelve of them, on the screen. "I see what you mean. The images are quite blurry."

"And that's after we had them enhanced and edited. I don't see—"

"Wait." She cut him off midsentence, pointing to the tenth photo. "Let me see this one."

He clicked on the photo to enlarge the image. Ivy drew closer to the screen. The profile was still blurred, but she saw something that put her pulse into overdrive. Could it be? He had gone off the grid, disappearing from public eyes. But she'd also heard rumors, ones that she had discounted as too odd to be true. The idea that Jonah Slater was working for a secret organization geared toward gaining justice for victims was too fanciful to be true. But the profile of Gabriella's abductor had strong similarities to the man himself.

Was it possible that Jonah Slater was actually responsible for the abduction of Gabriella Mendoza?

The girl had ties to Dallas, weak though they were. For the past three years, Gabriella had attended the McGruder Art Show there. What if during one of those times she had encountered one of the Slaters? It likely hadn't been Jonah, since he'd been in prison, but what if someone associated with a Slater had made contact? The abduction of Carlos Mendoza was an obvious attempt to bring him to justice. Had Gabriella Mendoza arranged a trade? Her freedom for Carlos's incarceration?

What an intriguing and delightful idea. And if Jonah Slater was involved, then things just got so much more interesting and a million times better.

"Do you see something, Ms. Roane?"

The question came from Stephan. She already knew the man had a less-favorable view of her than his employer. Stephan didn't trust her. If this had been a different kind of job, that might have concerned her at some point. With this particular job, his distrust made no matter.

Encompassing both men with her smile, she shook her head. "I'm sorry. I thought I saw a shadow...as if someone else other than those two on the snowmobile was there. I was wrong, it was nothing." She straightened. "You're right. This wasn't helpful at all."

"That was my belief, too," Mendoza said.

The man sounded tired, a bit forlorn. She had a cure for that.

"I do appreciate you showing me, though." He would never know how very much she appreciated it. "Even if it didn't give me any additional information, every stone needs to be turned and examined if I'm to find Gabriella and bring her home safely."

She gave one more dazzling smile, this one specifically for Luis. "And you have absolutely nothing more? No ideas at all? Conjectures on who the culprit might be? Thoughts on why she was taken?"

"No, none at all. We are at a standstill." His brow furrowed as angry frustration gleamed in his eyes. "There's nothing more I can give you."

Exactly what she had expected, but she had needed to make sure.

"Now I'd like to see what you have," Luis said. "You've been quite mysterious with your findings."

And there was a reason for that. Reaching down, she picked up the small briefcase she'd brought with her, placed it on the credenza and click opened the snaps. "I do have a couple of things I'm hoping you can shed light upon."

She slid her Glock 19 from beneath a concealed compartment and whirled. One bullet went into Stephan's ugly forehead, another to his chest. The man never knew what hit him.

Before Mendoza could react, she turned the gun on him. The old goat's eyes were wide as saucers. Ivy smiled. This never got old.

"But…why?" Luis said.

"Mr. Bianchi is tired of waiting. He will take care of matters from now on."

"But…but my treasure… Our agreement…"

"Has been canceled." She put a bullet in his head, one in his chest, and because it had been a special request, a bullet went into each of his knees and then one to his groin. Overkill in her opinion, but unless the deviations inconvenienced her, she did her best to please her clients.

The instant Mendoza went down, she double-checked her work. Assuming both men were dead without checking was sloppy wet work. She'd learned the hard way never to be sloppy.

Assured that both men's hearts had stopped beating, she returned the gun and silencer to her briefcase and then went to work. She downloaded the photos she'd been shown as well as a couple of other interesting-looking files onto a flash drive. There could never be too much information. She then uploaded a damaging computer virus that she kept on hand for times such as these. One could never be too careful.

Pleased with her day's work, Ivy closed her briefcase and, skirting Luis's body, walked out the door. Another gun was beneath her jacket, close at hand. Several guards eyed her as she went out, but that was the norm. Despite her disguise of a short blond wig and overgenerous curves, she was still a beautiful woman. Who wouldn't gawk?

No one tried to stop her. She, like so many, had been here for a business meeting with their employer. The goings-on behind those closed doors were not their concern. Of course, once they found two dead men, their feelings might change. But for now, she freely made her way to the black BMW she'd chosen for this particular job. Opening the door, she slid inside, started the engine and then she was off. Five miles down the road, she turned into a small lot and parked beside a red Lamborghini—a present to herself a few weeks back. She got into her shiny new toy and drove away.

The BMW had been stolen from a dealership in Caracas two days ago. Cameras from the dealership would show a stout woman with frizzy red hair and an unfortunate overbite helping herself to the car. The beautiful Ivy Roane was not a suspect.

She waited until she was a comfortable hour away from Mendoza's estate before she pulled off into a restaurant parking lot. Retrieving a phone from her briefcase, she pressed several keys.

Within seconds, a heavily Italian accented voice said in English, "It is done?"

"Yes."

"Excellent. Any witnesses?"

"None."

"How many?"

"Just the two you hired me for." She rolled her eyes. She didn't go about killing people for no reason. What was the point if there was no opportunity for gain?

"Very good. Your additional funds are being transferred now. Did you get any more information?"

"No." She knew better than to show her cards. "They had nothing else to give."

"Then you'll proceed as agreed?"

"Yes. I'll be back in touch soon."

"I'll be waiting."

She clicked off the phone and replaced it in her case. Then she pulled out another phone and sent a text message: "Phase one complete."

Immensely satisfied, she restarted the engine and pulled back onto the road. Settling back into the luxurious leather seat, she felt a small smile curve her lips as she considered what she had learned. Jonah Slater might be involved in this. If she played this right, she would get two prizes. Gabriella Mendoza would go to Bianchi for him to do God knew what with—wasn't her concern or business. And she, Ivy Roane, would have Jonah Slater's head on a platter.

Oh yes indeed, if everything worked out the way she wanted, this was going to be an epic win on all fronts.

CHAPTER THIRTY-THREE

Utah

Gabby threw the ball as hard as she could, watching with delight as Chamo raced after it. They still had a miscommunication on what he was supposed to do with the ball once he retrieved it, but he was getting better. At least he had stopped carrying it into the lake.

Her heart was so unbelievably light she felt as if it could burst with happiness. She wasn't pregnant. The day of her insemination was exactly one month ago yesterday. Every pregnancy test she had taken showed up negative, and today, for the first time in months, she had started her menstrual period. Never had she been so thrilled to see that arrive.

This morning, she had come downstairs to tell Jonah the good news. His face had lit up, and he had actually picked her up and whirled her around in a circle. Tonight, they were going to celebrate with a special dinner and a movie of her choice. And tomorrow…she shivered. Tomorrow, he was going to show her how to defend herself.

He had brought up the subject a few days ago, asking her if Raiza had trained her in self-defense. She had been intentionally vague, telling him that Raiza had trained her some, but she could always use some pointers from a professional.

His face had been serious and sexy at the same time as he explained that every person, man or woman, needed to know the basics of self-defense. And as she was being hunted, he said, she needed more than basics.

She could have told him his concern was unnecessary. As soon as Gabby had physically recovered from Rudy Bianchi's attack, Raiza had begun training her student. Raiza had combined her knowledge of jujitsu, Krav Maga, and old-fashioned street fighting to create her own type of self-defense. Training four days a week for almost a decade had turned Gabriella into the kind of fighter who could take on anyone. Not only had Raiza's training given Gabby the assurance that she could handle the Rudy Bianchis of the world, the discipline and knowledge required had instilled a confidence in her charge that could not be taken away.

No one, other than Raiza, had known about her training. If Luis had ever found out, he would have put a stop to it immediately. Raiza would have either been dismissed or even killed for doing such a thing. Her friend and trainer had known this but believed the risk was worth taking.

When Jonah had suggested the training, she had almost told him but had held herself back. Perhaps it was sneaky, but she wanted to show him what she could do. She looked forward to his delight.

Hearing a sound behind her, she smiled as she watched Jonah head her way, his long, lean limbs eating up the distance in seconds. His walk was all male and, to her mind, shiver inducing. There was a self-assurance and cockiness in his movements, making her more aware of him as a man than anyone she'd ever known.

"Have you and Chamo worked up an appetite yet?"

She could feel the blush coming before the color heated her cheeks. His innocent question called to mind other appetites. Unfortunately, other than a few heated glances she'd caught when he thought she wasn't looking, nothing, not even a kiss, had occurred since the night they'd arrived at the cabin. Even when they were lying in bed together and she could feel his body harden with want, he did nothing.

Taking the hand he held out for her, she went to her feet. "I was thinking I'd try to make breakfast this morning. I've watched you for weeks. I think I'm ready to try on my own."

His eyes glinted with humor. "I'll grab the fire extinguisher and be right there."

Laughing at his teasing, they walked hand in hand back to the cabin. Though Jonah's smiles were still rare, she loved that he was relaxed and comfortable enough with her to tease her.

She held back a sigh. Raiza had trained her to protect herself and to survive. She only wished she'd taught her what to do to make a man fall in love with her.

***

"Breakfast was delicious."

In the process of moving around the rubberized, overdone omelet on her plate to find an edible bite, Gabby looked up at Jonah and snickered. "It was not."

No, it hadn't been, but she'd looked so earnest and serious as she was cooking, he didn't have the heart to tell her just how bad it was.

"You'll get the hang of it. That was just your first try. Takes practice, that's all."

"Yes, but will our stomachs survive the practice?"

"How about this? You practice every other day, and for the rest of our meals, we'll rely on my limited skills and the microwave."

Her relief obvious, she dropped the fork onto her plate. "Sounds like a plan to me. Thank you."

Holding up a thin, charred, unrecognizable strip, he grinned. "Now, about this bacon."

She snorted with laughter and, without a hint of warning, threw a tiny scrap of bacon toward him. Without missing a beat, he scooped up a spoonful of omelet and flung the yellow lump toward her. It landed exactly where he had intended, in the middle of her forehead.

Her eyes went wide with surprise, but it took her only a second to catch on. Showing she knew how to get into the game, she took a handful of omelet from her plate and threw hard. Her aim was as true as any pro baseball player, smacking him in the face.

"That does it." He scooted his chair back. "The war is on."

Snagging the flour canister on the counter, he flipped the top, scooped a handful and threw. The white powder landed on her head, turning her hair instantly gray.

Letting out a carefree giggle, she jumped from the table and grabbed the egg carton on the counter. "One step closer, and it's eggs a la Jonah."

"Sounds like my kind of dish." He leaped for her just as an egg landed in the middle of his chest.

Her eyes wide with both alarm and laughter, she turned and sped toward the door.

Jonah was on her in a flash. "Oh no you don't." He grabbed her arm to pull her back into the kitchen. "We're not finished."

Gabby momentarily froze as those words clicked something inside her. He was here! He had found her. Shrieking with horror, she did the only thing she knew to do—what she had been taught. She whirled, delivering at uppercut to his jaw and a targeted kick to his stomach. Lost in terror, her only focus was survival. She didn't hear the harsh voice shouting her name. Preparing a double kick, one to his groin and again to his stomach, she shrieked again when her assailant grabbed hold of her, holding her arms at her sides, not allowing her to move.

"Let me go, you bastard! Let. Me. Go!"

"Gabby, calm down. It's Jonah. You're safe. You're safe."

"No. No. Let me go. You can't…you can't…" She couldn't breathe. Legs turning to jelly, she lost all strength and collapsed. Lost in a horror that she believed she had escaped, Gabby couldn't hear anything other than her own screams.

"Breathe, sweetheart. Breathe."

Jonah's voice finally penetrated her terrorized, frozen mind. She was here with him, she was safe. Rudy Bianchi was in prison where he belonged. He couldn't touch her. And she…

She looked up at Jonah, remorse replacing the horror. "I'm so sorry, Jonah. Did I hurt you?"

"Hey, it'd take more than that to damage a hard head like mine."

Instead of the smile Jonah hoped he'd see, her eyes filled with tears. His heart pounded with both sorrow and fury. Sitting in the middle of the kitchen floor, he held Gabby in his arms and cursed himself. He had been so damn focused on her courage and strength, he had completely missed that she was still hurting, still traumatized. The event could be pushed under the rug for only so long. She had received no formal counseling. As supportive and loving as Raiza had been, she hadn't been trained to deal with the emotional aspects of what a young girl had experienced at the hands of a rapist.

And clueless idiot that he was, he had no idea how to help her heal. But he could encourage her, talk to her. When she started her new life, he'd make sure she got the counseling she needed. He didn't care if he had to fly a therapist from one end of the globe to the other, she'd receive the best care money could buy.

"I can see that the self-defense training I suggested is a tad irrelevant. Now I'm thinking you should be the teacher."

She gave a watery giggle. "Sorry about that. I wanted to surprise you. Raiza was a martial arts expert. Had even competed when she was younger. Luis expected her to use those skills to keep me in line or protect me. He never expected her to teach me."

"In a way, I feel sorry for your grandfather."

She lifted her head from his chest. "Why on earth would you feel sorry for him?"

"Because he's such a coward and a bastard, so focused on himself, he'll never know what an amazing granddaughter he has."

"I don't feel very amazing."

"That's because you're sitting in the middle of a kitchen floor covered in eggs, bacon, and flour."

She peeked over his shoulder and winced. "My first food fight and I ruined it."

"No, you didn't. That's the great thing about food fights. There are no rules and they can begin or end anytime."

Her eyes glowed with both tears and wonder. "You knew this was on my list."

Before he could apologize for taking a peek at her list again, she cupped his face and put her mouth on his. Her soft lips tasted like heaven. Jonah groaned and pressed in deeper. She was sweetness, strength, and vulnerable, beautiful woman.

"Thank you, Jonah. You're the only man I've ever known who wants to make my dreams come true, even when they're silly."

"They're not silly." Settling her into his arms, he hugged her tight. "They're one of the many things that make you who you are."

She sat up and touched the bruise blooming on his jaw. "You mean like almost knocking you into the next county?"

He worked his jaw, ridiculously pleased that it hurt to do so. "You pack a hell of a punch."

She laughed and rose gracefully to her feet. "I'm glad you're happy about that."

Jonah stood beside her, and they both grimaced at the mess they'd made. "That's the only bad thing about a food fight. The cleanup."

"It won't take any time at all."

She was right. Less than half an hour later, the kitchen was set to rights. He noted that even something that simple seemed to please her. Several times, he caught her smiling as she cleaned the table and stacked the dishes in the dishwasher. She, who'd always had those things done for her, was genuinely happy to be able to do them for herself.

"Promise me something, Gabby."

In the middle of rinsing a plate, she stopped and looked over her shoulder. "Anything."

Ignoring what her words did to his heart, he said, "When you get set up…in your new life, you'll get some counseling."

"I promise. I really thought I was okay. But when you said those words…I don't know. Something just went off inside me. I remember Rudy saying those exact words."

"Those kinds of triggers aren't uncommon, but you need to know how to deal with them. If you feel up to it, maybe we should practice, using some of the other words you remember."

She grimaced but nodded. "That's a good idea."

Getting her agreement was the first step. The next step would be her allowing him to pay for her counseling sessions. He'd worry about that later. But he would not back down. Whatever she needed, he would make sure she had it.

CHAPTER
THIRTY-FOUR

Jonah watched from the porch as Gabby and Chamo played fetch. Chamo still hadn't gotten the hang of it yet as he tended to want to fetch the ball and take off. They'd been playing for over an hour, and Jonah could honestly say he'd never seen anyone more glowing or happy than Gabby. Or more beautiful. The expression on her face was priceless. This was one of her dreams—another one of her wishes that she'd written down—to play fetch with a dog. To see her simple wishes come true did something to his heart he hadn't yet allowed himself to think about. Each day, he grew more enchanted with her. She was so damn likable and fun to be around.

Since learning she wasn't pregnant, he had seen a light in her that was almost glowing in its intensity. Her laughter was a joyous sound that echoed around him, infiltrating all the parts he had believed frozen and dead.

The cellphone in his pocket sounded with a familiar tone. Jonah grabbed it and held it to his ear, never taking his eyes from Gabby.

"What's up?"

"Luis Mendoza is dead."

Considering all things, the news was not completely unexpected. Men of Mendoza's ilk usually met their fate in a violent fashion. And Luis Mendoza had deserved it more than just about anyone he knew.

"How'd it go down?"

"Assassin. Five shots. Head, chest, kneecaps, and groin. Definite execution."

"You know who's responsible?"

"Not yet. Might take a while. He had more than a few enemies."

"You're right about that. Those additional shots sound damn personal. What about Conti? He get a few shots, too?"

"Just two, head and chest. Word is Mendoza had a meeting with a private investigator he hired to find Gabriella. The PI left, and no one checked on Mendoza and Conti for a while. When the guards found them, they were cold. Had been dead for hours."

"Sounds like the private investigator had his own agenda."

"*Her* own agenda. And yes, it does sound personal." Justice said.

"Wouldn't surprise me if one of Mendoza's former associates used the ruse of a private investigator to take him out."

"Including Bianchi. He might've decided to take the initiative and just rid himself of Luis altogether."

The idea that Bianchi could be responsible worried Jonah more than if another of Mendoza's enemies had ordered the hit. Bianchi's focus on Gabby wasn't going to go away. Could this be a new path he was taking?

"We'll continue to monitor as we do our own investigating."

"I'll let Gabby know."

"How's she doing?"

"Better. She's definitely not pregnant."

"Can only imagine what a relief that is for her."

"Yeah. With this new development, getting her settled into a new life might need to wait, though."

Jonah told himself it wasn't selfishness on his part to suggest a delay. The possibility existed that if Bianchi was behind the hit, he had something else up his sleeve.

Still, the relief was there when Justice said, "I agree. At least a few weeks until things settle or become clearer. Could be that Bianchi might back off."

"You don't really think that."

"Unfortunately, no."

From any perspective, Luis Mendoza's death was good news, especially for Gabby. She no longer had to worry about her family hunting her down. And one less evil bastard in the world was always a good thing.

"Has Gabriella found anything more in her research?"

He'd called Justice days ago and given him the lowdown on what Gabby had uncovered about Luis and Rudolph Bianchi's decades old connection. "Not any more than what she found out before. Rudolph was once engaged to Flora Rossi, Luis's wife. After she eloped with Luis, an enmity began that lasted for decades."

"And to settle things, Javier, Gabriella's father, was supposed to marry Rudolph's daughter?"

"Yeah. Instead, he went to America for the summer, fell in love with Gabriella's mother, and married her."

Justice gave a grunt of disgust. "As screwed up as his thinking was, that's probably why Luis felt justified in killing his son and daughter-in-law. Javier went against his father's wishes."

"Plus, he was trying to remove Gabby from Luis's clutches. He had to know what the bastard was planning for his daughter."

"Just too damn bad Javier's escape plan didn't work."

"God only knows when that devil pact of joining Rudy and Gabby together was made."

"Rudy becoming a serial killer nixed that in the bud."

"Exactly," Jonah said. "So a baby would have settled things. But we're still coming up short on why it was so important to them. Could be a pride thing for Rudolph...but what was in it for Luis?"

"With Mendoza's death, that's something we might never know."

"Maybe so. I'll go break the news to Gabby."

"Also, let her know my people are working up several scenarios for her. Her interests are eclectic, so we had a lot to choose from."

"I wanted to talk with you about that. I know you have different monetary arrangements depending on what people need."

"We do."

"I'd like to double whatever you're providing for her."

"That's generous. Any reason why?"

Hell yeah, there were reasons, and judging by the amusement in Justice's tone, he knew what they were. Damned if he'd admit them aloud, though. "I just want to make sure she's got everything she needs. She's struggled enough. She deserves happiness."

"I agree. And we would gladly supply whatever she needs. Problem is, she wants very little help."

"What the hell? Why?"

"She said she appreciates the basic assistance we can provide. New name, new location, those things are a given. But she will only accept a small amount of seed money, which, by the way, she intends to repay when she can. She wants to start her life all on her own."

Jonah closed his eyes briefly. Hell, none of this should surprise him. For so long, Gabby had been dependent upon others. She'd never had the chance for independence. He couldn't blame her, but damned if he wanted her to have to scrounge for every single penny.

"Did you tell her the funds would be considered payment? She brought you a boatload of intel."

"I did indeed tell her that. It made no difference."

"How's she going to get settled? Hell, she's never been on her own. How does she know—"

"Gabriella is an intelligent young woman. She can figure things out, which is what she wants."

"Still, I think—"

"She'll have a handler. It's the one thing I insisted on. Her handler will help her set things up, make suggestions. But every decision will be Gabby's to make."

"As it should be. I'm going to try to encourage her to take more, though."

"Good luck." The amusement in Justice's tone said he didn't think it was possible. "I'll be in touch again soon."

Jonah pocketed the phone. Gabby and Chamo were now sitting in the grass beneath a shade tree. Gabby was writing in one of her notebooks. He swore she'd filled up at least a dozen since she'd been given her first one. Chamo lay beside her, his head on her lap. The dog's body language said he was relaxed, but Jonah knew that if a threat came for Gabby, he would be up in an instant, ready to defend her.

How would the news of Luis's death affect her? To Jonah, it was good riddance to a sleazebag, scum-sucking, murdering bastard. Gabriella was different from him, though. Would she grieve or be relieved that the man who'd done such horrific things to her no longer existed?

One of the many things he'd learned about Gabby was her unpredictability. She was often wise beyond her years, spouting homilies like she'd lived a thousand years. Other times, she was amazingly innocent.

Jonah had never met anyone more stubborn or courageous. She wanted to do everything for herself. Even wanted to repay Justice for the minimal assistance he was providing.

He had come to this job with a lot of preconceived notions about Gabriella Mendoza, and she had shot down every single one of them. And very soon, he would be saying goodbye to her—a woman he was quite certain he would never forget.

Gabby waved when she spotted Jonah. It had been such a lovely day, and there were so many things to be happy about. She was healthy and alive. Jonah Slater, a man she'd come to care about greatly, was headed her way with that intense, solemn look that caused shivers to zip up her spine. And she had the best, most loyal friend in the world who wanted to do nothing more than play fetch and adore her. How could she not be happy?

Sure, there were still things to worry about and consider. She had spent too many years dwelling on things she couldn't control or circumstances not to her liking. Many of those concerns might return, but that was for another day. Today, she would be content with what she had.

"From watching you, I couldn't tell who fetched the ball the most, you or Chamo."

She laughed and ruffled Chamo's silken head lying on her lap. They were both breathless from the play. "He's unique."

"That he is. As are you."

He dropped down beside her, and for several long moments, they gazed out toward the lake where blooming spring flowers surrounded the water, their golden-yellow petals creating a sunny outline.

She didn't say the words, because he wouldn't want to hear them, but she could live here forever and be perfectly content.

"I have news."

She tensed. For her, news was rarely good. "What's wrong?"

"Justice just called. Luis Mendoza was shot. As was Stephan Conti. They're both dead."

Gabby took in a breath, absorbing the news. She honestly didn't know how she was supposed to feel. If she'd had a normal relationship with a kind, loving grandfather, she would be filled with grief. But nothing between them had ever been normal, and Luis Mendoza had been as far from a kind, loving man as possible. Perhaps this was what justice looked like.

"Do they know who did it?"

"It was a professional hit. No idea yet who ordered it."

"Bianchi."

"Why do you say that so definitively?"

"It just makes sense. Luis was no longer useful to Rudolph. With my disappearance, they had moved past the purpose of their relationship. The one thing he wanted from Luis was me. Since Luis no longer had control over me, he was useless to Bianchi."

"Luis had many enemies. Could've been any of them."

"And they increased once his business associates began to be investigated and arrested. Because of me."

"Do you feel guilty about that?"

"Absolutely not. They were bad people doing bad things. They're receiving the justice they deserve."

"As did Luis."

She nodded slowly. "Yes. Maybe this was Bianchi's final revenge. He killed the man he hated for so long."

"That could put you in more danger. Bianchi's got a lot invested in you."

"I'm in just as much danger as I was before."

"If that was supposed to be reassuring, it fell flat."

"Sorry. I'm just saying that nothing's really changed. People will keep trying to find me, but they won't succeed."

"You're right. They won't. We'll see to that. How do you feel about Luis's death?"

"Numb…kind of empty. And maybe a little sad that I don't feel sad. Does that make sense?"

"Yeah, it does."

"Is that how you felt when your father was killed?" she asked.

"I felt sorrow that he hadn't been a good dad and neither of us would ever know what that would've been like. But it was also a relief to know he couldn't hurt anyone else."

"That's exactly the way I feel. And it's a grim justice that he was killed the way he murdered my parents."

"What will happen to your grandfather's estate?"

"My uncles and cousins will descend like vultures. They likely despised him almost as much as I did, but they'll want to profit."

"You know that you were probably left an inheritance."

"Doesn't matter. Luis's wealth was created from the blood of innocent people. I want no part of that. Anything I get I want to earn."

"Justice wanted me to mention that he will have several places for you to choose from for your relocation."

Her new life would happen soon. One that wouldn't include this man. She had hoped, prayed, and dreamed about starting a new life. She'd just never anticipated that she could dread it as well.

"Justice also told me you turned down anything but the most basic assistance."

"I want to earn my way."

Unable to be so close to him, seeing the concern in his eyes and not touching him, was impossible. She took one of his hands and held it between hers. "I need to do this. To prove to myself that I can. I've been dependent on others for so long, it's time I stand on my own."

"I understand, I just—" He released a jagged sigh and pulled her into his arms. "Promise me this. If something happens...if things get difficult, you'll let me know."

"I promise."

Gabby told herself she should be happy. All the hopes and wishes she'd written down were actually going to happen. The life she'd been dreaming about forever would soon start. She'd just never expected that it would break her heart.

CHAPTER
THIRTY-FIVE

"You can do this," she whispered. "I've got faith in you. You're brave and strong. You can do this...I know you can."

She had been repeating those words for the last ten minutes, but the woman in the mirror still didn't look convinced. Her dark eyes were filled with anxiety and more than a hint of fear. Gabby had all the confidence in the world when it came to bringing a man down with a right uppercut or a solid left hook. Bringing him to his knees with desire was something altogether different. Did she really have it in her?

She knew what she wanted in life and had worked hard to accomplish her goals. Things might have moved slower than she had wished, but that didn't diminish her accomplishments. She was far from perfect, and her mistakes were her own. She took responsibility for each one.

This was not a mistake. Okay, yes, she normally liked going into something already knowing the outcome. But she hadn't really known what the outcome would be when she'd partnered with Kathleen to bring her brother to justice. So far, that had worked out enormously well. This would, too.

Not that this was the same thing. Risking life and limb was so much easier than risking her heart. If Jonah rejected her, her heart would be scarred forever, without a doubt. Yes, she would go on, but she would hurt for the rest of her life.

The way she looked at it, she had two choices. Take this chance and have Jonah for a short while. Or not take the chance and never know how wonderful it could have been. When she looked at things from that perspective, how could she not take this chance?

She was stalling. Jonah was in charge of the meal tonight. He was downstairs doing his thing, and she was up here willing herself to be brave.

She was wearing a dress, the first she'd worn in months. It was simplistic but feminine. Whoever had purchased her clothes probably hadn't considered that she would need anything particularly dressy. It wasn't as if she'd be going out clubbing, not while she was being hunted. The fact that a dress had been included at all was a miracle. So her choice had been easy. This or a pair of jeans or sweats.

With short sleeves, a rounded neckline, and fitted bodice, the multicolored print dress in a cotton-polyester blend made her think of spring. The hem landed a few inches above her knees. She wore a pair of tan wedge sandals and was glad she'd given herself a pedicure this afternoon.

Her makeup supply was limited to mascara and lipstick, but she didn't want to go overboard anyway.

All in all, she thought she looked rather pretty. Now if she could just do something about the terror in her eyes. What if he said no?

***

Jonah lifted the Crock-Pot lid and sniffed appreciatively. Why hadn't he tried using this contraption before? His sister, Lacey, had sent the thing as a housewarming present. Figuring the gift was a joke, he'd stored the unopened box in the pantry. Yesterday, Gabby had discovered it, along with an enclosed recipe book. They'd sat on the sofa together and studied each page. If someone had told him a few months back that he'd someday read a recipe book and enjoy himself, he would've laughed his ass off.

Gabby made even boring stuff fun.

They'd decided on a roast recipe that looked simple enough. Five ingredients? Even a simpleton cook like him could do that. And judging by the fragrance, his first crock-potted meal was going to be a rousing success.

Gabby had already set the table, and he noted she had opened a bottle of wine. She was now upstairs getting dressed, which worried Jonah. She had told him she was going to wear something special tonight.

Most days, she wore jeans or sweats, which were hard enough to deal with. Gabby had a beautiful body, slender but curvy, with perfectly sized breasts and the most delectable ass he had ever seen. Their lifestyle in the cabin called for casual dress, and the loose-hanging sweats hid most of her charms. He knew what lay beneath but had worked hard to pretend he didn't. The jeans were harder to handle, since they molded to her body like a second skin, but he'd had a lot of practice forcing his eyes away from the more-tantalizing areas.

And now she was going to dress up for him in something that he was pretty damn sure was going to look spectacular. How the hell was he going to resist her?

Except for the pretense she put on to deal with her public persona, Gabby had lived her life without artifice. This was no different. She had made her attraction clear. Having been isolated for so long, it only made sense that she would want to explore the attraction. She might be twenty-seven years old, but when it came to experience, she was a neophyte. Pushing her away was better for both of them, but that didn't mean he had to like it.

Unlike Gabby, Jonah was not inexperienced. He knew without a doubt that they would burn up the sheets if he allowed himself to give in to temptation. He couldn't. It wouldn't be fair to either of them.

Jonah had done everything under the sun to avoid a confrontation. Hell yeah, he wanted her. Her sunny smile, soft giggle, delicate hands, long, slender feet, and everything in between turned him on like nothing ever had before.

But if they gave in to those needs, what then? It couldn't last. She would soon have a new life, a new name, a new everything. He couldn't be part of that life. How smart was it to start something that had no future?

He'd brought her here to protect her, not seduce her.

Turning at a sound behind him, Jonah felt his mouth go dry. All thought of seducing Gabby disappeared, because if he wasn't mistaken, she was going to take care of that all on her own.

She looked like springtime. Her long hair, gleaming almost blue-black beneath the lighting, curled around her creamy shoulders. The dress was simple and sweet and in no way could be considered provocative. So why the hell did he suddenly want to rip it off and devour the sweetness beneath?

Her smile was Helen of Troy, Cleopatra, and every other femme fatale he'd ever heard of rolled into one. He felt a vague amusement at his earlier arrogance. Experience be damned. Gabriella Mendoza could make the most experienced man in the world feel like an innocent.

"You look nice."

"Thank you." The compliment had been lame-assed and weak, not his best effort.

She smiled at him like he'd quoted poetry. "This is the first dress I've worn in months. I'd forgotten how much I enjoyed wearing them."

Jonah kept his eyes focused on her face, doing everything within his power not to let his gaze roam. When she'd walked in, he'd gotten a brief glimpse of her beautiful legs and had almost gasped. There were legs, there were world-class legs, and then there were Gabby Mendoza's legs. Without a doubt, he had never seen any lovelier.

Her eyes flicked to the counter behind him. "Dinner smells delicious."

Glad for the reprieve, Jonah turned back to the Crock-Pot and lifted the lid. "Yeah. I think we'll definitely need to use this thing more often."

He knew she was still standing behind him, likely waiting for him to turn back around. He could almost feel her disappointment in his response. He was torn between grabbing her for a long, passionate kiss or running out the door.

Dammit, he'd never run from anything in his life. He sure as hell wasn't going to run from this woman. She deserved better.

Manning up had never been so hard. He turned back to her, and she wasn't there. Hell, had he hurt her feelings? He started toward the living room and then jerked to a stop. Soft, bluesy, sensual music filled the air, calling to mind slow, hot kisses and bodies pressed together, moving in a rhythm as old as time.

He was in so much trouble.

Undaunted by Jonah's less-than-enthusiastic response to her first seduction attempt, Gabby selected classic love songs from the satellite music station on the television and headed back to the kitchen. So what if he had seemed more interested in the roast than in her? She refused to give up. She was nervous. Perhaps he was, too.

Surprising her, he was standing in the middle of the kitchen as if waiting for her to come back. "You look beautiful, Gabby. I should have told you that before. Like springtime."

"Thank you." She glanced down at her dress. "I don't know who supplied my clothes, but they did a remarkable job on such short notice. They all fit perfectly."

His eyes traveled down her body, and Gabby felt the heat all the way to her toes. That was the look she had hoped for. She held out her hand. "Dance with me."

She watched his throat move as he swallowed hard, and then he gave her the sweetest smile she could ever imagine. Pulling her into his arms, they began a slow dance.

Being held in Jonah's arms like this was a dream come true. He was about six inches taller than her five-seven height, and her head fit perfectly against his shoulder. She closed her eyes, breathed in his fresh, clean, masculine scent, and drifted, letting her body slide against his as they glided around the small kitchen. This was everything she had ever wanted, right here.

Jonah kept his eyes open and his mind clear. He would give her this, but he had to keep his thoughts on the future and what lay ahead. Getting romantically involved with Gabby was a sure disaster. She would leave soon for her new life, and he'd be off to another job. They'd likely never see each other again. He could not lead her on.

He looked down at her. Her head was on his shoulder, her eyes were closed, and a small smile played around her full lips. In that moment, he knew that if he didn't stop this now, there was no going back. He would kiss her, and that would lead to every fantasy he'd had coming true.

Dropping his arms, he gave her an impersonal nod. "I'll get the meal on the table if you'll pour the wine."

"Sounds good. I'm starving."

If she was disappointed in cutting the dance short, she didn't let on. Like so many times before, they worked together to get the meal on the table. When everything was set, the wine poured, they sat down.

Gabby held up her wine glass. "A toast." Looking him directly in the eye, she added solemnly, "To the here and now."

He heard her message loud and clear. She knew there was no future beyond what they would share here. She was wise beyond her years, and he hadn't given her credit for knowing what lay ahead.

Lifting his glass, he tapped hers. "To the here and now."

Their eyes locked, they each took a drink. Jonah felt as if he'd just made a pact, and he had no idea if it was a good one or a bad one. He knew only that this evening was not turning out the way he had planned. Gabriella Mendoza was a menace, not only to his peace of mind, but also his self-control.

The meal was delicious. After the toast, Gabby noticed a lessening of tension in Jonah's face. Poor guy probably thought she was going to jump his bones any minute. She knew he was trying to do the right thing. That was Jonah Slater, noble to a fault.

"I can't believe I made this." He scooped another helping from the platter.

"It's wonderful." Gabby laughed softly. "And you're definitely impressed with yourself."

"Damn right I am. This is what real food is supposed to taste like. Those frozen dinners are a thing of the past."

She took another bite of her meal and then put her fork down. The food had been wonderful, but she had enjoyed watching Jonah even more. Years from now, she would look back on their time together and smile. The memories would be poignant, sweet, and precious. In the short time she had left here, she wanted to make as many as she could.

Seeing that his plate was almost empty, she straightened her spine and took a giant leap, this time with her heart. "Jonah, are you attracted to me?" She knew the answer, but she needed to know where he stood. His reaction would help.

His mouth tensed, his fingers went stiff, his shoulders straightened. It seemed every part of him had a reaction to her words. She already knew the answer he would give, too.

"Gabby, you're leaving soon, and we can't—"

His hand was wrapped around his wine glass, his fingers so tense, she knew he would soon break the stem. Removing his hand from the glass, she held it gently in hers. "Years from now, I'm going to look back on tonight and I'll either smile and remember the beauty we shared, or I'll cry a little because we could have had something incredible and we didn't. That's your choice."

"Tell me what happens when you leave here, Gabby. Because you know that outside this canyon, we have no future."

"I'm not asking for a future with you, Jonah. I'm asking for tonight. And all the nights to come until I leave."

Jonah's chair screeched across the floor as he shoved it back. He threw his napkin over his plate and stood. Holding out his hand, he growled, "No going back. If this is what you want, then put your hand in mine. I've pushed you away as much as I can. But no more. While you're here, you're mine. Can you handle that?"

Placing her hand in his, she allowed him to draw her into his arms. Her hands cupping his face, she pulled him closer.

He resisted. "You didn't answer my question. Can you handle that?"

Her face within inches of his, she whispered, "I can handle anything you give me, Jonah. Question is, can you handle me?"

She never knew who kissed whom. Their mouths came together, and her world exploded. Everything Jonah had been holding back from her he put into his kiss. All the passion, the need, the wonderful heat that only he could give.

Jonah shut down every warning, every ounce of conscience. He had denied himself for as long as he could. This was what she wanted, and he had wanted her for what seemed like years. Regrets could not be part of the equation.

Without another word, he scooped her into his arms and carried her out of the room.

"Where are we going?"

"My bedroom."

He was surprised he was able to speak, even more surprised he could walk. His arousal was throbbing so hard, he ground his teeth to not give in to his baser desires. He wanted to lay her on the floor, any flat surface would do, and take her hard and deep. But Gabby deserved better.

He took the stairs two at a time. He had a moment of thankfulness that the door was open. Carrying her inside, he dropped her on the bed, and following her down, set his mouth on hers again. She gave as good as she got. Her mouth opening for him, she took his tongue, sucking and pulling him deeper inside.

He didn't remember tugging at her clothes. He was concentrating too hard on the silkiness of her skin, the scent of her arousal, the moans she released from her throat. His mouth traveled from that lovely throat down to her breasts. Coherency came in a flash, and he stopped.

"What's wrong?"

"I need to see you."

"What?"

He couldn't answer her if he tried. This moment was too special to rush. Ripping her clothes off and devouring her would satisfy a craving. But he wanted to savor every single second.

Sitting up, he feasted his eyes on the beautiful mounds before him. Luscious globes, creamy and perfect, just as he had imagined. His hands lifted them both, testing their weight, squeezing lightly. His thumbs brushed over her nipples, and he watched in delight as they tightened,

"Your breasts are sensitive."

"Yes," she breathed.

"Good." He leaned over and licked one nipple gently. Her body arched, and she gasped.

"Very good," he whispered. His lips latched on, and he suckled hard, pulling her deep into his mouth. The strangled moan she released urged him on, and his tongue flattened as he drew harder.

She couldn't catch her breath. Had never felt anything more wonderful in her life. Every part of her body felt alive. She wanted him everywhere. His lips, his tongue, his hands, those beautiful, long fingers dancing across her skin. Glorying in the beauty she had only imagined, she caressed his body, touching him everywhere she had dreamed. The shirt he'd been wearing was off one shoulder. His pants were unzipped but still buttoned. And one of his shoes was gone. She wanted him naked. She wanted to see him, too.

When he lifted his head, she pushed him slightly away from her and looked down at herself. He had been much more successful at getting her clothes off. Her dress was bunched around her waist, her bra was gone, and though she couldn't see that far down, she was fairly certain her panties were gone, too.

She giggled.

"What's so funny?"

"You've got way more clothes on than I do."

"Let me fix that." Standing, he dropped his pants, his underwear, and then his shirt. In less than two seconds, he was completely nude. She wanted to say something amusing but had no words. She had once thought Jonah's body was a work of art. She hadn't been wrong. He was muscle and sinew, hard planes and intriguing indentations. Her artist's eye immediately began to imagine painting him in the nude.

His penis was long and jutted past his naval. That was an appendage she had never carefully examined, had never wanted to exam. But with Jonah, there was nothing she didn't want to touch, to kiss, to taste. She leaned forward and put her tongue on the very tip. His taste was salty and masculine. Moaning her approval, she went for another taste but never got the chance.

With a growl, Jonah pushed her back on the bed and leaned over her. "Look at me, Gabby."

"That's what I was doing."

"That's not what I mean."

"Then what?"

"I need you to tell me if anything scares you. If I do something you don't want or doesn't feel right, you need to let me know. I promise I will stop."

The sincerity in his face, the earnestness in his eyes, moved her to tears. She knew he was aroused, that he was holding on to his control by a thin thread. She also knew he meant what he said. He would stop, now or at any time. This man had given her so much, but one of the most wonderful things he had gifted her with was the ability to trust. After all she had been exposed to, all that she had seen, she'd never thought she would have that.

She had no fear, no trepidation. She could give him those words but wasn't sure he would believe them. So she gave him her most confident smile instead and spoke softly, "Give me everything you have, Jonah. I want it all."

He gave her another hard, long stare, and then apparently believing her, he proceeded to do what she asked. And oh mercy, he had so much to give.

Jonah knew he would never get enough of her. His mouth devoured every inch, his tongue adoring every sweet hollow and secretive dip. He licked, nibbled, and when he heard her gasping, he repeated the process. When he knew he could no longer hold back, he opened the drawer of his bedside table and grabbed a condom, ripping it open with his teeth.

Surprising him once again, she took the rubber from his hand and slid it over his length. Then, with her seductress smile, she pulled him down to her.

Jonah slid in slowly, working himself in increments. She was wet, aroused, and so tight he almost lost all control. Every particle of his body was telling him to thrust and ride them both to oblivion. Gabby might be on board with everything so far, but she was too delicate and untried for him to take her fast and hard like he wanted. He allowed her to adjust, watching her face for any sign of discomfort or pain. She showed him nothing but acceptance and a need that matched his own.

When he was at last buried to the hilt, he gritted his teeth and held himself still. He didn't know what he was expecting from her. Maybe a little fear, perhaps a bit of uneasiness. Nothing could have prepared him for what she did.

"Why are you smiling?"

"Because you're inside me, and it feels even more wonderful than I imagined."

The only response he had to that was to kiss that smile and give her everything she asked for, all that he had.

Wrapping her arms around Jonah's back, Gabby opened herself and gave in to the burning desire. She had never felt so wonderful, so free, so incredibly alive. The need was building to a crescendo inside her, like a blaze was taking over, consuming her. Having Jonah inside her, thrusting, plunging, giving her incredible pleasure, was the stuff of fantasies and dreams. And just like always, he was making them come true.

The blaze became an inferno, coalescing into an incredible, devastating climax. Her world exploded, and Gabby shouted as she was flung to the stars.

She returned to earth to hear Jonah saying her name over and over again. His big body stiffened, and she felt the pulsing inside her.

With the knowledge that she was unbelievably blessed, Gabby wrapped her arms and legs around him, holding tight. She had been right. Years from now, she would look upon this night and she would smile. Jonah had given her that, too.

CHAPTER THIRTY-SIX

The next two weeks were the most magical of her life. No dream or fantasy could compete with her current reality.

She woke each morning in Jonah's arms, and they would make love until they were both breathless and replete. Jonah was an amazing lover, tender and ruthless in giving and taking pleasure. Sometimes, he would linger over her for hours, giving her exquisite pleasure before taking his own. Other times, he would take her fiercely and quick, as if it had been days since he'd had her. Each time was more beautiful than the last.

Having an intimate relationship with a man was a unique experience. The one extremely uninspired and short-lived relationship she'd had could not begin to compare with what she felt for Jonah. He fulfilled every need and desire as if he read her mind. He knew where to touch for maximum pleasure. He knew when to give and when to hold back, making her want him so much she wanted to scream. And she had, several times, but always with pleasure.

Their closeness had grown even deeper. Whether it was the shared intimacy or just the knowledge that they trusted each other, she wasn't sure. She only knew she would treasure and hold these memories close to her heart until her last breath.

They spent their days taking long walks with Chamo, trying out recipes in the Crock-Pot, watching movies, and making love. She knew she was living in a paradise that couldn't last, but she didn't let her mind dwell on what lay ahead. The here and now was all she could want, and that was enough.

They talked about anything and everything. Jonah was well versed in a variety of topics, and they'd even had some heated debates. She had learned that he had a stubborn streak a mile long and was set in his ways about many things. Silly, but she liked that about him, too. A man who knew who he was and what he stood for was incredibly sexy.

He'd opened up more about his family. She had learned about the other hideous things Mathias Slater was responsible for, including the death of Shelley Slater, Eli's wife before Kathleen.

And he had told her the truth of Mathias's death and how that secret could never be told. What a burden that must be for the entire family, especially Jonah's mother.

She'd learned about the contract someone had put out on the Slaters last year and how Kathleen and Eli, along with Jonah, had confronted the hired killer and shot her.

All the things he revealed, along with the things she already knew about him, fascinated her. Jonah's life had never been easy, but the man he had become would make any parent proud. Too bad his father had missed out on appreciating what a wonderful son he had.

In return, Gabby had continued to share her hopes and dreams. She told him about the paintings she'd left behind in England and how she was sure her grandfather had destroyed them. The day after that, Jonah had gone into town and returned with several canvases, paints, and art supplies. The last couple of days, she had spent hours in the upstairs loft, getting the feel for her art again. It was a heady experience to know there were no limits or boundaries she couldn't cross. She could create anything her heart desired, and no one could take it away from her.

She had started a portrait of Jonah, but she hadn't told him yet. Capturing him on canvas was much harder than she had anticipated. He was unique, and her feelings for him were so intertwined, that an objective rendering of his likeness seemed impossible. Whatever she painted, she wasn't sure she would ever be able to do him justice.

"You ready?"

She nodded and stood, mentally preparing herself for another lesson. She couldn't say she hated it. She usually ended up in Jonah's arms at the end of the session. The part before that happened was something she wished she didn't have to endure. She refused to stop them, though. There were definite trigger words she needed to overcome. Her initial response to the words wasn't a problem. She reacted just the way Raiza had taught her. The problem was in the aftereffect when her legs went weak as water and she either wanted to cry or throw up. Those things had to end. Going weak after a physical attack could mean disaster or death, which was exactly why she continued to work through the problem.

Since it was raining today, they'd opted to practice in the loft. Her art supplies took up very little space, and with almost no furniture, other than a chair and lamp, which Jonah had pushed to the corner, the room was the perfect venue.

Chamo was downstairs sleeping, two closed doors separating them. On their last session, they'd learned a valuable lesson. Whoever attacked Gabby would rue the moment he lifted a finger. Even Jonah, whom Chamo adored, wasn't allowed to raise his hand in a threatening way. Thankfully, Gabby had been able to stop the dog before he caused Jonah harm. But from then on, Chamo was far away when they practiced.

Today's lesson could well be the hardest. A nightmare a few evenings ago had prompted a memory of the vulgar names Rudy had called her. Jonah wanted to try several of them out to see what would happen.

"Okay?"

"Yes. I'm ready."

He came at her, as he had before. As he reached to grab her, she blocked his hand and pushed him away. He went after her again and then again, becoming more and more aggressive. She blocked, kicked, pushed, hit, did all the things she needed to do to fend off her attacker. Gabby could do this all day long.

Panting lightly, his skin covered in a slight sheen of sweat, Jonah continued to bombard Gabby with assault after assault. He was going easy on her at first, knowing from experience that she would settle into the session and handle anything he threw at her. She was incredibly talented, and it was all he could do to keep up with her sometimes. Not for the first time, he wished he'd been able to meet Raiza and thank her for what she had done for Gabby.

He wrapped his arms around her from behind. The next second, he was soaring over her shoulder, thankful for the mat that cushioned his fall. Since she knew what was coming, he had no choice but to woo her into a false sense of security. Getting her complacent and comfortable was the only way to draw out her fears.

An hour later, they were both panting heavily. "You want to take five?"

"Sounds good." She went to the corner where they'd placed a couple of bottles of water and towels. She twisted a top off and swallowed a mouthful.

He waited until the top was back on and she was half turned away from him. Grabbing her by the arm, he growled in his most menacing voice, "Come here, bitch!"

With a shriek, she swung the bottle, slamming it into his forehead, and followed with a right punch to his jaw.

Ignoring the sting, he came at her again, this time grabbing her around the torso, the exact same way he had before. "You're mine, whore," he snarled.

For an infinitesimal second, she froze, and Jonah felt his heart go into his throat, worried that this had been too much. In a blink, she recovered. She slammed the back of her head against his face and simultaneously hooked her ankle around his leg, throwing him off-balance. She followed through with an elbow to his stomach and a kick to his thigh.

Jonah backed away. Panting and hurting a little more than he'd like, he waited to see what happened next. In previous sessions, she'd gotten to a certain point and hadn't been able to continue. That didn't happen today. Her eyes glittering with determination, she went after him full force. Jumping on him, she threw him to the floor. Her knees dug into his upper arms, and her legs wrapped around him tight, pinning him to the floor without any way to move.

Glowering down at him, she snarled, "What did you call me?"

He grinned up at her and said with all truthfulness, "The most beautiful and talented woman in the world?"

For only a moment, he saw the blank look in her eyes and knew she had been lost in a memory. She recovered quicker than he could have hoped for and said, "That's what I thought you said," and leaned over and kissed him full on the mouth.

Since he was still pinned and unable to do anything other than respond to her lips, Jonah put all his efforts into that kiss. His tongue swept into her mouth, thrusting and retreating. Gabby groaned and loosened her hold. Jonah took full advantage of his freedom. Wrapping his arms and legs around her, he rolled until she was beneath him.

"That's more like it," she whispered.

"What? You like me on top?"

"I like you any way I can get you."

Groaning at the sheer sweetness of this woman, he proceeded to strip her from head to toe. Gabby eagerly complied, helping him as much as she could. When she was at last completely nude, he used his mouth once again, licking and kissing down her body. She tasted both spicy and sweet, of hot, willing woman. Silken limbs wrapped around him, and he wanted to devour her in one gulp. He could spend a thousand years loving her and never get enough.

Lifting her knees up, he spread her legs, all the while carefully watching her expression. Not once since their first time together had she acted remotely afraid or nervous. He would not take that for granted, though. The very thought of Gabby being afraid of him made him sick to his stomach.

The expression in her eyes and the smile on her mouth told him she had no fear, no concerns. Once she had gotten over her initial shyness with him, she had been uninhibited. Just like everything else in her life, she embraced the new experience of intimacy. She was sexy, giving. Sometimes playful, other times so incredibly sweet and innocent.

His eyes roamed from head to foot, taking in every glistening, panting, and silky inch.

"What are you doing?"

"Looking at you."

"But why?"

He smiled, detecting a little nervousness but no fear. "Because I want to. Because I can."

"Oh." She sounded surprised and then raised her head slightly to look down at her own body. "So what do you think?"

He laughed. "I think you're perfect, and I want to devour every inch of you."

"Well, don't let me stop you."

Still smiling, Jonah bent lower, inhaling the heady scent of sweaty, aroused woman. He licked at her, and she gasped. His tongued delved, and she arched. His mouth opened over her, and she melted, climaxing against his tongue.

He waited until she recovered and then slid deep into her wet heat. Her face was flushed, her eyes glittered with heat and satisfaction. And that Mona Lisa smile curved her mouth.

"You look very satisfied."

"I wonder why."

"Want more?"

"Always."

Jonah began a rhythm of thrusting and retreating, allowing himself to let go and enjoy the pleasure. He knew she was close again. He could feel her inner muscles clamping on to him, pulling. He watched her face, watched her reach for the pleasure, not only taking what he gave her but demanding more. He wanted to give her everything.

Determined that they go over together this time, he placed his thumb and forefinger at the top of her sex and pinched gently.

Her eyes went wide as the force of her orgasm slammed through her. As she exploded around him, he gave himself permission to let go, too. With a groan of delight, Jonah followed her into oblivion.

The sound of the rain falling outside while she was safe and secure in Jonah's arms was a wondrous, lovely feeling. Gabby sighed with sheer happiness. She could stay like this forever.

"I guess we should get up sometime."

The rough rumble of his voice beneath her ear made her smile. Snuggling deeper into his arms, she whispered against his neck, "Not yet."

He grunted his approval and held her tighter.

She loved his body, his sheer masculinity. From his hairy legs to his long muscular thighs, to his tight buttocks, hard flat stomach, broad, and powerful shoulders, and every inch in between. He was all man. She could spend hours exploring him, loving him.

"I'm going to paint you."

"Really? What color? I'm partial to lime green."

Giggling, she pressed a kiss to his salty skin. "On canvas, silly. Your body is a work of art."

He snorted. "When you get settled in your new life, you might want to make an appointment with an optometrist."

"My eyes are just fine." The mention of her new life took the smile from her face. She knew it was coming. It was what she had wanted for so long, what so many people had worked so hard to give her, but the very thought of never seeing Jonah again ripped at her like claws on the thinnest cloth.

"What's wrong?"

"Nothing, I just—" No. She couldn't tell him. Not only would it completely destroy this wonderful moment with him, they had an agreement. Once her time here was over, they were over, too.

"You just what?"

"I was wondering if you ever think about starting your own business again."

Jonah had told her that before he had uncovered evidence of his father's illegal activities, he had planned to leave Slater Enterprises and open his own consulting firm. With degrees in both business and finance, he had, understandably, wanted to create something that was just his.

"I like what I'm doing now. Working for Justice has given me a different perspective on life. On what matters most."

Another reason she admired this man so much. Life had slapped him down numerous times and instead of staying down, he got back up and focused on helping others. He hadn't achieved his goal of bringing down his fiancée's killer, but that didn't stop him from wanting to assist other people in gaining justice.

He twisted slightly, rolling her over onto her back so he could look down at her. "What about you? Do you want to be a famous artist someday? Show your art to the world?"

"Maybe some day. Not all of it, though. I don't think the world's ready for a lime green Jonah Slater."

He gave a shout of laughter and kissed her, his lips vibrating with amusement. Gabby wrapped her arms around him, laughing with him. Enjoying every precious moment, she once again allowed Jonah to carry her away to a sensuous, beautiful place that was meant for them only.

CHAPTER THIRTY-SEVEN

They sat on the front porch and watched the dawn break. This wasn't the first time she'd watched the sun come up since she'd been here, but sharing the beauty with Jonah made the event more beautiful and special. Especially since this was the last sunrise they would share together.

Today was the day. Grey would arrive soon with everything she would need to begin her new life. She was doing everything in her power to act excited. Dozens of people had worked hard, not only to ensure she was able to have a new life, but that she would also stay safe. Every detail had been carefully planned so those who were still searching for her would never find her.

She *was* grateful. The dream she'd had for years was about to come true. She had just never anticipated that when the time came to achieve that dream, she'd want something else instead.

The porch swing was large enough to accommodate them both with room to spare, but she moved as close as she could to the man beside her. The warmth of his body penetrated the coldness of her own. She inhaled, wanting to remember his scent, a combination of masculine musk and minty freshness from his toothpaste. She leaned her head against his shoulder, savored the comfort and the hardness, wanting him more than she could have ever imagined.

She hated to feel so needy…so weak. Her strength might not have always been apparent to others, but Gabby knew what was inside her. As a woman with a strong will and excellent discipline, she told herself she shouldn't feel this way. She was not fainthearted or a coward, so why—

She sat up as the realization hit her. No, she wasn't cowardly, but she was definitely dense. All the vulnerabilities she'd been feeling weren't because she was weak, they were because she was in love. For the first time in her life, she was in love and hadn't recognized the symptoms.

"What's wrong?"

As usual, Jonah's gruff morning voice caused shivers throughout her body. There were so many things he did and said that could turn her on in an instant. His rare smile, his husky, even rarer laughter. The way his eyes crinkled at the corners when he was in serious thought mode. The way his hands would smooth lovingly over Chamo's coat and the soft tender way they would glide over her own skin.

There were a million things she loved about this man, including his big heart and compassionate nature. And she was just now realizing them. It wasn't just sexual with Jonah. There was depth to her feelings, and she had been too caught up in the heat to recognize them.

"Gabby? What's wrong?"

She turned to him. She was once again in scary new territory, but there was no way she could keep the revelation to herself.

"I'm in love with you, Jonah."

The regret on his face tore an immediate hole in her heart. "Gabby…no. We agreed—"

"I know what we agreed, but love doesn't stop just because it's inconvenient."

"This isn't a damn inconvenience. This is your life we're talking about. I can't be a part of it. You have to let go of everything you know. That includes me. There's nothing else that can be done."

"It can work if we both want it to work. We could see each other in secret. No one has to know about it. We don't have to go out, be seen in public. We could meet in another city. We've both had covert training. There's no reason we can't use that for ourselves."

"You deserve more than that."

"But we can—"

"No. It won't work." He took her hand and squeezed it. "Listen, this is all new to you. This time here with you was wonderful, but it wasn't real. You'll have opportunities to meet other men. Once you do, you'll forget all about me."

In just a few short sentences, he had reduced the most wonderful moments of her life to meaningless sex and a fake romance. As if she would have fallen in love with any man who happened to be protecting her.

Torn between insult and heartbreak, she carefully moved away from him and stood. "That might be the most demeaning thing anyone has ever said to me. And believe me, I have a lot to compare it to."

"That's not what I intended at all. I'm just saying that you have no real experience with—"

"Stop, Jonah. You've had your say. Now let me have mine. I'm not an immature or silly young woman. I know my own mind and my own heart. My lack of experience has no effect on my intelligence.

"If you don't love me, I understand, but don't you ever put me in such a shallow, narrow box and tell me what I do or don't feel. You obviously don't know me as well as I thought you did."

"I'm sorry. Hurting you is the last thing I ever wanted."

"Well, congratulations. You just got your last thing."

The sound of an expensive engine heading toward them stopped her from making more of a fool of herself than she already had.

"Guess it doesn't matter anymore," she muttered. "Looks like my new life has arrived."

Jonah felt like shit. While every ounce of his willpower and grit were being used not to ask her to stay with him, his brain had apparently shut down. The bullshit speech he'd just delivered had proved that. To have someone like Gabby tell him she loved him was one of the most beautiful gifts he could have imagined. She was everything good and fine. Everything beautiful. She was what life should be. What he wished his life could have been.

And what had he done but tell her that her feelings weren't real. That wasn't what he'd meant. Though, it was obvious she saw him as some kind of romantic hero. Her eyes lit up when he came into a room. She laughed at his stupid jokes and hung on his every word. Yes, he believed her words. Gabby wasn't going to lie. But neither had she had a chance to live, not really. All that she'd seen of the world was what her asshole of a grandfather had allowed. She'd never had the chance to be on her own, make her own decisions.

He and Gabriella Mendoza had been thrown together by extraordinary circumstances. It only made sense that she would cling to him and see him as something special. Once she got out in the world and got another perspective, she would see things in a different way. She would eventually see him differently, too.

The idea of Gabby meeting and falling in love with another man hurt more than he'd thought possible. But his feelings didn't matter in this. She had a new life to look forward to, and he'd damn well not mess things up by encouraging something that wouldn't last.

Despite her obvious anger and hurt, he couldn't stop himself from grabbing Gabby's hand and holding it as they stood waiting for Justice to park the SUV. His boss hadn't told him anything about Gabby's handler, other than she had been a handler for about a year now and had successfully set up a half-dozen individuals with new lives.

Jonah had never seen his boss involved with anyone other than Irelyn. Since Irelyn hadn't been around in a while, he had wondered if Justice and the handler were involved. The tone of his voice when he was talking about her made him think there was some kind of affection between the two.

The instant the SUV parked, Gabby squeezed his hand gently just once and then pulled her hand from his, moving several inches away. Jonah felt that loss to the bone. It had been her way of separating herself from him. He understood her reasons, knew it was for the best. That didn't ease the pain.

The windows of the SUV were tinted, so he had no way of seeing inside. The doors didn't open for a moment, and Jonah tensed. What was the delay? What was—

The doors finally opened, both the driver's and passenger's sides. He recognized Justice's dark hair and broad shoulders immediately. His eyes veered toward the petite young woman emerging on the passenger side. Hair the color of sunshine, a smile that was both sweet and mischievous, and a chin that held more than a hint of Slater stubbornness. She also had the same color eyes as Jonah's.

Just what the hell was his sister doing here?

Grey watched Jonah's eyes widen the moment he recognized Lacey. For a lot of different reasons, he had kept the identity of Gabriella's handler a secret. And because Lacey had made the request. She knew her brothers saw her as a directionless and innocent young woman who needed to be protected from the harsher side of life. She had even admitted that she had cultivated that opinion. She said it was easier that way.

Eyeing the couple standing on the porch, Grey acknowledged another reason he hadn't told Jonah. The man was hurting. It might not be obvious to others, but having been put through the ringer himself, he knew the symptoms. Denying that your heart was being torn in two had very specific indicators. Jonah Slater had all the symptoms. Having something else on his mind might ease the blow to his heart.

"Lacey, what the hell are you doing here?" Jonah growled at his sister and then glared at Grey. "What's going on, Justice?"

"Simple," Grey said as he headed around the vehicle. "Lacey is my employee. She's Gabriella's handler."

Lacey made her signature move, which was to turn on the charm and distract. Grey had seen her do it several times and was always fascinated with the results. He wondered if it would work with her brother, though.

Her smile as bright as her hair, she threw herself into Jonah's arms. "It's good to see you, big brother. You look wonderful."

Jonah showed he was made of sterner stuff. He gave Lacey an abbreviated hug and released her. "I want an explanation. Now."

"I'm Gabriella's handler, of course. That's what's going on." She extended her hand to the silent, solemn woman at Jonah's side. "Guess there's no need for a formal introduction now. I am very pleased to meet you, Gabriella." She paused, then added, "Can I call you Gabby?"

"Absolutely," Gabriella answered as she shook Lacey's hand. "I'm very pleased to meet you, too."

There was an awkward silence as Gabriella eyed the man standing beside her. The wariness was understandable. Jonah wasn't bothering to hide his seething anger. But Grey saw the pain, too. As much as she had wanted a new life, her heart was breaking for the one she didn't think she could have. He felt badly for both of them, but he had gone as far as he could in interfering. They would have to work out the rest by themselves.

"Why don't we all go inside and get some coffee?" Gabriella asked. "This early in the morning, I'm sure we could all use another cup." Her smile and soft, coaxing voice helped diffuse the tension.

"Good idea," Jonah said. "But I still want an explanation."

Rolling her eyes at her brother, Lacey linked her arm with Gabriella's and headed to the cabin. Despite the anger radiating off Jonah, Grey was glad to have his initial thoughts confirmed. Lacey and Gabriella would get along very well.

Jonah waited until the two women had entered the cabin before growling, "You should've told me, Justice."

"Maybe, but Lacey wanted to surprise you. Seems she thinks you don't have a lot of confidence in her ability to make her own decisions."

"That's not true."

"Isn't it?"

Jonah shoved his fingers through his hair, thoroughly and completely disgusted with all of it. Not only was Gabby leaving, and he might never see her again, his little sister was in charge of getting her set up. That was a fuckload of shit to take in all at once.

"Let's go in and talk about what's going to happen. I think, if you'll keep an open mind, you'll see that Lacey will be the perfect handler for Gabriella."

With an abrupt turn, Jonah headed back to the cabin. If he stayed out here with Justice, he had a feeling blood would be shed. While that might make him feel better in the short term, he'd regret it later.

He walked in the front door to laughter. Both Gabby and Lacey were sitting on the sofa, already acting as if they'd been best friends since childhood. In spite of his anger at being blindsided, Jonah saw immediately what Justice meant. Lacey's sunny disposition had put Gabby at ease. Before they had arrived, Gabby had worn a pained expression. Now, color bloomed in her cheeks, and there was a definite spark in her eyes. He told himself that this should make him happier.

Pouring two cups of coffee from the carafe on the table, he handed one to Justice and then, taking the other one, dropped down in the chair across from the sofa. The two women barely acknowledged his presence as they continued to chat.

When there was finally a pause in the conversation, Jonah said, "How did you become a handler? I thought you were in France with Mom."

"I am. Well, most of the time anyway. I do all the preliminary work at the villa. Then, when it's time for a setup, I go to the location and get things in order. Then it's meet-and-greet time with my charge."

Jonah barely refrained from shaking his head. Her charge?

Apparently reading his thoughts, Lacey said in the firmest tone he'd ever heard from her, "Listen, Jonah, this is my job, and I'm damn good at it. Just because you and Eli think I should still be having tea parties and playing with dolls doesn't mean you're right. I'm twenty-five years old. I've been a caretaker for a woman who was a basket case for several months. I know you and Eli had your own issues, but don't demean my accomplishments just because they seem easy to you. Because, believe me, they weren't."

Shit, she was right. While he'd been focused on finding Teri's killer, and Eli had been focused on saving the family business, they had left Lacey in charge of their mother. Eleanor Slater was a loving woman, but after her husband's death, she had been exactly what Lacey called her—a basket case. They had depended on Lacey to handle things without giving her a bit of credit for doing so without complaint.

"I'm sorry, Lace. You're right. We never thanked you for doing that or told you what a good job you did."

She gave him a cheeky grin, but he saw the emotion simmering behind the smile. She had grown up, and he had completely missed it.

"So now that we've established I'm a mature adult, let's talk about what's next." All business now, Lacey turned back to Gabby. "You're going to love your new home."

Her departure happened in an inordinately short period of time. She had already packed her suitcases and art supplies. Chamo's crate and food, as well as his toys and blankets, sat beside her luggage. With Grey and Jonah doing the heavy lifting, everything was packed in the back of the SUV within a matter of minutes. The only things left were the goodbyes.

With a lump the size of Utah in her throat, she watched as Grey and Jonah shook hands. Then Jonah turned to his sister and enveloped her in a giant hug. The affection between them was real and incredibly sweet. Once, she had longed for that kind of connection with a family member. That had been a long time ago. Now she just hoped to heaven she never saw another member of her family for as long as she lived.

Grey and Lacey went on to the SUV and got inside. She appreciated their sensitivity. They had known she would want to say goodbye to Jonah without an audience.

Jonah stooped down and gave Chamo a big hug. She heard him whisper in the dog's ear, "Take care of her for me."

He stood and held out his arms for Gabby, obviously expecting her to walk into them, as she had so many times before. She couldn't do it this time. Couldn't hug him and then just walk away. She would lose it, she knew she would.

Instead of going into his arms, she held out her hand.

"A handshake? Really, Gabby? After all we've been through together?"

She stayed silent, her hand frozen in the air between them. Finally, Jonah had no choice but to comply. The handshake was firm and impersonal, just the way she needed it to be. Jonah had made it clear their relationship had ended. What remained was an impersonal and professional acquaintance. Nothing more.

"Thank you, Jonah, for everything."

"Gabby…don't."

"Don't what? Be mature? Keep the emotions to a minimum? I'm making this easier for both of us. You don't want emotions? You don't want love? Then this is what you get. A cool but sincere farewell.

"Thank you for everything, Jonah Slater. For your support, your courage, and your…" She swallowed hard around the lump that refused to diminish one millimeter. "For your…friendship."

Grabbing hold of Chamo's leash, she turned and walked away. She knew he watched her, and despite his words, she knew he was hurting. She could do nothing about that. He had rejected her. Yes, partly because of her need to leave everything in her past behind, but she knew it wasn't all that. They could have figured out something. He just didn't want to.

She opened the back door of the SUV. Tail wagging, his tongue hanging out of his mouth, excited for the next adventure, Chamo jumped up onto the seat. Without looking back, Gabby got into the vehicle and closed the door. No one said anything. It was as if everyone was waiting for a storm to break.

The SUV started up again, picking up speed as it headed down the drive. The storm broke within her, and she could no longer control its ravages.

"Grey! Stop!" Gabby shouted.

He slammed on the brakes, and the vehicle jerked to a stop. Gabby jumped out and ran to the man still standing in front of the cabin. His face a mass of churning emotions, he opened his arms, and she flew into them.

"I'm sorry, Jonah. I'm so sorry for leaving you like that."

His face buried in her hair, his voice was muffled. "Shh. Don't, sweetheart. I understood."

"You're the best thing that's ever happened to me, Jonah. Even if you can't love me, I need you to know that."

"Oh, baby…" The thick words sounded as if they had been wrenched from his chest. "I wish—"

She pulled away slightly to rain kisses all over his face. "I understand. Really I do." She backed away even more. "I just hated to leave things that way. These last couple of months have been the happiest times of my life. You've made so many of my wishes and dreams come true."

"I want you to have every dream and wish fulfilled, Gabby." His eyes glittering, he gave her a solemn smile. "The world is waiting for you, Gabriella Mendoza. Go make it a better place."

She pressed her lips to his, intending the kiss to be one of love and tenderness. Jonah gathered her close and ground his mouth against hers. She opened for him, and his tongue swept through, thrusting, tangling. Creating the soft, sensual world where only they could go. Need, hope, desire, and passion were all there. And there was love, on both sides. Whether he wanted to admit it or not.

Before she lost complete control of her senses, Gabby pulled away. "I've got to go."

Unable to bear more words from either of them, she turned and ran back to the SUV. Jumping in, she wrapped her arms around her middle and bent over double, holding her breath until the pain passed. She was vaguely aware that the vehicle was moving. Chamo made a whimpering sound of sympathy. Gabby wrapped her arms around him, buried her face in his neck, and let the grief take over.

CHAPTER THIRTY-EIGHT

Willoughby, Wisconsin

Her name was Jessica Olsen. Her parents had called her Jessie. Those closest to her called her Jess. She was an only child. Her mother, Maria, whose family originated from Barcelona, Spain, had met and married Jessica's father, Oscar Olsen, while vacationing with her family in Sweden. Both parents were deceased. Oscar died when Jessica was just a baby. She didn't remember him. Jessica had been twenty-one and away at college when Maria passed away suddenly of an undiagnosed heart problem.

Jessica grew up in Grand Rapids, Michigan. With a degree in art history from the University of Michigan, she had worked in art museums for the past seven years. She was fluent in both English and Spanish, and her hobbies included reading, hiking, and painting. She was an ardent animal lover and had a black Labrador retriever named Chamo. As soon as she was completely settled, she hoped to adopt more pets.

She had recently ended a five-year relationship with Ben Limskey, her college sweetheart, and was looking for a change. She hated large cities. Willoughby, Wisconsin, population just under fifty thousand, was the perfect size to start over.

At first, she had feared she wouldn't be able to pull this off. Becoming an entirely new person with a different background and memories seemed overwhelming. Her heart had still been aching, and for the first couple of days, she'd barely done anything but follow directions.

Having Lacey Slater as her handler was both surreal and wonderful. Even though Jonah was now in her past, Lacey helped to make the transition from brokenhearted to recovering a little easier. Lacey knew all sorts of wonderful things about her brother and had no issues with sharing.

That wasn't the only reason she loved having Lacey with her. The woman was both smart and savvy and a genius at decorating on a budget. And she knew how to find a bargain. By the fifth day of her move, Gabby had a beautifully furnished and decorated apartment at a fraction of what she had thought it would cost. She also had a fully stocked pantry and a closet full of pretty but sensible clothes that fit her perfectly.

Standing at that closet now, she contemplated what she would wear to her upcoming interview. The Willoughby Museum of Art and Natural History wasn't large, but it did boast several nice pieces. The most exciting part was that once a quarter the museum brought in exhibitions from all over the world. She was interviewing as the assistant to the director and hoped that her background of traveling to some of the most famous museums in the world would give her a leg up on any competition.

"With your height and exotic features, you could look elegant in a sack."

Gabby looked over her shoulder at the petite young woman standing at the bedroom door. Dressed in a pair of leggings and a long cotton T-shirt that would make most people appear sloppy, Lacey Slater was the epitome of elegance.

"Then how is it you can wear things that look as though they came from the dumpster, and you still look like a million dollars?"

"Cachet and confidence, my dear." Lacey waved a slender, elegant hand as if she were a queen waving to her royal subjects. "I am, therefore I am."

"You and your brother like to speak in riddles."

Lacey scrunched her nose. "Jonah is the most blunt man I know. If there's a riddle in him, it's covered in a ton of cement."

Gabby laughed at the image. Not only was Lacey incredibly down-to-earth, she had never once held back talking about her brother or her family. Jonah's sister was a walking encyclopedia on the Slaters and didn't mind giving her opinion on any of them.

Her brother Adam she called a sleaze. Her brother Eli had a gentle heart and determination of steel. And Jonah, she claimed, was one of the most sensitive, caring men in the world.

Before Gabby could tell her that bluntness and sensitivity didn't exactly go hand in hand, Lacey explained, "Prison damaged him, and Teri's murder just about destroyed him. But beneath that gruff exterior is a kind, loving man."

Gabby didn't disagree with her. She had seen the evidence of those qualities herself.

Pulling herself away from the painful and too-sweet memories, she returned to her perusal of her closet. "So what do you think I should wear for my interview?"

"The scarlet red with the to-die-for heels."

"You don't think that's a little too bold for an interview?"

"Go bold or go home. That's my philosophy."

Since she hadn't steered her wrong yet, Gabby reached for the suit and then jerked to a stop. The doorbell was ringing. Their eyes locked. They weren't expecting any deliveries and knew no one in town. And while it could be a neighbor welcoming them to the apartment complex, both of them knew they couldn't let their guard down.

Without speaking, Gabby went for the gun in her nightstand drawer. Lacey slid her own weapon out of her purse. Pressing her finger to her mouth, she jerked her head to indicate to Gabby she was going to check.

Gabby glanced down at Chamo, who was lying in the middle of the floor and acted as if nothing unusual was happening. Jonah had told her he would be able to sense danger, but maybe she should have trained him to be more on alert.

Following closely behind Lacey, Gabby went to the front window while Lacey peeked through the peephole at the door. They both gasped at the same time.

"What the hell is he doing here?" Lacey unlocked the deadbolt and pulled the door open.

"Hello to you, Lacey. Have you missed me?"

When Lacey didn't answer, Wyatt Kingston stuck his head inside the open doorway, grinning. "Mind if I come in? I don't think Lacey's going to invite me."

Before she could answer, Lacey poked him in the chest with a finger. "You got that right, buddy."

Still grinning, he grabbed her finger and kissed it. "Good to see you, too."

Before Lacey could push him out the door or aim her gun at him, which she looked ready to do, Gabby took hold of his arm and pulled him into the apartment.

"What are you doing here? Is everything okay? Jonah?"

Compassion softened his eyes. "Jonah's fine. I was just in the neighborhood. Thought I'd drop by and see if you ladies needed anything."

Lacey snorted as she walked away from them. "Tell that lie to someone who doesn't know you. You're checking up on us for my brother. He wants to make sure we're not in trouble, and he's too stubborn to make contact himself."

She waited to see if Wyatt would deny Lacey's words. Instead, he shrugged and said, "You've got to admit, Lace, Jonah's got his reasons."

Her training as a hostess came in good stead. What she wanted to do was ask questions about Jonah and why, if he was so concerned, he couldn't figure out a way to talk to her himself. Instead, she did the calm, adult, hostessing thing and said politely, "Have a seat in the living room. Lacey made some delicious lemonade this morning. Would you care for a glass?"

"Sounds good." And surprising her, he flung an arm around Lacey and pushed her toward a bedroom door. "We'll be just a minute."

Stunned, Gabby watched as they went toward the bedroom. Wyatt's expression was one of determination, but Lacey's was the most surprising. She had never seen her look so uncertain and vulnerable.

"Wait," Gabby said. "Lacey, everything okay?"

Lacey cut her eyes over at Wyatt and said, "I'm fine. We just need to get a few issues out of the way. Might want to put that lemonade in a to-go cup for Wyatt. He won't be staying long. I'll be back in five minutes."

Deep laughter was Wyatt's response, but the instant they entered the bedroom, he looked back at Gabby and winked. "She'll be back in half an hour." Before he closed the door, Gabby saw Lacey's face again. Temper had replaced the uncertainty, and Gabby wasn't sure who she was worried about the most.

Lacey and Wyatt? The thought made her smile.

CHAPTER THIRTY-NINE

Rome, Italy
Bianchi Compound

"You've accepted my money, Ms. Roane, but you haven't achieved the objectives for which I hired you."

She stood in front of the desk like some sort of naughty child pleading her case to a strict and humorless headmaster. The old man's face resembled an emaciated prune. His body had likely always been whipcord thin and now looked like a withered, bent stick. With one targeted hit, she could break him in two with one hand.

She hadn't liked Luis Mendoza; she liked Rudolph Bianchi even less. But liking her clients had never been a necessity. She could spend an unlikable client's money just as well as she could anyone else's.

"I disagree with your assessment, Mr. Bianchi. I achieved two of your objectives. I believe both Señor Mendoza and Señor Conti are spending quality time in hell because of me."

"That was a different contract, and I paid you handsomely for those hits. You have not achieved the final objective, which is the most important one. Gabriella Mendoza has not been found. You were to bring her to me. You have failed."

"I have not failed. I just haven't finished the job. Shooting someone is much easier than finding a lone woman who doesn't want to be found."

"So you believe, as I do, that Señorita Mendoza arranged her abduction so she could escape her grandfather."

"I do."

"At least we agree on that. However, that does nothing to fix the issue. I'm going to hire additional investigators. The one who brings Gabriella to me will receive payment, plus a sizable bonus. If you want that to be you, Ms. Roane, I suggest you do your job."

Considering the austerity and emptiness of this rotted old castle, this was a major concession from Bianchi. The man's miserly reputation was well earned. She knew the reason he wanted Gabriella found and could not fathom a kid growing up in this place. Hell, the man probably wouldn't live past the child's first birthday.

But it was not her place, or even of interest to her, why he wanted what he wanted. Money was her only priority.

His thin lips curled with arrogant amusement. "What do you say about that, Ms. Roane?"

Oh, how she wanted to end the old fart's life right this instant. Taking orders was her least-favorite part of her job. The people who hired her always thought they knew best. That she should have done something a different way or she wasn't fast enough. Some people could not be pleased no matter how smoothly their orders were carried out.

Being in the service industry as she was, she had to put up with a certain amount of kowtowing and public relations. It was the nature of the beast. However, the sheer unpleasantness of

Rudolph Bianchi made her want to end him much sooner than was wise. He was such a sourpuss.

But she wanted the money she had been promised, and she wanted the bonus. She would have both.

"You're right, of course. And I will do my job. Will you give me just one more day, sir, before you hire additional people? I believe I can convince you that your trust in me was not misplaced."

"What difference will one more day make?"

"I need to fetch something from my apartment in Paris. It will, I think, give you an insight into just how close I am to closing this case."

Watery eyes the color of old mud gleamed at her. "Is this a trick? An effort to delay the inevitable?"

The man might be old as dirt, but he was still crafty and alert. His intelligence was an inconvenience she could have done without.

"No trick. In fact, if you're not impressed with what I bring you tomorrow, I'll return your retainer money."

"Very well. I'll expect you at noon tomorrow. Don't disappoint me, Ms. Roane. I don't deal well with fools."

"You won't be disappointed. I promise."

Ivy left the mansion in a hurry. She had so much to set up before their next meeting. And she hadn't lied. Mr. Bianchi would definitely not be disappointed in what she brought to him. He would, however, be more than a little surprised.

A few miles down the road, she pulled into a parking lot and sent a text. The response she received was all she could have hoped for and more.

Game on.

***

Willoughby, Wisconsin

She had a job. It was all Gabby could do not to kick up her heels. Since she was wearing four-inch stilettos, she decided against that, but did do a little skip down the street. She was now the assistant to the director of the Willoughby Museum of Art and Natural History. The museum was split into two parts, and she would work on the art side. The job couldn't have been more perfect for her if it had been designed with her in mind.

She told herself that she had gotten the job on her own merits, but she wasn't completely sure. It was true that the interview had gone well. The ice-blue suit she'd chosen, and not the red one Lacey had suggested, did look good on her. And the instant she'd walked into the museum, she felt as though she were home. With almost no effort, she had smoothly answered the interview questions as if she'd been Jessica Olsen all of her life.

Maybe doubts would always be a part of her makeup, at least until she had some experience doing things on her own. For right now, today, she was absolutely ecstatic and couldn't wait to share her good news with Lacey.

She hadn't heard a peep from Jonah. Not unexpected. He had been more than clear on their need to never see each other again. And while she understood his reasoning that she needed to separate herself from everything and everyone she knew, there was a part of her that told her he had used that as an excuse.

She hated that whiny, insecure voice that would pop up at the most inconvenient times. Maybe that was just an aftereffect of having her heart broken. Whatever the reason, she didn't like the feeling. She might never see Jonah again, but she would never forget him and all that they shared. Concentrating on the good memories and not the pain would be the mature thing to do. If not for Lacey, she wasn't sure she would have done nearly as well.

It felt so odd and wonderful to have a friend. One she could share good news with. One who would be happy for her success. And one who was the sister of the man she loved.

But Lacey would be leaving tomorrow, and while she would be sad to see her friend go, Gabby knew it was for the best. The time had come for her to be on her own…have the life that she and others had worked so hard to achieve. It would be the height of hypocrisy and selfishness to squander the chance. Just because she had a broken heart didn't mean she couldn't have a valuable life. To have that life of meaning, she had to let go of the past.

Still, this clean break everyone insisted on was so damn painful.

She stumbled on a pebble on the sidewalk and realized she'd been walking down the street without any awareness of her surroundings. Just because she had escaped her past didn't mean she could take her safety for granted. For the foreseeable future, she had to take all precaution.

She stumbled on another pebble, almost tripping, and cursed her lack of foresight. She should have brought comfortable shoes to wear back home. It was only five blocks from the museum to the bus station, but in four-inch heels, that could feel like a mile. She glanced up at the street sign. One more block to go. She winced as the toe pinching began in earnest.

Her mind on getting to the bus station and sitting down as soon as possible, she didn't see the man until he was almost on her. She spotted him out of the corner of her eye. He was running across a parking lot, toward the sidewalk. His fierce expression wasn't necessarily alarming. The gun in his hand was.

"Stop! Thief!" An old man, eighty if he was a day, hobbled after the man. "He just robbed my store!"

If she had given herself time to think things through, she might have made a different decision. But the hard look on the thief's face, combined with the desperation of the old man, made her decision for her. The man was a yard and a half away when he pivoted to avoid a collision with her. Intending that there be a collision, Gabby made an abrupt move, putting her body directly in his path. She swung hard and made contact with his right arm, knowing from experience that his arm would go numb, along with his gun hand. He dropped the weapon, snarled a curse at her, and pivoted again, trying once more to run. Gabby stuck her foot out, tripping him. The thief teetered before falling face first onto the pavement.

The man rose to his knees and scrambled for the gun.

Gabby kicked the gun out of the way and then pressed her spiked heel into the man's back. "Stay put."

Before she could do anything else, a uniformed policeman ran toward them. "Are you okay, ma'am?"

"I'm fine, Officer." She moved away and watched as the policeman hauled the man to his feet and handcuffed him.

The old man, winded from running, grabbed hold of her hand and shook hard. "Young lady, thank you. You stopped him."

"It was nothing, really. Just happened to be at the right place at the right time. Anyone would have done the same thing."

Gabby was doing her best to downplay her role when things went from bad to worse. A van with the local news station emblem on its side drove up and parked at the curb. Two people jumped out, one of them holding a camera, the other holding a microphone.

She held back a sigh. This was what she got for requesting a small town to relocate in. Any kind of excitement, even something this mild, was sure to bring attention.

Dozens of people milled around, excitedly chattering about what they'd seen and what happened. The old man continued to talk to the news media, explaining in painful detail about how Gabby had saved him.

When a microphone was shoved in her face and a smiling reporter began to ask questions, she knew without a doubt she was in big trouble.

***

Utah

"Five days. She's there five damn days, and she blows her cover."

Over a thousand miles separated them, but Lacey's huff of exasperation came through loud and clear in Jonah's ear. "It wasn't exactly her fault, Jonah."

"Fault or not, she's got to get out of there. No way in hell can she stay there now."

"How do you even know what happened? It's not exactly national news."

"I have an alert on my phone."

"An alert?"

"For news from Willoughby, Wisconsin."

"I see."

The amusement in Lacey's voice barely penetrated his worry. "I'm going to call Justice. We'll—"

"I've already talked to Grey. He said, and I agree, that we need to wait."

"Wait!" Jonah barked. "Wait for what? For her to get kidnapped, taken back to those bastards?"

"Calm down, big brother, and listen. We're in a small town in Wisconsin. Not only does she have a new name, she's got a new hairstyle. Even had it lightened a bit, with streaks of gold. Looks fantastic, by the way."

When he let loose what sounded like a feral growl, she added with more solemnity, "Seriously, Jonah, she barely looks like the same person. I'm not sure even you could recognize her. Besides, the chances of this news reaching Italy is almost zero. And even if it did, no one would recognize her. New name, new look. It's no big deal."

Jonah ground his teeth. Didn't anyone get this? "The chance exists. That's what counts. She needs to get out before something happens that we can't control."

"You mean that you can't control, don't you?"

"What's that supposed to mean?"

"She's not your responsibility anymore."

"I didn't keep her safe just to have her put her life in jeopardy the moment she's out of my sight."

"Wow. It's like déjà vu all over again. For a second, I was hearing Daddy talk."

The hurt slammed into him, followed by the knowledge that she had a point. He had sounded a lot like his old man.

"Low blow, Lace."

"Justified, Jonah. Now, do you want to talk to her? Because if you do, you'd better check that attitude. She's had a pretty emotional day and doesn't need any shit from you."

"You've got a foul mouth, Lacey Lou."

She snickered at the nickname he'd given her when she was a baby. "I learned from the best. So, are you going to behave?"

"I'll be on my best behavior. Promise."

He heard whispers and then Gabby, sounding a little husky, said, "I didn't do it on purpose."

"I know, baby. I'm just worried about you."

Gripping the phone in her hand, Gabby held back tears. It had been a roller coaster of a day. Her emotions were all over the place. First the job offer, then the chance to stop a thief, followed by the horror of all the attention she had gotten. And now talking with Jonah. She hadn't been sure she'd ever hear his voice again.

"I think you should leave. We can put you back in a safe house until we get you a new identity and location."

"I'm not going anywhere. This is my home now."

"That makes no sense. The primary purpose of you disappearing from the public eye is to keep a low profile. That's been shot to hell."

"I live in a small town, thousands of miles away from the Bianchis. There's absolutely no reason for anyone in Italy to hear about this incident. By tomorrow, it will be old news here. All the way in Italy, it won't even register."

She cleared her throat, adding firmly, "The matter is settled."

And because she wanted to hear him say something other than give her dire warnings or a stern lecture, she said, "I got a job today."

"You can get another one somewhere else."

Gabby closed her eyes. What had she expected? Jonah would always look at her through a lens of protection. She had been his charge, and that was what he would always focus on first.

"Your job with me is over, Jonah. I'm not your responsibility anymore. You're not my protector or my keeper. I'm on my own now and—"

"I'm aware of that. Just because I want to keep you out of the clutches of that son of a bitch doesn't mean I'm trying to take away your independence. I'm trying to keep you alive."

She drew in a trembling breath. They were going in circles and would never agree. Yes, there was the possibility of danger, but if she moved every time the possibility existed, she would be on the run for the rest of her life.

It was now or never. "I appreciate your concern, but the matter is settled. Goodbye, Jonah."

"Wait!"

She ended the call and dropped the phone on the kitchen counter. With a smile that felt both frozen and fake, she said, "Let's celebrate my new job."

***

"Okay. I'm going to tell you something. Being the pigheaded man that he is, Jonah would deny it, but I swear it's true."

"What?"

"I don't think he and Teri would have lasted."

They were sitting in Gabby's living room. An empty pizza box sat between them, along with an empty bottle of wine. She hadn't told Lacey about her hopes and wishes books. Jonah was the only one who knew about them, but this had been on her list. She had wanted to have a girls' night with a friend to share secrets and giggle. They had started out with giggles, but now, with full stomachs and two glasses of wine each, the secrets were coming out.

"Why don't you think they would have stayed together?"

"Because they didn't have anything between them, not really. They started dating at the same time they began digging up dirt on my dad and Adam. That's all they concentrated on. If they'd been dating like a normal couple, I think the relationship would have ended with just a few dates."

"But why?"

"Other than their shared interest of revealing the corruption of the Slater empire, they didn't have much in common. Mind you, I only saw them together a few times. They were trying to keep their relationship a secret, but whenever Jonah talked about Teri, it always revolved around their investigation. There was affection there, but the tender feelings you'd expect to see when a man talks about the woman he loves weren't there."

Lacey's smile was soft, almost wistful. "I only saw you two together for a couple of hours, but there was more emotion and tenderness between you than I ever saw with them."

"Really?"

"Absolutely. Jonah couldn't keep his eyes or his hands off of you."

"He couldn't?" She blushed. "I don't even remember him touching me."

Lacey's green eyes, so much like Jonah's, glinted with laughter. "That's probably because you were touching him, too. You guys have it bad."

"It doesn't matter. Even if he admitted his feelings, we couldn't be together."

"And why not?"

"Because I need to stay hidden."

"So? You can stay hidden and still have a relationship. No one has to know."

She had a feeling Lacey's boss wouldn't agree with her opinion, but that was one of the many things she liked about Jonah's sister. Lacey definitely had a mind and an opinion of her own.

"That's exactly what I told Jonah. He said it wouldn't work."

"Look up stubborn in the dictionary and you'll see Jonah's picture."

Despite her misery, Gabby laughed. The woman definitely had a way with words. It was obvious she adored her brother, but she didn't hold back her thoughts when she believed he was wrong.

"Is that what you and Wyatt have done? Kept your relationship hidden?"

Brightness left Lacey's eyes, and Gabby wanted to call her words back. "I'm sorry. That's none of my business."

"No, you're right. And saying it's complicated is a cliché, but that's because clichés are often all too true. Our relationship is beyond complicated."

"But why? It's obvious he's crazy about you."

"Is it?" Her smile was sad. "Tell Wyatt that. Maybe he'll believe you."

They went on to talk about other things, but Gabby kept thinking about Lacey's words. Relationships were complicated. Perhaps hers and Jonah's was more so than most, but did that really mean they couldn't have one? Apparently, no one knew that Wyatt and Lacey were in a relationship. Why couldn't that work for her and Jonah?

Her mind veered away from her biggest doubt, but the voice inside her head wouldn't let it lie. Was Jonah using her need to stay hidden as an excuse to not be with her? She knew he had feelings for her, but maybe that's all he had. Feelings didn't necessarily equate love, at least not the forever kind.

And without a doubt, hers were forever.

CHAPTER FORTY

Rome, Italy
Bianchi Compound

The night was silent and still. A soft, warm breeze, fragrant with the aroma of late spring flowers and freshly cut grass, ruffled her hair. Ivy smiled at the incredible feeling of well-being. She loved night jobs the most. There was such an air of romanticism to the event. It got the blood pumping and her adrenaline going like nothing else. The best sex she'd ever had was right after a successful nighttime hit.

She glanced over at the man a few feet away from her. That definitely wouldn't be happening tonight. She'd been around some disgusting people in her life. In her line of work, that was a given. But she could categorically say that this asshole beat them all for sheer repulsiveness. The man was a maggot.

Still, in this at least, he was her partner. She looked forward to the end of that partnership very soon, too.

But first, there was this job. Then on to the next—the pièce de résistance, one might say. Her blood pumped harder at the anticipation. How long had it been since she'd had such excitement for a job? Maybe it was because of the personal nature. Taking out an adversary as opposed to killing for money had its own rewards. What a rush!

"You ready?"

Ivy nodded, jerking her attention back to the job at hand. Time for fun later.

They had discussed the entire scenario beforehand. She needed this man's knowledge to get them into the house and then the bedroom. Once there, he was to stand back and let her take over. She hoped he lived up to his end of the bargain. There was a gleam of wildness in his eyes that made her feel uneasy about his sanity. Having to kill the bastard before she got her money would seriously piss her off.

"Let's go." He spoke just above a whisper, but she could hear the rampant excitement in his voice. He enjoyed the kill, too. Thankfully, that was all they had in common.

She followed him, noting how much at ease he was while breaking into the house. For a man who lived like a pauper, Rudolph Bianchi was incredibly well guarded. With more guards than some royal palaces, this place should have been impossible to breach. But this man acted as if he'd done this a million times. She had a feeling he had.

They entered through the cellar, the dank smell quickly entering her nostrils and making her grimace. She doubted that anyone had been down here in the last decade.

"Let me get the security system turned off."

Allowing someone else to take the lead was unsettling. She'd called the shots in every job she'd had until now, and rarely did she have a partner. This creep might be good at killing, but when it came to dealing out death, there was no one better than Ivy Roane.

After a series of punches on the keypad and several beeps, the indicator lights disappeared. The system was now disarmed.

He grinned, the wild-eyed look now rampant. "Come on. There's a shortcut."

He opened a squeaky door and disappeared. Ivy followed as he started up a spiral staircase that appeared to wind on forever. When they finally reached the top, he pressed a finger to his mouth to warn her. This close to their target, guards would be present. Since this death had to look like a natural one, having a guard see them would put a serious hitch in their plans.

Instead of going through the door, she was surprised to see him open a small compartment in the wall. "It's a small elevator… an electronic dumb waiter. Years ago, this room was the main kitchen. The house was remodeled about twenty years ago, but the elevator should still work."

He fitted himself into the elevator, and she was surprised to see that she could fit in as well. She climbed in after him, and he pressed a button. Within seconds, the door closed, a humming noise commenced, and then they were moving upward at a surprisingly rapid pace.

The old man's suite was on the fourth floor. When the elevator reached its destination, the door slid open, and they climbed out.

Ivy straightened and looked around. Another surprising and pleasant surprise awaited her. They were already in the master suite. As long as no guards were there with him, they could get this done much quicker than anticipated.

Both taking soft steps, they went through a sparsely furnished sitting room and stood before large double doors. "He's in there."

"I'll take it from here," Ivy said.

"But I get to watch."

"You can stand at the door and see everything. There's no need for you to do anything."

"But I want him to see me. He needs to know I'm here. That's part of our deal."

"You can come in once he's ingested the poison, but not before."

"Fine."

Ivy refrained from rolling her eyes at his petulant tone. Putting up with unpleasant people wasn't her forte. She had done away with more than one irritating person over the years. This man, with his arrogance, believed he was safe. And unfortunately, the fact that he held the purse strings meant he was right. At least for now.

Without another word, Ivy entered the room. Just like the other rooms she'd been in, this room was stark to the point of being austere. The old man lived in a multimillion-dollar mansion, was worth billions, and yet the house looked as though he couldn't afford a decent decorator.

The massive room held a king-size bed and a nightstand that appeared to be holding more than a half-dozen prescription bottles. A double dresser stood against the wall across the room, and a chair and a floor lamp sat in front of a massive hearth. That was it. Though the room was dim, she could see well enough to notice the lack of color. The room reflected the joylessness of the man who occupied the bed.

She went to that bed, noting he had to have at least six quilts covering him. Rudolph Bianchi was a skinny man, but the bulk from the quilts made him seem larger.

"Mr. Bianchi. Wake up."

He blinked up at her in confusion, not recognizing her at first. She'd seen that look in the eyes of a mark many times. Waking up to an intruder in your room was startling enough. Knowing the intruder was also a killer added a different dimension to the disorientation.

"What are you doing here?"

And they always asked the same damn question.

"I promised you an update on the case."

He struggled to rise, and Ivy obligingly assisted him by putting the stack of pillows lying beside him against the headboard.

She watched him struggle to sit up and reached out to help him. He swatted her hand. "Get your hands off me, girl. I can do it."

"Whatever."

It took a couple of minutes for him to sit up properly. By the time he did, his face was almost purple with the effort. In gasping wheezes, he said, "How did you get in? Why...are...you...here?"

Hmm. Perhaps poison wouldn't be necessary. Testing the theory, she said, "I have a gift for you."

"What kind of a gift? This is totally...inappropriate." He coughed so hard she wouldn't have been surprised to see half a lung hanging from his mouth. Hell, the man might not live long enough for her to have their little talk.

"Before I give you the gift, I wanted to let you know that your attitude toward me was most annoying. I don't make a habit of killing off my clients. Bad for business. But, since no one will know I had a hand in your demise, I made the exception.

"You're not a very nice man, Mr. Bianchi, and it's not been a pleasure knowing you." She glanced over her shoulder. "Come on in. Let's see if we can do this without any additives."

Rheumy eyes widened with disbelief as her partner came through the door. "No..." Bianchi gasped. "It. Can't. Be."

"Oh yes, it can," the smiling man said. "Good to see you, old man. You look even worse than the last time I saw you."

"But you're supposed to be…" Clutching his chest with one hand, he reached for a bottle beside the bed with the other.

Ivy was there before him, pushing all the bottles out of his reach. "Now, now, now. Let's not ruin a good thing. It's time nature took its course."

The man stood over Rudolph Bianchi. "Just so you know, all of this was my idea. You thought you were so smart…so crafty. You're nothing but a bag of bones and a rotting heart. One that will be stopping in…" He pressed a hand over the old man's mouth.

"Stop that," Ivy snapped in a harsh whisper. "Smothering him could produce evidence that might cause questions. He's dying. Just give him a minute or two more."

With an exasperated sigh, he removed his hand from the old man's mouth. "I've waited this long. Guess I can wait a little longer. You know, for a woman who kills for a living, you're incredibly squeamish about getting it done."

"Not squeamish. Professional. Amateurs ruin it for the rest of us."

A rattling sound came from the man on the bed. They both returned their attention in time to see him slump onto his side. Touching his neck, Ivy checked for a pulse. She couldn't find one, but that meant nothing. The old bag of bones might still be revived.

"We'll give him five more minutes and then leave."

"No problem."

When he dropped to his knees, Ivy backed away. "What the hell are you doing?"

"Getting what I really came for."

He slid a giant hand beneath the mattress. She could see his arm moving and knew he was searching for something.

"If you steal anything, people will question his death. We need to make this look like natural causes."

"Don't worry. This isn't something…" He grunted with the effort and then said, "Hardly anyone knows about this."

"And what is this 'this' that you speak of?"

He withdrew a small black pouch from beneath the mattress and stood. Grinning like an idiot, he dangled the bag in front of her. "My inheritance."

"What is it?"

"Nothing for you to be concerned with." He glanced down at the dead man on the bed. "Let's get out of here before we get caught."

She didn't like secrets. She didn't like it when her clients withheld valuable information. But she would wait to see where this might lead. Perhaps she could get even more than she'd ever anticipated.

"Very well. You go first."

"On to the grand prize?"

"Yes." She allowed herself a smile. "The grand prize indeed."

CHAPTER FORTY-ONE

Dallas, Texas

"I'm telling you, we need to get her out of there. She's not safe."

The man barely raised a brow at Jonah's demand. "She disagrees. And I happen to agree with her."

"Dammit, Justice. She's never been on her own. She doesn't know the kind of danger she's in. She—"

"Is a very intelligent young woman who has faced more danger than most people do in a lifetime. You told me yourself she's better trained in hand-to-hand than you are. And on top of that, she shoots like she was born with a gun in her hand."

"She's still traumatized. She has triggers…some she isn't aware of."

"And she's getting counseling, just as you suggested. Her first session was yesterday. She texted Lacey that it went well."

"That doesn't mean she will stay safe."

"You want to tell me what the real problem is, Jonah? Do you really think she's in danger, or are you wanting to relocate her just so you can spend time with her again?"

Jonah ground his teeth till he thought they'd crack. Why the hell didn't people get it? "My only concern is for Gabby's safety."

"So if we did move her to another location, I'm assuming you're okay with not knowing where she'll be. Kingston can take care of her relocation. I'll assign her a new handler. She'll be completely off your radar. Would that work for you?"

Seething, Jonah glared at his boss. "You're an asshole, Justice."

"Can't argue with the truth." His smile more than a little triumphant, he waved a hand toward the sofa. "Have a seat. Calm down. Want a drink?"

Without waiting for an answer, Justice went to the bar and poured two generous portions of his best scotch.

Jonah raised a brow when Justice handed him the glass. "Either you're about to give me bad news, or you're trying to help me drown my sorrows."

"Neither, actually. I wanted to talk to you about Irelyn."

"You've heard from her?"

"You might say that."

Jonah noted that not only did Justice seem almost happy, a rarity in itself, he hadn't picked up the second drink he'd poured. Tension zipped up his spine as dawning suspicion hit him.

"She's here, isn't she?"

"Yes. I thought it best if I was present when you saw each other again. She—"

"Is quite capable of speaking for herself."

Surging to his feet, Jonah turned to face the woman who'd done the one thing he had been determined to do. Still beautiful beyond description, Irelyn Raine stood before him. Dressed in a white off-the-shoulder blouse and black leggings and her ink-black hair pulled back from her face, she was casually elegant and incredibly lovely. She was also nervous. She was as hard to read as Justice, but he detected a definite uneasiness in her demeanor.

"Hello, Irelyn."

"Good to see you, Jonah."

She accepted the drink Justice handed her, and Jonah noticed the lingering touch of their fingers. Didn't surprise him. Justice might be hard as steel, but when it came to Irelyn, there was a softening. One he might not even be aware of.

She gave Jonah a solemn look. "Grey has told me that you'd likely shoot me when you saw me again. I'm glad to see he was wrong."

"There was only one person I wanted to shoot. You took that away from me."

"For good reason."

"That wasn't your right, Irelyn. It was mine."

"Killing isn't a right, Jonah. It's a burden. One I took on for you."

"I didn't ask you to take it. And killing the man who murdered Teri would not have been a burden."

"That's easy to say until you actually take a life." She took a long swallow of her drink, set the glass back on the bar, and then sat down across from him. "I know you're angry. If I were in your shoes, I would be livid. If you can't forgive me, I completely understand. But you need to know that if I had to do it all over again, I would."

"At least tell me he died knowing the reason."

"He did. The words he heard before his last breath were her name."

"Did he..." Jonah cleared his throat, tried again. "Did he tell you where her head is?"

"No. I'm sorry. He said he didn't know what happened to her body. That once it was done, he left. He mentioned that your father's right-hand man, Cyrus Denton, took possession of her remains."

Pain slashed his heart. Was Denton the man who'd dismembered Teri? If so, she would never be found. Denton had died the same night as Mathias.

"Perhaps it's time to put Teri to rest for good, Jonah."

Justice's voice broke into his tortured thoughts. "Just like that? Put it behind me? Get on with my life."

"What's your alternative?"

"My alternative?" His eyes moved from Justice's and burned into Irelyn's. "My alternative was taken away from me."

He stalked to the elevator door. Before leaving, he turned back to Justice. "Find Gabby a new name and location. Tell her it was my idea. Dealing with her anger will be a damn sight easier than dealing with her death."

The instant the door closed on Jonah's fury, Irelyn turned to Grey. "Well, that went well."

"What did you expect? Gratitude?"

"No. Maybe in time he'll see that I did him a favor."

"Why did you do it?"

"I told you. So he wouldn't have to."

"Because you're a killer and he's not?"

"Do you see it another way?"

"You think of yourself as a killer."

She raised her brow at that. "And you don't?"

"You'll never forgive me for that, will you?"

"Have you forgiven me?"

"You consider the two the same?"

"Why shouldn't I? Isn't that why you made me do it? An eye for an eye?"

"Quoting the Bible now, Irelyn?"

The smile she gave him was both sad and angry. "I think I should go."

"Stay." He blurted it so fast, it was almost incoherent.

She cocked her head. The movement was so familiar, so poignant, Grey's chest went tight with the memories.

"Why should I?"

"Because you want to. Because I want you to. Do you need more than that?"

She rose to her feet and went to him then. Laying a palm on his cheek, she reached up and kissed him softly on the mouth. "I think I do. I think we both need more than that."

Myriad emotions churning through him, it was all he could do not to grab her and make her stay. Make her listen. Instead, Grey watched her walk away once again and wondered if this time might be the last.

Chapter Forty-Two

Willoughby, Wisconsin

Gabby stood in the middle of her living room, the phone gripped so hard in her hand she vaguely wondered if there would be indentions where her fingers were digging in.

"Rudolph Bianchi is dead? You're sure, Grey?"

"Yes. His body was found by his butler yesterday morning."

"But how? Was it an assassination, too?"

"Natural causes. He had a massive heart attack."

Her legs like overcooked asparagus, she collapsed onto the sofa. "I don't know what to think. How to process this. Does this mean it's over? That I'm free?"

"I'm not ready to have you contact the press and announce your whereabouts to the world, but yes, I think very soon we can say this is over. You'll be able to live as Gabriella Mendoza if you like. Or you can stay Jessica Olsen."

It was too much to take in at once. She had just gotten used to being someone else, and now the possibility existed that she could go back to being herself. The mind boggled at the possibilities.

"Does Jonah know?"

"Not yet."

"Can I call him?"

"I thought you might want to. Be prepared, though. He might not be in the best frame of mind."

"What happened?"

"Let's just say that he's revisiting his obsession with taking down Teri's killer."

Teri again. The woman Jonah couldn't forget. How silly for her to think he could love Gabby. Despite Lacey's insistence that Jonah's feelings for Teri wouldn't have stood the test of time, to him, Teri would always be his only love.

As if he hadn't noticed her lack of response, Grey continued. "But if anyone deserves to be able to tell him, you do. He'll be glad to hear good news for a change."

"Do you know where he is?"

"Last I saw him, he was here in Dallas, insisting on getting you relocated somewhere else."

"I'm glad I didn't. Everything went back to normal the next day. My new employer hadn't even heard about the incident. Neither the photograph in the paper nor the news segment on television looked like the old me."

"That's what Lacey told me. So, how are you liking your new job?"

"It's fun. A little monotonous at times, but I'll take that over running for my life any day."

"I hope soon that'll be a thing of the past."

"But you want me to be cautious still. Is there something about this I don't know? Some other threat?"

"Not that I know of. I'm just not fond of coincidences, even happy ones. The deaths of the two people who were your biggest threats coming so close together is a little too convenient for my peace of mind."

Even as much as she wanted to shout about her freedom from the highest building in Willoughby, she agreed with Grey. There was no harm in waiting. Besides, she liked her life right now. The stability after the storm of being on the run was reassuring and calming. Peaceful. There was only one thing missing. One person for whom she would give up all that stability and peace. And he was still in love with another woman.

"Maybe you should tell Jonah instead. He probably doesn't want to hear from me right now."

"I disagree. I think you're exactly who he needs to hear from. The sooner the better."

Grey was right. She should be the one to call Jonah and let him know her nightmare might be over for good. He deserved to hear the news from her.

What would he say? Would he see this as a new beginning not only for her, but also for them? Could she convince him that he was the man she wanted for all time? But even if she did, would that make a difference? Would she learn that it was as she feared? That he had used her need for anonymity as an excuse? Jonah was obviously still in love with his fiancée.

"Gabriella? Everything okay?"

She shook her head to clear it. Keeping Grey Justice on hold while she tried to figure out her love life wasn't the most polite thing to do.

"Sorry. Yes. Just thinking things through."

"So you'll call Jonah?"

"Yes. Thanks, I will. And Grey?"

"Yes?"

"Thank you again for everything. Without you, I'd still be locked away. There's no telling what might have happened to me."

"You're the one who instigated it. I just provided the tools."

She didn't agree but knew there was no point in arguing.

"We'll talk soon. Continue to keep as low a profile as possible until we're sure it's clear."

"I will."

After the call ended, Gabby stared at the phone in her hand. A part of her wanted to call Jonah right away and let him know about Bianchi's death. She knew he would be relieved. Another part hesitated. If she told him and he didn't see the need to change their relationship, how would she deal with that?

Shaking her head at her indecision, Gabby hit the speed-dial key for Jonah. When his voice mail announced he wasn't available, she couldn't decide whether she was relieved or sad.

She wouldn't leave a detailed message. The possibility always existed that it could get into the wrong hands.

"Hey, it's me. Just heard some interesting news. The one we were worried about is no longer a problem." And because she was a coward when it came to telling Jonah what she wanted, she added, "Call me back if you want details, or you can contact your boss."

She held the phone several more seconds, wanting to say something, anything that might change the way things were between them. Finally, realizing that there would be a huge amount of dead silence on the message, she ended the call with nothing more than a simple, "I miss you."

***

Dallas, Texas

Jonah listened to the message three times. He'd been in the shower when she called, and while he hated that he'd missed talking to her, he was glad for the time to think. He didn't like what was going on. His instincts had been honed in prison. Anticipating and expecting trouble at every turn made for a paranoid, uneasy existence, but it had kept him alive.

This was no different. His gut was telling him that no way in hell had they just lucked out with both of Gabby's tormentors having up and died. Luis Mendoza's death had been understandable and less worrisome. There were so many who had wanted him dead. Whether it had been Bianchi or a dozen of his other enemies, a hit had been only a matter of time. But now this? Didn't matter that Rudolph Bianchi was an old, sickly man and could've croaked at any time.

The stink of conspiracy was all over this. Question was, who and why?

Instead of calling Gabby, he punched in Justice's number. Jonah didn't waste time on pleasantries. Justice would be expecting his call.

"Do you believe Bianchi's death is just a convenient coincidence?"

"No."

"Something's up."

"I agree."

"What did you tell Gabby?"

"That she needs to continue to take precautions until we know she's safe."

"How'd she feel about that?"

"I think she's having trouble digesting everything, but she's a smart woman. She won't put down her guard until she's certain."

Holding the phone to his ear, Jonah strode to the closet and pulled out his go bag. The need to ensure Gabby's safety was becoming a living thing. The longer he thought about it, the more concerned he became.

"I'm heading there now. I'll call her on the way."

"The plane's at the airfield, fueled and ready to go, waiting for you."

Jonah huffed out a humorless laugh. "You know me a little too well for my peace of mind."

"I just know what a man does for a woman he loves."

Arguing with him would do no good, especially when he knew Justice spoke the truth. He did love Gabby, and he would do anything for her.

"I'll call you when I get to her apartment."

"You'll find a packet on the plane with Gabby's apartment keys, along with other vital information you might need."

Jonah snorted. "Must be nice to be a know-it-all."

"It helps in times of trouble. I'll let you know if anything develops."

Grabbing a couple extra weapons, Jonah was out of his apartment and striding toward his SUV within minutes. Once he was on the plane, he'd call Gabby and let her know he was coming. He had a feeling the only person who would be surprised that he was headed to her was Gabby herself.

***

Willoughby, Wisconsin

The flight was less than two hours long, but the arrival of the rental car had been delayed. Just to be sure she was safe, he had called Gabby when he boarded the plane, once when he was in the air, and then the minute he landed.

She probably thought he was the most paranoid asshole in the world. Didn't matter. Something wasn't right. He'd been around too long, seen too much evil, to take for granted that Bianchi's death was just a happy coincidence. The more he thought about it, the more certain he became. Until he could get to Gabby, he would not relax.

His mind whirled, backtracked, and then went around again. He had to get to her. Had to protect her, make sure she was safe. He had to—hell, he had to tell her he loved her. Couldn't live without her. If necessary, he'd change his name, too. Whatever it took. He wanted to be with her, no matter what. And if he hadn't been driving, he would have reached up and kicked his own ass for waiting so long to realize just how much she meant to him.

Of course he had loved Teri, but Justice was right. The time had come to let her go. The guilt would always be with him. Since his own father was responsible for her death, how could it not? But guilt accomplished nothing. He wanted a future with Gabby. If she would still have him.

The cellphone beside him rang with Justice's ring tone. Jonah grabbed it and hit speaker. "What's up?"

"Are you at Gabriella's yet?"

"No. I'm about ten minutes away. Why?"

"Get there quicker."

Already speeding, Jonah punched the gas. The urgency in Justice's tone worried Jonah almost as much as the words. "What's wrong?"

"We tracked down the payment Mendoza made to the investigator he hired—the one that killed him. Had to go through several phony accounts before we found the real one. The money went to an account in the Bahamas. Payee was Ivy Roane."

"Dammit. She's not dead."

Jonah's gut clenched. They had feared this might happen. Last year, Ivy Roane, a contract killer, had been hired to destroy the entire Slater family. With Justice's help, Eli and Kathleen had taken down the man responsible for the contract. But Ivy Roane hadn't cared that her employer was dead. She had been determined to carry out the job. She had almost succeeded. With Eli and Kathleen, along with Jonah and a few more of Eli's men, they had successfully foiled Ivy's plan. After being shot multiple times, the woman had plunged into the ocean, miles from land.

"How the hell did she survive?"

"Miracles can happen to even the most evil of people."

"You have any idea how to find her?"

"We're working on it."

"Eli and Kathleen know yet?"

"I was just about to call them. They'll want to up security on everyone."

"Yeah. It'd probably be best if my mother stays in Italy until this is resolved. Is Lacey with her?"

"Yes. I've called her and told her to be on alert. I've got Kingston headed to Wisconsin, too. He can stay at Gabriella's apartment and be prepared for what might go down, while you get her to a safe house."

"I'll take her to my place again."

"That should work."

"So what's Ivy's connection with Mendoza and Bianchi?"

"Both men hired her. Mendoza retained her to find Gabriella. I'm assuming she posed as a private investigator to get to him. Bianchi likely initiated the whole thing."

"So she pretends to be a PI to get to Mendoza. Then she does him and Conti. Then she kills Bianchi?"

"That's the working theory. There was no autopsy on Bianchi, so who knows?"

"But why murder the man? That's not her MO. Murdering clients doesn't exactly get you repeat business."

"I agree. Something's off."

"She's got an agenda, and it somehow involves Gabby."

"Until we figure what the hell is going on, we'll keep everyone on alert."

Jonah ended the call and pressed the accelerator down to the floor. How the hell had Ivy Roane gotten mixed up with Mendoza and Bianchi? What was he missing? She wouldn't have killed Bianchi without benefitting in some way. Killers like her didn't kill just for the fun of it. There had to be some kind of gain.

Who could—

If he hadn't needed to get to Gabby as soon as possible, he would have slammed on the brakes. How the hell had they missed this?

Grabbing the cellphone, he punched Justice's number. The instant the man answered, Jonah said, "I know who's behind it."

CHAPTER
FORTY-THREE

Standing beneath the spray of gushing hot water, Gabby tried to push down the excitement. Just because Jonah was coming didn't mean anything other than he was concerned about her. Given his need to protect and control, she shouldn't have been surprised when he'd called and told her he was on his way. Plus, the other two times as well. Jonah Slater was ever the protector.

But she wanted so much more. She wanted a partner, a lover, a companion, a friend. And she wanted all of those in Jonah. Would he ever want that, too?

It should help that she agreed with some of what he had told her. She hadn't had a chance to live, not truly. She'd never dated anyone. Never had the chance to be free and independent.

But if all the threats were gone and she could finally have the freedom to do all the things she had missed out on, would she still want to be with Jonah? She knew to her soul that the answer was a resounding, one hundred percent yes. She loved him, now and forever. Being out of danger was not going to change her heart.

The guilt he felt over his fiancée's death continued to influence him, preventing him from moving forward. Just because she saw the problem for what it was didn't mean she knew how to fix it.

Finishing the shower, she wrapped a towel around her hair and one around her body. She wanted to be dressed when Jonah arrived…ready for battle. She refused to give up on them. Making him see the light wouldn't be easy, but nothing worthwhile ever was.

Telling herself that her new optimism wasn't a façade to cover heartbreak, she hurriedly dried her hair. The new style was one she never would have considered, but thanks to Lacey's insistence, she had changed her mind. Her hair was five inches shorter and framed her heart-shaped face like a dream. The added golden highlights made her eyes seem darker and more mysterious. And it was much faster and easier to style.

She applied a minimum of makeup and slid into her lingerie. If she hurried, she could order Chinese from the new restaurant the next block over and have dinner waiting when Jonah arrived.

Steering her mind away from how she was going to persuade Jonah to give their relationship a try, Gabby slipped into one of her favorite summer dresses, a white sleeveless sundress with a lovely flared skirt. By habit, she slid the silver bracelet over her hand—the reason she wore it every day barely registered anymore. It was one of several safety features she had suggested. A tracker in a bracelet was much less invasive than having one inserted in her body.

The shoes she'd bought to wear with the dress were the most uncomfortable she'd ever owned, but they made her legs look a mile long. Jonah loved her legs.

Deciding to wait until he knocked on the door to put them on, she finger hooked the shoes by the straps, grabbed her cellphone, and headed to the kitchen.

Preoccupied with finding the takeout menu she'd stashed in a drawer, she didn't notice anything off until she heard the sound of a throat being cleared. Gabby whirled around. A woman she had never seen before stood in the middle of her kitchen. An amused smile on her sultry, exotic face, she was quite possibly the most beautiful woman Gabby had ever seen. She also had the coldest eyes imaginable.

"Who are you?"

The woman laughed, flashing white, perfect teeth fitting for a toothpaste ad. "I'll be honest. After all the things I've heard about you, I assumed you'd either squeal like a little mouse or cower in the corner, whimpering like a puppy." She shook her head. "Men always underestimate women, don't you think?"

Surprise turned to alarm. Her heart in her throat, she looked behind the woman. Where was Chamo?

"If you're looking for the dog, not to worry. He barely felt the tranquilizer dart I shot into him. He'll wake up in time for breakfast tomorrow. There's no fun in harming a defenseless animal. People, on the other hand, are rarely defenseless."

She smiled again, and Gabby knew without a doubt the woman was a cold-blooded killer. But why was she here?

Backing up slightly, Gabby reached into the drawer behind her. The gun, one of five she had stashed around the apartment, was gone.

"If you're looking for your SIG Sauer, I'm afraid it's no longer there. All five of your guns have been confiscated. I have to say, I'm impressed with your arsenal of weapons. They were another pleasant surprise."

The gun might not be there, but the woman had missed the other weapon taped to the top of the drawer. Keeping her face impassive, she slowly eased it from the sleeve.

To distract from any noise she might make, she demanded in an overloud voice,

"Who the hell are you, and what do you want?"

A flush of delight brightened the woman's face. "Considering what your grandfather told me about you, I can't tell you how pleased I am that you're not the mealymouthed, timid creature he believed you to be."

"Luis hired you?"

"Yes, but to be fair, our association didn't live up to his expectations. You see, he hired me to find you and bring you home. I had a different agenda."

"You're the contract killer hired by Bianchi."

Beautiful eyes flashed with surprise. "Okay, now you're just trying to freak me out. No way could you know that."

"It doesn't take a brain surgeon to figure that out. No one had reason to hate Luis more than Rudolph Bianchi."

"Except for you, of course."

"Hiring a sleazy contract killer isn't my style."

"Don't try to get on my bad side by insulting me. I have extremely thick skin."

"Are you here to kill me?"

"Of course not. That would defeat the whole purpose."

"And that purpose is?"

"Turning you over to my employer."

"Both of your employers are dead. There's no one who's trying to find me anymore."

Shrill laughter echoed through the apartment. The eerie noise was so indistinct and odd, Gabby at first thought her mind was playing tricks on her. That hideous laugh was often featured in her nightmares. She told herself the sound was an auditory mirage brought on by fear.

The sound grew louder…closer. And she knew. With the speed of an out-of-control wildfire, a nauseating chill zoomed through her whole body. It couldn't be. It. Could. Not. Be.

The woman shifted slightly, and Gabby got her first glimpse. For the first time in twelve years, the evil monster was in her presence. He looked so different from the memory she had of him that she at first told herself this was someone else. Then she saw his eyes. They were the same. Dull gold with flecks of mud brown gleaming with a terrible light. She remembered those eyes peering down at her, hovering over her.

Don't panic…don't panic. She worked to control her breathing as she tried to hide the horror she was feeling.

Focus on the here and now, not the memories, Gabby. You've trained for this.

Except for the eyes, everything else was different. A scar ran down the left side of his face, causing the corner of his mouth to droop slightly. His nose was bumpy, larger, too, as if it had been broken more than once and hadn't been set correctly. When he was younger, he'd had thin, coal-black hair. The hair was gone, replaced by a multitude of dark, elaborate tattoos. Even his body was different. Twelve years ago, he'd been slender, almost skinny. Now, he looked muscular enough to move a boulder with his broad shoulders. Prison had not been kind to Rudy Bianchi. The ordinary, unattractive man now resembled the brute he was inside.

"Ciao, Bella. It's good to see you at last. Did you receive the gift I sent you?"

He didn't need to explain his words. She knew exactly what he meant. Nausea surged up, but with a strong gust of fury, Gabby fought it back. She would not panic.

Ignoring his reference to the artificial insemination, she asked, "So you and your grandfather hired this woman to kill Luis?"

"Actually, my grandfather encouraged Luis to hire a private investigator to find you. Which he did, never knowing that she was an assassin sent to gather all the intel he had before putting a bullet in his brain."

He grinned, showing the wide space between his front teeth. "And I was the one who recommended this dear lady to my grandfather." He nodded toward the beautiful and deadly woman standing beside him. She looked slightly bored with the whole matter.

"Luis and Rudolph never knew they were hiring their own killers. Though, to be fair, Rudolph kind of did his own thing once he saw me. My grandfather was ever the contrarian."

She turned her attention to the woman again. "You conned them both?"

Eyes the color of a cold winter sky gleamed with pride. "A con within a con within a con. One of the more enjoyable and lucrative jobs I've had."

Gabby took a breath, found her center. She had two things going for her. They didn't know that she could defend herself. And they didn't know that Jonah was on his way here. Between the two of them, these two didn't stand a chance.

Sidling over to the pantry, Gabby reached behind her and into the small bin labeled potatoes where she'd taped her Glock to the inner wall. She touched empty space.

The woman smiled again. "Told you."

Yes, she had, but Gabby had had to make sure.

How far away was Jonah? She had no clue. He had called when his plane landed, but that was almost an hour ago. Could she keep them talking until he arrived? She had only one weapon at her disposal. She needed two.

She directed her gaze to Rudy once more. "You think you're going to take me back to Italy and force a child on me?"

That same creepy laugh erupted from Rudy. "Do you actually think I want a brat? I want what was denied me all those years ago. I got beaten up for my troubles and absolutely no satisfaction. You're a lot older than what I prefer but I'm willing to make an exception." His grin sickly evil, he added, "You owe me, bitch."

Disgust roiled through her, but she refused to give in to the feeling.

"So you weren't in on Rudolph and Luis's plan?"

"Not hardly. My grandfather played yours like a violin. He knew Luis would do anything to get his prize."

"And that prize would be?"

"Wouldn't you like to know?"

The woman standing beside him released a loud sigh. "While this reunion is touching, there's the little matter of what I came here for. Can we please get on with it?"

Gabby latched on to the woman's words. An ominous feeling joined her fear. "What did you come for?"

"Why, Jonah Slater, of course."

Why hadn't she seen it before? Jonah had told her about the woman who'd been hired to kill all the Slaters. They had believed she was dead. Jonah had described the woman perfectly. "You're Ivy Roane."

Another beautiful smile flashed across her face. "I see my reputation precedes me."

"I wouldn't call that a compliment."

"But you're not me." She held up a slender, perfectly manicured hand. "I'll save you the insult. We're both glad we're not each other."

The gun still pointed at Gabby, the woman shifted her gaze to Rudy. "I have things I need to set up. If we're to proceed with your plan, I suggest we get started."

There was a plan? Gabby told herself that was a good thing. That meant she would have some time to come up with her own. Because, dammit, she would not be taken by Rudy Bianchi, and Jonah would not be killed by this sleazy contract killer.

Wanting to give Jonah more time, she continued Rudy's distraction. "What prize did my grandfather want from Rudolph?"

"The Rossi sapphire, of course. The Rossis presented it to Rudolph when Flora jilted him. Your grandfather always resented that he had it."

Hard to be insulted or outraged when your life was on the line, but she was. All of this trouble just for a jewel? "So my child was to be a payment?"

"The gem is worth millions." He gave her a dirty up-and-down look. "Much more than any brat you could produce."

"Enough!" Ivy snapped.

Knowing she couldn't wait any longer to act, Gabby swung her arm up and threw the knife. Her satisfaction at Rudy's squeal of outrage was short-lived when a bullet ripped through her arm.

"Dammit, don't kill her," Ivy snapped.

"The bitch stabbed me."

"You should learn how to move faster."

"She's gonna die now."

"Not yet, you idiot," Ivy snapped. "She's got a job to do."

Holding her arm, Gabby fought the piercing pain as her eyes searched for an escape. They had her cornered, but if she could—

The small pop sounded like an explosion in the silence. It hadn't been a gunshot. The sound was too hollow. She glanced down at her bleeding arm. A dart-like object protruded inches from where the bullet had entered.

Her vision blurred, and a numb feeling spread throughout her body. Her muscles went heavy, useless. She tried to speak, to scream. Nothing happened. Her legs folded, and she felt herself falling. Strong arms caught her before she landed. The hideous sound of Rudy Bianchi's laughter followed her into unconsciousness. Her last thought was a silent scream for Jonah.

***

He didn't bother knocking. Using the key from the packet Justice had provided, he pushed the door open, gun at the ready. The instant he entered, he noticed two things immediately. The scent of an expensive perfume that he knew didn't belong to Gabby—she didn't wear perfume—and the silence. If Chamo had been in the apartment, he'd be having a barking fit. The emptiness screamed at him.

She was gone.

Even though he was sure, he still went from room to room. He found Chamo in the guest bedroom, unconscious but unharmed. His breathing and heartbeat were good. He didn't bother to tell himself that since Ivy didn't kill the dog, that meant something. He knew better. A killer had Gabby. One who could kill without batting an eye.

His first call was to Justice. "She's gone."

Justice released a soft curse, then said, "I'll check the video feed and get the trackers activated."

His heart leaped. "She has a tracker?"

"Yes. On a bracelet she wears every day. Plus, she has an additional one on her phone. She was the one who suggested them, along with giving Lacey a key to her apartment."

Jonah's heart clenched. That was his Gabby. Incredibly brave and ever practical.

"Can you tell how long ago she was taken?"

"Within the hour. I called her when I landed."

"We should have her location in minutes."

"I'm taking her dog to the vet. Looks like he's been drugged."

"I'll be back with you soon."

Jonah gently lifted Chamo into his arms and carried him to his car. The dog whined a little but never opened his eyes. He was a beautiful, loyal companion to Gabby. She would be heartbroken if he didn't recover.

Five minutes later, he was delivering Chamo into the capable hands of an emergency vet's office. He gave a vague explanation of what he thought had happened, and the veterinarian assured him that they would take good care of the dog until Gabby could pick him up.

Returning to Gabby's apartment, he searched every room to determine how it might have gone down. He found drops of blood in the kitchen in two different places, with no trail between them. Two people injured? Gabby and Ivy?

A sick feeling was growing in his gut. When he had been in prison, Mathias had put out a contract on him. Cyrus Denton, Mathias's head henchman, hadn't liked the fact that Mathias was trying to have his own son killed. Denton had used some of his contacts to get Jonah to a safe place.

Did Rudy Bianchi have the same kind of pull? Jonah had already determined that Rudy was behind the whole thing, but was there more? Money could pay for a lot of things, including a get-out-of-jail-free card. Was Rudy with Ivy? Had they abducted Gabby together?

There had been little to no struggle. Gabby could defend herself, but two armed attackers would be harder to fight off. They had likely taken her by surprise and held guns on her. A tranquilizer had been used on Chamo. Had Gabby been able to get off a couple of shots, or did the blood on the kitchen floor belong to her?

Only by concentrating on what needed to be done was he able to push back the panic surging inside him. He could not lose her...he wouldn't. He didn't care what Rudy Bianchi and Ivy Roane had cooked up between them. They wouldn't win. Not this time.

CHAPTER FORTY-FOUR

The pain in her arm woke her. Disoriented, she worked to get her mind focused on what was going on. Voices were close… both spoke English. The man's was heavily accented Italian. The woman's held a hint of Irish. Reality crashed and panic zoomed to the surface. Rudy Bianchi and Ivy Roane. They had taken her. Jonah wouldn't know what had happened. He wouldn't—

Wait. Yes, he would. He would know, and he would come for her. She needed to stay alive, and she needed to find out where they were taking her and what they planned.

The two killers sat in the front seat like normal people on an outing, and were either unaware or uncaring that she could hear everything they said. She feared it was the latter, as the plan they discussed was simplistic but as deadly as they come. Jonah was to be lured. Ivy would then make an example of him to his family. Apparently, she had decided to forgo vengeance for all the other Slaters. Jonah would be the sacrificial lamb.

And Rudy. Rudy planned to enjoy her the way he hadn't had the chance twelve years ago.

Neither she nor Jonah was expected to survive this ordeal.

With her wrists and ankles zip-tied, duct tape covering her mouth, and a bullet wound in her arm, she had little choice but to wait until she got the chance to escape. Attacking them now would only get her shot again.

There was hope. Grey would be tracking her location. Her bracelet was intact. Also, based on what Ivy had described as her plan to lure Jonah, the woman had Gabby's phone. Both items held trackers. Plus, the camera hidden in the doorframe at her apartment would reveal her attackers' identities.

And while it was only a matter of time before she was found, Gabby didn't intend to wait. A trap was being set for Jonah, and she could not allow that to happen.

She imagined all the things that might be going through his mind right now. He would want to save her, that was a given. But what kinds of torture was he putting himself through? Even though this was a totally different situation, he would no doubt compare this to Teri's abduction. And he would do everything in his power to rescue her without an ounce of concern for himself.

While she appreciated and loved him for his self-sacrificing heroism, she didn't intend him to do this on his own. Or even with assistance from Grey's people. She was going to do everything she could to save herself. It was what Raiza would expect of her, but more important, it was what she expected of herself.

She could almost hear Raiza's voice whispering in her ear. *Wait. Watch. Act.* That set in her mind, Gabby tamped down her fear and pain as she continued to listen.

"The house is down this road, just a couple more miles."

"I still don't like that we didn't take her back to Rome. I have a special place I'd already picked out. No one would've ever found her."

Ivy restrained herself from releasing a disgusted sigh. Maintaining a pleasant demeanor around this creep was getting harder.

She would be glad when this job was over. The money might be good, but there was just so much whining she could put up with. This freak was supposed to have killed at least six girls, but she couldn't imagine him having enough gumption to harm anyone. Yes, he looked the part, but from what she could tell, he was a spoiled child hiding in a giant's body.

"If you had planned to keep her longer, taking her there would have made sense. But you said yourself you only want her for a few days."

"Yes, but I have dreamed of this for a long time. Having her exactly the way I imagined would make this much more pleasurable."

Talking sense to him was a waste of time, so she didn't bother. "Turn right at this road. The house is about half a mile from here. It's perfect for what we need. Isolated but no trees or bushes. We'll see Slater long before he makes it inside."

As Rudy made the turn, he glanced over his shoulder at the woman lying in the backseat. "I've got what I wanted. Slater's your problem, not mine."

Ha. That's what he thought. If let loose, Jonah Slater would make mincemeat of Rudy Bianchi. She had only one goal—to kill a Slater. And this one was the one she wanted to kill most. He had been the one to shoot her in the head. Even though the bullet had only grazed her scalp, she had bled profusely. If not for a local fisherman spotting her in the water and pulling her out, she would have either drowned or been eaten by sharks. It was way past time for her to return the favor to Jonah Slater. Only her aim would be truer than his had been. The bastard would be dead before he hit the floor.

Before they'd entered Gabriella's apartment, she had insisted the money owed to her be paid in full. She also wanted to get a hold of that sapphire. For such a braggart, he had been ridiculously closemouthed about the thing. If the jewel was indeed worth millions, then she had one more reason for wanting Rudy dead.

Of course, if she killed him, there was always the risk of ruining her reputation. People tended to balk at hiring a killer who might turn on them. She was willing to take the risk, though. The money she'd made with this job, plus the millions she could make off the jewel, would go a long way in easing any unemployment woes.

The house appeared. Late afternoon had turned to dusk. It had rained earlier, and now a thick fog was settling around the old two-story farmhouse. Peeling white paint and black shutters hanging haphazardly from the soiled windows completed the picture of a secluded and desolate structure. The setting couldn't have been more perfect.

She had rented the house a couple of weeks ago. The seventies décor was hideously outdated, but for their purposes, it couldn't have been better. No one around for miles to hear those pesky hair-raising screams some people tended to make when they were being tortured.

Not that she planned any kind of torture herself. Not her thing. One shot through Slater's heart ought to take care of her part. Anything more complicated or fancy and there could be problems. She'd waited too long to accomplish this goal. It was time to get the job done and get on with her life.

"Park around back. You can carry her in through the kitchen. There's a bedroom off the kitchen."

"I need a lot of room."

She wasn't even going to ask why. "Then you might want to carry her upstairs. There's a big room on the right when you get to the landing."

Grunting his approval, Rudy pulled around back and parked. Ivy got out of the vehicle. She had plenty of time to get things in order for her meeting with Slater. And while she was doing that, Rudy would be out of her hair, enjoying himself.

"Hold on. I need to make a quick recording for Slater."

She clicked record on the girl's iPhone, shooting Gabriella from several angles. Her eyes fluttered, and Ivy figured she was feigning unconsciousness. Didn't matter. She was tied up like a steer. No way could she get loose.

Satisfied, she nodded at Bianchi. The girl was his to do with what he wanted.

If she'd had a conscience, she might have spared a moment of pity for what lay ahead for Gabriella Mendoza. Since she had none, she walked away from the vehicle without a second glance.

CHAPTER
FORTY-FIVE

Jonah paced Gabby's small living room, waiting for Justice's call. The fear was there, so real and palpable he could feel its icy fingers clawing at his chest. He knew Gabby was tough and resilient. She had been through so much and had conquered every challenge put before her. She would survive this ordeal, too.

But God help him, he needed to get to her!

The instant his phone buzzed, he barked, "What do you have?"

"We were right. Both Bianchi and Roane were there. Cameras revealed Gabriella was unconscious when Bianchi carried her out the door."

"Do you know where they are?"

"A little community called Walcott Creek about an hour away from you. Looks like they've got her in an old farmhouse. I'm reading the public records as we speak. The house was rented a couple of weeks ago by a woman who claimed she wanted the place to be alone. Said she was writing a horror story."

His jaw tight, Jonah grabbed his weapons and left the apartment. Figuring the stairs would be faster, he bypassed the elevator and ran down the stairs.

"Send me the address."

"I will, but—"

"Don't start with me, Justice. I'm not waiting for Kingston."

"I didn't figure you would, but you know this is a trap."

"Not yet it's not. They won't be expecting me. They have no idea I'm in the area."

"Maybe so, but Kingston is on his way. He'll be there in a couple of hours. If you—"

"Fine." Throwing the bag into the passenger seat of the car, Jonah jumped in, started the engine, and slammed on the gas. "Send him on. The more the merrier. I'm not waiting, though."

"Law enforcement in that rural of an area is scarce, but I can—"

"Gabby has a better chance if I go in alone and surprise them."

"Dammit, Jonah. Getting killed won't bring Teri back."

"This has nothing to do with Teri."

"The hell it doesn't. You're still hung up on not being able to save one woman you love, and you're going to get yourself killed trying to save another woman you love."

"Stop the psychobabble and send me the damn address."

"Already sent. Just…" Justice blew out a harsh breath. "Just remember that Gabriella and a lot of other people need you to stay alive."

Ending the call, Jonah entered the address Justice had sent into the GPS on the dashboard. Travel time was a little over an hour. Unless he hit a roadblock, he intended to beat that time by half.

***

Gabby didn't struggle as she was carried upside down over Rudy's shoulder. Her arm throbbed with an unending ache, but she told herself when the time came she could use it. Every ounce of her strength would be needed to bring down this gorilla.

As she bounced around on Rudy's shoulder, she heard Ivy in another part of the house. She was no doubt setting her trap for Jonah. She would use the video she'd recorded as a lure. Gabby's cellphone had Jonah's number stored under JS. It would be no problem for Ivy to figure that out. She would send the recording, and he would come.

Could she take care of both Rudy and Ivy before Jonah arrived?

She mentally rolled her eyes. *One at a time, Gabby.*

More than aware that she was doing everything she could not to think about what Rudy was planning to do once he got her to the bedroom, she concentrated on her surroundings. Being upside down made that a little more challenging.

The first room they entered smelled like stale coffee and garbage. The tile floor was old and cracked, as was the wood paneling on the walls. Shag carpeting in another room told her that decorating was not a priority for whoever owned the house.

They started up the stairway. With every creak of the wood, Gabby became more and more tense. She didn't know if Rudy planned to begin his "fun" as soon as he put her down, but she had to be ready. It didn't matter that he was almost twice her size. She knew where to hit and how hard.

When he reached the top of the stairs, he had to stop and catch his breath, which further encouraged her. He might look like a muscle-bound wrestler and be stronger than an ox, but he wasn't fit, nor was he fast. She could definitely work with that.

A door creaked open. The bedroom where he said he needed room for what he had planned. Gabby breathed in a silent, bracing breath, readying herself for battle. He had gotten away with almost killing her before. This time, things would be different.

***

Ivy gazed in the mirror, a slight smile lifting her full lips. While Rudy had his fun, she was preparing for her own. The outfit she'd chosen for this first part was from her favorite designer. The formfitting light peach maxi dress showed only the slightest hint of cleavage but had a long slit up the right side. When she walked, it opened enough to reveal a peek of her long, sleek leg. The dress was classy and sophisticated, but also sexy. Just like the woman who wore it.

She allowed her hair to curl around her shoulders but pulled the strands back just enough to show the lovely diamond earrings dripping from her ears.

She would, of course, change in plenty of time for the final confrontation, but she wanted Jonah to see that she was alive, well, and still incredibly beautiful. He needed to see that his bullet hadn't caused the damage he had hoped. Ivy Roane was not only alive, she was thriving like never before. The man needed to know how badly he had failed.

He would fail again.

The recording of an unconscious Gabriella was only a few seconds—there was no need for more. The girl was easily identifiable. Besides, this wasn't about Gabriella at all. She was just a tool to be used. This was all about Ivy and the hatred she had for the Slaters. She would dangle the bait, and when Slater arrived, she'd yank the hook. He wouldn't know what hit him.

One last lipstick touch-up and she was all set. Turning away from the gorgeous woman in the mirror, she picked up the girl's iPhone. Really? JS? How incredibly careless. She had originally planned to send an email with an attachment to Eli Slater's business and make her demands known. This way was so much better, as she could target the person she wanted most.

She clicked open the JS contact and then touched the FaceTime icon. In seconds, Jonah Slater's ruggedly handsome face appeared.

"Who is this? Where's Gabby?"

"Sorry, darling. Gabby's a bit tied up right now. And how very sweet that you have a nickname for our girl."

"Where is she?"

"Not so fast, Jonah. Please tell me you remember me. My ego just couldn't take the rejection."

"Ivy Roane."

The furious way he whispered her name, blended with the glittering fury in his eyes, caused delightful shivers up her spine. He might be a thousand miles away in Texas, but the man had a potent charisma that she found incredibly exciting. The image of a nude, tied-up Jonah Slater flashed through her mind, and she mentally adjusted her timeline. There was no harm in extending their time together. She had never done that before, but she was willing to make an exception for Jonah Slater. And why shouldn't she have a bit more fun than usual with a kill? She had certainly earned it.

"Miss me, Jonah?"

"What the hell have you done with Gabby?"

"Do check the text I sent you. The recording isn't the highest quality, but I think the message will come across loud and clear."

She waited patiently, knowing he would be checking his text and seeing the lovely, unconscious Gabriella all tied up.

The recording was only nine seconds long. Either he watched it several times, or he couldn't bring himself to speak. She imagined it was a bit of both.

At last, his face appeared on the screen again. "What do you want?"

A rush of triumph flushed through her. This was what she had lived for, why she had worked so hard to recover. The pain and agony she saw in his eyes were exactly as she had dreamed.

"We have some unfinished business to resolve."

"Where the hell is Gabby? What have you—"

"Really, Jonah. You do have a one-track mind. While you're dillydallying, poor Gabriella is becoming reacquainted with an old flame. Would you like to see video feed of that, too? I'm sure Rudy wouldn't mind."

"What do you want?"

The fear in his voice made her want to laugh. She had anticipated that Jonah would care for the girl, but this was so much better.

"You're in love with our dear girl, aren't you? How absolutely marvelous." She sighed. "I do love a good rescue story. Will you arrive on your white steed, sword in hand, ready to slay the dragon, and save the day? How very romantic."

"Damn you, tell me what you want."

"A trade, of course. You for her."

"Where and when?"

"Now, now, we're getting ahead of ourselves once again. Here are the rules. You come alone. If I see even the slightest hint that you've brought someone with you, the girl gets a bullet between her lovely eyes. I don't imagine you would be able to overcome the guilt of that, would you?"

"How do I know you won't kill her anyway?"

"You don't. Rest assured, though, she will die if you don't come. Are you willing to take that chance?"

"Where?"

"I'll text you the address. Don't keep me waiting too long. I can already hear our girl screaming."

She clicked off the call and settled back into her chair. Even taking the Slater private jet, travel time would take a couple of hours. Then he would have to find some transportation. Still, she would take no chances. The Slaters were a sneaky bunch. She didn't trust that he wouldn't send someone in his stead.

Time to set up for scene two.

***

Jonah parked a quarter mile from the house and ran the rest of the way. Though his first instinct was to smash through the door, he'd be dead before he took three steps inside. Just because they didn't know he was coming didn't mean they wouldn't be prepared. Ivy Roane was a trained killer—she would expect the unexpected. And since her one goal was to kill Jonah, he couldn't take the chance of dying. If he died, then so did Gabby.

Rudy Bianchi wasn't a trained killer, but what he lacked in knowledge and skill, he more than made up for in fucked-up craziness. No way in hell would Jonah underestimate either of them.

He could see why Ivy had chosen this location. Not only did the ramshackle house look as though a mass murder had already occurred here, but there was no place to hide. No trees to stand behind, no bushes either. The place was out in the open. Anyone looking for a threat would see him coming. When he did go in, he'd have to go in hard and fast.

Fortunately, trees surrounded the outer edges of the property. Jonah crashed through the woods, uncaring of the sounds he made. He was far enough away that no one could hear him. When he had a good view of both the front and the back, he stopped. Dropping his weapons bag, he took out the field binoculars and scanned the house. Three entry points, front and back doors, plus a cellar door at the back, which might be his best bet. An SUV was parked in the back. He saw no movement, but the house blazed with lights. Keeping a low profile didn't worry them, which told him that either they didn't care if anyone happened by, or they believed they were so isolated that no one would notice. He was betting on the second.

When Ivy called, he'd pulled off onto the side of the road. The last thing he wanted was for her to see or hear something that would get her suspicions up. She needed to believe he was still far away, preferably Dallas. The video had been hard to watch, as she had intended. Seeing Gabby's pale, unconscious face, the tape across her mouth, the blood on her arm, he had wanted to shout his fury. Why the hell had he let her go? If she had stayed with him, they never would have found her.

The cellphone in his pocket buzzed with Justice's ring tone. Jonah pushed the regret down where it belonged. Castigating himself for his poor choices would not save Gabby's life.

He held the phone to his ear as he unzipped his weapons bag. "Yeah?"

"Here's what we know. Bianchi escaped about a month ago. Had a visitor come in, and they traded places. Idiots had no idea he'd escaped till now. As far as we could tell, Rudolph didn't know about it either."

This didn't surprise him. The most bizarre shit he'd ever seen had been while he was in prison. Overcrowding, lack of training, and carelessness could make for a deadly combination.

"There's a worldwide BOLO out for him."

"Doesn't matter. He won't survive this encounter."

"Understood."

"You have the blueprints?"

"Just texted them. Kingston is less than fifteen minutes away."

"I'm not waiting. He can come in when he gets here and help with the cleanup. Either way, I'll call you when it's over."

There was silence and then, "I'll talk to both you and Gabriella soon."

"Roger that."

Setting the phone to silent, he pulled up the blueprints and studied them as he dressed, then strapped on his weapons. Since stealth and speed were a necessity, he opted for his SIG P226 and a KA-BAR knife sheathed and strapped to his hip. A Bersa Thunder 380 CC, compact but deadly, went into his ankle holster.

The blueprints confirmed his earlier thoughts. The cellar had a stairway and door that led to the kitchen. It was his best bet to get inside without getting caught.

He grabbed up his binoculars again to take another quick scan. Still no movement. Only one light was on upstairs. A chill zipped up his spine. This was where Bianchi had taken Gabby. He didn't ask himself how he knew. *He knew.*

A blood-curdling scream cracked the silence of the night. His heart in his throat, Jonah took off running. Stealth be damned.

CHAPTER FORTY-SIX

Huffing and puffing like he'd just run up a mountainside, Rudy dropped Gabby onto the bed. Since her hands and legs were bound, she did what was expected of her. She rolled around on the bed and moaned beneath the tape on her mouth. The arm she'd been shot in had gone numb, but the bounce on the bed woke the pain with a vengeance. She told herself that was a good thing. Pain she could work with. Numb meant useless.

"Do you know how long I've dreamed of this, Gabriella? The ones I had before you were merely practice. The ones after you were sloppy seconds. Everything else was practice for what I'm going to do to you."

Gabby lay on the bed and stared up at the monster she'd feared for years. This was the man she'd envisioned while training. Every punch to a face, kick to a belly, and stomp to a head had been aimed at Rudy Bianchi. And though he looked different from her memories and nightmares, he was still the same slimy bastard she'd longed to destroy.

An icy calmness washed over her. Pain disappeared, fear vanished. Everything became crystal clear. All the events and hardships she had been through in her life had led her to this time, this moment. Every night she'd woken up screaming. Every tear she'd shed. Raiza's training and support. Jonah's strength and encouragement. And her own indefatigable spirit. All of these had culminated in her becoming the woman she was now. The woman who would finally get her revenge.

She gave Rudy a glare filled with all the loathing she felt.

His grin was crooked because of the scar, but no less creepy. He leaned over her. "Here, let me remove the tape. I remember how wonderful your screams sounded."

Her fury and hatred were so great, she barely registered the pain as he ripped the tape from her mouth.

"You're the most forgettable man I've ever met, but much uglier than I remember."

The outrage in his eyes would have been funny if she'd be in a humorous mood. She wasn't. This was serious. She needed to get rid of this creep and get downstairs. Jonah would be coming soon, and she needed to be ready to help him.

"You're going to regret those words."

In a way, he was right. For right now, he needed to see her as weak and terrified. Putting on her most convincing act, she shivered. "Don't hurt me, please."

"I'm going to do more than that."

She waited. The urge to jump up and ram her head into his gut was strong, but the risk of injury was too great. Patience would pay off.

He leaned forward again. His giant fingers grabbed the top of her dress, clearly intending to rip it off her body. Using her upper back as leverage, she kicked with both feet as hard as she could. A pain-filled grunt was followed by a shrill shriek loud enough to rattle the windows.

With a fierce, quick pull, she broke the ties at her wrists and then released a shrill scream at the agony in her arm. Pain increased her rage, kept her focused. She bent down, snapped her ankle ties and jumped off the bed. Rudy was still struggling to get back on his feet. Before he was halfway up, she jumped him, taking him down again. His head slammed into the floor with a satisfying thud.

Roaring with anger, Rudy rolled over, pinning Gabby to the floor. His face blood-red with fury, he swung a fist toward her jaw. She managed to jerk her head back, avoiding the brunt of the impact, but he still managed to clip her chin. Her ears rang, and her head and heart thundered.

Giant hands went for her throat. Her hands on his upper arms, she held him away from her body, then in a move she'd practiced a thousand times, she grabbed hold of his right wrist and forearm, trapping them against her. At the same time, she hooked his right leg with her ankle, bucked her body upward, and flipped him. The instant his back hit the floor, she delivered a swift series of punishing blows to his face, each blow a targeted hit designed to stun and impair. After a dozen or so, she sprang to her feet.

Barely conscious, face a bloody mess, Rudy no longer looked like the monster of her nightmares. He was a pitiful excuse for a human being whom she had just beaten to a pulp. She had to get out of here before she killed him. As much as she wanted him dead, she refused to let him force her into being his killer. He didn't deserve a quick death.

Turning, she searched for something to secure him. Her eyes latched on to the bedside lamp. Her mind on her task, she never saw the giant hand that swiped at her. A stunning blow on the back of her head sent her crashing to the floor. Shrieking and screaming, she kicked at him as he grabbed her ankle and dragged her toward him.

"You're dead, bitch."

She kicked hard, heard a crunch, felt the warm splatter of blood. His grip on her foot loosened, and she scrambled to her feet. Not wasting any time, she grabbed the lamp and whirled around. Rudy was somehow standing again but was teetering, ready to fall. The crunch she had heard was his nose, which was now a bloody mass of flesh. Swinging the lamp, she watched his eyes widen briefly as he registered what was coming. The glass dome crashed into his skull. His eyes rolled back in his head, and he dropped like a rock at her feet.

Sobbing breaths wheezing from her lungs, Gabby stood over him, working with all her might not to collapse on top of him. She had to get out of here. Ivy was downstairs, preparing a death trap for Jonah. She couldn't let that happen.

She drew in another breath, then another. As she calmed, her body began to register aches in various places. She embraced the pain, knowing it'd help her stay conscious and focus on her next steps.

Swiftly wrapping the cord around Rudy's wrists and ankles, she tied it in a crude knot. Her heart pounded in a frantic rhythm. Something was telling her to hurry, a sixth sense warning that more danger was imminent.

She took another quick look around, cursing the fact that Rudy had no weapons on him. He had been relying on his strength to control her. Gabby didn't waste time on wishes. She had to get—

A loud crash downstairs had her head swinging around. And then, "Gabby!"

Jonah! He was here. And walking into a trap!

Empty-handed, Gabby sprinted out of the room.

The scream he'd heard was one of agony. Crashing into the door like a freight train should get their attention away from Gabby. He stopped in the middle of a small hallway. The woman he had hoped to never see again was walking down the stairs toward him, an HK45 pistol in her hand and an ugly sneer on her face.

"You Slaters have the absolute worst timing," Ivy drawled. "It should have taken you hours to get here."

"Where is she, bitch?"

"Now that's just rude. You don't knock, you don't ask how I am. I—"

"I asked you a question. Where's Gabby?"

"She's preoccupied at the moment. While she and Rudy are getting reacquainted, you and I have some unfinished business."

"Get the hell out of my way."

"I don't think so."

Jonah didn't bother with another threat. He had to get to Gabby. He fired at the same time she did. The bullet slammed into his chest, knocking him back several feet and into the doorjamb. He vaguely acknowledged that he was thankful he was wearing Kevlar. The breath was knocked out of his lungs, but that was all. He was disoriented for only a second, his dazed mind telling him to get his ass up. He needed to save Gabby.

"You've ruined my favorite dress, you bastard!"

A bright red bloom of blood covered Ivy's right side. She was still standing, her hand over the wound.

Jonah lifted his gun again. Something moved behind Ivy. His heart stopped, and the breath he'd just gotten back left his body again.

Even as a small voice whispered to him that she was still alive, he knew if he lived to be a hundred, he would never get this nightmare vision out of his head. What might have been a white dress at one time was covered in blood and barely hanging on her body. Her face was deathly white, but her eyes…her eyes gleamed with life and purpose.

Sensing her presence, Ivy made a quick turn, swinging her gun toward Gabby.

"Gabby! Get back!"

Like an avenging angel, Gabby shouted as she flew toward Ivy at the same moment Jonah fired off another round.

His mind screaming, Jonah raced to where both women lay on the steps, neither of them moving.

Jonah's voice, thick with anguish, woke her. She blinked up at him. His eyes were wild, his face devoid of color. "Jonah? What's wrong?"

"Where are you hurt?"

"Hurt? What—"

Memory returned in a flash. Rudy Bianchi. And Ivy. Where was Ivy? She tried to sit up, but Jonah held her shoulders, preventing her from moving. "Where's Ivy?"

"She's dead."

"You're sure?"

"One hundred percent this time. Now tell me where you're hurt."

"What about Rudy? I left him tied up and unconscious upstairs."

"I'll get to him in a minute. First, tell me where you're hurt. You've got blood all over you."

"Most of it is Rudy's."

"That's my girl," he whispered. "But you are hurt. Where?"

"My left arm. I think there might be a bullet in it. Kind of numb right now. The rest are just bruises and stuff."

He lifted her in his arms and carried her into the living room. Laying her on the couch, he quickly checked her arm. "Looks like it's stopped bleeding, but try not to move. I'm going to check on Rudy, make sure he's still out. Kingston should be here any minute. The police, too."

She cupped his cheek with one hand. "You're okay, too?"

"I'm fine." He took her hand and pressed a kiss to her palm. "Be right back."

They had both survived. She lay on the couch and closed her eyes, allowing peace to wash over her. She could barely comprehend that this was over. All of it. If—

Her eyes popped open. Something wasn't right. An odd feeling nagged at her, her senses telling her she had forgotten an important detail. She could practically hear Raiza's voice telling her to get her ass up and—

She shot up from the sofa. When she had been in the apartment with Rudy and Ivy, she had thrown a knife and hit Rudy in the upper part of his body. He had pulled it out. But what did he do with it?

Think, Gabby, think. He had pulled the knife out of his shoulder and…put it in his back pocket. She hadn't seen any kind of weapon in the bedroom. Nor had she seen a knife in his back pocket.

Where was it?

She took a step, had to make an abrupt stop as the room whirled around her. Grabbing hold of the closest object, the back of a chair, she steadied herself. The numbness in her arm had been replaced with a bone-throbbing ache. The rest of her body had joined in symphony, making her one big ache. Didn't matter. She had to get to Jonah.

She walked into the hallway and spotted Ivy sprawled on the stairs on her side. Blood pooled around her body. Her beauty destroyed, she was now a mass of bone and blood. Jonah's second shot had blown off most of the left side of her face.

Sidestepping the body, Gabby ran up the stairs. Her head jerked up at a growling curse. Jonah and Rudy were on the landing, arms wrapped around each other, locked in a death battle.

Gabby looked around for a weapon—anything she could use. Her gaze turned back to Ivy. The woman had been a trained killer. Surely she would have a secondary weapon somewhere.

Knowing she had only seconds, she raced down to Ivy and ran her hands up and down the woman's body. Nothing. Holding back a sob, she rolled her over on her back. There had to be something that—

Her hand touched her outer thigh. She jerked the dress up. A holster, holding a Ruger LCR revolver, was attached to her right thigh. Sliding the gun from the holster, Gabby ran back up the stairs, praying she wasn't too late.

They were still wrapped in a life-or-death struggle. Rudy had Jonah pinned to the wall. The knife she had forgotten about was gripped in his hand and was covered in blood. She already knew the blood was Jonah's.

"Jonah!" she screamed. "Get away from him!"

Rudy twisted his head toward her, shouted, "You're next, bitch!"

Taking advantage of Rudy's distraction, Jonah wedged an arm between them and pushed hard. Rudy stumbled backward, and without a second thought, Gabby unloaded the gun into his chest.

She didn't wait to see him fall. Jonah was slumped against the wall, covered in blood. She went to her knees, grabbed his face in her hands. "Jonah. Look at me."

"He's dead."

"Yes, he's dead. Come on. You need to lie down."

"You're finally free."

"Yes." Tears poured from her eyes. "Thanks to you, I'm finally free. Now let's get you somewhere to lie down."

"Think I'll just do that here." He slid down the wall and landed with a thud.

She went to her knees beside him and looked into his eyes. They were glassy and full of pain.

"Where are you hurt?"

He gave her a crooked smile. "Be easier to say where I don't hurt."

Gabby fought back the panic. She couldn't lose him. She couldn't.

"I need to find something to staunch the bleeding."

"Don't. Just..."

"Jonah? Stay with me. Please."

His eyes closed, another small smile curving his mouth. "You did most of it. You're a badass."

"I—"

A noise, like glass breaking, sounded downstairs. Gabby squeezed Jonah's hand and then ran to the top of the stairway. Wyatt Kingston stood at the open door.

"Wyatt! Hurry! Jonah's hurt!"

She ran back to where Jonah was sitting. He was slumped over, his face death white, his eyes closed.

Her mind screamed in denial.

CHAPTER FORTY-SEVEN

Madison, Wisconsin
Madison Memorial Hospital

He existed on a cloud. Muffled voices, anxious whispers, and tear-filled voices were distant and indistinct. There was pain, but it existed like a far-away entity, distant, but also threatening.

Hands touched him, some competent, others gentle and kind. A couple of times, he felt kisses on his brow. And once he felt soft lips on his mouth. That one had made him want to smile, because the lips belonged to someone he loved.

As long as he stayed here, cloaked in this puffy cloud, he didn't have to face the pain. Didn't—

The face of an angel appeared in his mind. Gabby. Beautiful, courageous, wise beyond her years. But tears pooled in her chocolate-brown eyes. She was crying. He didn't know why or what. He knew only that he needed to do something to stop them. Seeing Gabby cry tore at his heart like nothing else could.

With Herculean effort, Jonah left his place of peace and returned to the pain-filled brightness of the living.

"Welcome back."

A middle-aged woman with twinkling blue eyes beamed down at him. She was a stranger but seemed amazingly pleased to see him.

He opened his mouth to ask her what was going on and realized he couldn't. Something was blocking his ability to speak. A wave of anger washed over him. What the hell was going on?

"Now, now. I can see you're getting upset. Don't you worry. The doctor is on the way, and we'll get that tube out of you. Just relax."

Wasn't easy, but unless he wanted to pull the damn thing out himself, he would wait. But they needed to hurry. He had questions, and he wanted answers. Where was Gabby? Was she okay? How badly had she been hurt? Were Rudy Bianchi and Ivy Roane really dead? What had Gabby gone through before he arrived?

What happened after he collapsed was a blur of images and frantic voices. What happened before would be ingrained in his memory for all time. He was in love with a warrior woman. There was no other way to describe Gabriella Mendoza. She had faced her worst nightmare, the monster who'd taken her innocence and almost killed her, and won. Hell, she'd beat the shit out of him and then tied him up in a neat little bow.

Bianchi had surprised him, though. Jonah had eased open the door, expecting to find the bastard still tied up, hopefully unconscious. Instead he'd found an empty room. He had been about to back out and shout a warning to Gabby when he'd felt a presence behind him. He'd twisted around but not in time to avoid the knife going into his lower back. Lucky for Bianchi because it had just missed the protection of his Kevlar vest.

Jonah had managed to get in some good slugs but Bianchi had gotten in a few more stabs, too. And then his warrior woman had shown up.

She'd helped him with Ivy, too. Leaping toward the assassin like an avenging angel, Gabby had distracted the woman, allowing him to take the kill shot. That she had almost been shot, too, made him shudder. At such close range, it would have been instant death. Thank God he'd been able to stop that from happening.

His eyes roamed around the room. Where was she now? How long had he been here? His mouth felt as if he hadn't had water in a year. His throat hurt as if he'd swallowed a truckload of gravel. And his chest…his chest felt as if a giant elephant was dancing a jig right in the center.

The doctor finally arrived. Not nearly as cheerful sounding as the nurse had been, he briefly explained that Jonah had undergone surgery for a knife wound that had nicked a kidney. He also explained he had a cracked rib, a slight concussion, and twenty or so stitches all over his body.

No wonder he felt like shit.

Jonah pointed at the tube in his mouth. He couldn't say a damn thing until it was out of him. Giving gruff instructions to the nurse, he proceeded to remove the tube. Jonah cursed him in silence, telling himself the sooner he got this over with, the sooner he could find out what was going on.

But most important, where the hell was Gabby?

***

The driver eyed her warily as she stepped onto the bus. She likely looked like a victim of abuse. The bruises on her face and around her neck were obvious evidence of violence. If she told him she was no victim and had been the winner of the fight, she doubted he would believe her. Besides, she didn't feel much like a winner right now.

Since the trip would take several hours, she went to a seat in the back and settled in for a long ride. A few passengers glanced her way, but she didn't meet anyone's eyes, so no one bothered her.

He would be angry with her when he woke. She was sure of that. But she couldn't stay. She had waited until she was sure he was going to be all right, and then she'd slipped out of the hospital. Checking herself out when the doctor kept insisting she needed more rest hadn't been easy, but she had persevered. The bullet wound in her arm throbbed like a toothache, an ugly reminder of what had happened. Her only other wounds were superficial. There was no need to stay longer. Her doctor had argued about emotional trauma but hadn't been able to dissuade her. She had needed to leave. Staying would cause much more emotional trauma than she could handle.

Her phone buzzed, and she braced herself as she clicked to read the text message. Her breath hitched when she saw it was from Lacey.

Hey, where are you?

She quickly responded, *Is Jonah okay?*

Yes. He's awake, asking for you. Where are you?

He was awake. He was going to be all right. Even though the doctor had reassured her repeatedly of that fact, she hadn't been completely sure. But now…she closed her eyes. Now she could breathe so much easier.

Her phone buzzed again. She opened her eyes and read, *Gabby, what's going on?*

She stared at the blinking cursor. Lacey was waiting for a reply, like *I'm on my way*, or *Be there in a few minutes*. No way would she expect what Gabby was doing. Nor would she understand why.

She glanced out the window and took a moment to compose the words in her head. Explaining why she had left without a word to anyone was going to be difficult. Especially since she had no good explanation other than she'd had to leave.

Giving a mental shrug, she texted, *I left the hospital. I'm on my way home.*

What??????!!!!!

The multiple exclamation and question marks almost made her smile. Lacey had a tendency to overuse punctuation to emphasize a point.

As she texted her answer, she imagined the exclamation marks were going to get another major workout soon.

I need to check on Chamo. And I need to go back to work.

There was no answer for the longest time, and Gabby didn't think she'd ever felt lower. Lacey would be hurt and disappointed in her. But she had told the truth. She was worried for Chamo. He probably thought she had abandoned him. She knew he was healthy—she had called the clinic to make sure of that—but she wanted to get him out of there as soon as possible. He was her family.

And she did need to get back to work. Her employer knew what had happened and was understanding of her absence, but she had a business to run. Gabby had been gone for three days. She needed to return and do her job.

Finally, her phone buzzed again, with a two-word text: *I see.*

The mild response hurt worse because she could practically feel Lacey's disappointment in her. And no, Lacey didn't see. She couldn't. Nor was there any way for Gabby to explain without spilling her guts and sounding like the pitiful person she was.

Gabby could think of nothing else to say. She powered off her phone and slid it into her backpack. Then, pushing her seat back into a reclining position, she closed her eyes and let the tears flow.

***

Jonah glared at his sister. They'd finally gotten the frigging tube out of his throat, and though he still felt like reconstituted dog crap, at least he was able to talk. "What the hell do you mean she left? How could she just leave? She's injured. There's no way in hell they'd release her."

"Other than the wound on her arm, which just required a few stitches, she's fine."

"She sure as hell isn't fine. She was attacked, drugged. She's got bruises. Hell, there's no telling what she went through with that bastard."

"He didn't rape her. She told me he barely put his hands on her before she was beating him to a pulp."

Lacey sounded inordinately proud of that fact, and in spite of his anger, Jonah was, too.

"I still don't get why she would leave."

Lacey shrugged. "She signed herself out. She said she needed to get back home, to Chamo and her job."

Just like that? While he'd been unconscious, she'd walked out on him? Why? What the hell had happened to make her abandon him this way?

He didn't think he would have been more surprised if she'd come into the room and shot him point-blank. Her leaving made no sense. She was finally free. Finally out of danger. Why the hell would she leave?

He glared accusingly at his sister. "Did you say or do anything that would make her leave?"

Eyes flashing with temper, Lacey returned his glare with her own. "Did *I* do or say something? No, I did not. How about you, big brother?"

"I haven't had a chance to talk to her. If you hadn't noticed, I've been unconscious."

"Which is about the only time you don't piss someone off."

"Thanks, Lacey. Your sympathy is so heartwarming."

She huffed out a long sigh. "I know you're a hero, Jonah. No one, especially me, would dispute that. But how many times have you hurt Gabby and she took it? Maybe she's had enough."

"I didn't hurt her on purpose. I wanted her to have a chance to live."

"What about what she wanted? All of her life, she's been manipulated and told what to do, what to think. Maybe she's tired of people telling her what she needs."

"She knows why I did it."

"Does she?" Lacey shook her head. "Jonah, she's in love with you. How many times has she told you that and you rejected her? And before you interrupt to tell me she only thinks she's in love with you, let me stop you there. Gabby isn't a flighty, immature person. She knows her own mind, her own heart. She knows what she wants.

"For heaven's sake, she instigated her own abduction, arranged for her brother to be brought to justice, and fought two killers, one of whom she beat the ever-living shit out of."

Putting her hand on her hip in a pose she'd learned when she was just a little girl, she batted her lashes at him. "So what do you think, brother mine? Mightn't you be a tad bit of a know-it-all, tight-ass, arrogant jerk?"

"You got a nasty mouth on you, Lacey Lou."

"Like I've always said, I learned from the best."

He rested his head on the pillow and thought about what he had done…and what Gabby had put up with from him. His intentions had been honorable, but Lacey was right. He had treated Gabby as if she didn't know her own mind. The woman had proven herself over and over again. She was strong, brave, tenacious, and intelligent. A warrior woman with a gentle, loving heart.

"Hand me my phone."

A smile of triumph lighting her face, she opened the cabinet beside his bed and handed him his phone. He glanced at it and groaned. "Battery's dead."

"Here. Use mine." She handed her phone to him and stood there expectantly.

"A little privacy would be nice."

"Fine. But you'd better say nice things, or I'll have Wyatt kick your ass for me."

"Why Wyatt?"

An odd expression flickered across her face before she caught herself and gave a careless shrug. "Why not?"

"Something going on with you two?"

"Don't be ridiculous." She nodded toward the phone in his hand. "Get to calling. She had to get a new phone, but her number is the top one on my recent calls list."

She scooted out the door before he could question her further. Wyatt and his baby sister? *No way in hell.*

Pushing aside that worry for now, he punched the call icon and waited for Gabby to answer. He told himself he knew what he was going to say, but when the call went immediately to her voice mail, he choked.

"Gabby. It's Jonah. Where are you? Why'd you leave?" And then, because he apparently didn't sound enough like an asshole, he added, "I can't believe you just walked out without saying goodbye."

Jonah ended the call before he could say more stupid things. Why did his vocabulary always turn caveman-style with her? Hell, was it any wonder she left?

Lacey stuck her head back inside the room. "Well?"

"Got her voice mail."

"That's not good. You suck at leaving messages."

"You're so good for my ego, Lacey."

She grinned. "Thanks. I try."

"Do me a favor?"

"What?"

"Tell Justice I need to see him."

"What are you going to do about Gabby?"

"I'm going to let her make her own decision this time."

"That's it?"

"Well, I didn't say I was going to play fair."

Closing his eyes, he smiled, the plans already coming together in his mind.

The door squeaked open. Jonah sat up expectantly and then hissed out a pain-filled breath. Dammit, that hurt.

Eli stood at the open door. "Heard you were awake and causing an uproar."

"It's the Slater curse," Lacey said.

"Ha. That's the least of the Slater curses." Jonah croaked the last word, wincing at the pain. Maybe he should rest his voice awhile. When Justice arrived, he planned to do a lot of talking.

"Mind if I talk to Jonah alone, Lace?" Eli asked.

"Not at all. It'll save me from causing him more injury." She glared at Jonah before she walked to the door. "Next time you call her, be nice."

She walked out before he could say anything about her eavesdropping.

As Eli came closer, Jonah noted how relaxed and peaceful he looked. A little over a year ago, he'd looked like a completely different man, but then he'd met Kathleen and his entire life had changed.

"How's Kathleen doing?"

"The bed rest is getting to her, but it won't be too much longer. She insisted I come and check on you. We were both worried about you."

"I'm fine. Could've been a lot worse."

"Yeah, it could've. How are you feeling?"

"Like someone beat the hell out of me."

"Well, there's a reason for that." He glanced down at his watch. "Mom's flying in this afternoon. I'm going to pick her up at the airport."

Jonah grimaced. "Guess I scared her a bit."

"You scared all of us more than a bit."

While he hated the reasons behind her coming, he would be happy to see his mother. It had been too long. And dammit, he wanted her to meet Gabby.

"Did you know Gabby left?"

"No, but based on what I've heard, I'm not surprised."

"Apparently, I'm the only one who is."

"You think she should've stuck around?"

Jonah dropped his head into the pillow with a sigh. "If you're here to lecture me, save it. Lacey's already laid into me."

"Little sis does have a way with words, but I'm not here to lecture you."

"Good."

"I'm here to tell you I know exactly how you feel."

"How's that?"

Eli came closer. "We've skirted around this long enough. It's time to bring out all the garbage in our family closet."

Talking about his family's dirty laundry was one of his least favorite pastimes.

"We've got some messed-up stuff."

"Yes, we do. Question is, does it define us?"

Their oldest brother, Adam, was a reflection of Mathias, but the rest of his children were not. Eli was one of the most ethical people he had ever known. He'd worked his ass off trying to restore the Slater name and right the wrongs that had been done. Their sister, Lacey, was an intelligent, strong-willed person with a generous, giving heart.

And Jonah, despite his penchant for being an idiot about certain things, wanted to do the right thing.

"It's time to let go of the past, Jonah."

"I'm getting there."

"It's okay to be in love with another woman, too. Loving Gabriella doesn't mean you loved Teri any less."

"Thanks, but I've already come to that conclusion on my own."

"Really? When?"

Hell if he knew. Maybe it was when he hadn't known if Gabby was alive or dead. Or when he'd realized that Rudy Bianchi had taken her. And maybe it was the moment she'd passed out in his arms all those months ago. He'd just been too thickheaded to realize how damn lucky he'd gotten.

He had loved Teri, but that didn't mean he couldn't love Gabby, too. And he did love her. Every beautiful, stubborn, kindhearted, sweet inch of her. She had brought light back into his life and made him want to live again.

He felt a lightening of his chest and an easing of his spirit. Gabby deserved the best of everything, and Jonah was going to make sure she got it.

Whether she would include him in her plans was entirely up to her. He could only pray he hadn't screwed up beyond her ability to forgive him.

CHAPTER FORTY-EIGHT

Three weeks later
Willoughby, Wisconsin

Standing on the balcony, Gabby looked down at the giant crowd of people and breathed in a sigh of almost giddy satisfaction. The sense of accomplishment from a job well done was a heady experience. She doubted she would ever get used to the feeling.

The art show for local artists was an annual event for the museum, but she had helped make the occasion one that people would talk about for months. Her organizational skills, combined with the knowledge acquired through her studies and travels, had helped turn the fundraiser into a rousing success.

Wouldn't Luis roll over in his grave to know that the trips he had insisted she take every year had enabled her to be successful at her job? The irony was beyond amusing.

Thanks to Grey Justice, she had learned more about Luis Mendoza in the last few weeks than she had in a lifetime of being his granddaughter. Grey had told her he could get her as much information as she wanted. She decided she wanted to know it all. Every single solitary detail. Then and only then would she put the past where it belonged.

All the things she'd uncovered about Luis beforehand—the elopement with her grandmother, the enmity between him and Rudolph because of that—were very true. She had also known of his love of art. His home was filled with some of the finest pieces in the world. She just hadn't known about his obsession. Apparently, there was a mini museum beneath the monstrosity of the Mendoza mansion. Treasures and one-of-a-kind pieces that only he and a chosen few were allowed to see. Those had been the true objects of his affection.

When the Rossis, her grandmother's family, gifted Rudolph Bianchi a priceless sapphire as a token of their regret for what their daughter had done, a new obsession had been born. The one jewel that Luis couldn't have had become what he wanted most. And Gabby had been his pawn.

The reasoning behind Rudolph Bianchi's desire for a great-grandchild still wasn't clear. Had he convinced himself he loved Flora Rossi so much that he had to have her great-grandchild? She would never know. Gabby speculated that his need was more about revenge than anything else. Rudolph had known about Luis's weakness and had played him quite brilliantly. Holding something like that over his enemy's head had to have been a boon to Rudolph's damaged pride.

The priceless jewel had been found in a safe-deposit box Rudy had rented at a Rome bank. It had been returned to the Bianchi family, and rumor was, every person who had an ounce of Bianchi blood was trying to get their hands on it. Gabby couldn't care less what happened to the stone or where it ended up. There was way too much heartache and pain attached to the thing.

She had also received word through Grey that her cousin Antonia wanted to talk with her, to apologize. She'd claimed that she had made the information on the artificial insemination easy to access in order to help Gabby. She'd said it was the only thing she could think to do. She confirmed what Gabby had surmised—that Luis had threatened Antonia's family if she didn't comply with his orders.

Knowing the truth helped, but she hadn't yet been able to contact Antonia. Maybe someday she could. For right now she wanted to stay as far away from her relatives as possible.

Now that she knew all those things, she told herself she could finally move on. If only it were than easy.

Some things had been remarkably easy—such as becoming Gabriella Mendoza again. After explaining things to her employer and why she had used a false identity, the woman had been sympathetic with what she had endured and surprisingly enthralled by the drama.

The last couple of weeks had been the busiest of Gabby's life, but not nearly enough to ease her heartache. Not a day had gone by that she didn't question her decision to walk away from Jonah.

Lacey texted her frequently. If she had thought she would lose her friend over this, she had been happily mistaken. Jonah's sister didn't hold a grudge against her for leaving. In fact, whenever they talked about Jonah, Gabby was usually the one who defended him.

She knew Jonah. He was a good, honorable man. He had given her so much, and even if she never saw him again, she would love him forever. But he hadn't followed her as she'd hoped. Maybe it had been a silly, immature thing to do, but she'd felt she had no choice. She had told Jonah that she loved him, wanted to be with him. And in return he had insisted that her safety would be in jeopardy if they stayed together. All of that was over now. All the obstacles that had kept them apart were gone. But still he hadn't come. She supposed that was her answer. Hurt like hell, but at least she knew the truth. He didn't love her. Not the way she had dreamed and hoped.

She had a wonderful life to look forward to living. She would make her own way, her own choices. And while she would always grieve for what might have been, she would never for one moment regret what they had shared. Nor would she regret the love she had offered him.

Her only regret was he would never know the amazing life they could have had together.

"Gabby?"

She turned to see an older woman headed toward her. With iron-gray hair and a sweet, infectious smile, Dorothy Dockery, or Dee Dee, as she liked to be called, was the perfect employer. She had given her the opportunity of a lifetime. By trusting Gabby, she had allowed her to thrive and grow. The charity event was Dee Dee's baby, but she had turned the bulk of the planning over to her assistant without a hint of hesitation.

"Did you need something, Dee Dee?"

"Yes…well, maybe. I'm not sure. There's a deliveryman at the back door. He said he has more pieces to display. I don't remember ordering anything else. And I'm not sure where we would put them at this late date."

"That's odd. I'm not expecting anything else."

"Would you go chat with him, dear? He's waiting in the storage room."

"Of course."

Glad to have something to do other than dwell on what could never be, Gabby squeezed Dee Dee's hand and took off down the stairs. Halfway down, she jerked to a halt, all breath leaving her body. In a room filled with dozens of elegantly dressed people, one tall, lone, incredibly handsome man stood out. Dressed in a black tuxedo, his dark hair glistened beneath the chandelier lights. And his eyes…those beautiful, mesmerizing eyes the color of brilliant emeralds, gleamed up at her.

He had finally come.

She was a vision. Never in his life had he seen anyone more breathtaking. Dressed in a shimmering gown of silver and white, she exuded elegance, class, and sheer loveliness.

He walked slowly toward her, his heart thudding so hard, he wondered if the crowd around him could hear the thundering beat. He knew he was taking a big risk coming here like this. She might decide to ignore him altogether, or she could just give him a giant wallop, sending him crashing into the wall. He likely deserved both.

It had taken considerable willpower not to come to her as soon as he was released from the hospital. Probably would have been the smart thing to do. But in his heart, he felt he needed to do more. For the last three weeks, he had worked tirelessly night and day. And whether she rejected him or not, he was glad he'd done this for her. At least he would have gotten one thing right.

He stood at the bottom of the stairs, waiting for her. Her face was composed, but he saw the questions in her eyes, the trembling of her mouth. She was nervous, too.

She reached the bottom step, and he held out his hand. "You look lovely."

Her eyes dropped to the hand, and his heart stopped beating. She wasn't going to take it. She was going to reject him, as he had rejected her. It was nothing less than he deserved.

Finally, she took his hand, and he was able to breathe again. He pulled her down to the main floor and just let his eyes roam over her. He wanted to kiss her until they were both breathless, he wanted to glide his hands over her silky skin, and he wanted to lick and nibble every succulent inch of her with excruciating slowness until they both passed out with pleasure. He also wanted to hear her laugh, see her smile, listen to her talk about the endless subjects that interested her. He wanted everything.

"You're looking well."

Her voice shook a little, and he knew she was more nervous than he'd thought.

"I'm one hundred percent again."

"I—" She looked around at the crowd. Most everyone was preoccupied, admiring the art or mingling in small groups, but several people were looking at them curiously.

"Could we go somewhere private and talk?"

"Yes…of course. But I need to…" She took a shaky breath. "There's a deliveryman at the door in the back. I need to handle that, and then I—"

He smiled and squeezed her hand gently. "I'll go with you."

"Okay."

He let her lead him through the gallery and around the pockets of people. A few nodded or smiled as they passed. One older couple tried to engage them in a conversation. Like everything else Gabriella Mendoza did, she handled them with ease, smoothly extricating herself before they managed to corner her.

When they were at last at the door, she turned. "I'll be just a moment."

"No worries. I'll go with you, and maybe we can find a quiet place to chat."

"Okay."

She went through the door, and Jonah followed. A young man stood next to several large crates. Dressed in a dark green uniform, he had the look of a man who was eager to do his job and leave.

"Hi. Are you authorized to sign for this delivery, ma'am?"

"Could I see the paperwork? I'm not expecting anything."

"Sure thing." He handed her several pages.

As Gabby looked down at them, Jonah nodded. The young man winked, smiled, and backed out of the room in a flash.

"I don't understand." Her brow furrowing, she looked up from the pages and looked around. "Where did he go?"

"He had to leave. I told him I'd take it from here."

"Take what from here? What's going on, Jonah?"

"Look down at the pages again, sweetheart. What do you see?"

Confused, Gabby looked down again. The list was itemized alphabetically, but nothing on it made sense. She hadn't ordered anything, and the things listed weren't items the gallery would likely consider showing.

A café in Italy, sunset in London, sunrise in Paris, red roses with dew.

Eclectic, but still…

She shook her head slowly. "I still don't get—" Her breath caught in her throat. Maltese puppy with a pink bow, black and white dog, gray and white kitten.

Her eyes filling with tears, she looked up at Jonah in wonder. "These are mine."

"Yes."

"You brought all of my paintings here? From the house in England?"

"Two hundred twelve paintings, eighteen unfinished works of art, and two dozen pages of doodles."

She shook her head. "I can't believe you did this for me."

"Don't you know by now that I would do anything for you?"

"But you—"

"I love you, Gabby. I have for a very long time. I was an idiot. I never should have sent you away. Never should have let you go."

"Oh, Jonah." Dropping the pages, she threw her arms around his neck and showered him with kisses. "I can't believe you did this. Can't believe you don't hate me for leaving you."

"Hate you? How in the world could I hate the most wonderful, precious, and perfect gift I've ever been given? I just hope I'm not too late."

"It could be fifty years from now instead of three weeks and it would never be too late. My love is forever."

"As mine is for you."

He kissed her then, claiming her lips as she had claimed his heart. Never in his life had he believed he could fall in love again. This beautiful, talented, courageous woman had taught him how to live again, love again. And he was never going to let her go.

EPILOGUE

Three months later
Dallas, Texas

"Here, let me get that for you."

"Thanks." Gabby gazed dreamily at the reflection of the handsome man standing behind her, zipping up her dress. The last three months had been a whirlwind of joy. Not a moment had gone by that she hadn't wanted to pinch herself to make sure it was not a dream. She had lived on hopes and dreams for so long, but now her reality far outreached anything she could have ever imagined.

Tonight was their first outing as man and wife. Since neither of them had wanted a large wedding or had the patience to wait for any kind of planned event, they'd been married within a week of Jonah's arrival in Willoughby. Only Jonah's family, along with Grey and a few of Grey's employees, had attended. Gabby had no family on her side to attend, but as Jonah's mother quickly pointed out, she had plenty of family now.

And what a marvelous family they were. She had fallen in love with them. She had already loved Kathleen and Lacey. Then she'd met Eli, who was exactly as Lacey had described him—kind, gentle-hearted, and handsome. Violet and Sophia were a delight, making her laugh within seconds of meeting them. And the newest addition, Kathleen and Eli's son, Jonathan Daniel Slater, was a bundle of sweetness. They were the perfect family.

The only Slater she had been nervous about meeting was Jonah's mother. There had been no need. From the moment their eyes met, Gabby had recognized a kindred spirit. Eleanor Slater's spirit had been almost extinguished by her former husband, but Gabby saw a spark still simmering.

The wedding had been an intimate, beautiful moment, joining her together with the man who held her heart so tenderly in his big hands. With just a few words, she had become not only a wife, but also a sister, aunt, and daughter. She had so much more than she'd ever dreamed possible. All because of the amazing man standing behind her.

Their honeymoon had been two weeks of glorious bliss, starting with a private island in the Caribbean and ending with a stay in their cabin in Utah. And because Jonah had known how much Gabby had missed Chamo, he had arranged for him to be at the cabin when they arrived. No doubt about it, Jonah Slater was a miracle…her miracle.

How was it possible to love him more today than yesterday? And she knew she would love him even more tomorrow.

"You keep making my dreams come true, even the ones that seem impossible."

Warm hands kneading her shoulders, Jonah leaned down and pressed a kiss to her neck, making her shiver and feel flushed at the same time.

"My number-one goal is fulfilling every single one of them, especially the ones you never believed were possible."

Closing her eyes, she leaned back against his hard body. They were due at Kathleen and Eli's house in about half an hour. They would arrive at the gala together, as one unit. Not only was this hers and Jonah's first outing as a married couple, it was Eleanor's first social event since she had lost her husband. All the Slaters would be surrounding Eleanor as one front, because that's what real families did.

"Then maybe I need to add to my collection."

Both of their gazes shifted to the bookshelf where five notebooks stood, filled with her hopes, wishes, and dreams, many of which had already come true. Beside the notebooks was a stack of ten empty ones. Jonah had presented them to her on their wedding day, along with a gorgeous Montblanc writing pen.

"I'll get you a bigger shelf."

Happy tears pooling in her eyes, she whirled around and threw her arms around him. "I love you so much, Jonah Slater."

"And I love and adore you, Gabby Slater. I might make your dreams come true, but you are my only dream."

She leaned back in his arms. "But I want to give you something more."

His grin sexy and suggestive, he growled, "We don't have time."

"Oh, you'll get that, too. Don't worry. But that's not what I mean."

Seeing her sincerity, Jonah went serious. He was learning much about his sweet wife, and one of the things he'd picked up on was her need to give in return.

Leaning his forehead against hers, he whispered, "There is one gift I'd like to have, but it would be for both of us."

"What's that?"

"A baby."

He felt the shock go through her. "I'm not saying anytime soon. But it's something I've been thinking about."

"But I thought you didn't—"

He pressed his fingers to her lips. He didn't even want to hear her say the words. They were so damn wrong. Before Gabby, the probability of him ever fathering a child was zero. But she had made him see many things from a different perspective, including fatherhood.

"Our child will have two parents who love him or her beyond measure. That's something my beautiful wife taught me."

"What?" she whispered.

"Love will always win."

Her face glowing, she threw her arms around him again. "Yes, it will."

He squeezed her hard for another second and then stood back. "We need to get going if we're going to be there on time, but I have something for you that can't wait."

"Jonah…no. You've already given me so much."

Not nearly as much as she had given him. "Just a few more things."

Pulling away, he opened a cabinet in the bookshelf and took out three wrapped packages. He held an oblong one out to her. "This one first."

Her eyes shining with laughter, she shook her head and took the package. "You are too much."

He watched as she carefully unwrapped the package, extending the excitement. Once unwrapped, she clicked the box open and laughed softly, "Thank you, it's beautiful. In fact, it's the same style of drawing pen I lost when I—" She held the pen up to the light. "How odd. There's a nick on the side…almost like my old—"

Her breath hitching, her eyes went wide. "Is this? Oh, Jonah. Did you find…how did you find it?"

"Your purse was in evidence lockup at the police station in London. I called a guy who called another guy."

It had been a little more complicated than that. The procedure hadn't exactly taken an act of Congress, but it had been close. The joy on her face made every bit of the effort worthwhile.

He held out the second package. Since she suspected what it contained, she practically snatched the box from his hand. He laughed watching her tear into the paper like a child at Christmas.

Her voice was a low whisper, thick with emotion. "My parents' photographs. You even had them framed."

"Now this." He held out the third box, larger than the other two.

Her hands shaking, she took the box from him and just stared at it for a few seconds.

"Gabby?"

She looked at him then, her eyes flooded with tears, her mouth trembling. "I don't know what I did to deserve you, Jonah Slater. But I swear I will spend the rest of my life thanking God for you."

His chest tight, Jonah swallowed past a lump. "Exactly how I feel." He nodded at the box. "Open it."

Going slower this time, she carefully unwrapped the box and then opened the small leather case that held her mother's necklace.

"I thought it would look nice with your dress."

Holding the box to her chest, she wrapped her arm around his neck and kissed him.

His heart fuller than he'd ever thought possible, Jonah lost himself in her taste. This woman, with her courage, sweetness, and incredible zest for life, had brought him back from the edge of darkness. He didn't know what he had done to deserve her, but he would spend the rest of his life cherishing Gabby, the only gift he would ever need.

Dear Reader,

Thank you so much for reading Too Far Gone, A Grey Justice Novel. I sincerely hope you enjoyed Jonah and Gabby's love story. If you would be so kind as to leave a review at your favorite online retailer to help other readers find this book, I would sincerely appreciate it.

If you'd like to be notified when I have a new release, sign up for my newsletter. http://authornewsletters.com/christyreece/

To learn about my other books and what I'm currently writing, please visit my website. http://www.christyreece.com

Follow me on Facebook. https://www.facebook.com/AuthorChristyReece/ and on Twitter. https://twitter.com/ChristyReece

ACKNOWLEDGEMENTS

Special thanks to the following people for helping make this book possible:

My husband, for your love, support, numerous moments of comic relief, and almost always respecting my chocolate stash.

Scott Thompson, for your expert advice on guns and weapons. Any mistakes are my own.

Joyce Lamb, for your awesome copyediting skills and fabulous advice.

Marie Force's eBook Formatting Fairies, who always answers my endless questions with endless patience.

Tricia Schmitt (Pickyme) for your gorgeous cover art.

The Reece's Readers Facebook group, for all your support and encouragement.

Anne Woodall, always my first reader, who goes above and beyond, and then goes the extra mile, too.

My beta readers, Crystal, Julie, and Alison for reading so quickly and your great suggestions.

Kara Conrad for reading an almost finished version and making excellent observations and suggestions.

Linda Clarkson, proofreader extraordinaire, who, as always, did an amazing job. So appreciate your eagle eye, Linda!

Hope Frost for your help and assistance in a multitude of things. You are so very kind!

And to all my readers, thank you for your patience. Your emails, Facebook, and Twitter messages about Jonah's book were very much appreciated. Though the story took me longer to write than I anticipated, I hope you feel it was worth the wait!

ABOUT THE AUTHOR

Christy Reece is the award winning, NYT Bestselling Author of dark romantic suspense. She lives in Alabama with her husband and a menagerie of pets.

Christy loves hearing from readers and can be contacted at Christy@ChristyReece.com.

Discover the exciting world of LCR Elite

A Whole New Level Of Danger

With Last Chance Rescue's philosophy of rescuing the innocent, the Elite branch takes the stakes even higher. Infiltrating the most volatile locations in the world, LCR Elite Operatives risk everything to rescue high value targets. Unsanctioned. Off the grid. Every operation a secret, danger-filled mission. LCR Elite will stop at nothing, no matter the cost, to fulfill their promise.

Running On Empty
An LCR Elite Novel

The Danger Has Only Begun

Having survived a brutal childhood, Sabrina Fox believed she could handle anything. That was before she watched the love of her life die before her very eyes. Brokenhearted, her emotions on lockdown, she finds purpose and hope as an LCR Elite Operative rescuing victims from some of the most volatile places in the world.

Covert ops agent Declan Steele is used to a life of danger and deceit, but when the one person he trusted and believed in above all others sets him up, he'll stop at nothing to make her pay. Finally rescued from his hellish prison, Declan has one priority—hunt down Sabrina Fox and exact his revenge.

Trusting no one is a lonely, perilous path. Sabrina swears she's innocent and Declan must make a decision--trust his heart or his head. As memories of their life together returns, he realizes just how treacherous his torture had been and the target of his revenge shifts. But when Sabrina is taken, retribution is the last thing on his mind. With the assistance of Last Chance Rescue Elite, Declan races to rescue the only woman he has ever loved before it's too late.

Turn the page to read an excerpt of Running On Empty

RUNNING ON EMPTY
AN LCR ELITE NOVEL

CHAPTER ONE

Republic of Congo
Central Africa

A whomp-whomping noise woke him. His mind, though dulled from malnutrition and brutal beatings, could still recognize the unmistakable sound of a helicopter. He touched his eyes, felt them blink—the only way he knew they were open. How long had he been inside the tank this time? A week? More?

They'd dumped him here after his last interrogation. Not because he had refused to give them information. He'd been here a long time and hadn't given them shit. Would never give them shit. No, this time the punishment had come from managing to break free for a few seconds and slamming his fist into his torturer's gut. For the first time in forever, he had felt a spark of triumph...of life. Yeah, it'd gotten him a more severe beating and then thrown into this dark, dank hellhole, but damn, it'd felt good.

He didn't even think about when they'd let him go back to his regular cell. He preferred being able to see sunlight instead of pitch-dark nothingness, but it was all relative. Hell was hell. At least in here, myriad insects weren't sucking out the last of his blood.

The helicopter noise grew louder, like it was hovering over-head. New prisoners coming in? When he'd first arrived here, he'd glimpsed a few. But that'd been a long time ago. Months? Maybe years? He had no concept of how long he'd been here. Since he heard the occasional pain-filled scream, he knew some were still here. Had they given up all hope? Did they exist in a state of dull mindlessness, waiting and hoping to be killed, thinking that only death would give the final release of pain?

Odd how he could wonder about them but feel not one ounce of sympathy. Torture did that. Turned a normal, caring human being into an empty shell—hollowed out and lifeless. No heart, no soul, no humanity.

Gunfire erupted. Sounded like military grade. M4s, maybe? AK-47s? Whoever and whatever, there were several of them. Had someone tried to escape?

He noticed that his heart rate had picked up. That hadn't happened in a while. He mentally shrugged. Whatever the reason for the fireworks, the speculation had given him a brief reprieve from misery.

A loud clanging noise sounded outside his cell. Apparently, it was time for another interrogation. Or would he be taken back to the hole he called home, where the endless sounds of her treachery whispered in his ears? Wouldn't his torturers get a kick out of knowing that he'd rather take a beating than listen to that soft, soothing voice of betrayal?

Hurried footsteps came closer. He didn't bother to raise his head. They'd get here soon enough.

Piercing light penetrated his sight. He squinted his eyes shut. Damn, that hurt. Covering his face with his arm, he lay still. Waited to be hauled out, for an attack…more pain. Coercion, more voices of betrayal. No point in getting to his feet. Why make it easy for them? Besides, if he tried to stand, he'd just fall.

Then he heard a voice. One he hadn't heard in a very long time. "My God, it is you. It's really you!"

Was he dreaming? No, he no longer did that. Dreams were for those with hope. So if this wasn't a dream, was this reality? After all this time…after all the shouting, cursing and praying. After giving up completely, had someone actually come for him?

Seven days later
Somewhere above the Atlantic Ocean

Declan Steele returned from the dead a changed man. Eyes that had once been vibrant blue and glinting with life were now dark, murky…empty. The strong, muscular body that had once carried a comrade ten miles through a sizzling-hot desert was unrecognizable. Thick, dark-as-midnight hair had been replaced with a dull, wild mane that reached well past his thin shoulders. An emaciated wraith, more than thirty pounds underweight, with a bitter twist to his sensuous male lips, stood in his place.

His appearance wasn't the only change. Hatred seethed and burned within him. He was a hardened, embittered, heartless creature, determined to achieve only one goal—vengeance.

After his rescue, he had been taken to a large private home, where he had been allowed to shower, alone and with clean water. Fresh clothes had been provided, and food that wasn't covered in maggots or mold had been set before him.

A doctor had given him a physical, declaring him malnourished and anemic but in good shape considering what his body had endured. The doctor had remarked that his captors had been amazingly humane in allowing aid workers to attend to him from time to time. Declan had stared blankly at him. Humane? The word apparently had a different meaning for the physician, because he'd seen no humanity in any of the bastards who'd tortured him daily.

The health aid workers had been beneficial in one aspect, though. Apparently, one of the physicians from the group had told of a tall, dark-haired prisoner with a slight Scottish accent and predilection for quoting Robert Burns. And that had gotten the attention of his former fellow EDJE agent Jackson Sands.

"We've been working like mad to get you out. The minute I heard the description of the prisoner, I knew it had to be you." Jackson shook his head. "Still can't believe it…we thought you were dead, man. Everyone thought you were dead. That you'd been killed in that explosion in Florence. But then I heard about…" He lifted a broad shoulder. "I just had to make sure. We worked around the clock to save you."

Jackson had been repeating these words since his rescue. Damning himself for asking, Declan said, "Who?"

The other man's eyes widened. Was it the shock of Declan finally speaking or the rough gravel of his damaged voice?

"Who what?"

"Who's been working like mad?"

"Oh…sorry…my team. I have my own security business now." He jerked his head toward the two large, silent men across from him. "Meet Neil Erickson and Kyle Ames. I couldn't have done it without them. Took us a couple of months to pull this off."

The men remained silent, watching. Declan gave them a nod of acknowledgment and returned his attention to Jackson. "The Agency wasn't involved?"

"They don't know we found you. I'll leave it up to you, when you're ready, to let them know you're alive. Sabrina doesn't know, either. I haven't been in touch with her since…well, since we thought you were killed. I—"

At the mention of that name, Declan turned away. Discussing the woman and his plans for her was out of the question. This was between the two of them and no one else.

Jackson blew out an explosive sigh and shut up. Declan could tell he made the man uneasy. At one time, he'd been the type to go out of his way to put people at ease. It had been one of his gifts. Those kinds of talents weren't worth shit anymore.

He had worked with Jackson, had once thought of him as a friend. Even though he had no feelings left in him for anyone, he respected that the man had possessed the balls to carry off a rescue op. A soft emotion like gratitude didn't fit him anymore, but he owed the three men, Sands, Erickson, and Ames. They'd risked their lives for him. He wouldn't forget it.

The blue sky and puffy white clouds outside the airplane window were invisible to him as he thought about his next move. He was headed back to the States. He hadn't asked about their destination. Where he went, where he lived, all of that was meaningless. His heart pumped for one reason only now. To repay the scheming, red-haired witch who'd put him in that hellhole. Sabrina Fox would pay with everything she had. And when he finally put a bullet between her lovely, lying green eyes, she would know exactly how it felt to have your heart ripped out by the one person you loved and trusted above all else.

And then it would be over for both of them.

Made in the USA
San Bernardino, CA
17 March 2018